CHOCOLATE WISHES

Trisha Ashley was born in St Helens, Lancashire, and now lives in the beautiful surroundings of North Wales. Her novel, *A Winter's Tale*, was a *Sunday Times* bestseller and shortlisted for the Melissa Nathan Award for Comedy Romance 2009. Although Trisha loves chocolate, she would not describe herself as a chocoholic – she can give up anytime she wants, honestly . . .

To find out more about Trisha please visit www.trishaashley.com

TRISHA ASHLEY

Chocolate Wishes

AVON

AVON

A division of HarperCollins*Publishers*
77–85 Fulham Palace Road,
London W6 8JB

www.harpercollins.co.uk

A Paperback Original 2010

1

A catalogue record for this book is
available from the British Library

ISBN-13: 978-1-84756-114-5

Set in Minion by Palimpsest Book Production Limited,
Grangemouth, Stirlingshire

Printed and bound in Great Britain by
Clays Ltd, St Ives plc

Mixed Sources
Product group from well-managed
forests and other controlled sources
www.fsc.org   Cert no. SW-COC-1806
© 1996 Forest Stewardship Council

FSC is a non-profit international organisation established
to promote the responsible management of the world's forests.
Products carrying the FSC label are independently certified
to assure consumers that they come from forests that are managed
to meet the social, economic and ecological needs
of present and future generations.

Find out more about HarperCollins and the environment at
www.harpercollins.co.uk/green

My grateful thanks go to the following people for so kindly and generously giving up some of their valuable time to help me, and if I have sometimes warped their information to fit my weft, I would like to make it clear that it is none of their doing.

To Annie and Guy of www.scentedgeraniums.co.uk with special thanks for the chocolate-scented geranium, an inspiration in itself. To Gareth and Christopher East of The Chocolate Factory, Hutton le Hole, North Yorkshire, www.The-Chocolate-Factory.co.uk whose expert knowledge is reflected in their delicious chocolate. And last, but certainly not least, to Rev. Canon Frances Wookey, Vicar of Hanley Swan & Welland and Rural Dean of Upton, who bears absolutely *no* blame whatsoever for the views or goings-on of my extremely alternative Vicar!

I think it is time my wonderful agent had a dedication all to herself, so this one is for Judith Murdoch, with love and thanks.

Prologue

Mortal Ruin

When the normally innocuous radio station she always listened to while she was working suddenly started pumping out Mortal Ruin's first big hit, 'Dead as My Love', Chloe Lyon was in the kitchen area of her small flat, carefully brushing a thick coating of richly scented dark criollo couverture chocolate into moulds, to make the last batch of hollow angels before Christmas.

That seemed pretty appropriate, because a hollow angel was what Raffy Sinclair had proved himself to be, but it meant that it was a couple of minutes before she had a hand free to reach across and snap down the off button. By then they'd moved on to Eric Clapton's 'Tears in Heaven', so it was becoming obvious that the guest on *Desert Island Discs* (she'd missed the start) had much happier memories of 1992 than Chloe did. In fact, she'd take a bet on the next song being Whitney Houston and 'I Will Always Love You', and that really *would* finish her off.

But the music carried on playing in her head even after the radio was silenced and it was already too late to suppress the memories. The dark, viciously searing tide of anger and pain at Raffy's betrayal was rushing in as sharply as if it had all happened yesterday and she was once again that love-struck nineteen-year-old, thinking she'd found a kind of magic more potent than any of her grandfather's chants, charms and incantations.

She'd loved that Clapton song, though Raffy'd teased her that it was mawkish. But then, as well as being keen on Nirvana, he'd had a worrying penchant for Megadeath and older bands like Iron Maiden, Judas Priest and Black Sabbath, all of which influenced the lyrics he wrote for his own band, Mortal Ruin. This obsession with the dark side was part of the reason why she'd never mentioned her grandfather to him – he might have been *too* interested had he known about her connection with Gregory Warlock.

But actually, there had simply not been enough time to explore their family and backgrounds, since they'd met and fallen in love at the start of her first university term and those few weeks spent intently engrossed in each other encompassed the whole span of their relationship.

It wasn't surprising that *she'd* loved *him* at first sight – he was tall and handsome, with long black curling hair, a pale, translucent skin and eyes the greeny-blue of the Caribbean Sea in a holiday brochure – but he'd seemed as transfixed as she was . . . And anyway, the Tarot cards, when she consulted them, had told her that change was coming and she would meet her soul mate, so she'd naturally assumed he was the one.

Big mistake.

She hadn't believed it was the end, even after that final argument on the last night of term, when he'd told her he and the other three Mortal Ruin band members had decided to gamble their futures on a recording contract and he'd asked her to go with him, rather than head home for the holidays as she'd intended. She hadn't explained why she absolutely *had* to go home either, though she might have done if she hadn't been so angry – or if he had been capable of talking about anything other than Mortal Ruin by that point.

If only she'd known she wouldn't be going back for the next term . . . If only they hadn't had that final, bitter argument, so she never even gave him her home address . . . There was a whole series of ifs, but they probably wouldn't have made any difference in the end, because he turned out to be *so* not the man she'd thought he was.

A hollow angel: dark and handsome on the outside, an emotional void within. A Lucifer echoing with false promises.

Of course, she hadn't known that then. Looking after Jake, her baby half-brother, while waiting for her mother to come back from her latest fling, she'd had plenty of time to worry about what would happen when Raffy finally got her letter. She'd sent it via her former roommate, Rachel, to hand to him when he came to his senses and went back to look for her. Because, despite their last argument, she'd been quite sure of his love and that somehow they would find a way of being together, of working things out. He'd told her he loved her often enough . . .

Even in her darkest moments she'd believed that, right up to the day she received the note from Rachel, telling her that Raffy had returned briefly at the start of the new term and she had given him the letter, but after reading it he'd simply crumpled it up and shoved it in his pocket without comment.

She hadn't needed the tear-stained confession on the next page to know how easily and quickly he had replaced her, or how little she meant to him. Out of sight, out of mind.

It was not so easy for her to forget him, when his music seemed to be out there everywhere, assailing her at unexpected moments, but eventually her searing anger had cauterised the wounds and given her a certain measure of immunity.

So why now was she sitting at the kitchen table weeping hot, scalding tears?

Saltwater and chocolate are *never* a good combination.

Chapter One

There Must Be an Angel

You know those routines most people have, the ones they fall into automatically when they wake up? Well, until a few years ago, my morning rota had 'read Tarot cards' neatly sandwiched between 'brush teeth' and 'breakfast'.

It was just the way I was brought up, and nothing to do with magic – or not the sort my grandfather practises, where the effects of his rites are so hit-and-miss that most positive results are probably sheer coincidence, like the way the sales of my Chocolate Wishes went stratospheric right after he gave me part of an ancient Mayan charm to say over the melting pot. Fluke . . . I thought. I have to confess that I've never been entirely sure.

But really, apart from the novelty value of the concept, my success was probably more the result of my having finally perfected both my technique and the quality of my moulded chocolate, mostly by trial, error and experimentation – and the really good thing about working with chocolate is that you can eat your mistakes.

What originally sparked the whole thing off was coming

across a two-part metal Easter egg mould at a jumble sale when my half-brother, Jake, was a small boy. I made lots of little chocolate eggs and put messages inside them from the Easter Bunny, then hid them all over the flat and court-yard for him and his friends to find.

And while I was making them I started thinking about fortune cookies, which are fun, but not really that good to eat. And from there it was just a short bunny hop to creating a line of hollow chocolate shapes containing 'Wishes' as an after-dinner novelty and selling them in boxes of six or twelve.

The 'Wishes' are encouraging thoughts or suggestions, inspired by the Angel card readings that have replaced my earlier devotion to the Tarot, and I'm positive that each person will automatically pick the appropriate Chocolate Wish from the box – their own guardian angel will see to that!

It was all very amateur at first, but now the Wishes come in printed sheets and the boxes are also specially made to hold and protect the chocolates in transit, because most of my orders come through the internet, via my website, or by word of mouth.

Nowadays I favour mainly criollo couverture chocolate, the best and most expensive kind, which not only tastes delicious but has a superior gloss and good 'snap'. I temper it in the machine Jake christened the Bath and then, with an outsize pastry brush, coat specially made polycarbon moulds in the shape of angels or winged hearts until I have a thick enough shell. When they're cold, I 'glue' the two halves together with a little more chocolate – but before I do that, I put in the 'Wish'.

And I am so much happier since I began to read the Angel cards instead of the Tarot! They never seemed to come out right when I read them for myself and I often wonder if my future would have been different if I hadn't always looked for signs and portents before I did anything. Do we make our own futures, or do our futures make us?

Granny, who was of gypsy descent and taught me how to read the cards in the first place, said they only showed what *might* be the future, should the present course be held to; but I'm not so sure. She would have approved of the Angel cards, though, which is more than my grandfather (whom Jake and I call Grumps, for obvious reasons) and Zillah, who is Granny's cousin, do.

But I truly believe in angels and have done from being a small child when Granny, who despite her Tarot reading was deeply religious, assured me that the winged figure I glimpsed one night really *was* a celestial visitor, rather than a figment of my imagination. (And my friend Poppy saw it too, I do have a witness!)

Why an angel should appear to an unbaptised and ungodly child of sin is anyone's guess, unless it was my own personal guardian angel making an early appearance in my life, to counter Grumps' influence and set my feet on the right path. But if so, she hasn't visited me since in that form, though sometimes I can hear the soft susurration of wings and feel a comforting presence that is almost, but not quite, visible. And the Angel cards . . . maybe she guided me to those too?

Granny died when I was twelve, but she too did her best to counter Grumps' influence, flatly forbidding any kind of baptismal ceremony involving his coven, or involvement in its rites until I had reached the age where I could make a considered decision for myself – a resounding 'No way!' She had already done the same for my mother, though unfortunately without instilling in her any alternative moral code.

That February morning, when I shuffled the pack of silky smooth Angel cards and laid them out on the kitchen table, they predicted change, but at least they also assured me that everything would work out all right in the end, which was a great improvement on coming face to face with the Hanging Man or Death over the breakfast cereal and trying to interpret the reading as something a little less doom-laden than the initial impression.

Rituals completed, I went to wake Jake up, which took quite some effort since, at eighteen, he could sleep for Britain. I made sure he ate something before he set off for sixth form college, dressed all in black, from dyed hair to big, metal-studded boots, a cheery sight for his teachers on a Monday morning.

When he'd gone – with a cheeky 'Goodbye, Mum!' just to wind me up – I checked my emails for incoming Chocolate Wishes orders and printed them out, before going through to the main part of the house to see what Grumps was up to. Our flat was over the garages, so the door led onto the upper landing, and was rarely shut, unless Jake was playing loud music.

In the kitchen Zillah was sitting at the table over the remnants of her breakfast, drinking loose-leaf Yorkshire tea and smoking a thin, lumpy, roll-up cigarette. As usual, she was dressed in a bunchy skirt, two layers of cardigans with the bottom one worn back to front, a huge flowered pinny over the whole ensemble and her hair tied up in a clashing scarf, turban-fashion. Grumps says she was bitten by Carmen Miranda in her youth and after I Googled the name, I suspect he is right. Today's dangly red earrings made her look as if she had hooked a pair of cherries over each ear, so the fruit motif was definitely there.

She looked up – small, dark, with skin not so much wrinkled as folded around her black, bird-bright eyes – and smiled, revealing several glinting gold teeth. 'Read your tea leaves?' she offered hospitably.

'No, thanks, Zillah, not just now. I'm running late, it took me ages to get Jake up and on his way. But I've brought you another jar of my chocolate and ginger spread, because yesterday you said you'd almost run out.'

'Extra sweet?'

'Extra sweet,' I agreed, putting the jar down on the table.

It's really just a ganache of grated cacao and boiled double cream, with a little finely chopped preserved ginger added for zing. It doesn't keep long, though the way Zillah lards it onto her toast means it doesn't have to.

Zillah turned up on the doorstep the day after Granny died. She'd read the news in the cards and come to burn her cousin's caravan – metaphorically speaking, anyway, because she'd had to make do with burning Granny's clothes and personal possessions on the garden bonfire instead.

Grumps seemed unsurprised by Zillah's sudden appearance, as if he'd been expecting her, which maybe he had, and his purported magical skills aren't a *complete* figment of his imagination. She'd never given any suggestion of remaining with us permanently, yet here she still was several years later, cooking, cleaning and caring for us, in her slapdash way.

She handed me the fresh cup of tea she'd just poured out, put two Jammie Dodger biscuits on the saucer and said, 'Take this in to the Wizard of Oz then, will you, love?'

'Grumps is up to something, isn't he?' I asked, accepting

the cup, because although he is taciturn and secretive at the best of times, I could still tell. I only hoped he wasn't about to try some great summoning ceremony with his coven, because on past form all they were likely to call up was double pneumonia.

Zillah tapped the side of her nose with the fingers holding her cigarette and a thin snake of ash fell into her empty cup. I hoped it wouldn't muddle her future.

In the study Grumps was indeed sitting at his desk over a grimoire open at a particularly juicy spell, which he was probably considering trying out when the weather improved. (The coven practised their rites in an oak grove, skyclad, and none of them was getting any younger.)

His long, silver hair was parted in the middle and a circlet held it off a face notable for a pair of piercing grey eyes and a hawk-like nose. His midnight-blue velvet robe was rubbed on the elbows, so that he bore more resemblance to a down-at-heel John Dee than a Gandalf, but it was a look that went down well with the readers of the beyond Dennis Wheatley novels he wrote as Gregory Warlock. Sales had been in the doldrums for many years, apart from a small band of devotees, but they were suddenly having a renewed vogue and his entire backlist was about to be reprinted in their original, very lurid covers.

Grumps is one of those annoying people who need very little sleep, so that by the time I pop in to see him in the mornings, he usually has achieved quite a heap of hand-written manuscript. There are often lots of letters too, because he corresponds with equally nutty people all over the globe, and since his handwriting is appalling I take everything away and type it up on my computer.

When I was younger there was a time when I thought

10

Grumps was a complete charlatan. You can imagine what it was like growing up in a small town like Merchester, with a relative who both looked and proclaimed himself with every utterance to be totally, barking mad. For example, his eccentric clothing, the ghastly novels and his definitive book on the magical significance of ley lines. (Leys are straight lines that link landmarks and sites of historical and magical importance.) Add to all that the rumours of secret and risqué rites in remote woodland, and you will begin to see my point.

Yet as I grew older I came to realise that he believed completely in what and who he was and then it ceased to bother me any more: if he wasn't embarrassed by it, then neither was I.

Now I picked my way towards the desk through a sea of unfurled maps that covered the carpet, each crisscrossed with red and blue lines showing both established and possible new ley lines. The crackling noise as I inadvertently trod on one drew Grumps' attention to my presence.

'Ah, Chloe – I believe I have found the solution to my financial problems,' he announced in his plummy, public-school-educated voice, looking distinctly pleased with himself. He is distantly related to lots of terribly grand people, none of whom has spoken to him since he chose his bride from a fortune-telling booth at the end of a Lancashire pier, at a time when one simply didn't *do* that kind of thing.

'Oh, good,' I said encouragingly, putting his tea down on the one empty spot among the clutter on his desk.

'Yes, it came to me and I acted upon it, once the clouds of confusion sent by Another to conceal it from my knowledge were suddenly dispelled.'

Grumps has a private income, but he'd settled Mum's huge debts six years before, after her last, permanent, vanishing trick. Besides, his investments weren't paying out in the way they used to and even the recent four-book contract his agent had secured wouldn't be enough to cover the bills and still enable him to purchase rare books and artefacts in the manner he seemed to think was his birthright. Even now his desk was littered with auction catalogues sporting bright Post-it notes marking things that interested him.

'Great,' I said cautiously, because Grumps' good ideas, like his spells, have a marked tendency to backfire or fizzle to nothing. 'Did Zillah read the cards for you and spot something nice?'

'She did, and foresaw change.'

'She always does. You'd think we lived in a sort of psychic whirlpool.'

'Well, change there certainly *will* be, because I am selling the house and we are moving to Sticklepond.'

I'd started gathering up the loose sheets of paper inscribed in a sloping hand, which were the latest chapter of *Satan's Child*. Now I stopped and stared at him. 'We're moving? But how can that help?' Then the penny dropped. 'Oh, I *see*. You mean you and Zillah are downsizing to a small cottage? That's a good idea, because now that sales of Chocolate Wishes have taken off in a big way through the internet, I can easily afford to make a home for Jake on my own.'

'No, no,' he said impatiently, 'I am not downsizing – the opposite, in fact – and there will be room for us all. An estate agent recently approached me with an advantageous offer for this house from someone who has taken a fancy to it, just at the very moment when I happened upon an advertisement for the Old Smithy in Sticklepond, which a friend had sent me, and which had somehow got mixed up among some other papers. It became apparent to me that this was a *sign*, and I therefore moved quickly.'

He pushed the grimoire aside and handed me a leaflet that had been underneath. It pictured a low, barn-like building, set longways onto the road, with a small ancient cottage at one side and a larger Victorian house at the other, like mismatched bookends.

'It's Miss Frinton's Doll Museum!' I said, recognising it instantly, because it's not only just up the road from Marked Pages, the second-hand bookshop run by my friend Felix, but almost opposite the pub where I meet up with him and Poppy two or three times a week.

'It *was*, though of course not for some time – it has lain empty. I knew it was for sale prior to this, of course, I just hadn't realised its significance.' He indicated the larger house with a bony finger adorned with a substantial and oddly designed silver ring. 'This is the main residence, where the Misses Frinton lived. There would be abundant room for my library and for Zillah to have her own sitting room, as she has here. The front room of the small cottage at the other end of the building was the doll's hospital – and I thought it would be ideal for your chocolate business, with enough room for you and Jake to live behind it, although it needs a little updating.'

'When estate agents say that, it usually means it's semi-derelict.' I wished there were photographs of the interior of the cottage as well as the house in the leaflet.

'Not derelict, just neglected. It used to be rented out, so there is a kitchen extension with a bathroom over it

and two bedrooms. It is larger than your current accom-
modation.'

'It could hardly be smaller,' I said, though of course
without Mum we had more space, especially since I'd packed
up all her belongings and stacked the boxes in Grumps'
attic on the first anniversary of her disappearance. But since
Chocolate Wishes had taken off, I really needed a separate
workshop.

'The cottage also has a walled garden behind it,' he added
slyly, because he knew I longed for a garden of my own.
Here we just had a gravelled courtyard and although I did
grow lots of things in tubs and pots and in my tiny greenhouse, including herbs both for cooking and for Grumps'
rites, salad vegetables, strawberries and a small fig tree, there
were limitations . . . especially for my cherished and
constantly growing collection of scented geraniums,
currently over-wintering on every available windowledge
in the flat.

I was sold.

'The cottage is linked to the main house via the Smithy
Barn, the former doll museum, and my intention is to open
a museum of my own there,' Grumps explained, 'one dedicated to the study of witchcraft and paganism. I will be
able to display my collection and increase my income, thus
killing two birds with one stone.'

'Well, goodness knows, you have enough artefacts to
stock *ten* museums, Grumps!' I exclaimed. 'But you surely
wouldn't run it yourself? I can't see you selling tickets to a
stream of visitors!'

'I fail to see why not,' he said testily. 'I will open only
in the afternoons, from two till four, and can have my
desk in one corner and let visitors roam freely, while I

get on with my work. Zillah has said she will also take a hand.'

'But if you don't keep an eye on the visitors, half your collection will vanish!'

'Oh, I think not: I will put up placards pointing out that any thieves will be cursed. In fact, I might have it printed on the back of the tickets.'

'That should go down well,' I said drily.

'It will serve: they will ignore the warning at their peril. I shall have signed copies of my books for sale too, of course, both fiction and non-fiction.'

After my first surprise, the idea began to grow on me. 'Do you know, I think you might be right and it would be quite a money-spinner, because since that Shakespeare connection was discovered at Winter's End, hordes of tourists come to Sticklepond. At least one café and a couple of gift shops have opened in the village lately, and passing trade at Felix's bookshop is much better. There's a strong witchcraft history in the area too.'

'Precisely! And besides,' he added as a clincher, 'the Old Smithy is on the junction of two important ley lines; *that* was what was so cunningly obscured from my vision by the malevolence of Another. There may even be a third – I am working on it.'

'I expect the conjunction of the ley lines was a major selling point the estate agents managed to miss,' I said, ignoring the second mention of a mysterious and malevolent opponent, which was probably just a figment of his imagination.

He gave me a severe look over the top of his half-moon glasses. 'Its unique position imbues it with magical energy, my dear Chloe, and since the museum area is large,

15

my coven may meet there with no diminution of power. Rheumatism has affected one or two of them,' he added more prosaically, 'and they have suggested we move to an indoor venue.'

'Yes, I can see that the museum would be ideal, provided you put up good, thick curtains,' I agreed absently, still turning over the whole idea of the move in my mind. 'What about Jake, though? He has to be able to get to sixth form college and he isn't going to want to move away from his friends, is he?'

Though now I came to think of it, a fresh start in a new village might be a good idea for my horribly lively brother. He's outgrown his childish pranks, but will still forever be 'that imp of Satan' to those inhabitants of Merchester who've been his victims.

'Jake may borrow my car and drive himself to school until he has taken his final examinations, and then of course he will be off to university,' Grumps said. 'He likes the old Saab for some reason. In the holidays, he can help me in the museum and I will pay him.'

Grumps seemed to have it all thought out.

I looked down again at the leaflet. A cottage of my own with a garden, separated from my grandfather by the width of a museum, and with room for my Chocolate Wishes business, sounded like bliss . . .

'So, have you actually seen the property and made an offer for it, Grumps?'

'Yes, of course – and the people who want to buy this house have also been to view it, though you were out at the time. I thought I would wait until everything was signed and sealed before I told you.'

'I certainly didn't see this coming!'

'If you *will* read Angel cards instead of the Tarot ... Angel cards – pah!'

'They seem to work for me, Grumps.'

'Not, apparently, very well: Zillah saw the changes coming and she has already decided on her rooms in the new house.'

If Zillah knew and approved, then really, there was no more to be said: it looked like the Lyons were on the move.

A thought struck me. 'When Mum finally decides to stop playing dead and comes back, how will she find us?'

'Like a bad penny,' he said bleakly.

Chapter Two

Satan's Child

On the way back to the flat, with a lot to think about and a chapter of *Satan's Child* and three letters to type up, I found Zillah still in the kitchen stirring something savoury-smelling in a large pot. The cat, Tabitha, was draped around her neck like a black fur wrap, her tail practically in the stew.

Hygiene was possibly not Zillah's strong point but neither she nor Grumps (nor even Tabitha) ever seemed to suffer ill effects. Nor did Jake and I, come to that, because although I did some of our own cooking in the flat, we shared quite a lot of meals. We must all have been immune.

'Zillah, if you have time, maybe you had better read my cards,' I suggested. 'Grumps just told me that we're on the move.'

Zillah silently turned down the heat and put a lid on the pot, then fetched her Tarot pack and handed the cards to me to shuffle. Under my fingers they felt cool, snakily smooth and almost alive.

'You could read them yourself,' she grumbled as I gave them back, but she began to lay them out in a familiar pattern on the table. The cat, bored, disentwined herself and stalked off, holding up a tail like a bottlebrush that has seen better days.

'You know I've given up reading them, especially for myself, because there never seemed to be good news. I simply don't think I could bear it if I saw yet another dark stranger scheduled to enter my life bringing change, because it never turns out well,' I added gloomily.

It would have been really useful if the cards had ever given me some helpful hints about whether the changes would be good or bad too, especially regarding my ex-fiancé, David.

'It's all in the reading and how you interpret it, Chloe, you know that,' Zillah said. 'You don't have to make a self-fulfilling prophecy.'

While I puzzled over that one, she looked at the cards that showed what was currently going on in my life.

'Hmm . . . no surprises there, *or* in what will happen if you continue on your current course.' She turned over more cards and pondered.

'But my course *is* about to be changed, isn't it? Not only are we moving, but Jake will be off to university later this year.'

I'd had the maternal role for my half-brother thrust upon me and I'd done my best, torn between love and resentment, but although I adore Jake, I couldn't say I wasn't relishing the idea of being my own woman again.

That my own childhood had been a happy and secure one was entirely due to Granny but, though kindly and affectionate, Zillah seemed to have been born without a maternal gene

19

and could not take her place. That hadn't stopped Mum from thinking Zillah could quite easily assume Granny's role as mother substitute when she was off with her latest lover, though – but then, *she* didn't have the maternal gene either.

At least Zillah loved us in her own unique way, even if, like Grumps, she didn't find children terribly interesting until they were capable of holding a conversation.

'It doesn't say anything about Mum turning up again, does it?' I asked, following this train of thought. 'Only it would be just like her to walk back in, now there aren't any responsibilities for her to shoulder, what with Grumps having paid her bills and Jake an adult.'

My mother had spent less and less time at the flat until she had finally vanished altogether from a Caribbean cruise six years previously and was currently presumed by everyone except the family to be dead. *We* presumed her to be fornicating in sunnier climes, even if this time her absence had been inordinately prolonged. Her disappearance had coincided with David jilting me, too: cause and effect.

Zillah ignored me, turning over the cards showing what was happening with my relationships, which was not a lot apart from a platonic and fraternal one with my old friend Felix Hemmings, the bookseller of Sticklepond.

Through the thin spiral of smoke from her latest cigarette I automatically began to read the meanings upside down, and groaned. 'Oh, no, *please* don't tell me another man really *is* coming into my life? I can't bear it!'

'Maybe more than one person,' she said, frowning. 'Perhaps there's unfinished business with someone you knew before?'

'No way! Now I've realised I'm stuck in some endless

Groundhog Day cycle of love and rejection, I'm not even going to *look* at another man.'

'You can't call two failed relationships an endless cycle, Chloe.'

'Two? Have you forgotten Cal, or Simon or—' I stopped, unable to remember the faces, let alone the names, of some of my more fleeting boyfriends.

'I did not mention *men*, but in any case they were obviously unmemorable. And can we help ourselves if love strikes?' She thoughtfully fingered the card depicting a tower struck by lightning.

'We can if it strikes twice,' I snapped. 'But even if I'd been tempted to take any boyfriend seriously after David jilted me, they weren't prepared to take on Jake too. He's the ultimate love deterrent.'

I shuddered, recalling some of the hideous pranks my inventive half-brother had got up to over the years in order to get rid of my boyfriends. I was sure Grumps had had a hand in some of the more fiendish tricks.

'He *was*, but he's now an adult, and once he's at university he'll have other things to think about.'

'So he will . . . and it seems like only five minutes since *I* went off to university, too,' I said with a sad sigh, for that had been my one, abortive bid for independence, the year after Jake was born. It had been all too easy for Mum to absent herself for longer and longer periods, leaving me literally holding the baby, but I'd thought if she didn't have me to fall back on, then she would be forced to stay at home and behave like other mothers.

How wrong I was! I got back at the end of the first term to find she had dumped the baby in Zillah's unwilling hands, leaving me a scribbled note with no idea of when she would return. Jake was touchingly happy to see me, making me guilty that I had been so engrossed in my love affair with Raffy that I had hardly thought of him for weeks. Grumps and Zillah were also happy to have me back, in their way, but *I* was the one who could have done with a mother's tender care just then, rather than have to take on the role myself.

But surprisingly, in the end, Zillah proved to be a tower of strength when I most needed one . . .

I looked at the spread of cards again and asked hopefully, '*Can* the future be altered, Zillah?'

'People can change, and then the future also changes. Or perhaps the true future remains fixed, the other is merely a warning to put us on the right path to our fate.' Her gnarled hand reached out and flipped over the final cards. 'Your future has interesting possibilities.'

'What, you mean interesting in the Chinese curse sort of way?'

'Well, what are the angels telling you?' she asked acerbically.

'That change is coming, but it will all turn out right in the end.'

'Whatever "right" means, Chloe.' She swept the cards together, tapped them briskly three times and wrapped them up in a piece of dark silk.

Back in the flat I felt unsettled, which was hardly surprising when a positive Pandora's Box of painful recollections kept escaping from where I thought I'd had them safely locked away. Memories not only of my first love, Raffy, which even after so many years evoked feelings of loss and betrayal far too painful to dwell on again, but also of my ex-fiancé, David.

We met in Merchester's one upmarket wine bar and he

had seemed so different from any of my other, short-lived boyfriends. He was several years older, for a start, solid and dependable. Maybe I was looking for a father figure, having never had one? He was a partner in a firm of architects, so more than comfortably off, and even Jake's attempts to get rid of him (culminating in the plague of glowing green mice in David's flat – I have *no* idea how he worked that one) just made him go all quiet and forbearing. He said Jake would grow out of it – which he had, only not until David's presence in our lives was history.

And Jake *had* been the sticking point in the end. It was odd how I had remained completely blind to the fact that David was so jealous of my close relationship with my half-brother until that last day, only a couple of weeks before our wedding. I'd also assumed he understood that whenever my mother was away, Jake would stay with us after we were married, for the first few years at least. But as Zillah often says, men don't understand anything unless it is spelled out for them in very plain language.

'Jake could live with your grandfather and his housekeeper,' David had suggested when Jake was twelve and my mother had performed her latest vanishing trick.

I let the 'housekeeper' bit go, since although Zillah certainly wasn't that, her role in our lives defied definition. 'Hardly, David! Social Services aren't going to take kindly to a twelve-year-old living with a warlock, are they?'

'Now, Chloe, don't exaggerate, when you know that's just a *nom de plume* he adopts for his books. He may be a little eccentric, but the whole persona . . .' He smiled indulgently, his teeth very white against his tanned, handsome face. 'It's a publicity thing, isn't it?'

'No, it's how he *is*. I keep telling you.'

'You'll be saying your mother is a witch next, Chloe, and has simply flown off on her broomstick.'

'Oh, no, she never showed any inclinations that way and although Jake *is* interested in witchcraft, luckily it's only from a historical point of view. It's just a pity Granny isn't still around to help me bring him up, but he isn't a bad boy really, just lively.'

David shuddered.

'What? You *like* him, you said so!'

'Yes, of course I do, but that doesn't mean I want to live with him. And there's no reason why you should have to sacrifice your entire life to bringing up your half-brother, is there? Fostering might be the making of him.'

'*Fostering?* I can't believe you would even suggest that!' I stared at him with new eyes. 'Anyway, it's going to be only for a few weeks at most, until Mum comes back. The longest she's ever been away is three months.'

David's expression softened and he came and put his arms around me. 'Darling, you have to accept that she isn't coming back this time – she's dead. I know it's hard, but look at the facts.'

The facts, as Mum's friend Mags had reported them, were that Mum had simply vanished into thin air one night from the cruise ship taking them between Caribbean islands (a holiday won by Mags, who was ace at making up advertising slogans).

'Mags was lying and she isn't dead,' I explained. 'She's probably somewhere in Jamaica with a man, and when she gets tired of that, she'll come back again. She has a very low boredom threshold.'

'Look, darling, she was seen on the ship the evening after it left Jamaica, wasn't she?'

'Someone wearing one of her more flamboyant dresses and with dark hair was seen, but I suspect it was Mags.'

'But your mother's friend is blonde – and why on earth should she go to so much trouble anyway?'

'A wig? My mother often wore one when her hair looked ratty. And they were in the habit of covering up for each other.'

'Come on, Chloe! Look, it's been several weeks now, and I think, however hard it is, you'll have to accept that she had too much to drink – which you know was one of her failings – and went over the side in the small hours without anyone noticing. This time she *isn't* going to reappear as if nothing has happened. Which brings us back to what to do about Jake.'

'Nothing, because you're wrong. I expect she'll be back in time for our wedding, but if she isn't, then Jake can come and live with us, can't he? I mean, you always realised he would have to do that whenever Mum was away, didn't you?'

David was slow to answer, probably imagining the chaos one very lively boy could cause to his immaculately ordered life and minimalist white flat. I had already unintentionally caused enough of that while cooking chicken with a dark cacao *mole* sauce in his kitchen: chocolate *does* seem to get everywhere . . . And evidently he hadn't understood the strength of the bond between Jake and me.

'I'd like it to be just the two of us, for a while at least, darling,' he said eventually. 'You have to accept she's not coming back and that other, permanent arrangements need to be made. I mean, your grandfather's got a private income, hasn't he? He could send Jake to boarding school.'

'I don't think his private income would stretch that far

and anyway, Jake would hate it. He's always seen *me* as more of a mother figure than Mum. I'm the security in his life, and so it would simply be another betrayal. And his friends are all here in Merchester.'

'Then he'd hate being transposed to a city flat, wouldn't he?' David said quickly.

'Yes, but we did say we'd find a house in the country, one you could commute from. That could be somewhere round here, couldn't it?'

'I meant *much* later, when we want a family. I'd like to have you to myself for a bit. Anyway,' he added with a wry smile on his handsome face, 'I'm starting to think I'm allergic to the country because I come out in this damned rash every time I visit Merchester.'

'You can't really call Merchester country,' I objected, but it was true about the mysterious rash, because even now an angry redness was creeping up from the collar of his shirt.

I reminded myself to speak to Grumps about that . . . He and David had not really taken to each other, mainly because David spoke to him like an adult humouring a child: *big* mistake. He tended to take that tone with Jake too, and according to most of the locals, he'd never been any kind of child at all, but an imp of Satan.

'Look, Chloe, I really can't live with your brother. It isn't fair to ask me.' He ran his fingers through his ordered dark chestnut locks in a distracted way that showed me just how perturbed he was. He even loosened his silk tie – good grief!

'You'll have to find some other solution,' he announced with finality.

'I keep telling you Mum isn't dead!' I snapped, losing

patience. 'She bolts all the time, but she'll be back eventually: I've read the cards and I know I'm right. What's more, so has Zillah.'

But although they had told us that Mum was alive, they couldn't, of course, show us where she was or how long she would be gone.

'It's Jake or me,' he said quietly.

'But, David—'

'Do you love me?'

'Yes, of course,' I said, which I did, even if not with the searing passion of my first love. 'But—'

'Me, or Jake,' he repeated. 'I don't want to be hard-hearted, but it simply won't work having him to live with us – and I'm certainly not moving here, which I'm sure you were about to suggest next.'

'Well, yes, but it would be only until Mum comes back.'

He sighed long-sufferingly. 'Which she isn't going to do.'

He put on his jacket, which had been hanging neatly over the back of a chair in the chaotic kitchen area of the flat, where the paraphernalia of my budding Chocolate Wishes business covered every surface. In fact, there was a glossy smear of tempered couverture down one immaculate sleeve, which I decided not to point out.

'The wedding's in less than a fortnight, so you had better make your mind up fast, Chloe, hadn't you?'

'You can't really mean you'd end it all over this, David?'

'Yes, I do. Make other arrangements for Jake or you can call off the wedding.'

I still didn't really think he meant it and I might have tried to soften him up a little, but I was distracted at that moment by catching sight of the imp of Satan himself through the window. He seemed to be closing the bonnet of David's car . . . But no, David was always careful to lock it, so how could Jake . . . ?

The door slammed behind David and he strode across the gravel and got into his sports car without, so far as I could see, a word or look at Jake, who was standing innocently by with his hands behind his back.

The engine roared into life and then coughed a bit, before the car sputtered off down the lane. It sounded pretty ropey; I'd be surprised if it got him home without breaking down.

It hadn't, either. He'd phoned me when he finally got back, incandescent with rage. 'That child did it – and that's the last straw, Chloe, I mean it. Make other arrangements for him, or this is the last you'll ever hear from me.'

So that was it, and though I was heartbroken, I was also relieved that I had discovered how jealous he was of my love for Jake before we got married. I'd already known he resented my closeness to my old friends Felix and Poppy, but thought he would get over that. Funny how you can be so blind, isn't it?

I called off the wedding, which was both expensive and difficult at that late stage, and, resigning myself to perpetual spinsterhood, settled back into my life as before.

Except that this time, Mum *didn't* come back. And the awful thing was, none of us missed her.

28

Chapter Three

Chocolate Wishes

I was jarred back to the present by the realisation that Radio Four was now traitorously playing 'Darker Past Midnight', yet another damn song of Raffy's! Is there no escape from him?

You hear it everywhere since it was used as the theme song for a film. And it's still running as the soundtrack to that hugely popular car advert – the one in which a man is driving through the night alone, when suddenly a girl appears, sitting next to him, and you're never quite sure if he's imagining her or if she's a ghost . . .

This time it was the introductory music to a supernatural story, so clearly no radio channel is safe any more. But still, at least the hated sound of it brought me back to the present, because sitting about in a murky swamp of unwanted memories, feeling like one of love's rejects, was not going to get me anywhere.

My first impulse (apart from switching off the radio) was to phone up my best friend, Poppy, who together with her mother runs a riding stables called Stirrups just outside Sticklepond, and tell her the news about the move. But she was probably taking a lesson, or was out with a hack, and, even if she wasn't, half the time she forgets to take her mobile phone with her, or it isn't working because she's dropped it in a bucket of water.

Felix, my other best friend, was going to an auction that day to buy more books he didn't have room for: Marked Pages was bursting at the seams.

So in the end I just did what I always did at that time: typed up Grumps' letters on the computer and put them into envelopes ready to post, then started on the latest instalment of *Satan's Child*.

The new episode was surprisingly gripping, with a very scary bit when the tall, dark and compelling warlock hero (who from the detailed description looked amazingly like photographs of Grumps when younger) was inside the pentagram, while a really nasty demonic beast was testing the boundaries and trying to get in.

In fact, the scene was so realistic that I started to wonder if Grumps . . . But no, *surely* not? He just has a fertile imagination, that's all, as evidenced by his constant hints that some mysterious rival was loosing the slings and arrows of outrageous magic at him, which was probably, as Zillah said, 'all my eye and Betty Martin' (though don't ask me who Betty Martin is, I have no idea).

But I made a mental note that once we had moved to the Old Smithy I would take care to avoid entering the museum area when the coven was meeting. Maybe I could make a little sign for Grumps to hang on the connecting door between the cottage and the barn:

DO NOT DISTURB:
IN FOR A SPELL

I'm a fast touch-typist so it didn't take long to input everything. Then I printed the manuscript out ready to take it across in the morning when I collected the next lot.

I sort of fell into being Grumps' PA when I returned after that disastrous first term at university. It gave me something to occupy my mind with, while looking after Jake and waiting for Mum to come back from her latest fling, other than worrying about my future and what would happen when Raffy finally got my letter telling him everything . . .

I wrenched my mind back from the brink of yet another pointless trip down Memory Lane and reflected that I seemed to have managed pretty well without a Significant Other for the last few years. Among my blessings I had good friends (OK, only two, Felix and Poppy, but it's *quality* not quantity of friendship that counts) and a social life, though that mainly involved meeting up with them at the Falling Star in Sticklepond.

I didn't think I'd made a bad job of bringing Jake up either, considering his lively disposition: the police never pressed charges, even when he painted the Arbuthnot statue in front of the Town Hall blue. (Luckily there was a downpour soon afterwards and the emulsion was not quite dry, so most of it washed off.)

And the saying 'Who needs men when you've got chocolate?' was *literally* true in my case, since discovering a passion for it and then building up my successful Chocolate Wishes business had certainly put the icing back on the slightly jaded cupcake of life.

Little did the purchasers of my expensive chocolates know that they were whipped up practically on the kitchen table in the kitchen end of our living room. I made the chocolate shells in big batches and often spent the evenings sitting putting in the Wishes and sealing the two halves together with melted tempered chocolate (because if you don't use tempered chocolate, you get a white line round the join). I had the TV for company if Jake was out with his friends, or shut into his room, doing whatever teenage boys do – and whatever that is, it's probably *much* better that their big sisters don't know anything about it.

The flat – and probably me, too – always smelled deliciously of chocolate. Maybe that's why Felix, who has a sweet tooth, had started to look at me in a new, slightly appraising light . . . unless I was imagining it? I didn't think I was, though, unfortunately. I first noticed it about the time Grumps gave me that allegedly Mayan chocolate charm to say over the melting pot and the business took off like a rocket, though as I said, I'm sure the two events had nothing to do with each other: it was simply all my hard work paying off.

I had only part of the charm anyway. Grumps was trying to decipher the rest, which was written in some form of ancient Spanish, having specialised in dead and buried languages at Oxford. One of the letters I'd just typed up was to the archivist in Spain who had found the original document among some collection of papers he was cataloguing, though like Grumps his principal interest was in ley lines.

Since I'd just created a whole new batch of Wishes I had enough to keep me going for a while, so I packed and labelled that day's orders ready to post later with Grumps' mail.

All the time I was working I was thinking about the Old Smithy and the little cottage that I would have to myself once Jake had gone off to college, and especially what I could grow in the walled garden. Certainly a greater variety of herbs and, if there was room for a bigger greenhouse for over-wintering them, I'd have lots more varieties of scented geraniums. Pelargoniums were my newest passion. There were so many kinds I hadn't got yet . . . even one that was supposed to smell like chocolate!

And I would have tubs of hyacinths and those small, frilly Tête-à-tête daffodils in early spring, lavender and roses, nasturtiums, snapdragons and hollyhocks . . . My mind ran riot with horticultural possibilities.

But I still couldn't imagine Grumps running a museum, even a witchcraft one! He wasn't in any way gregarious, besides being over eighty and very set in his habits, so I expected Zillah would end up collecting the entrance money and issuing tickets. But since she used to operate the Tarot-reading booth on a Lancashire seaside pier with Granny, I imagined she'd take to it like a duck to water, especially since, unlike Grumps, she was hugely inquisitive about people.

Maybe she'd do Tarot readings on the side, and make herself a little nest egg?

Jake came home briefly to eat and change, before going out to an eighteenth birthday party. Zillah had given me some goulash, having made gallons, so that's what we had, together with crusty bread. I didn't mention Tabitha's tail to Jake, because I hoped perhaps it hadn't *quite* gone into the stew pot. The goulash tasted OK, anyway.

We followed it up with blackberry crumble, out of the freezer, with ice cream and then, while Jake filled any remaining interior spaces with about half a pound of crumbly Lancashire cheese (he is a bottomless pit as far as food is concerned), I broke the news of our imminent move to Sticklepond.

He stopped shovelling food in and stared at me through a lot of thick, blue-black hair. When it isn't dyed, it's the same dark brown as mine and our colouring is quite similar, apart from his brown eyes. Mine are the typical Lyon grey.

Jake's father was an Italian waiter Mum met on holiday, while mine was Chas Wilde, the former manager of the Pan's People-type dance troupe she performed in during the late sixties and early seventies, along with her friends Mags (Felix's mother) and Janey (Poppy's). Mum told me herself she only had me as an insurance policy after Wilde's Women disbanded, since Chas was married and so paid up without a murmur to keep her from letting the cat – or the baby – out of the bag.

But none of the three of them was much good in the motherhood stakes, which is probably why Felix, Poppy and I have such close bonds of friendship: we've always looked out for each other.

Jake resumed chewing, swallowed, then said, 'Grumps showed me the house agent's leaflet and asked me what I thought of the Old Smithy ages ago. I didn't think he was going to buy it, though. I just thought he was interested because it's at the junction of two important ley lines.'

'Yes, that does seem to have been his driving motivation,' I admitted, 'but also he's had a very good offer for this house, much more than it's worth. Did you know that he intends reopening the Old Smithy as a museum, too?' And I told him about Grumps' plans.

'So, you and me are to move into the little cottage, then?

How do I get to college from Sticklepond – can I borrow your car?'

'No way! But Grumps says you can use the Saab.'

'Even better. I look stupid in your baby Fiat.'

'I'm going to try and get the Old Smithy key tomorrow and have a look, but it has two bedrooms and there's a bathroom, though I don't think any of it is terribly modern. One room downstairs was extended into a shop front for Aimee Frinton's doll's hospital.'

'For *what*?'

'One of the Frinton sisters mended dolls and teddy bears. There used to be a lot of doll's hospitals, before mass-produced cheap toys took over. Grumps thinks it would be perfect for making Chocolate Wishes and I could even sell them directly to the public, if I wanted to.'

'You'll be practically round the corner from Felix's shop, too,' Jake pointed out in a casual manner that didn't fool me in the least, 'so you can see a lot more of him.'

'I see quite a lot of him already,' I said mildly. Having done his best to get rid of potential suitors for years, Jake had recently started to try to push me and Felix together – maybe that's what gave Felix the idea in the first place? I suspected it was because Jake was about to fly the nest and felt guilty at leaving me alone, but little did he know how much I was looking forward to some me-time!

Anyway, it was pointless, because I simply couldn't feel that way about Felix – he was more like family. Wilde's Women finally folded in the early seventies, when Janey suddenly married and had Poppy and then, as I've said, Mum had me for her own dubious reasons. Felix was a few years older, having been Mags' teenage mistake, so he was always a protective older brother figure to us.

So, you see, that's why I loved my friend like a brother, my brother like a son and my mother . . . not at all. Was it any wonder I'd always had trouble with relationships?

'Poppy's only a couple of miles out of Sticklepond on the Neatslake road, so I can see a lot more of *her* too,' I added pointedly.

Jake looked at the clock and rose to his feet. 'I'd better go. Ben's picking me up in a minute.'

'Well, remember, Jake—' I began warningly.

'I know, I know,' he interrupted me good-humouredly, shrugging himself into the long, black leather coat it had taken me ages – and hundreds of Chocolate Wishes – to save up for. 'No drugs or drinking to excess, and safe sex – I should be so lucky!'

'Jake!' I exclaimed, but he was gone.

I felt like every exhausted mother of a teenager, trying to walk the fine line between keeping him safe and coming across as boringly old and uncool.

And the irony of it was, I wasn't even a mother.

I rang Stirrups up later and told Poppy about Grumps buying the Old Smithy.

'But that's *amazing*!' she exclaimed. 'We were only discussing it at the last Sticklepond Parish Council meeting, because my cousin Conrad told me it had been sold and it was going to reopen as a museum. Didn't I tell you?'

'Well, you might have done, but I'd forgotten.' She and Felix are both on the Parish Council so they often tell me what they have been discussing, but it had never seemed either interesting or relevant – until then.

'I can't think why Con didn't tell me who was buying it!' she said.

'Grumps probably swore him to secrecy, you know what he's like. And why were you discussing it at the meeting? I wouldn't have thought it would need planning permission, since it's already been a museum. And the shop in the little cottage shouldn't either, because that was Aimee Frinton's doll's hospital.'

'I don't suppose either of them will need permission and we weren't so much discussing it as chatting at the end about how many tourists the Shakespeare manuscript find at Winter's End brings to the village, which is why we've got all the new gift shops and cafés and the Witch Craft Gallery to cater for them. Even Stirrups is doing much better and Marked Pages gets lots more passing trade. So everyone was really pleased the Old Smithy is going to be both a family home and museum again. They hope it will be something suitable, like the doll's—'

She broke off abruptly, so I expect she'd tried to put dolls and Grumps into the same mental picture frame and failed dismally to marry the two.

'No, of course it won't be dolls, will it? Silly me!'

'The only sort of doll Grumps might have in his museum is a poppet.'

'Poppet?'

'An image of someone used in magic.'

'You mean like a voodoo doll? Pins and stuff?'

'Sort of. They can be used for good things as well as bad.' I paused. 'So, do you think perhaps a museum of witchcraft and paganism might not be _quite_ what the Parish Council is hoping for?'

'Well . . . no, not exactly. But I'm sure it will be hugely popular,' she added hastily, 'though I don't quite know how Hebe Winter will take it.'

'You mean that having been the only witch in the village for so long, she might take umbrage when Grumps arrives?'

Poppy giggled. 'Chloe, you can't call her a witch. She goes to church and everything!'

'But Winter witches do, don't they? In any case, she's a much whiter witch than poor old Grumps. I'm pretty sure he strays across the line into the grey bits from time to time, though always with the best of intentions.'

'I think your grandfather is scary.'

'You know he's all bark and not a lot of bite, really.'

'I can't forget that when I was small he used to look at me as though he would like to turn me into something froglike. The fear has never quite worn off.'

'He doesn't see any point in babies and children until they're old enough to hold a sensible conversation,' I explained. 'It isn't that he doesn't love us, in his own way.'

'Yes, I suppose so,' Poppy said, not sounding totally convinced. 'But your granny was adorable.'

'She was, wasn't she? And though Zillah couldn't take her place, I'm very fond of her, too.'

'Hebe Winter calls herself a herbalist, rather than a witch,' Poppy said, reverting to the previous topic. 'I've heard some of the potions, like the love philtre, really work – and actually, I bought one!'

'Poppy! Who are you thinking of trying it on?' I demanded, because although neither of us had been lucky in love, Poppy still hadn't totally given up hope of finding Mr Right, and she was such a truly special person she deserved all the happy-ever-afterness going.

'Oh, no one,' she said hastily. 'It was just an impulse, Chloe. You know me – I can't love anything without four hoofs and a mane.'

38

'I think that's a slight exaggeration. You just haven't met the right man yet, that's all.'

'I think I often have, it's just that they don't think *I'm* the right girl. And nobody at all wanted to meet me from that internet dating site I joined.'

'Probably just as well, because you can't tell what kind of men you're in contact with. They could be really weird.'

'I suppose you're right and at least if you're going to be living nearby we can meet more often, so that will be fun.'

'And Felix too – we can be three singletons together,' I agreed. 'The Lonely Hearts Club of Sticklepond. Meanwhile, perhaps you'd better keep the news about who's bought the Old Smithy to yourself for a bit, Poppy, if you think it might make an upset. Let it suddenly burst on Sticklepond as a *fait accompli*.'

'But you'll tell Felix, won't you?'

'Yes, I'm going to ring him in a minute, but I'll swear him to secrecy too. In fact, the reason why I'm ringing you now is because I've arranged to get the keys to the Smithy from Conrad tomorrow, and I thought you might be able to get away and meet me for lunch in the Falling Star afterwards, so I can tell you all about it.'

'Hang on, I'll just ask Mum how we're fixed.'

She covered the phone, but I could still hear her shouting: 'Mum! Chloe wants me to meet her for lunch tomorrow – could you manage? What . . . ?'

But although Poppy's mother has an equally healthy pair of lungs (despite being a chain smoker), the other end of the conversation was just a faint noise in the background, so she must have been upstairs.

Poppy came back on. 'Mum says that's OK. It's a quiet day for lessons and the work experience girl can help her muck out and clean the tack.'

'About twelve then – and you can tell me what you've been doing recently.'

'Not a lot. Staying up all night with a pony with laminitis is about the most exciting it's got lately,' she said sadly. 'Oh, except that at the last Parish Council meeting, before we started talking about the museum, Miss Winter said the bishop is still looking for a non-stipendiary vicar to take over All Angels, because the alternative is to amalgamate our parish with another one and none of us is keen on that. That's what the *last* emergency Parish Council meeting was about, and there's yet another one this evening, so perhaps he's actually found us a vicar now – but I'll tell you about it tomorrow.'

'I can hardly wait.'

'At least we will be back in the village hall tonight. We had to have the last meeting in the church vestry because the Scouts were clearing away their jumble sale, and it was freezing. Mr Merryman, the temporary vicar, seems a very nervous man, though I don't think the fact that three of the council were already wearing Elizabethan dress for the Re-enactment Society meeting afterwards really helped – Miss Winter as Queen Elizabeth the First is quite terrifying! And then Mr Lees, the organist, was practising fugues all the way through, so that was really gloomy.'

'I can imagine. And what did you say a non-stipendiary vicar was, again?'

'Someone who has got ordained but doesn't need a salary, basically.'

'Oh, right – an economy vicar. And tell me again, who's on the Parish Council as well as you and Felix and Miss Winter as chairman?'

'I don't think you ever listen to a word I say,' she

complained, but complied. 'Well, there's the Winter's End steward, Laurence Yatton . . .'

'Oh, I know – elderly, silver-haired and handsome, drives an old Land Rover.'

'Yes, that's him. And you've probably seen his sister Effie, too. She used to be a gym mistress in a private school but now she works off all that excess energy by running the Brownies, the tennis club and the Elizabethan Re-enactment Society. Then there's the vicar and the village policeman, Mike Berry.'

'I've met Mike a couple of times in Felix's shop with his girlfriend, Anya, the one with red dreadlocks.'

'Yes, she's very nice, isn't she? She's an old friend of Sophy Winter, who inherited the Winter's End estate the year before last and she runs the gift shop there when the house is open to the public.'

'Is that everyone?'

She counted up: 'Me, Felix, Miss Winter, the vicar, Mike, Laurence and Effie . . . Yes, that's it.'

'Small, but perfectly formed,' I commented.

When I rang Felix he wanted to come over to the Old Smithy with me, but I wouldn't let him. It was hard to explain, but I felt I wanted to be on my own this first time, especially when I saw the cottage where Jake and I would be living. He agreed to meet me and Poppy at the pub at twelve, though, to hear all about it.

'In fact, I might as well shut for the whole day; the village is as quiet as a grave and probably will be until Easter, when Winter's End reopens.'

'Oh, I think it might get slightly livelier before that. Don't forget, Jake will be moving in too.'

'Oh my God!' he said, though actually he had suffered much less from Jake's practical jokes and general awfulness than any of my boyfriends had, probably due to being just a friend rather than a potential suitor who might take me away.

'Not to worry, he seemed to grow out of that phase ages ago,' I assured him. 'Or maybe he just stopped because I'd finally given up on men?'

'But you haven't really, of course, you've just been busy like me and the years have slipped away,' he said. 'Then one morning you wake up and think how nice it would be to have another person there to share things with, someone undemanding and comfortable and—'

'Like a cosy pair of slippers?' I suggested sweetly. 'Well, you are older than me, Felix, so I'm not saying I might not feel like that one day, but if I do, I'll get a dog.'

Chapter Four

Falling Star

As usual I couldn't fall asleep that night until I heard Jake come in, which he did fairly quietly considering the size of his big, black boots. But I still got up extra early next morning, so I had time to pick up the latest chapter from Grumps and pack Chocolate Wishes orders, before driving over to Sticklepond.

I collected the key from the house agents on the way there – the main branch is here in Merchester – and promised Poppy's cousin Conrad that I would lock it up carefully behind me and return them later.

'Not that I've shown the property to anyone else since the Misses Frinton accepted your grandfather's offer, of course,' Conrad said quickly. 'And even before that, once he'd expressed an interest in buying it, because he told me—' He broke off, looking embarrassed and uncomfortable.

'He told you that if you did, he would put a curse on you, one that would render your life unutterably hideous?' I asked helpfully.

'Er . . . yes,' he agreed sheepishly. 'Of course, he was joking – I know your grandfather!'

He didn't sound too sure about it, though.

The Old Smithy is at the very end of the High Street, almost opposite the Falling Star, where I was to meet Felix and Poppy later. As I drove past, Mrs Snowball, the publican's ninety-year-old mother, was outside the front door donkey-stoning a square of the grey pavement into sparkling whiteness. She'd done it all her life and old habits died hard. Behind her, the meteor-shaped brass door knocker sparkled blindingly in the weak February sunshine.

The Falling Star is much older than the Green Man, the more popular pub at the other end of the village, and since it was once a coaching inn, I suppose it made sense at the time to have the blacksmith nearby.

The Old Smithy itself is a collection of mismatched parts that have been rendered into a vaguely cohesive whole by the application of a lot of whitewash. As I arrived I was just in time to see the museum sign being loaded into a large van, presumably at Grumps' direction, to be repainted. He must be pretty sure of himself, because I didn't think he'd exchanged contracts yet, though I could have been wrong – he was infuriatingly secretive.

Following Conrad's directions, I parked in the small grav-elled area behind the museum, which was sheltered by a bronze-leaved beech hedge. I had the most enormous bunch of keys, some of them so ancient as to be collector's pieces, but luckily they were all labelled.

I started with the Victorian house, which was quite substantial and also, since it was where the Frinton sisters had lived, perfectly comfortable and up to date as regards bathrooms and electrical wiring. If the décor was a trifle on the gloomy Victorian side, then so too was Grumps. But the scarlet Aga in the enormous kitchen struck a surprisingly modern note and Zillah would adore it. By the time she had swathed the windows in bright lengths of fabric in clashing colours, littered the place with lace-edged runners, splashily painted toleware jugs and hideous ornaments constructed out of seashells, it would look like an explosion inside a traditional gypsy vardo, just as our present kitchen did.

A door from an inner hallway gave access to the museum, which was quite big, with a wooden floor and lots of ceiling lights. There were rows of empty glass display cabinets and a fixed mahogany desk near the museum entrance, with a cash drawer and a yellowing roll of admission tickets, all a bit sad and dusty. The room was certainly more than large enough to accommodate all of Grumps' treasures, even if he divided one end off for his meetings. I hoped it would be the end *furthest* away from my cottage.

And the cottage was the thing I most wanted to see – so of course I'd left it till last, like you do with the most exciting-looking present under the Christmas tree. But now I found the key for the door and entered what would be my new home with a feeling of excited anticipation.

I went down two shallow, worn steps, straight into what had been the doll's hospital, with a glazed shop window built out onto Angel Lane, round the corner from the museum. Presumably the Misses Frinton had had the extension done long before planning regulations became so restrictive.

A polished wooden counter ran right across the front of the room and behind it were worktops, a sink and racks of drawers labelled with fascinating things like 'Teddy Bear Noses', 'Doll's Eyes – Blue' and 'Whiskers – Large, Black'.

There were several electric sockets where I could plug in the Bath – the machine that tempered the couverture chocolate – and even a small double gas ring, presumably once used for melting glue, or something like that, but now perfect for a *bain-marie*, or for making toffee. The place was ideal!

Behind it was a small sitting room that looked as if it had been used most recently for storage, since the one bare bulb dangling from the ceiling shone down onto flattened cardboard cartons littering the balding lino floor. The deeply recessed window facing onto the garden was murky and festooned with furry cobwebs, but had a seat built in beneath it. There was an open fireplace bordered by art nouveau purplish-pink glazed tiles, and a twisting staircase went up in one corner behind what I had thought was a cupboard door until I opened it.

The kitchen had been added onto the back at some more recent point in time, with a very utilitarian white bathroom above it – though I was just grateful it had one at all and not just an outside toilet! But Grumps had said something about the Frintons having had tenants in the cottage in the dim and distant past, so I suppose they had updated it a bit then.

Upstairs, as well as the bathroom, were two bedrooms and a small airing cupboard housing the water tank and an ancient immersion heater – all mod cons provided! And although the cottage smelled chilly and unused, it didn't seem damp and the thick stone walls would keep the heat in in winter, and out in summer.

Finally I went out through the kitchen into the garden,

which was surrounded by a tall wall of mellow bricks, with matching paths in a herringbone pattern, slimy with damp and disuse. Large, half-moon beds ran around the walls and there was a big central round bed in which was a tree – plum, I suspected. It looked half dead, but plum trees love to fool you like that.

It was all very overgrown, and at this time of year it was hard to tell what was there. It would be exciting to see what came up in the spring, and to clear and replant parts of it. There was certainly lots of room for my pots and my little greenhouse – there was even sufficient space to have a bigger one, when I could afford it.

I absolutely loved it – it was like having my very own Secret Garden – and I decided then and there that I would have the back bedroom overlooking the courtyard, leaving the front for Jake, even though it was slightly larger.

When I finally looked at my watch it was already noon and I had been there for hours, although it felt more like minutes! I left hastily, retracing my path through the Old Smithy and the house, locking the doors behind me, one by one.

When I emerged the road was momentarily deserted, though to the right I could just see Felix's swinging sign for Marked Pages, the first of the High Street shops. They were increasing steadily in number: as well as the Spar near the Green and an old-established saddlers, there was now a new café-cum-craft gallery (Witch Crafts), a delicatessen and a couple of gift shops. Another teashop was in the throes of being renovated.

The Shakespeare find at Winter's End a couple of years ago had really revitalised the village, so Grumps was lucky to have got the Old Smithy, especially at what seemed to be a very advantageous price. I wondered how he'd managed that.

There was no sign of Felix and Poppy until I crossed the road to the Falling Star and saw them waving at me from the bow window of the snug. Mind you, if I didn't know them so well, I wouldn't have recognised them behind the thick bull's-eye glass panes, because they looked like dubious sea creatures seen dimly lurking in green waters.

As usual I tried to avoid stepping on the clean square of pavement as I went in, because it seemed an unlucky thing to do. Mrs Snowball was now sitting behind a tiny reception desk under the stairway (the inn lets rooms, mostly to business reps), knitting something voluminously pink and fluffy while watching a portable TV. She looked up at me, described a suspiciously pentagram-like shape in the air with one needle, and grinned gappily.

Oh God, not another of them? She'd never done that before!

Slightly shaken, I turned right into the snug, where Felix was now at the bar buying me a ladylike half of bitter shandy (I was driving, after all). He turned and gave me a hug – a tall, loose-limbed man with soft, light brown eyes, floppy hair and the sort of nose that has a knobbly bit in the middle. It's a nice face, in its way, but you can't call it handsome.

'Hi, Chloe – you look lovely,' he said warmly, though I was just wearing jeans garnished with cobwebs and the odd streak of garden slime, but he'd probably just said exactly the same to Poppy, because he's nothing if not kind. I sometimes think I'm imagining that he's trying to move our relationship onto a new, more romantic footing and actually I do truly hope so, because I like things just the way they are.

'Is that my drink? I'll carry it, then you can manage the other two,' I said, kissing his cheek. He smelled, not unattractively, of old leather book bindings.

'Look what Felix found for me!' called Poppy, gaily waving a paperback copy of *I Had Two Ponies* by Josephine Pullein-Thompson. 'The last one of hers I hadn't got!'

'Great,' I said, sitting down next to her. She smelled of sweet hay and horses, and I expect I was permanently chocolate-fragranced, with just a hint of scented geranium, so anyone with a good nose could guess blindfold what the three of us did for a living.

'I thought I had a Heyer for you, Chloe, but the cover was torn,' Felix said.

While Poppy loves old children's pony adventure books, I collect vintage Georgette Heyer hardbacks in those lovely, misty, dream-like paper jackets. Felix also looks out for the rarer volumes Grumps would like to add to his already huge, esoteric and eclectic library, which is probably where most of his income goes.

Poppy was almost as excited about my moving to the Old Smithy as I was. 'But I still think it was mean, not letting us view it with you.'

'I just wanted to see it on my own the first time,' I explained. 'I'll have to come back and measure for curtains and furniture, so perhaps if you can both get away, you can see it then?'

'I've been in the museum and the doll's hospital, but not for years,' Poppy said. 'So, what's the rest like?'

I described it all in detail, but I may have dwelled rather longer on the garden than the rest of it put together. Anyway, they both generously volunteered to help me clean and paint the cottage.

'Or anything, really, that you need another pair of hands to do,' Poppy added. 'Now, do you want to hear our news?'

'*Our?*' I looked from one to the other of them, with a raised eyebrow. 'You're getting married and you want me to be bridesmaid?'

'Don't be silly,' Poppy giggled.

'It would be nice to settle down with someone, though, wouldn't it?' Felix suggested rather pointedly. 'Just not Poppy!'

'Yes, because the three of us are so like family that it would be like marrying a sibling,' she agreed. 'Completely out of the question.'

'It certainly would be,' I agreed heartily, and Felix looked gloomy.

Poppy said, 'What I meant was the news from last night's emergency Parish Council meeting.'

'Did you tell them that Grumps had bought the museum?'

'No, though I expect we both looked totally guilty. Luckily, something else was distracting Miss Winter, because she usually has eagle eyes. You remember I told you that the bishop was trying to find a non-stipendiary vicar to take over All Angels?'

I nodded. 'Have they found one?'

'Yes, and the brilliant thing is that he's buying the vicarage too!'

'And he's the kind of vicar you were telling me about, who doesn't need to be paid?' I asked. 'A freebie?'

'Well, in effect,' Felix agreed. 'Basically, it's someone who's been ordained but is either still following another career, or so rich he doesn't need a salary. Hebe Winter is terribly pleased about it, but the bishop didn't say a lot about the new vicar except that he used to be some kind of pop star. And she seemed to think that when he came to look at the vicarage he should have called in to see her too, so she *was* a bit narked about that.'

'I expect he came when the estate agents had that open day and perhaps he hadn't even made his mind up to move to Sticklepond then. But isn't that exciting news, Chloe?' Poppy's cheeks glowed and her eyes, the soft blue of washed-out denim, sparkled. 'An ex-pop star! I thought it might be Cliff Richard, but Hebe says that's daft.'

'It is daft. Everyone would know if he'd taken holy orders,' Felix pointed out.

'Yes, but then who on earth could it be?'

'I think one of the Communards got ordained,' I offered.

'I didn't know that,' Felix said.

'You'll have to come to church and see him when he arrives, whoever he is,' Poppy suggested.

'Come on, Poppy, you know I haven't been inside a church in my life! Grumps would have forty fits, the earth would tremble and the spire crumble to dust.'

'No, I'm sure it wouldn't. Remember the angel in the churchyard?' she reminded me. 'I think she was trying to tell you something, so perhaps you *should* try it and see.'

'What? Which angel?' Felix demanded. 'Have you two been keeping secrets from me?'

I hesitated. We'd never discussed the angel with anyone except Granny, and at this length of time it was hard to know how much of what we remembered was real and what imagined.

'Oh,' I said as lightly as I could, 'it was something that happened when we were little girls. Poppy had come to stay for a couple of nights because Janey was in hospital and since

51

Mum was away too, we were in a bedroom in the main part of the house, near Granny. The window looks down over the wall into the old churchyard and the first night we both saw . . . well, we saw a white figure. With wings.'

'An angel,' Poppy agreed positively.

'But surely the churchyard is full of white marble angels?' suggested Felix. 'Two over-excited and tired little girls, late at night . . . the imagination does play tricks.'

'The angel was moving and we could see her clearly even though it was a misty night – swirly mist, like in horror films, only this wasn't frightening.'

'Her face was a bit scary though,' Poppy put in.

'Scary?'

'I didn't really mean *scary* – just sort of beautiful, but remote,' she explained. 'And then Chloe's granny heard us whispering and came in, and when we told her and looked for the angel, she had gone.'

'There had to be a rational explanation,' Felix said.

'No, it was a holy sign,' Poppy insisted. 'We were going to stay up and watch for it again the next night, I remember, but your mum came home, Chloe, so we moved back into your room in the flat.'

'You know, I'd forgotten that! And Granny said she didn't think we would see it twice anyway.'

'Oh well,' Felix said good-naturedly, 'I can see you both believe in it, so I'll have to believe it too. But I see now why you have a thing about angels, Chloe.'

'We all have guardian angels, Felix. I told you that when I read the oracle cards for you.'

He looked over his shoulder nervously, as if his might be standing right behind him. 'Let's have another drink,' he suggested.

'Not for me. I have to get back and type up some letters for Grumps, and then make a big batch of Wishes because my stock of hearts plummeted what with Valentine's Day coming up – I had loads of orders this morning.'

'And the blacksmith's coming out any minute now,' Poppy said. 'Honeybun's cast one of his shoes and it's hardly worn, so I want to walk the paddock and try and find it before he gets there.'

'I suppose I might as well go back and open the shop up then,' Felix said. 'I'm thinking of putting a sofa into the front room and a coffee machine to attract people in – what do you think?'

'It's a good idea. And you can leave out leaflets for Grumps' museum when he opens, and we can have information about your bookshop on display,' I said. 'Mutual publicity.'

'Oh, but just wait until Hebe finds out about the witch-craft museum!' Poppy said, shuddering. 'Sparks will fly!'

'I sincerely hope you're wrong,' I replied. 'I get enough of that with Jake and those firesticks he's borrowed from a friend!'

Chapter Five

Pay Dirt

Grumps *had* exchanged contracts, so life suddenly became very hectic and I wished he or Zillah had given me a bit more warning about the move.

My Angel card readings kept helpfully suggesting I spend a day at the seaside, or visit a garden to soothe my soul ready for a major but fortuitous change of direction, but there wasn't time. My batteries would simply have to recharge themselves with solar power.

By some alchemy (or so he said), Grumps had managed to get the purchasers of our home to let us stay there for two weeks while the Old Smithy was cleaned and repainted inside and out. They were a pleasant pair of middle-aged American antique dealers and I wondered why on earth they had fallen in love with a shabby chunk of Victorian Gothic, situated right next to a graveyard. I didn't want to rock the boat by asking them, though.

Felix recommended the painters and decorators he'd used when he moved Marked Pages from Merchester to Sticklepond a few years before, and he also suggested a local cleaning firm called Dolly Mops. Grumps must have promised them each an enticing bonus if they finished in record time, because the work was well under way when I went back with Poppy only a couple of days after my initial visit, in order to measure for curtains.

Grumps did not revisit, but ordered everything from afar, choosing the interior paintwork colours from the gloomier end of the Farrow and Ball range and stipulating that all the original William Morris wallpaper was to remain. But Zillah had free range in the kitchen, her sitting room and her own bedroom suite, where a bold paper featuring an unlikely combination of giant red peonies against a blue trellis was destined to reign supreme.

It was lucky that Grumps' new home was also Victorian Gothic, because it meant that most of the furniture and curtains he already had turned out to fit perfectly. Even his huge range of bookshelves could be accommodated in the room that was designated as his new study.

Our flat was a more recent addition, furnished with a mixture of the cheap modern stuff that my mother had favoured and bits and pieces I'd picked up in junk shops. Most of it just wouldn't fit, and anyway, it was such a pretty little cottage that I yearned to go all chintzy and cabbage-rosy.

Of course, Jake wanted his new bedroom painted black, like his present one, and threw a teenage hissy fit when I said the whole house was going to be cream with touches of the old-rose purply-pink colour of the tiles in the sitting-room fireplace, or as near as I could get to it. But in the interests of fraternal harmony we compromised eventually: he was to have one wall painted purple, plus some new black and purple curtains and a matching bed throw – very retro. It sounded vile, but could easily be fixed when he grew out of this phase . . . if he ever did.

Grumps had opted to have the removal men pack everything up, and then unpack again at the other end, but Jake and I decided to do our own. Jake, because he was at just that secretive age when your most treasured possessions might be misinterpreted by alien (or even sisterly) eyes, and me because I didn't have a huge amount of stuff . . . apart from the Chocolate Wishes equipment and stock, about a million ornamental angels and dozens of potted geraniums. And I had to make arrangements to move the geraniums, the mini greenhouse and all the pots and tubs of plants in the courtyard myself, since the removal firm refused to take them.

'Poppy and I found some rose-patterned Laura Ashley curtains for the cottage in a charity shop in Ormskirk yesterday,' I told Grumps, when I went in to collect the latest chapter of *Satan's Child* and a letter that seemed to consist of several pages of barely veiled but mysterious threats. It was addressed to a book reviewer who had dared to say rude things about his last novel, *The Desirous Devil*. 'And a lovely coffee table – it's a big brass tray on knobbly black wooden tripod legs.'

Grumps had generously given me a cheque to buy anything I needed for my new home, but I was making it stretch as far as possible. Anyway, it's much more fun (and a lot more ecologically sound) to search out stuff from charity and junk shops, though there wasn't much time. It was just as well Stirrups was quiet at this time of year, so Poppy could get away occasionally and help me.

I wasn't really expecting Grumps to be terribly interested

in what I was saying, so I was surprised when he stopped scribbling on a bit of paper, looked up and said, 'I seem to recall that there are one or two pieces of furniture stored in the attic. Perhaps there might be something you would want among them? In any case, someone should decide what is worth taking with us, or can be left for the Meerlings.'

'Marlings,' I corrected. 'OK, I'll sort that out, Grumps. And you've reminded me – that's where I put Mum's stuff, so I'd better go through it, hadn't I? She isn't going to want any of her clothes when she does come back now – they'll be out of fashion – though I suppose I'll have to keep her personal possessions.'

The day I put them up there was not a happy one. For some reason, Jake had been totally convinced Mum would turn up on the first anniversary of her disappearing trick and was correspondingly so deeply upset when she didn't, in an angry, thirteen-year-old sort of way, that he took it out by trashing his bicycle with a tyre wrench and then vanishing for hours. In his absence I had shoved all her possessions into old suitcases and boxes, clearing the flat of any lingering trace of her presence, and I hadn't thought about them since.

'Label anything Lou might still want and it can be transferred to the attic of the new house,' Grumps suggested.

'OK. There shouldn't be much.' I paused. 'Do you think she *will* ever come back? It's been a long time.'

'You would need to ask Zillah that, but I would much prefer she didn't. Life is more tranquil without her, and Zillah assures me that she is alive and well.' He held out the slip of paper he had been covering in his black, crabbed writing and added, 'The ancient Mayan chocolate charm I gave you was, if you remember my saying so, incomplete.

I think I have managed to translate a little more with the help of my friend in Cordoba. He wrote to me this morning with some suggestions. You might want to add the additional lines when you are preparing your chocolate.'

'Since the ancient Mayan people didn't have a written language, I can't imagine how they could pass down a charm for chocolate making anyway, Grumps!'

'There is such a thing as oral history, you know, Chloe, and no reason why such a thing should not have been written down by one of the early Spanish *conquistadores* – as it was – and carried back to Spain.'

'Yes, but—'

'Just have faith. The last version worked, to a certain extent, did it not? Business boomed.'

'My sales *did* rise,' I admitted, though I was sure that had more to do with the excellence of the chocolate and the novelty of the concept, rather than the brief incantation of some probably spurious spell over the tempering pot.

Just out of curiosity, when he had managed to decipher the whole thing I thought I should try a sort of blind chocolate tasting session, with Felix and Poppy as the guinea pigs, to see if they thought it made any difference to the taste.

I found one or two dust-sheeted gems among the rolls of moth-eaten carpet and broken furniture up in the attic – a white Lloyd Loom chair and matching small ottoman that would be lovely in my bedroom. I put them to one side and labelled them for the removal men, along with a small mirror that some long-gone Victorian miss had adorned with a frame of shells. A few were broken or missing, but I had an old sweet jar full of seaside treasures that Jake and I had collected when he was a little boy, so I could easily replace them.

Other than that, there was just a sad huddle of Mum's stuff. There weren't any books (like Zillah, she didn't read anything except magazines) and not much paperwork, since when it became clear that she wasn't coming back any time soon, Grumps had taken her bank and credit card statements so he could settle her affairs, though I was sure he was under no legal obligation to do that. We thought escaping her spiralling debts was part of the reason she took off in the first place.

I'd packed up what was left, together with her costume jewellery, makeup and beauty aids. Most of her extensive wardrobe I'd crammed into a huge cabin trunk that was already up here.

Now I opened the lid, releasing a wave of Je Reviens and a lot of unwanted memories of when I had been a small child, convinced it was my fault that my mother didn't seem to love me very much . . .

I'd brought a roll of strong plastic bin bags with me and began to fill them with clothes. There were a lot of expensive labels in there, and even though they were out of date I could probably have made some money selling them on eBay. But there was not much time and, besides, I just wanted to clear as much of her out of our lives as possible. Time for Jake and me to have a whole, fresh new start.

As I filled the bags and repacked the old suitcases, I carried them all the way down to the front hall and stacked them ready to go to a local charity shop, so I was getting tired, hot and grubby by the time I reached the last couple of boxes. The first and largest one was full of bric-a-brac, teddy bears and various trashy holiday souvenirs, so I labelled that for the attic and moved it over with the furniture that was going to the new house.

Finally I was left with just a large shoebox of old letters. I hadn't looked at them when I was packing her stuff up, but now I found myself sitting under the skylight on the Lloyd Loom chair with the contents spread across the top of the ottoman. I wasn't sure why I wanted to read them; I didn't really think they would suddenly illuminate some depths that my shallow and self-centred mother had kept hidden because I was sure she hadn't got any. What you saw was what you got.

There wasn't a huge collection, though some dated back to just before I was born. My mother had scrawled remarks on a couple of the envelopes like 'Yes!!!' and 'Result!!!' so I started with those – and hit pay dirt with the very first one. Then, with horrified illumination dawning, I went through all of the rest, finishing with a couple of notes in Mags' distinctive handwriting.

After that, I just sat there unconscious of time passing, my lap full of secrets and lies, until I heard the unmistakable thumping of Jake's big boots on the wooden attic stairs. Hastily bundling all the letters together, I thrust them back into the box and crammed on the lid, wishing what I had learned could be as neatly packed away and forgotten.

'What on earth are you doing up here?' Jake demanded, ducking his head to get through the low doorway. 'The lights and radio are on in the flat, but Zillah hadn't seen you for hours. I thought you'd vanished.'

'Like Mum' was the unspoken inference. I'm sure that's why he had always got rid of my boyfriends – every time I'd gone out with one of them, he'd been afraid I wouldn't come back.

'Sorry, Jake. Grumps asked me to sort things out up here ready for the move, and I lost track of time.'

'You look a bit pale.'

'I'm tired, I've been up and down stairs with bags of stuff. But I've just about finished now and I found this lovely Lloyd Loom furniture for my bedroom. What do you think?'

'It's a bit *girly*,' he commented, his attention clearly elsewhere. 'But I like that huge trunk with all the travel stickers on it! Do you think Grumps would let me have it?'

'It would take up an awful lot of floor space in your room, you know.'

'Maybe, but I could store loads of stuff in it, so the rest of my room would actually be much tidier,' he suggested cunningly.

'I suppose it would fit at the foot of your bed, if you really wanted it, and Grumps won't mind because he said I could have anything from the attic.' I handed him the roll of labels. 'Here, write "Cottage – front bedroom" on this and stick it on top.'

He did that and then I asked him to carry the last boxes and bags down to the hall.

'OK,' he said, grabbing two heavy bags in each hand as if they weighed practically nothing, 'but I really came to find out what's for dinner.'

I passed a weary hand across my forehead. 'Oh, I don't know . . . I haven't thought about it yet.'

'Zillah says she's doing steak and kidney pudding, mushy peas and crinkly chips, but you have to say now if you want any, before she starts cooking.'

'You have that, if you fancy it, Jake. I'm meeting Felix and Poppy this evening, and by the time I've showered all this filth off, there'll only be time for a snack. What are you doing tonight?'

'I promised Grumps I'd help him with something,' he said mysteriously, and then laughed at my expression. 'No, I'm not about to become part of the coven, cavorting about with a lot of wrinklies, or do anything else daft! He just wanted me to research someone called Digby Mann-Drake on the internet for him.'

'Digby *Mandrake*? That sounds even more bogus than Gregory Warlock!'

'Mann with a double "n" and it's hyphenated. I expect he made the Mann bit up, since he seems a bit Aleister Crowley – all fancy robes and "Do what thou wilt shall be the whole of the law",' said Gregory Warlock's grandson, casually knowledgeable. 'In fact, he sounds a nasty piece of work altogether and he's been sending veiled threats to Grumps, because he wanted to buy the Old Smithy, only he fell ill at the crucial moment.'

'Opportune,' I commented, thinking that this sounded awfully like the plot of *Satan's Child*. Could this Mann-Drake possibly be the Secret Adversary, both of the novel and in real life? The man who had tried to prevent Grumps realising the significance of the Old Smithy's magical position? The plot thickened. 'Do they know each other, Jake?'

'They were at Oxford at the same time, but I don't think their paths have crossed since, until now. Grumps wants to probe Mann-Drake's weak spots so he can protect us if he tries any mumbo jumbo,' he said with cheerful irreverence. 'That's why he wanted the information. I'll see you later.'

I carried the shoebox of letters down to my room, then dashed back up to the attic one last time in order to blast the inside of the cabin trunk with Jake's very overpowering Lynx aftershave, which entirely vanquished the scent of Je

Reviens. There was no need for both of us to wallow in miserable memories.

I showered quickly, so I had time to do an internet search for one of Mum's correspondents, who turned out to be an actor, printing out his photo and some information to take with me to the Falling Star, where I was meeting Poppy and Felix.

Zillah must have come into the living room just after I'd finished that and gone back into the bathroom to apply a bit of slap, because there was a plate of dinner on the table covered by a hot, inverted soup bowl. I hadn't thought I was hungry at all until I lifted the bowl off and the aroma of steak and kidney pudding and chips hit me, but I ate it in five minutes flat, standing up, before dashing out.

Indigestion was on the cards – if I could tell heartburn from heartache these days.

Chapter Six

Stupid Cupid

We were all sitting round the table in the snug at the Falling Star, Mum's collection of letters and the computer print-outs spread over the table between our glasses.

'So, let's get this straight, Chloe,' Felix said, making a valiant attempt to untangle my incoherent narrative. 'When Lou got pregnant with you, she didn't just tell Chas Wilde that he was your father, she told *another* man he was too?'

'Yes, as a moneymaking scam. Since they were both married, once she threatened to tell their wives they agreed to pay her to keep quiet about it. She had quite a little racket going.'

I hadn't thought I could feel any more disillusioned about my mother, but this sank my perception of her to whole new depths and I'm not sure anything could survive down there, certainly not love.

'Gosh!' said Poppy, wide-eyed. 'So your father could be either of them?'

'Yes – or neither, because there's no guarantee it wasn't someone else entirely, is there?'

'Oh, I don't know,' Felix said thoughtfully. 'Since she seems to have got pregnant as a means to an end, it probably *is* one of them. It's still quite likely it was Chas Wilde, like she always told you, you know.'

'Yes, he's always taken an interest in you and sent Christmas and birthday presents, which he didn't do for either of *us*,' Poppy agreed, 'and called in to see you when he's in the North.'

When I was a child those had been short, awkward visits, with me desperate to know why, if he was my daddy, I wasn't allowed to call him that, or ask him anything else that puzzled me, like why he didn't live with me and Mum. But later, when I was old enough to understand, we had grown closer and easier with each other. I hadn't seen a lot of him since Mum vanished, but we kept in touch by phone and email.

'But all that doesn't prove he's my father, just that Mum convinced him he was,' I pointed out, and then looked down despairingly at the letters. 'I wish now I hadn't read these so I would still believe Chas *is* my father, because at least he's kind and nice, despite being stupid enough to let my mother use him!'

'But, Chloe, he may very well turn out *still* to be your father,' Poppy said.

'I know, and I want it to be Chas,' I said, picking up one of the envelopes from the table, 'because when you read this letter he sent to Mum when I was ten, after he'd finally confessed everything to his wife, he made it clear he was still going to carry on supporting me – that he *cared* about me.'

'He is a nice man,' agreed Poppy, 'and he certainly paid for one weak moment, didn't he?'

'Through the nose – and maybe for someone who wasn't his child after all. Have a look at these two sets of photos I got off the internet and tell me if you think I look like any of them. The ones of Chas are from when he was younger, so he looks different.'

Felix and Poppy put their heads together over the photographs and Felix asked, 'Who is this other man?'

'Carr Blackstock, an actor, mostly theatre work, especially Shakespeare, but he has appeared in one or two things on TV. When I Googled the name, he was the only one who came up, so it must be him.'

'He looks slightly familiar,' Poppy said, then added hesitantly, 'though actually that might be because you look a bit alike. Slightly *elfin*, if you know what I mean – like Kate Bush.'

'Elfin? I don't look at all elfin,' I said with disgust, '*or* like Kate Bush. I wish people wouldn't keep saying that!'

'Well, it certainly wasn't me who got called "Pixie Ears" at school!' she retorted.

'No, you were "Pudding" because you ate everyone else's jam roly-poly and custard on Wednesdays!'

'Only because I needed the energy. I burned up loads of calories mucking out my ponies before school every morning,' Poppy said with dignity.

'Now, girls!' Felix said mildly. 'I think we're straying from the subject in hand – and I have to agree with Poppy that if I had to pick one of these two as being related to you, then Carr Blackstock would be the man. It's hard to tell from printouts, but he even seems to have the same unusually light grey eyes.'

'I think my printer cartridge is fading. But anyway, Grumps has grey eyes.'

'Yes, but ordinary grey ones,' he said.

'There's nothing at all ordinary about Grumps!'

'That's true, they *are* a bit piercing.'

'What do you know about this actor?' asked Poppy, and I fished out the information sheet from the bottom of the heap. One of us must have slopped his or her drink, because it was a bit damp and wrinkly.

'He's been married to the same woman *for ever* and they have four children. Mum must have got him in a weak moment, like Chas. It doesn't say a lot about men's faithfulness, does it?'

'We're not all alike,' Felix said, which was quite true in his case. He is the faithful-unto-death sort and divorced his wife several years before, only when she had a very blatant affair. 'But your mother must have been stunning at the time, if that's a mitigating factor? And we all make mistakes in life, of one kind or another.'

'He must have been furious about making that one, because apart from his really terse answer to her news about the pregnancy, there aren't any letters until my eighteenth birthday, when he sent the note saying he wasn't going to pay any more and he'd never been entirely convinced I was his child anyway.'

'I suppose that was fair enough, because they didn't really have DNA testing then like they do now, so he wouldn't have been able to prove it one way or the other, would he?' Felix said.

'But if he'd actually *seen* you he'd have spotted the likeness,' Poppy said.

'I don't think there is a likeness.' I scrutinised the photos again. 'You're imagining it.'

'He's just the most like you out of the two of them, that's all,' Felix conceded.

'Or the least *unlike*. And whether he believed it or not, he paid up, just like poor old Chas, so Mum must have thought she was on to a good thing until the money stopped coming in altogether when I was eighteen.' I tossed the picture back on the heap. 'And then the truly awful thing is that she thought she'd try the same trick all over again – by getting pregnant with Jake!'

Poppy's pale denim-blue eyes widened. 'Oh, no, not Jake too!'

'Yes, only this time it didn't work out.'

'No, well, I suppose it wouldn't, these days,' Felix said. 'Things have changed and a lot of men wouldn't care, except for being made to pay Child Support. And they could find out for sure if the child *was* theirs first, through a DNA test.'

'Lou was never the brightest bunny in the box, so that didn't seem to have occurred to her until too late,' I said, then gave a wry smile. 'And the man she tried to trick into believing he was the father was very fair, so it wasn't going to wash if he ever set eyes on the baby! I think for once she was telling the truth when she told me that Jake's father was an Italian waiter she met on holiday. He had to get those lovely dark brown eyes from somewhere.'

'When she knew she wasn't going to get any money out of it, I suppose there was no point in lying about who the father was,' Poppy agreed. 'So at least you don't have to worry about Jake's paternity, only your own.'

'Mags and Janey both seem to have been in on Lou's original scam and it's clear that Mags at least thought it was all highly amusing,' Felix said, looking up from reading one of the brief notes in his mother's scrawled handwriting. 'Especially about Chas, since he'd never shown any sign of being anything other than a happily married man until he let Lou seduce him.'

'Well, he could have said no,' Poppy said fair-mindedly. 'And so could the other man.'

'They could have, but they didn't,' Felix said. 'Lou knew what she was doing and she put it about a bit. In fact, all three of our mothers seem to have, though at least yours settled down after a few wild years and got married, Poppy.'

'That was just a timely combination of desperately missing horses and falling for Dad. Once he'd gone, she started trying to work her way through the male members of the Middlemoss Drag Hunt.'

'Quite literally,' I said and Poppy giggled.

'I suppose so! Still, at least she hasn't brought any of them home since that time I caught her in a loose box with one of the whippers-in when I was thirteen. And on the whole, she's not *really* been bad as a mum.'

'She certainly turned out the best of the bunch from that point of view,' Felix agreed, 'though that isn't saying much. Chloe's is a bolter with a blackmailing habit, while my unrespected parent dumped me on my grandparents the minute I was born and is still playing the field in her fifties, while nominally living with a smarmy git half her age.'

'At least she's *around*, Felix,' I pointed out, because Mags got lucky with a legacy from an elderly lover and opened the Hot Rocks nightclub in Southport a few years ago. The said smarmy git is the manager. 'If she hadn't had a business to run, she might have decided to vanish with Mum.'

I'd never believed Mags' version of events about the night Mum disappeared. Lou and Mags had always been thick as thieves, whereas Janey had tended to go off and do her own thing after the Wilde's Women years were over, though they all remained friends and sometimes hung out together at Hot Rocks.

'God knows what Lou is up to all this time, or where she is, though I suspect Mags could give me a hint if she wanted to, Felix,' I said.

When she'd switched from taking all those holidays to Jamaica on her own and started visiting Goa instead, I'd wondered if that was a clue to Mum having skipped the Caribbean.

He looked uncomfortable. 'I have asked her and she swears she has no idea.'

'Yes, that's what she told me, but I don't believe her.'

'And I asked Mum if Mags had told her anything and she said she hadn't,' Poppy said, 'though that means nothing when they've always lied and covered up for each other.'

She indicated the stuff on the table, which Felix was now neatly repacking into the box. 'What are you going to do about this, if anything?'

'I don't know, I'll have to think about it. It's been a shock finding out my father might not be Chas. But there's no point in telling any of it to Jake, because it would only upset him and anyway, it looks like she was telling the truth about who *his* father was, at least. She even gave him a holiday snap of them both together, though it isn't terribly clear.'

'He must have been nice, because Jake is,' Poppy said loyally. She'd always adored Jake, who had never played tricks on her (apart from mild ones, like whoopee cushions and plastic flies in her coffee) and called her Auntie Pops.

'I'm certainly not going to do anything hasty. Even if I wanted to, I have too much on at the moment, trying to keep my business running while sorting and packing and getting ready for the move. I'm dismantling my greenhouse tomorrow.'

'I could come and help,' offered Felix.

'No, that's OK, Felix,' I said quickly, since he is pretty useless as a handyman, besides being the kiss of death to anything breakable, being all elbows and feet. 'It won't take me long. It was dead easy to put up and I still have the instructions.'

'Really, Chloe, we make a good team,' he insisted. 'We'd get it done twice as fast.'

'Really, Felix, we *don't* – especially where panes of glass are concerned.'

He looked slightly hurt, so I added, 'But I'll definitely need your help on moving day.'

I felt in need of another drink, so went to the bar to get a round in.

When I got back, Poppy suddenly announced, 'I've got a date for tomorrow night!'

'Where from? I thought you'd given up on internet dating sites and decided the private marriage bureaus were too expensive.'

'Who with?' Felix demanded, in bossy big-brother mode.

'Just a man I met through *The Times* lonely hearts ads,' she said casually. 'We've talked for hours on the phone and now we're meeting up.'

'Where?' I asked, distracted from my own problems. 'I hope you're being sensible and it's somewhere very public, with other people about?'

'Yes, you have no idea what kind of man he really is,' agreed Felix. 'People can say anything.'

'I do know. I told you, we've talked for hours and we have

so much in common. And it's OK, because we're meeting in Sticklepond, at the Green Man.'

'Do you know what he looks like?' I asked.

'Yes, he's medium height and a bit like Tom Cruise.'

'If he looked like Tom Cruise he wouldn't need to meet women through the lonely hearts ads,' Felix said suspiciously.

'He's probably exaggerating a bit, but I expect he's very nice really,' I said quickly, seeing Poppy's face fall. 'Did you tell him what you look like?'

'I said I was fair and blue-eyed and an outdoors type and he thought that sounded perfect, because he was very energetic and loved outdoor pursuits.'

'That does it,' Felix announced. '*I'm* coming too!'

'No, you're not. Three's a crowd and I don't need a chaperone!'

'I didn't mean exactly *with* you, Poppy, just in the pub to see how it goes. But don't go off anywhere with him. I'll have my car, but I might lose you.'

'Oh, *honestly*, Felix!' she said, but actually I was glad to see him focusing on Poppy instead of me. I can take care of myself, but Poppy is distinctly soft-centred.

Then suddenly, quite out of nowhere, I had a blinding flash of illumination – Felix had all the characteristics Poppy had recently listed to me as being what she wanted in a man! He was single, kind, honest, not a sex maniac or a weird obsessive, and attractive.

And if Felix really yearns to settle down to a comfortable family life before it's too late, then he's barking up the wrong tree as far as I am concerned, but he and Poppy would be perfect for each other. Except that she only sees him in a brotherly light, of course, and Felix thinks of Poppy as a mate, only the wrong kind.

We've all three of us been unlucky in love and, by some strange coincidence, we had our worst moments at more or less the same time, though in different ways. While I was having my heart torn to shreds by Raffy at university, Poppy was away getting her riding instructor's certificates and falling heavily (in an unrequited, *Villette* kind of way) for one of the married staff and Felix's marriage was thrashing about in its death throes.

I suppose in our separate ways, we'd all got an education, just not the kind we'd hoped for.

By the time we'd got together again we were ready to slip back into our old, comfortable companionship without any need for extensive emotional post mortems, mainly, I suspect, because all three of us were harbouring one or two secrets we didn't, for once, want to share.

I certainly was. And the longer I went without telling anyone, the harder it became to confide even in Poppy, to whom the whole of my life, up to the point I left for university, had been an open book.

Chapter Seven

Brief Encounters

Although my discoveries about my mother had upset me deeply, there wasn't really any time to sit about brooding or to work out what, if anything, to do about it.

I still had lots of packing to do, including bubble-wrapping my extensive collection of ornamental angels, many of them given to me as gifts. I was also trying to make a large enough stock of Chocolate Wishes to tide me over until I could start up production again in the cottage, so the Bath was chugging away pretty well non-stop as it heated and stirred the couverture, and trays of chocolate-coated angel and heart moulds covered every surface, hardening before I could put in the Wish and seal them up.

It would be wonderful when I had a separate workshop, because chocolate making had taken over the flat!

Meanwhile, not even imminent house-moving could stop Grumps' steady output of one or two chapters of novel per day, or his incessant correspondence: cranks of the world, unite! I told him again this morning that email would be easier and quicker, and I could show him how to do it in no time, but he said the devil was in the machine and it could stay there.

Then he added that that had given him an idea, and started scribbling away, my presence forgotten, so I tiptoed off and left him to it, though I don't suppose he would have noticed if I'd blown a trumpet in his ear and then slammed the door.

'So, how did it go?' I asked Poppy when she called round on the morning after her date. 'Did he turn up?'

'Yes, but I didn't realise it was him for ages. We were both sitting separately in the pub for half an hour, each thinking the other one wasn't coming. Felix was in another corner, hiding behind a newspaper like a spy. He kept peering over the top of it.' She gave her irrepressible giggle. 'In fact, it was like a singles night for the severely shy!'

'I thought your date told you he looked like Tom Cruise? He should have been easy to spot.'

'Actually, he looked more like a spinning top. He had a small head but a huge stomach and little legs.'

'I don't think Tom Cruise is very tall, is he?'

'No, but at least he's good-looking! This one had a face that could stop clocks.'

'That bad?' I said sympathetically.

'Worse! I mean, I've no objection to *homely*, but Cruise Missile was *gargoyle* ugly! But eventually, when no one else turned up, the penny dropped that it must be him, because he was constantly watching the door as if he was waiting for someone.'

'Cruise Missile? Is that what he called himself in the ad?' I asked incredulously. 'You didn't tell us that bit!'

'It didn't seem important,' she said simply. 'Just a name to grab the attention.'

'It seems to have hooked you, all right. What did you call yourself?'

'Riding Mistress.'

'*Riding Mistress?*' I looked at her and she gazed innocently back at me. Considering what her mother is like, I can't believe how naïve she can be sometimes, but she has a very literal mind, which must account for it.

'Well, that's what I am, isn't it?'

'Ye-es . . .' I said slowly, 'but – well, never mind. What did you do next, sneak out of the back door under some pretext and leg it?'

'No, I went over and asked him if he was waiting for Riding Mistress, and he was, only I could see *he* was really disappointed in me too.'

'I don't see why,' I said loyally, though it's true that Poppy's idea of making an effort to dude herself up a bit was usually confined to applying rose-tinted lip salve and running a comb through her slightly frizzy, damp-sand-coloured hair, usually the comb she has just used on Honeybun's tail.

'He told me straight out why he was disappointed: it was because he'd thought I would be wearing riding breeches and carrying a whip!'

'Oh dear, one of those.'

'He certainly was. We hadn't been talking more than five minutes – and he didn't even offer to buy me a drink – when he said he'd been a very bad pony and why didn't we go back to my place so I could *school* him. I was a bit gobsmacked.'

'I take it you didn't oblige? How did you get away?'

'I caught Felix's eye and mouthed, "Help!"'

'The gallant knight to the rescue – good old Felix!'

'Not immediately: he got up and slipped out of the back door and I thought for a minute he'd abandoned me, though of course I really knew he wouldn't. I panicked a bit and I was just stalling Cruise Missile by telling him my mother was at home mucking out, when Felix came in again through the front door, marched right up and said, "There you are, Poppy! The children are crying for you – please come home with me, darling. I'm so sorry we argued!"'

'I think he's been reading Victorian melodramas again,' I said. 'So then . . . ?'

'I got up and smiled at Cruise Missile and said I was sorry, it had all been a mistake, and then we left and went back to Felix's shop. It was horrible at the time, but after a bit it all seemed sort of funny and it was a pity to waste a night off, so we went to see a film in Southport. We did try phoning to see if you wanted to come with us, but there was no reply.'

'Yes, the phone rang,' I remembered, 'but I was at a tricky bit with a big angel for a personalised card reading, so I couldn't answer, and then I forgot about it. I've swung into major production. The whole place smells like a chocolate factory.'

'It always does,' Poppy said simply. 'I like it.'

It was no surprise that Felix phoned to give me his version not ten minutes after Poppy left, and it was similar, except that he insisted Poppy's would-be date was sinister and creepy.

'In all fairness, I think Poppy unintentionally sent out all the wrong signals. He sounded to me more sad and insignificant than anything,' I said.

'Dangerously weird,' he insisted. 'I can't imagine how, growing up with a mother like Janey, she manages to stay so . . .' He paused, racking his brains to describe the puzzle that was Poppy, the Maria von Trapp (bar the singing) of Sticklepond.

'Sweet and innocent?' I suggested. 'That's just what I thought.'

'I'd say trusting and credulous. I've told her to stop answering that kind of advert.'

'Did she agree?'

'No, she said just because there was one rotten apple, it didn't mean the whole barrel had gone squishy. You'll have to make her see sense.'

'But she gets lonely, Felix, and I can't always go out with her, I'm too busy with the business and trying to keep track of what Jake is up to.'

'Jake's legally an adult now, you don't have to do that.'

'He might be legally adult, but he's still my little brother and part-boy, part-man. I want to make sure he stays on the right track until he goes to university. Then I'll have done my best and it'll be out of my hands.'

'Yes, and then you will be free to get what you *really* want out of life.'

'I seem to already have most of it, though I'm *so* looking forward to a bit of freedom too – being alone and doing my own thing,' I said brightly. 'I expect I'll be spending all my spare time in that lovely little walled garden after I've moved. I can hardly wait.'

'Hmm,' he said, sounding discouraged, which was my intention.

I tried a bit more manoeuvring: 'At the moment things are so frantic, getting ready for a move at such short notice, that I wouldn't have time to keep an eye on what Poppy's up to anyway, even if I wanted to.'

'Someone needs to, because what she's doing really could be dangerous.' He sighed long-sufferingly. 'I suppose *I* will have to.'

I made encouraging noises, even though I'm not entirely sure that Poppy will appreciate continually being shadowed by Felix on dates with potential suitors. But if they are all as dreadful as the first one, which seems quite likely, she may start to see what's under her nose in a new light. They *both* might.

I reminded him, as I already had with Poppy, that I was not telling Jake anything at all about what I'd discovered in the attic. Mum's behaviour had damaged him enough, he didn't need to know that she only had him in order to try to extort money. I wished *I* didn't know that that's why she'd had me, but I'd cope – I always had.

Apart from packing his own belongings up, Jake has been pretty useless the last few days, glooming about like a slightly Goth Lord Byron (but without the limp).

When I asked him at breakfast one morning whether he was upset about the move, he said tersely: 'No. It's a girl.'

I looked at him in surprise. 'I didn't know you had a girlfriend at the moment, Jake. You kept that quiet.'

'I *haven't* got one, that's the trouble.'

'You mean, you fancy someone, but she won't go out with you?'

He sighed heavily. 'She doesn't even know I exist! She's new – her parents just moved to the area – and she seems only to want to work all the time. If she isn't in class, she's in the library.'

I wished Jake would be a bit more like that! 'She sounds nice,' I said kindly. 'What terrible timing having to move college just before your exams, though. That's probably why she's concentrating on her studies.'

'She's dead set on going to Oxford too,' he said, even more gloomily.

'Are you doing the same subjects?'

'Yes, that's why I see her all the time. Only she doesn't seem to see me.'

I didn't really know how she could miss him – tall, brown-eyed, handsome, and all in black from dyed hair to big boots – but I saw an opportunity for some sneaky advice. Nagging him to revise always had the opposite effect, but revising to impress a girl could have a valuable knock-on effect . . .

'You've got things in common then, Jake, and that's a really good start. If I were you, I'd hang out in the library at the same time she does – ask her if you can check something in one of the books she's using, that kind of thing. Show her you're serious about *your* studies too.'

He gave me a suspicious look, but reluctantly conceded I might have something.

I cleaned and mended the pretty shell mirror, then covered it in bubble wrap and put it in the ottoman in the attic, together with a few more breakable things, like our box of Christmas decorations and a particularly pretty, but very fragile, spun-glass angel ornament.

While I was up there I noticed that Jake must have already transferred some of his more dubious treasures to the cabin trunk, because it now had a large padlock affixed to the hasp and, when I tried lifting the end, it weighed a ton.

I only hoped the removal men could still get it down the narrow and steep attic stairs.

Jake did seem a little more cheerful since we'd had the conversation about the girl he liked at college, so perhaps my advice about how to get to know her was paying off? I hoped it paid off in better exam grades, too.

Chas phoned me up that evening, which took me by surprise, even though he does do that from time to time. And I suppose I must have sounded a bit odd, because he asked me if everything was all right.

I wasn't ready to discuss what was on my mind yet, so I just told him I was tired, and all about the imminent house move.

He was kind and interested as usual, so that I found myself wishing again that he would turn out to be my father after all, though it would be even better to have one who didn't make furtive phone calls from his mobile only when his family weren't about!

Poppy came over to the flat after the next Parish Council meeting, which seemed to be taking place thick and fast because of all the changes going on in Sticklepond, and told me that the cat still wasn't out of the bag about Grumps and the Old Smithy.

'But I'm terrified I'm going to let it slip, and I'm sure Felix and I look really guilty all the time.'

I could just imagine Felix and Poppy avoiding each other's eyes and looking shifty, though the news would have to come out sooner or later.

'Luckily they had some other news to distract them, or they might have spotted it,' she said.

'Oh?' I looked up from enfolding the last of my collection of ornamental angels in bubble wrap. 'Have they finally found out who the ex-pop star vicar is, then?'

'No, they still don't know a thing about that, either. It's just that an old cottage called Badger's Bolt has been sold, after being on the market for absolutely ages, probably because it has spring water instead of mains and it's a bit isolated – up a track near the edge of the Winter's End estate. I only know where it is because we buy hay from Mr Ormerod, who has the farm next to it.'

'I can't see what's so fascinating about that, Poppy. People buy and sell houses all the time.'

'Yes, but Badger's Bolt is important because it comes with the two pieces of land in the village where the tennis club and lido are, and if there's a new owner then the lease might go up when the current one expires.'

The so-called lido field was a grassy picnic area next to a curve in the river, which had been partly dammed by large boulders to form a large, shallow pool where in summer the local families splashed about.

'Didn't you tell me ages ago that they were trying to raise money to buy the tennis club and lido? I'm sure I bought raffle tickets for it.'

'That's right, and Effie Yatton's been organising it, but they haven't got enough money yet, and now maybe the new owner won't want to sell. But Conrad said he was a very pleasant elderly man, a Mr Drake, so perhaps he will be happy to keep things as they are,' she added optimistically.

'I wouldn't have thought an elderly man would *want* an isolated house a long way from any amenities and with a dodgy water supply.'

'He might not know the water pressure isn't that good,

especially in summer. I don't suppose Conrad mentioned it.' She giggled suddenly. 'Do you remember when Felix moved into his shop and we found that trapdoor in the kitchen floor, under the lino?'

'Yes, leading to a cellar with a stream running through a stone channel, right in the middle of it, which he knew nothing about. His face was a picture when you told him having cold running water in the house was probably a luxury when the place was built.'

'It's a pity there isn't something like that at Badger's Bolt. This Mr Drake told Conrad that he'd also bought the title of Lord of the Manor of Sticklepond when it came up for auction, and Hebe Winter thinks that is a sign that he will take a benevolent interest in the village generally.'

'I would have thought the Winters were Lords of the Manor.'

'No, some of these old titles don't seem to go with local families, they get sort of detached and then sometimes they auction a whole load of them off. Miss Winter said she wanted her great-niece to buy it, but since it was just an empty title she thought the money could be better spent on the estate.'

'She's probably right. It sounds like something you would just buy for vanity, like a fancy numberplate.' I folded the top of the box down and taped it shut, then wrote 'Angels – sitting room' on top with a big, black marker pen. 'Let's have some coffee, and then you can tell me why you're clutching a copy of *The Times*.'

'I've marked some men in the lonely hearts column and after that last disaster I want to know what you think before I contact them. You might be able to tell better than me if they sound weird.'

They *all* sounded weird to me, or desperate. But then Poppy is also getting slightly desperate (though she is not at all weird), since she would love to marry and have children before it is too late.

I'd resigned myself to having neither, unless you counted mothering Jake, who hadn't so much fulfilled my maternal yearnings as made them wither on the vine.

Chapter Eight

Good Libations

Eventually, just as even the heroic patience of Grumps' buyers was wearing thin, the day of our removal to the Old Smithy dawned clear and bright.

The day before, Poppy had brought her big horsebox over, and we'd taken all my pots and tubs and the dismantled greenhouse across to the Old Smithy and put them in the walled courtyard. The pots of scented geraniums had to line all the windowsills, since it was too cold to put them outside yet.

When we'd done that, Poppy showed me the housewarming present she and Felix had bought me between them: fixed to the wall next to my new front door was a painted oval sign, decorated with red geranium flowers, which read, 'Angel Cottage'.

'Angel Cottage, 1 Angel Lane' sounded wonderfully soft and downy and safe, a home I could nestle into, like a cygnet under its mother's wing. But I wasn't sure what Grumps would make of it – angels on one side, pagans on the other! Still, there was a good chance he would never even notice.

You know, Sticklepond was a very Angel sort of place, what with Angel Lane and the old church of All Angels, the graveyard of which seemed full of marble ones. Felix told me a nearby stonemason specialised in them, and I often admired them over the wall.

And now there was my Angel Cottage too. It had been immaculately cleaned by Dolly Mops and was now repainted a soft, warm cream throughout, with one deep, old-rose, purply-pink wall in the little living room, to match the old tiles around the hearth.

The only exception to the colour scheme was the dark purple wall in Jake's room, of course, which actually didn't look quite as bad as I'd thought it would, even after I had hung his retro red, black and purple curtains.

Poppy helped me to hang the rest of the curtains before she had to dash back to Stirrups. She'd spent so much time in the previous two weeks helping me to scour the local junk and charity shops for furniture and furnishings that Janey was starting to complain, even though she was quite capable of going off on a bender herself at a moment's notice. (A bit like Mum, though at least Janey's disappearances lasted only a few days and she *always* came back.)

But we had done as much as we could anyway and by the next day this would be my new home – and maybe a whole fresh new chapter in my life too, as a contentedly single and successful businesswoman.

The team of removal men swung into action at dawn next morning. They had already spent days packing up the house, with Zillah and Grumps increasingly marooned in the kitchen and study respectively, among the packing cases.

Jake and I were all ready to go, we just had to strip our

beds and pack up the last few things, like the kettle and coffee mugs. Then the contents of our flat were loaded into a small van and whisked away to Sticklepond, while the rest of the men were only just starting to fill a huge pantechnicon with Grumps' worldly goods (*and* otherworldly ones), as though they were doing some challenging kind of three-dimensional jigsaw puzzle.

Felix and Jake were to direct unloading operations at the cottage, so Jake drove Zillah over in my Fiat, with Tabitha complaining bitterly in a basket on the back seat.

When I rang his mobile later to see how they were getting on, he said he and Felix had just screwed our bed frames together (I made a note to check those out before sleeping on them) and put the mattresses back on, and Zillah had already got the Aga going in her new kitchen and was dispensing stewed tea and biscuits.

'*And* she put butter on Tabitha's feet before she let her out!'

'I think that's supposed to make cats come back to the new house, though goodness knows why,' I said. 'Tell me when the phone landline starts working, won't you? And I hope we can get broadband quickly, because I don't want to have to conduct my business from the library or an internet café.'

'OK, though Felix has broadband and I'm sure he would let you use his computer . . . and here comes *my* stuff, so I'll have to go,' he said, then rang off. I expected he would spend hours rearranging his new bedroom, ignoring the rest of the cottage, but at least Felix was there to make sure all the boxes and furniture went into the rooms they were labelled for.

Back at the old house, Grumps had written solidly in his

study while it was emptied around him, so that his tall, Gothic chair and matching desk were the last things to go into the van – and therefore would be the first items out at the other end, meaning there would be very little disruption to his work. Clearly, there was method in his madness.

Finally, I drove him to Sticklepond in the Saab, wrapped in a midnight-blue velvet cloak against the chill and with a sort of embroidered fez over his long, silver hair. I dropped him off at the door, then turned round and went right back to take a last look alone around the old house and say my goodbyes. It was just something I felt I needed to do, before I could move on.

All the rooms echoed hollowly under my feet and looked strangely forlorn, especially the kitchen without Zillah's bright cushions, throws and curtains. I wandered through the house, remembering mainly the happy things, like Granny and the strangely pagan-crossed-with-Christian version of Christmas we celebrated every year, Jake's face as a small child, unwrapping presents (the one from Mum I always bought for her, because she never had any idea what he really wanted) and the night Poppy and I saw the angel . . .

I tried not to let memories of the bad times seep in, the moments of heartbreak and despair, but it was still all a bit poignant. It was more than time to move on and, I wondered, maybe I could leave the past behind me, like an outgrown shell and slip into a more expansive future?

In fact, a fresh start in a new place was just what we *all* needed – the Angel cards this morning had more or less told me so. I was sure Zillah had got her last reading wrong and the only visitors from my past likely to bother me were the ghosts I had just laid to rest.

I placed a big glazed pot of tulips on the kitchen windowsill, with a note welcoming the new owners to their home. Then I left, dropping the keys off with Conrad on the way to Sticklepond.

In our cottage Jake was still upstairs, which was much as I had expected, but Felix had lit a fire in the sitting room and was unpacking kitchen stuff into the wrong drawers and cupboards, though it was a kind thought, as was his having plugged in the little freezer and fridge the moment they were brought in.

'I thought I'd make a start,' he explained, 'but I'll have to go in a minute. I've got someone coming for a complete set of leather-bound Dickens and I'm hoping to offload some Thackeray onto them too. Is there anything else you'd like me to help you with, first?'

'No, you've done wonders, Felix, I'm really grateful. And I *love* the house sign that you and Poppy gave me!' I said warmly, giving him a hug. 'I'm going to make our beds up now and then everything else can wait until tomorrow.'

After he'd gone, I found a new little bookcase with a slanting top that fitted neatly under the steep staircase, with a card from Felix saying it was especially for my Georgette Heyer collection. He was so kind! In fact, he would make someone a wonderful husband, preferably Poppy. It certainly wasn't going to be me, and any other woman would undoubtedly resent his close friendship with us, so Poppy was the only possible candidate, when I came to think about it.

Grumps' removal men had gone into reverse, and were now unloading and unpacking everything, though it was such a mammoth task that they would have to come back next morning to finish.

Once I was sure everyone had a bed to sleep in that night, I suggested we went over to the Falling Star for a bar meal. We were all exhausted, with the possible exception of Grumps. Even Jake looked tired, though he didn't seem to have done much more than drive Zillah across and then spend the rest of the day rearranging his bedroom and sticking posters – all featuring the blood red/funereal purple/dead black range of the spectrum with lots of skulls, dragons and swords – onto the freshly painted walls.

When we trooped into the snug, which was empty as usual, since the regulars preferred the music, dartboard and slot machine of the public bar, they all came and peered at us through the hatch as if the circus had come to town.

I certainly don't usually merit this kind of attention, but I suppose as a group we did look a bit unusual, what with one near-Goth dressed head to foot in black and only needing a large axe in order to be a dead ringer for the Grim Reaper, an elderly Merlin in a rubbed velvet jacket and embroidered, tasselled fez, and a small, round gypsy clad in several brightly clashing layers and with a shocking-pink scarf wrapped around her head like a turban. But I expect they will quickly get used to seeing the family about the village and we will be a seven-day wonder.

The young, pink-haired barmaid, Molly, was the exception, since she showed no sign of surprise or interest at our appearance, apart from eyeing Jake in a slightly speculative manner. There was no sign of Mrs Snowball, who kept early hours, and that was perhaps a good thing.

Grumps, who rarely enters pubs, was very gracious about scampi in a basket and plastic sachets of tartare sauce – more gracious than Zillah, actually, who was affronted by the modest prices and said she could have cooked the meal at home for a fraction of the cost, and much better too. But she said it without her usual gusto, so she was definitely tired. I tend to forget she must be nearly as old as Grumps, because her face has been seamed, lined and folded like an old brown linen table-cloth for as long as I've known her.

We went back to the Old Smithy and had what Grumps called a libation of good single malt in honour of our new home, then we all went to bed. It had been a *very* long day.

Chapter Nine

Drawing the Lines

Grumps, needing little sleep, had already knocked out a chapter of *Satan's Child* and was in the museum by the time I'd seen Jake off to college next morning (in Grumps' Saab, with huge warnings about being careful and not driving too fast).

Although I'd managed to find the toaster and the Pop-Tarts, Jake's current breakfast of choice, the whereabouts of the porridge oats and jar of honey was still a complete mystery to me. I think my box packing and labelling must have been getting a bit random by the time I got to the kitchen, because I kept finding the most unlikely combinations, but I sincerely hoped I'd screwed the lid on the honey tightly and it was the right way up, wherever it was.

I slipped silently through the door leading from the cottage into the museum. Grumps had his back turned to me, but even so he immediately said, 'The removal men are here again already, Chloe, unpacking in the house.'

It's always unnerving that he can tell who is behind him

without looking – but equally unnerving that when he is completely absorbed in something he can be so totally *unaware* that even a herd of elephants stampeding through the room wouldn't penetrate his consciousness.

'Well, that's good, Grumps and, going by yesterday, unpacking is much, much quicker than packing, so they should be done very soon and then you can get back to normal.'

Whatever normal is, in Grumps' case.

'Zillah is directing their activities.'

Zillah was more likely to be in the kitchen with Tabitha, smoking a roll-up fag, drinking tea and studying the cards, so I said, 'Do you want me to go and help? I can tell them where to put things.'

'Thank you, but I do not think that is necessary, for they seem to know what they are doing. But they are currently in the study, so I thought I would come in here for a time. They should not be long, since they need not unpack my books. Jake will help me arrange them tomorrow, it being the weekend, since he tells me he is eager to earn enough money to purchase a pair of firesticks. Interesting – he must demonstrate these weapons when he has them.'

'Actually, I don't think they are weapons, Grumps, just a form of entertainment, like juggling. One of his friends has been letting him use his, but he wants his own.'

'Everything is a weapon when used the right way, Chloe. Do not underestimate the power of light or fire.'

I thought that was a bit of a sweeping statement, but let it pass because Grumps can be really weasely in arguments, so I often found I'd switched to his side without realising it and was arguing against my own original point. Jake was getting to be good at this too. Perhaps he could become the first Goth politician in the House of Commons? Or the post of Black Rod could become that of Black Firestick? That would liven things up a bit.

'Those cleaners Felix recommended were extremely thorough,' Grumps was saying approvingly, and it was true, because both the cottage and house sparkled, and here in the museum the glass display cases had been cleaned and polished inside and out, and the mahogany desk by the door shone like oiled silk.

'Oak floors,' Grumps pointed out, 'very fortuitous for our meetings.'

'Yes, I suppose if you can't meet in an ancient oak glade, at least here you will have the equivalent under your feet.'

'True.'

I would be able to stop worrying about him catching a chill, too. Performing magical rites totally starkers might sound kinky, but actually Grumps' love of nudity harks back to a more innocent age of healthy naturism and has nothing to do with any Five-fold Kiss or Great Rite goings-on. In fact, when Granny was alive, she used to go and sit on the sidelines as a sort of indulgent chaperone, knitting, with flasks of hot tea to thaw everyone out afterwards. Zillah took over the role, but she told me these days she usually stayed in the car instead, smoking and reading magazines by torchlight, till the coven came back.

'Well, if you don't need me, I'll go and start sorting out the unpacking in the cottage—' I began.

'Ah, but before you go, there *is* something I need your assistance with, Chloe. Here, take this compass and box of chalks and I will bring the maps and yardstick.'

It appeared that he wanted me to help mark out a huge

pentagram on the floor at the far end of the museum, which he obviously deemed to be of much more importance and urgency than my unpacking.

But there was never any point in trying to deflect him from a course he was truly determined on, so I meekly took the chalk and did what he told me. Naturally, this involved a lot of measurements and constant references to a large-scale map, on which he had drawn the conjunction of the two important ley lines.

Well, that was fiddly, but eventually it was done to his satisfaction and I promised to buy a huge roll of masking tape and some hard-wearing paint later that morning and make the pentagram permanent.

The windows, which were fortunately mostly at the back of the building, were to be hung with dark blue velvet, and a curtain of the same material would frame the pentagram end of the room, a bit like a stage, so that area could be shut off when the museum was closed.

'The curtains are delayed. They should have been deliv ered today, but they have promised they will be finished by the end of the week – in good time for the full moon, you know.'

'Oh? Well, I hope they do, because it's a big job to complete so quickly, isn't it?'

'They *will* finish in time,' he stated positively, then cast a satisfied eye around the room. 'It will all work very well: the visitors will think the pentagram is part of the exhi-bition, since there will be an illustrated history of the Old Religion hung around the walls at that end.'

'They have something similar in the hall at Winter's End, Grumps – but mostly about Alys Blezzard, the family witch.'

'She was little more than a herbalist, like Hebe Winter,'

he said dismissively. 'But my history will be comprehensive and all-embracing.'

'Do you know Hebe Winter, Grumps? I haven't met her, though I have seen her about.'

'Our paths have crossed once or twice in the past.' He delved randomly into the nearest packing case and came up with a particularly scary-looking Balinese mask. 'Now, why would that be in the Fetish box?'

My reply was drowned out by a thunderous knocking at the museum door, which proved to be two workmen with the freshly repainted museum sign.

We went out to see the board fixed into place over the entrance door, standing at the edge of the pavement out of the way of the ladders.

Across the road old Mrs Snowball, who had evidently just finished her daily paving stone purge, called 'Coo-ee!' and flapped a hand at Grumps.

He bowed in her direction, gracefully doffing his fez, before turning back to admire his sign:

GREGORY WARLOCK'S MUSEUM OF WITCHCRAFT
A CELEBRATION OF ALL THINGS PAGAN

There was also a folding wooden billboard that would stand on the pavement outside the door when the museum was open, enticingly listing the delights to be obtained inside and also the charges for entry.

I hadn't had any hand in this, so I read with interest that the museum would open from two until four on five days a week, from Easter to September, and weekends only off-season.

ADMISSION: FOUR POUNDS
NO CONCESSIONS
NO CHILDREN UNDER 12 YEARS OF AGE
PARKING AT REAR OF BUILDING

'We have plenty of time to get it ready if you mean to open in early April, Grumps.'

'Yes, though all the exhibits need arranging, and a guide-book and perhaps some pamphlets must be produced. But I am sure it can be done in time, and then Zillah says she will be happy to take charge of the desk when I am otherwise engaged.'

'I don't suppose it's that much different from reading fortunes at the end of a pier, so she will probably enjoy it. And I can help out too, of course, if you need me,' I offered.

'You have your own little business to run,' he said graciously.

'Yes, but I can still give you a hand if things are really busy in peak tourist season. I'll set up the Chocolate Wishes equipment this afternoon and then Jake's going to see if he can reconnect us to broadband when he gets back, so I can print off my new orders.'

That had to be the first priority, and then getting the cottage sorted out. But after that, finally, I could get at my potentially lovely walled garden!

'Jake will work at the museum in his university vacations, I have spoken to him about it. For one day,' Grumps added, with a magnificently sweeping gesture at the Old Smithy, 'all this will be his. Except the little cottage, of course – I am arranging to have that transferred into your name.'

Stunned, I turned to stare at him. 'In *my* name? You mean . . . I'll *own* it? But Grumps—'

'But me no buts,' he said grandly.

'It's so kind of you, Grumps!' I stood on tiptoe to kiss his cheek, which he suffered me to do rather in Jake's manner, though I know they both quite like it, really. Then an unwelcome and probably unworthy thought struck me. 'But what if Mum comes back? Won't she expect—'

'Your mother has chosen her own path and deserves nothing more from any of us. If she returns after I'm gone, then I would strongly advise you to send her on her way again. Any share of my inheritance she might *think* she deserves has already gone to pay off her debts.'

This was very true . . . and already I was feeling possessive about my little cottage! I was happy for it to be Jake's home for as long as he needed it, but there was no way I could share living space with my mother ever again.

Having finished their job the workmen packed up their tools and departed and Grumps fell back a bit, so that he could admire the sign again. The weak late February sunshine gilded his long, silver hair under the fez and shone off the bald patches on the seat and elbows of his quilted velvet robe. For the first time I noticed he had only thin, red leather Moroccan slippers on his feet and I was about to urge him to go back in, since the cold from the pavement would be striking upwards, when there was a screeching noise from the road behind us. A small white Mini had jarred to an abrupt stop and was quivering by the pavement.

A tall, silver-haired, imposing woman unfolded herself from it and confronted Grumps: Hebe Winter, soon to be not the only witch in the village. Though actually, going by the way old Mrs Snowball had been carrying on, Hebe may have had company all along without realising it. Perhaps she was the only *solitary* witch in the village.

'Hello, Hebe,' Grumps said, doffing his fez again, as he had done to Mrs Snowball.

'*You?*'

'Yes, me,' he agreed, quite mildly for him. 'How are you, my dear? Still dabbling in the shallows of alchemy, turning herbs into money?'

She didn't appear to register what he had said, for she'd now spotted the museum sign and an expression of outrage appeared on her patrician features. 'Can it be possible that it is *you* who have bought the Old Smithy – that you intend to *live* in Sticklepond?'

'It can and it is. We moved in yesterday.'

'*We?*' She acknowledged my presence for the first time by favouring me with an unimpressed stare, but of course I was wearing old jeans and a fleece for unpacking and moving things, not dressed to receive august and slightly scary visitors.

'With my family,' Grumps explained. 'This is my grand-daughter, Chloe.'

That didn't even merit another glance – she had weightier matters to get off her narrow chest now she had spotted the new sign. 'You cannot seriously expect to open such an ungodly museum in Sticklepond, nor introduce your dubious ways into my parish, and think that I would do nothing to prevent it?' she demanded. 'I felt the threat coming, yet I thought it concerned our lack of a perman-ent vicar to guide and protect us, not the establishment of a Mecca to the Dark Arts in our midst!'

'Oh, come off your high horse, Hebe,' Grumps said testily. 'You know I am not a threat to anyone, even if I am opening a museum of witchcraft. Does it not seem a good idea to you? I had thought you would approve.'

'Approve of you bringing your dubious practices to Sticklepond? I think not!'

'Then you may be pleased to learn that some of what you would prudishly consider to be my more *dubious* practices have, unfortunately, currently been curtailed by cold weather and old age.'

This was all very interesting and there was obviously some history between them. In an unusually expansive moment Grumps once let drop that when he first moved to Merchester and started his coven, one or two local witches he had invited to join him had taken exception to the nudity aspect of his rites. I expect it was an innovation too far, even though they must have seen that he was a scholarly, rather than an any-excuse-to-have-an-orgy type of warlock.

'Be that as it may, I cannot approve of your ungodly ways,' Hebe said firmly. 'And there is *nothing* to celebrate in paganism!'

'It would have been far worse if Digby Mann-Drake had bought the place. He wanted it, you know – only I clinched the deal with the Frintons while he was unable to act, due to a septic appendix. Dear girls, the Frinton sisters – we sorely miss them at our meetings.'

Her bright blue eyes widened. 'The *Frintons*? You mean they were . . . ?'

'If you will practise in solitude, it is hardly surprising that you don't know these things, Hebe,' Grumps chided, but she didn't seem to hear him, because another thought seemed to have struck her.

'What was that you said about Mann-Drake?' she asked sharply.

'You have heard of him, then?'

100

'Of course. He's an even bigger charlatan than you!' she said rudely.

'You must not underestimate him, my dear Hebe – nor me. He is not just a harmless exhibitionist, but uses what powers he has for unworthy ends, corrupting and debasing impressionable young people.'

Hebe was now looking worried. 'A Mr Drake snapped up the title of Lord of the Manor when it came up for auction – for a hugely inflated price, even though it confers no benefits whatsoever – *and* he has purchased an isolated house at the edge of the village, Badger's Bolt. Drake is not an unusual name and I thought nothing of it, but now I wonder if it could be Mann-Drake?'

'It is quite possible, for though the Old Smithy is in the most fortuitously powerful position, the whole village is, as you might say, magically wired,' Grumps said thoughtfully. 'That would be very bad news for us all, believe me, Hebe. My presence would be the least of your problems.'

'It may not be him and so we will deal with that situation if it arises,' she said, rallying. 'But even if it does prove to be true, although *you* may be the lesser evil, we still do not want you or your museum in the village. But I expect our new vicar, when he arrives, will know how to deal with you!'

'Bell, book and candle?' he smiled. 'My dear Hebe!'

'Wait and see. I myself am not entirely without power around here, dabbler in alchemy or not,' she snapped, so obviously that barb had pierced her armour.

'Same old Hebe – and what a *very* angry aura!' Grumps said admiringly as she drove away after some clashing of the gears. Then he turned back to the matter in hand. 'The signs are satisfactory, so let us go back indoors, Chloe. I have work to do.'

'But Hebe Winter, Grumps – won't she make trouble for you? I mean, she's very important in Sticklepond, isn't she? She seems to run the place, according to Poppy. Poppy and Felix are on the Parish Council and they tell me about things.'

'The museum will be good for the village and, in any case, she has no teeth in this matter. Nor does the vicar, if he should try to interfere. They will have much more to worry them should their Mr Drake turn out to be Mann-Drake.'

'Is Mann-Drake his real name?' I asked curiously.

'He was plain Drake when we were at Oxford, but I believe he later hyphenated it with his mother's maiden name.'

'Jake mentioned that he was researching him for you and he didn't sound like good news.'

'He was always a nasty piece of work, though his great charm of manner initially fools many people. But do not fear: I know how to protect my own,' he assured me, and then went off to see if the removal men had finished with his study so that he could reoccupy it.

I went back to the cottage, plugged in my radio, and began sorting out my chocolate-making supplies and stock. All the little drawers and cupboards were really handy for storing moulds, packaging, sacks of couverture like big, richly fragrant chocolate buttons, ribbons and Wishes.

I'd printed out a fresh copy of the Mayan chocolate charm Grumps had given me, with the new part added, and now Blu-Tacked it to the front of one of the cupboards over the Bath. If Grumps and his Spanish friend ever manage to translate the last bit, I might frame the whole thing.

I stacked my entire stock of gold boxes of Chocolate

Wishes on the shelves around the shop area, along with the empty boxes for the large chocolate angels with personalised readings inside, which I made to order: it was lovely to have enough room for everything, at last!

All the time I was working, my mind was still running on the conversation between Grumps and Hebe Winter, so when everything was shipshape I got out my Angel oracle cards and shuffled them.

They seemed to indicate major problems to overcome, but that success would be entirely possible.

Felix closed his shop in the afternoon and came to offer any help I needed – he is so sweet! I'd been out for masking tape and paint by then, so I got him to help me finish the pentagram on the museum floor.

I told him about Grumps and Hebe and he said the sparks would probably fly. Already Hebe had called an emergency meeting of the Parish Council tomorrow, now that the cat was out of the bag.

Grumps wandered back in just as we'd almost finished our task and regarded Felix with approval. While we were children Grumps tolerated his presence around the house, just as he had Poppy's, but now that Felix goes to huge lengths to find the obscure volumes he wants, he has moved up several rungs in Grumps' estimation.

'I came to tell Chloe that Zillah has a huge pan of stew ready and Jake has rung to say he will eat at a friend's house and be back later.'

'He didn't ring *me*!' I said suspiciously. 'And which friend? I hope he isn't going to drink when he has to drive back, and—'

'There is no need to panic, Chloe. He did try to call you

earlier, but there was no reply, so he left a contact number with Zillah. I don't need the car tonight and he is a sensible boy. You,' he added to Felix, more in command than invitation, 'may join the rest of us for dinner. We don't dress.'

'Not at all?' Felix blurted, and then went pink.

'He means you can come as you are,' I explained, and he stopped looking aghast, just scared but gratified. He'd often eaten with Jake and me in the flat, of course, but had never before been invited to dine with the whole family.

But if he was expecting some kind of Addams Family frog stew, he must have been very pleased to discover that it was just a solid lamb hotpot with suet dumplings, followed by sultana-stuffed baked apples and custard. In my opinion, the baked apples would have been better for a little grated chocolate in the stuffing; but then, as far as I am concerned, almost anything would.

Chapter Ten

Comparative Evils

I turned the Bath on for the first time the following afternoon, so that the cottage became filled with the lovely, familiar smell of chocolate as it was heated and stirred. I find the soft chugging noise it makes very soothing, too . . .

Later Poppy, on her way home from the latest Parish Council meeting, sat on the worktop watching me coat the Wishes moulds with chocolate using my large pastry brush, a technique I learned through trial and error. I can get the chocolate shells just the thickness I want this way and, after making so many, it comes automatically to me.

Since she was wearing the breeches, gilet and paddock boots in which she had presumably earlier mucked out several horses, this might not have been the most hygienic idea, but it was a bit late to point this out. Anyway, I was too grateful at having a mole on the Parish Council to quibble at a few germs.

'I thought Miss Winter had called the emergency session to finally tell us who the new vicar was – I'm dying to know! But it was all about your grandfather instead,' she said, finishing a quick résumé of what had been said, for my benefit.

'Felix and I knew what it was about, but I assumed he would have told you.'

'No, and I don't see why it couldn't wait until the regular meeting on Thursday, because none of us felt there was anything urgent about it and anyway, there was nothing we could do to stop your grandfather opening his museum, even if we wanted to!'

She giggled. 'Poor Mr Merryman said there already was a witchcraft museum up at Winter's End, and I thought Miss Winter was going to turn him into stone.'

'He's quite right though, Poppy. They do have a large display about Alys Blezzard and witchcraft, we saw it when we visited last year, do you remember? So I don't know why she's so against Grumps, except they seem to have had some kind of disagreement years ago.'

'She said he practised the Dark Arts. She's very keen the vicar meets your grandfather.'

'Well, it takes one to know one and, honestly, from the way she went on you'd think Grumps was a Satanist!'

'I expect she sees herself and what she does differently. The Winter womenfolk seem to manage to combine the occult and Christianity quite successfully somehow: you can tell that just by the way Hebe wears a cross and a pentacle round her neck all the time!'

'Well, Grumps doesn't do that, but he's perfectly harmless, and even when he does try some of the dodgier stuff it never works out right, so she's no need to worry. In fact, it seems that if Grumps hadn't bought the Old Smithy, someone who really *does* walk on the dark side would have done!' And I told her what I knew about Digby Mann-Drake.

'But of course magic doesn't *really* work anyway, even if Grumps is genuinely deluded that it does – and presumably this Mann-Drake is too. Grumps told Miss Winter about him trying to buy the Smithy and then she remembered that it was a Mr Drake that had purchased the title of Lord of the Manor and was also buying Badger's Bolt.'

'Oh, I *see!*' Poppy exclaimed, enlightened. 'It might be the same person and *that's* what she meant about us perhaps having to deal with a greater evil than your grandfather. She said the Mr Drake who's bought Badger's Bolt could turn out to be even more undesirable, though she didn't say why.'

'According to Grumps the village is a magical hotspot, being on the junction of two ley lines, so even if he failed to buy the Old Smithy, Mr Mann-Drake might still want to come here. I can't imagine why he would want to be Lord of the Manor, though!'

'Perhaps it *is* a different Mr Drake after all,' she suggested. 'Let's hope so. By the way, Felix and I confessed that we knew you and I told them you made and sold Chocolate Wishes. They couldn't have any objection to *that.*'

'I wouldn't have thought so. And where did you say Felix has got to?'

'He had to go back and open the shop. One of his special clients is coming and anyway, he can't keep shutting all the time, even if it is off season, or he'll never make a living.'

'I think he'll always do most of his bookselling via the internet, like me with my Chocolate Wishes, even if I let the public into the workshop when the museum is open. Passing trade is just the icing on the gingerbread, but I can have jars of chocolate lollies on the counter for the children, and I thought about making treacle toffee witch's cat ones, too. Do you remember when I used to make them for Jake and his friends on Hallowe'en and Bonfire Nights?'

'Yes, that's a good idea. It's quiet for passing trade up this end of the High Street, but once the witchcraft museum opens, you'll probably get a lot more.'

I finished coating the last heart moulds and gave Poppy a couple of ones I'd made earlier that had broken while I was taking them out.

'Oh, yum,' she said. 'You are clever, Chloe, making such lovely chocolate!'

'Well, you make brilliant Yorkshire puddings, don't forget, while mine come out like crispy cowpats and I have to cheat and use frozen ones.'

'But your fruitcake is wonderful too, so you're multi-talented.'

'*Anyone* can make a fruitcake, Poppy. It's dead easy.'

'Maybe, but yours tastes extra special.' She licked the last of the chocolate off her fingers and added, 'And your chocolate always tastes different too, especially since you started using that spell your grandfather gave you. You *do* always say it while you're mixing up the chocolate, don't you?'

'Yes,' I admitted, 'but only because it was so kind and thoughtful of him to find it for me, not because I think it affects the taste! He gave me a couple more lines recently that he and the friend he corresponds with about it have managed to decipher. He said that might be all of the original and the rest of the document may be a later addition – a sort of added bonus. Not that I really believe any of it *is* some ancient Mayan charm passed down through the *conquistadores*, of course.'

'*I* do and I think the spell works,' she declared. 'I mean, you made good chocolates before, but now they're on a different plane.'

'But they're only hollow chocolate shells, Poppy, it's not like a box of truffles,' I said, though actually I do experiment with lots of those, for home consumption. 'The message inside is the important thing, that's why people buy them. They're a novelty and an after-dinner treat.'

'They're magic,' she insisted, and I abandoned trying to change her mind, since she gets these stubborn moments. 'Speaking of magic, that brings us right back to Hebe and the meeting, doesn't it? Did you say the temporary vicar intends coming to visit Grumps?'

'Not just intends – we actually walked here together, because he said he would rather get it over with. He looked a bit nervous, poor man, though I tried to reassure him.'

'What did you tell him? Come back later, armed with a large stick and a bottle of holy water?' I was pouring the last little bit of tempered chocolate into lolly moulds, to use it up.

'I told him he should forget what Hebe said and just welcome Mr Lyon to the village, shake his hand, and go away again.'

'Very sensible.'

'But I don't think that he will take my advice, because he went all scared and stubborn and said if your grandfather was practising witchcraft, then he must try and persuade him to mend his ways, and also not open a museum likely to poison the holy tranquillity of the village.'

I stopped tapping the mould to release air bubbles and stared at her. 'There's never been much holy calm about Sticklepond, has there? Even I know that! Is he a *complete* idiot?'

'Yes, but a nice one and he means well.' She glanced quickly over her shoulder, as if the devil might be standing there – or Grumps. 'You don't think . . . ?'

'Grumps doesn't suffer fools gladly, but he was in quite a good mood this morning when I collected the latest chapter of his book. He was looking forward to spending the day arranging things in the museum and labelling them, so he may not be too harsh with poor Mr Whatever-he's-called.'

'Merryman.'

At that moment a small, youngish, balding man wearing a clerical collar scurried past the glazed shop window, as if the devil himself were after him. He turned his head and gave us one terrified glance, then took to his heels and ran.

'*Not* so Merryman,' I commented and sighed. 'Grumps must have had a change of mood.'

'Oh, poor thing!' Poppy said. 'He's so nice, too.'

'Poppy, have you got your eye on him? He *is* single, isn't he?' I asked suspiciously.

'No, and I'm pretty sure he's gay, actually, because he keeps showing me pictures of his friend Gerry.'

'Oh, right.'

'But I phoned a man from the lonely hearts column last night – not one I showed you before – and he sounded lovely! I'm sure the first one I met was just beginner's bad luck. We're going to meet at the Green Man on the day after my birthday.'

'Poppy, this is just like fishing through a hole in the ice – you don't know what's going to come up on the end of the hook! Felix will have fits.'

'*You* may have given up on men, Chloe, but I've changed my mind because Mr Right has to be out there somewhere.'

'But yours may not read *The Times*. Do *Horse and Hound* do a lonely hearts column?' I suggested.

Chapter Eleven

Birthday Wishes

Poppy had to come into Sticklepond again on the Thursday for the regular Parish Council meeting and she seemed to be developing the habit of calling by on her way home so she could tell me all about them. This time Felix came too and immediately started dropping hints about hot chocolate, until I gave in and started grating cacao.

Personally, I think adding anything else other than a bit of honey or raw cane sugar to it ruins the whole, delicious experience, but Jake loved his loaded with whipped cream and even marshmallows (yuk!) and both Felix and Poppy liked hot, frothed milk with theirs.

'The meeting wasn't very exciting tonight,' Poppy said, taking a cautious sip and emerging from her mug with a white moustache. 'Probably because we'd already discussed everything at the emergency session!'

'Is it ever?'

'Well, *I* think it is, what with all the discussions about the witchcraft museum and speculating about the new vicar,' she said, and then suddenly got a belated attack of conscience.

'You know, I suppose we really shouldn't be discussing Parish Council business with other people, Felix!'

'Isn't it a bit too late for that now? And I'm *not* "other people"', I said indignantly. 'Haven't we always told each other everything . . . or *almost* everything, because I suspect we all have one or two deep, dark secrets.'

'I haven't,' Felix said. 'I'm an open book.'

'You're a nice if slightly time-worn edition, attractively foxed,' I said kindly. 'And you both know I wouldn't discuss Parish Council business with anyone else, though I'll swear silence, if that helps?'

'Of course we know you wouldn't tell anyone else, don't we, Felix? I was being silly,' said Poppy. 'Go on, tell Chloe what happened.'

'OK, but not a lot *did* happen that I recall, except that Hebe Winter told poor Mr Merryman that he was a weak vessel who'd failed to avert a threat to all our mortal souls, or something like that.'

'I thought he was going to cry!' Poppy put in. 'So I told her your grandfather wasn't so bad, but then she said yes he was, he was the *Antichrist*!'

'I think that might be going a little too far,' I said. 'I mean, Aleister Crowley he is *not*! And even if his magic practices do stray across the line sometimes, it's never even bordering on satanic.'

Or I hoped not, anyway . . . No, on reflection, my guardian angel would definitely have had something to say about that!

'Oh, no, I'm sure he's not,' Poppy agreed. 'I think Miss Winter is now pinning her hopes on the new vicar taking a stronger line about it, when he finally arrives. Apparently, he intends moving into the kitchen wing of the vicarage where Mr Harris lived after he found the stairs too much, while the rest of the repairs are finished. That's what the Minchins say, anyway. He's keeping them on, which they're very relieved about.'

'Who are the Minchins?' I asked.

'They're a brother and sister in their fifties, who looked after the vicarage for Mr Harris, and they have a sort of flat over the kitchen, with its own back stairs,' she explained. 'Salford Minchin has served time in prison for murder, so they were worried they might be out of a job.'

'Yes, I imagine they might!'

'It was more of an accident really, I think – Salford found his wife with another man and things got out of hand. Don't they call that a *crime passionnel* in France?'

'Yes, and I suppose if he doesn't remarry, it's unlikely he'll do it again,' I agreed.

'Miss Winter found out that the vicar had paid a flying visit to Sticklepond last week to see how renovations were progressing, but he didn't tell anyone except the Minchins that he was coming, so she was furious about that,' said Felix.

'When Effie Yatton asked Maria Minchin what he was like, all she could say was that he was younger than Mr Harris and not anything like any vicar *she'd* ever known,' Poppy said, with a giggle.

'Apart from Methuselah, it would be difficult to be *older* than Mr Harris,' Felix said. 'He looked transparent the last few years, as if he was already half gone, but he was so absent-minded towards the end that I think he just forgot to die.'

'Maybe God finally tied a knot in his handkerchief to remind him?' Poppy suggested. 'He should certainly have retired years ago, but I expect it slipped the bishop's mind.'

'On purpose, because it was probably more convenient to forget about him and Sticklepond altogether, while he could,' Felix agreed. 'The new vicar must be stinking rich, because there's a positive army of workmen all over the vicarage.'

'And he must be kind,' Poppy said, 'because he's having the Minchins' flat repaired and redecorated first.'

'But you still have no idea who he is?' I asked her, because the mystery was finally starting to pique my curiosity.

'No, the bishop hasn't replied to any of Hebe's letters and when she rang his secretary, she said he'd gone on holiday.'

'I think he's just avoiding her,' Felix said, with his attractively lopsided grin. 'There must be something odd about the new vicar that the bishop doesn't want her to find out, until it's too late.'

'Well, whatever it is, I expect she'll beat him into shape, just like she has with Mr Merryman, don't you, Felix?' Poppy asked.

'Probably, and I feel sorry for the poor man already. Since she cornered him after his first service to make her views clear about the happy-clappy guitar-playing stuff, she's got poor Merryman so cowed that she only has to say, "That's the way we have *always* done things in Sticklepond," and he shuts up, even if he's proposing something totally innocuous, like taking the Sunday school children on a nature ramble round the churchyard, instead of colouring in pictures from the Bible in the vestry.'

'But it's Effie who runs the Sunday school, and she thought it was way too chilly for that kind of thing,' Poppy pointed out fair-mindedly. 'And if the new vicar is someone *famous*, like Cliff Richard, Miss Winter won't really be able to browbeat him, will she? I mean, I don't suppose he's used to being told what to do.'

'Poppy,' I said patiently, 'it isn't going to *be* Cliff Richard, so don't get your hopes up! Believe me, it'll be some sixties one-hit-wonder pop star that no one remembers.'

Jake, having for once in his life followed my advice, had become friendly with the girl he liked at college to the point where he now picked her up in Grumps' car every day and brought her home again.

She lived on the other side of Sticklepond in a converted barn, just next to the start of the track to Badger's Bolt. I thought this might not turn out to be the most salubrious of addresses, if Mr Drake was who we suspected he was.

Her parents phoned me up before they would let Jake drive her anywhere, and I had to assure them that not only was he a very careful driver (which he is, really, it's just me fussing), but also that Grumps' ancient Saab was incapable of breaking any speed limits, except downhill with the wind behind it.

Presumably at that point they had not yet set eyes on Goth Boy, or heard all the gossip about Jake's grandfather and the museum, because they gave their permission.

Anyway, Jake now seemed much happier, so far as I could tell through all that black hair, though I wished his taste in music would lighten up a bit. And he'd brought the girl back on the way home twice, so I could have the honour of making her real hot chocolate. Her name is Katherine, though she told me she is always called Kat, and seemed like a nice girl, so far as I could tell – she chatted away, though unfortunately very quietly and without moving her lips, so I had no idea what she was saying. I just smiled and nodded a lot.

We were by then all unpacked and more or less settled, and Chocolate Wishes was fully functioning again, which was more than could be said for the little village post office when I tried to send off my first lot of orders. I expect they will get used to it, though, and surely they *want* lots of business?

My pots of geraniums lined every deep windowsill, their fragrant leaves scenting the air and making the cottage feel like home, and now I could at last make a start on the garden. Felix helpfully blasted the slime off the herringbone brick paths with his power hose, revealing the lovely colours, and then insisted on helping me put up the little greenhouse, though I only really let him pass me the tools and prop things. When I could afford a proper, bigger greenhouse, I decided, I would get it delivered and erected without telling him first!

I started to clear out any obvious weeds and pruned everything that would take it, but for the rest I'd have to wait and see what came up in spring. One of the half-moon-shaped beds seemed pretty empty, apart from a climbing rose and a quince up the back wall, so I'll make it a herb garden, dividing it up like the spokes of a wheel and using as edging some of the small stack of old bricks I found under a hummock of ivy in the corner.

Another bed was earmarked for my baby Brown Turkey fig tree and I hoped the plum tree in the middle – if it was a plum – would burst into leaf and fruit eventually. It was all very exciting – to me, at any rate! And all the exercise was good for me too, because I had to go and soak the aches away in the bath afterwards, lying like a slightly strange

Ophelia among a scattering of dried attar of roses-scented geranium leaves.

The nicest thing about living in Sticklepond was that Poppy could drop in much more often, after meetings or whenever she had to call into the village for anything, and Felix sometimes locked up his shop and walked round for a cup of coffee or chocolate and a chat in the afternoon.

By now I'd started popping into Marked Pages on the way back from the post office every morning. Felix had installed a comfortable leather sofa and coffee machine in the front room – I even found Grumps in there one day. The lure of a bookshop practically on his doorstep must simply have been too much for him.

Then there was the Falling Star – it was much easier to meet my friends there now than when I had to drive all the way from Merchester, and back again afterwards.

My life was not exactly a social whirl all of a sudden, but it was very companionable and *much* more fun.

Poppy had been a bit inclined to be gloomy about birthdays ever since she turned thirty and saw the signpost pointing in the direction of forty, so I made her a special iced fruitcake decorated with a plastic horse the same shade of conker brown as Honeybun, her beloved steed, and took it up to Stirrups as soon as I'd sorted out the Wishes orders that morning.

I'd got her to shuffle the Angel cards last time she visited, so I could do her one of my special, big chocolate Fortune Angels with a personalised reading inside it, which I gave her as my present.

That and the cake cheered her up no end, especially

since the fortune was an extremely encouraging one, all about new persons coming into her life and doors opening, though that's never a good portent when it comes up for me.

But at least my bad news was broken gently through the Angel cards (unless I succumbed and got Zillah to read the Tarot or leaves), and while they might still *infer* that I was doomed, they also assured me that they meant doomed in a *good* way and I wasn't to worry about a thing.

Janey had given Poppy a lipstick in the same vibrant red that she used herself, screwed up in a striped paper bag that smelled of Uncle Joe's Mint Balls, so I think she may have forgotten it was Poppy's birthday until our cards had arrived that morning, and a spare lipstick was all she had by her. Poppy hardly ever bothers with makeup at all, but had put some on to show willing, though it was definitely wearing her and not the other way around.

'Give the lipstick a miss this evening,' I said, because we were to meet up with Felix at the Falling Star for more celebrations, 'unless you wear a lot more makeup with it.'

'I don't really think it's me, do you? Anyway, makeup is wasted on the horses – they don't care what I look like!'

'Well, *we* do,' I said, because I was always trying to persuade her to have her light-coloured eyelashes dyed and at least wear a bit of tinted moisturiser, since even if she did spend most of the day with her four-legged friends, there was no reason why she shouldn't look pretty while doing it. When the sun bleached gold streaks into her sandy hair in summer it looked really pretty, and a good hairdresser could keep it like that all the year round.

* * *

Jake had gone to dinner at Kat's house, so it looked as though her parents had got used to him and this was a seal of approval!

Felix, Poppy and I pushed the boat out and had a birthday feast of scampi and chips in a basket at the Falling Star, though actually the two of them bickered throughout about her next lonely hearts column date, the following evening.

It sounded like the scenario would just be a repeat of the last one, with Felix glowering over the top of his newspaper in the pub corner, like a jealous dog over a bone – though I thought maybe I would go with him this time out of sheer curiosity and we could peer over the paper together.

They made up their quarrel when he gave her her present, which was a tiny oil painting of a horse in the primitive style, and then after that she got tiddly and extremely giggly on gin and tonic.

We went back to the cottage for hot chocolate, the smell of which got Jake, who had by then returned, down from his room for long enough to wish his Auntie Pops a happy birthday and let her kiss him, in that terribly resigned way teenage boys have. You'd think it was an endurance test. Is there a Duke of Edinburgh's Award for that?

The hot chocolate didn't have a noticeably sobering effect on Poppy so we finally sent her home in a taxi, singing something about a galloping major. Goodness knows where she got *that* from. Janey would have to drive her down next morning to pick up the Land Rover.

'You know,' I said to Felix as the tail-lights of the taxi vanished round the bend, 'if her mum hadn't decided to work her way through all the eligible young farmers in the area and the local hunt, Poppy might have found Mr Right somewhere among their ranks.'

'I can't see her as a farmer's wife, and she doesn't like hunting, does she?' he pointed out.

And it was true that Poppy had taken a sudden aversion to hunting living creatures for pleasure when she was about ten, and didn't follow the hounds, even when they turned exclusively to drag hunting.

She was so terribly soft-hearted and I really didn't want to see that heart bruised or broken by careless hands, like mine was, even if I had successfully cemented it back together with tempered chocolate, so it wasn't just as good as new, but *better* than new.

But I knew she longed for love and marriage and even children, so I would much rather she fell for a decent man like Felix . . . if he fell for her in return, of course!

Chapter Twelve

Desperate Dates

It was the evening of Poppy's Desperate Date and I was going as emergency backup with Felix. It wasn't just an excuse for an outing, I was curious to see what rabbit she had pulled out of the hat *this* time.

I collected Felix from Marked Pages on the way and we were just cutting through the car park of the Green Man, when a familiar voice called out, '*Chloe!*'

I swung round, startled. 'David?'

My ex-fiancé was standing next to a snazzy red sports car, the keys in his hand. He looked just as handsome as ever: age didn't seem to have withered his beauty and it couldn't have staled his infinite variety because he never had any. His predictability was one of the things I'd appreciated most about him six years before: a calm harbour after the storm.

While I was still standing transfixed, he slammed the car door shut and strode over. 'I knew it was you!' Looking delighted, he kissed me on both cheeks, then held me away slightly and said, 'And you look absolutely wonderful!'

I felt flattered, since I didn't think I did really. My hair needed cutting and my nose was probably pink from the chilly breeze.

'You look pretty good too,' I said, finding I was quite happy to see him once I was over that initial surprise. Now he was closer I could see new lines on his face and some silver among his dark chestnut hair (he is several years older than me, after all), but it just made him look distinguished. Nature is unfair to the sexes like that.

'You remember my friend Felix, don't you?'

'Yes, of course,' he said with a brief, polite smile. 'Nice to meet you again.'

'Yes, you too,' Felix said unenthusiastically. 'I'll go on into the pub, Chloe – see you there shortly.'

He walked off and David turned his full attention back to me. 'I've often thought about you, Chloe. How have things been with you and what are you doing here?'

'I was about to ask you the same thing!'

'I have friends who live nearby and we sometimes meet up at the Green Man. But today I had a client over in this direction, so I stopped for a quick bar snack.'

'You never did move out into the country then, David?'

'No, I stayed in the city and I'm still living the bachelor life in my flat . . . though actually, that might be about to change. How about you? I don't suppose you're still in Merchester?'

'No. In fact, we've just moved to Sticklepond.'

'*We?*' he queried quickly.

'The whole family – Jake, Grandfather, Zillah. Grumps bought the Old Smithy at the other end of the High Street.'

'Oh?' He digested this information. 'Jake's still at home? He must be . . . how old now?'

'Nearly nineteen and off to university this autumn, if he ever actually gets down to some exam revision.'

'And your mother never came back? I was right about that?'

He might as well have added, 'Told you so!' But then, he'd never believed me when I said I knew she was alive.

'No, she never came back.'

'So – no husband, children, significant other?' His hazel eyes looked deep into mine. 'You surprise me.'

'Not at the moment,' I said, not wanting to come across as Little Miss Desperate, which I wasn't in the least. 'My Chocolate Wishes business is thriving and that, plus being Grumps' PA, takes up most of my time these days.'

He looked at an expensive watch. 'Look, I've got something on and I'm running late, but I'd love to catch up with you soon. We could even meet here one evening – how about it?'

'I usually go to the Falling Star down the other end of the village with Poppy and Felix. You remember Poppy, don't you?'

'Oh, yes,' he said, in the sort of voice that meant he had totally forgotten about her, though six years ago Poppy had been all set to be my bridesmaid at the registry office. 'The Green Man might be better, though, because I'd like to catch up with you alone the first time – I feel I have a lot to apologise for!'

'Oh, no, really you haven't,' I assured him, taken by surprise.

'I've always regretted not being more understanding at the time, Chloe,' he said with rather a wry smile.

'No, I meant it, David, because later, when I wasn't so upset, I could see *your* point of view too.' This was true, though admittedly not for an awfully long time afterwards and the way he had detailed his secretary to help me cancel the wedding plans and return the presents had only added insult to injury.

'Look, how about if we meet early one evening at the Falling Star for a chat, then, before your friends get there?' he compromised. 'Can you make it Friday?'

'OK,' I agreed, because I really couldn't see why not. Although I'd felt surprisingly pleased to see him again, I didn't think there were any embers left to stir into a flame, so it *would* just be a friendly chat.

'There's no reason why we can't be friends now, is there, Chloe?' he said with his attractive smile, seeming to read my mind – and really, there wasn't.

In the pub, Felix was already established in a dark corner with a good view over the room. He was inclined to be sulky and sarcastic about David's reappearance in my life, even when I told him that I wasn't about to fall for him all over again, and that I saw no reason why we couldn't have a drink together for old times' sake.

'I think having anything to do with a man who could let you down like that is a big mistake,' he warned me, and would have said more, except that Poppy came in just then. She gave us a little half-wave, got a glass of mineral water and settled into a table near the door.

'I do wish she would let me advise her about makeup and clothes a bit,' I muttered. 'I'm no fashion plate, but I do make an effort when I go out.'

'At least she's not wearing jodhpurs with the down-filled gilet that makes her look three feet wide,' he said.

'No, though actually they suit her better than that blouse, because she's not a spot, ruffle and pussycat bow sort of girl.'

The pub door opened and I nudged him. 'Look, that must be the date!'

A tallish, thin man with thick grey hair had come in, and paused on the threshold, looking around the room. Then he walked across to Poppy, holding out his hand.

'He looks fairly normal,' Felix said critically.

'Actually, he looks rather nice,' I agreed. 'He's older than I expected, though – early fifties, I should think – but that grey hair with the tan and the bright blue eyes are a pretty good combination.'

So far as we could tell, he and Poppy seemed to get on well too, and we started to feel pretty redundant as watch-dogs. But when they got up to leave together, Felix was still all for following them, to make sure Poppy was all right, and I was still trying to dissuade him when Poppy walked back in again, alone.

She was pink and smiling dreamily. 'Gosh, he's *sooo* nice – and he seemed to like me! He couldn't stay long tonight, so when he left *I* pretended to go too, then doubled back. We're having lunch tomorrow.'

'Where?' I asked.

'At his house – he loves cooking.'

'Dodgy.' Felix shook his head.

'No it isn't. He's really not that kind of man at all and I'll be fine. He wants to show me his garden.'

'But you aren't interested in gardening,' I said.

'I'll pretend. I don't think *he's* terribly interested in horses either, but he said he'd like to see my Honeybun.'

'I bet he did,' muttered Felix darkly and I gave him a sharp dig in the ribs. He was acting like a dog with two bones, neither of which he particularly wanted himself, but liked to have put by in case of sudden famine.

'OK, you can go, but keep your phone on and I'll call after about an hour to see if you're OK,' he said. 'We can have a codeword for emergency rescues.'

'Like "help"?' I suggested.

'This is serious, Chloe,' he said severely.

We adjourned to the Falling Star's dark, cosy snug, which was more our ambience than the slightly trendier surroundings of the front bar of the Green Man. Established in our usual window seat, Poppy waxed lyrical about her date. Apparently he was a former university lecturer who had taken early retirement, a widower, and he lived not far away, in Crank.

'That figures,' said Felix, who was determined to be disagreeable, and then he told her about David's sudden appearance and described what he said was my spineless agreement to meet him again, despite everything he had done to me in the past.

'He jilted me, that's all, and it was pretty mutual in the end, when we couldn't agree over Jake.'

However, Felix didn't find an ally in Poppy, because she was on my side. She didn't see why David and I couldn't meet casually after all this time if I really wasn't still attracted to him, and neither could I. In fact, I was quite looking forward to it.

Back home, I passed through the museum, where Grumps was unpacking one of the last boxes and took no notice of me at all, and on into the house.

As I expected, Zillah was in the kitchen, which had already taken on an even more exotically gaudy aspect than our last one. I think the bright red Aga must have gone to her head.

Today she was wearing a red cardigan back to front under a purple one the right way round, with a corsage of orange felt roses pinned to the bosom. She'd added to the effect by wrapping a shawl covered in shrieking pink flowers over the whole ensemble and what looked suspiciously like a checked tea towel wound turban-wise around her head.

It was a gloomy day but the lights were off, since she hated artificial light unless it was essential, not counting the big, flat-screen TV that was constantly on in the corner by an easy chair. When she smiled her teeth flashed white and gold in the light cast by the flickering screen.

'There you are,' she said, as though she'd been expecting me – indeed, she had two flowered china cups in front of her and was already pouring tea.

'Zillah, I've just met the person from my past that your Tarot reading warned me about, but it was only David, after all.'

'David?'

'My ex-fiancé, remember? You bought a feather fascinator in six colours for the wedding ceremony.'

'Ah, yes, *him*.'

'He was just getting into his car outside the Green Man, so we had a chat. I'm meeting him in the Falling Star early Friday evening.'

She looked up from swirling her teacup round and round, her bright eyes sharp. 'Is that wise?'

'Why not? A lot of water's passed under the bridge since we were engaged to be married, so there's no reason why we can't meet as friends, is there?'

'Hmm,' said Zillah, removing my now empty cup and scrutinising the tea leaves at the bottom. 'If you remember, I said that more than one person from your past

127

might reappear and affect the course of your life,' she reminded me.

'*Might* – so maybe not. And anyway, people from my past can only affect me if I let them, can't they?'

'You've already agreed to let one of them do that, Chloe.'

'No, I haven't. Although it was nice to see David, I've no intention of falling for him all over again – or anyone else that might pop up from my past. You have a look at my tea leaves: they'll show you.'

'Sometimes you can't see all aspects of the future until it's unfolded.'

'Then I'll keep mine tightly creased. But maybe you could read the cards for Poppy? She's getting so desperate for love that she's abandoned the internet dating sites and started ringing up men advertising in the newspaper. Felix and I are both worried about it. That's what we were doing at the Green Man earlier, keeping watch to see if her latest date looked OK . . . though I have to admit he looked very nice.'

'I would have thought your angels would have told her what her future held,' Zillah said, a trifle tartly.

'They have. I did a reading for her birthday, but it was all a bit general.'

'Oh, bring her to me, then,' she sighed, putting my teacup down. 'And whatever you say, your life *is* about to change greatly. The cards and the leaves don't lie.'

'No, but that could simply be interpreted as meaning all the changes involved in moving here and Jake going off to university in the autumn and that kind of thing, couldn't it?' Then a horrid thought struck me: 'Oh God – perhaps the cards mean Mum's about to turn up again and *totally* disrupt everything!'

Although I would have been quite pleased to have had word that she was definitely all right, I wanted it to be in the form of a postcard from a long, long way away. Call me selfish, but I really didn't want to share my little cottage with *anyone*, and especially not with my chaotic and totally self-centred mother.

On the other hand, I could ask her who my father really was – if she actually knew. It was a problem I was going to have to deal with at some point, though I was not yet sure exactly how.

Chapter Thirteen

Ashes of Roses

Jake and I had dinner with Grumps and Zillah and she came right out and told them I was going to see David again!

Grumps looked up from his plate of seafood risotto (Zillah likes to try out new recipes from magazines, though she spices them up with peculiar little additions of her own), and said that if my former fiancé crossed the Old Smithy threshold he would ill-wish him, and that went for any of the other men who had let me down in the past.

Then Jake said, 'Good idea, Grumps – I'll help!' so clearly that news didn't go down too well.

'What does Felix think?' Jake added, removing a clove from between his teeth and laying it on the side of his plate beside two more. I'd wondered what the hard black bits were until I'd tried to bite into one – but then, I think cloves are good for the teeth, aren't they?

'Why should it matter what Felix thinks? And anyway, David won't be trying to cross your threshold, Grumps. We're just having a friendly drink to catch up on what we've been doing the last few years, not rekindle the romance.'

'That may be what *you* intend, but *he* may have other ideas,' Grumps said. 'You're a fool. Felix is much the better man.'

'I'm sure he is, but I'm not romantically interested in either of them. Nor do I expect an orderly line of all my previous boyfriends to start forming up outside the door any time soon, so this is all much ado about nothing.'

I shot Zillah a dirty look, but she just gave me a glinting, minted smile and carried on eating.

The following day was pretty busy. For a start, Grumps had surpassed himself and written three whole chapters of *Satan's Child* in the early hours, plus several very long letters, so that it was mid-morning before I got round to printing off a whole sheaf of new Chocolate Wishes orders. I was usually on my way back from the post office by then, via Marked Pages for a cup of coffee, but I was still labelling the last boxes at lunchtime when Poppy burst through the door, looking even pinker and more dishevelled than usual.

'Hello, what are you doing here?' I asked, surprised, but with my hands automatically continuing to slap address labels onto the parcels and adding them to the pile, like a one-person production line (which is what I am, I suppose). 'Weren't you having lunch with your Desperate Date today?'

'I did! I was!' she cried, flinging herself into the nearest chair. 'Honestly, Chloe, you're never going to believe this!'

'Did he make a pass at you? Well, I did warn you, Poppy – and wasn't Felix supposed to be calling your mobile in case you needed rescuing? You had a secret codeword and everything.'

'Yes, and thank goodness he *did* call, because I pretended

he was my mother telling me that Honeybun was taken ill and I had to go straight home.'

I looked at her with a raised eyebrow. 'Did he fall for that one?'

'He didn't look *entirely* convinced,' she admitted. 'I don't think I'm a very good liar. But he said he'd phone me and we'd have to do it again.'

'Do *what*?'

'Have lunch in the garden.'

'That doesn't sound *too* dreadful, Poppy, though February is hardly ideal picnic-in-the-garden weather, is it, unless he has one of those patio heaters?'

She shook her head. 'There was no heater and he'd laid lunch out on a table in a sort of summerhouse with three open sides. I wished I hadn't left my padded jacket in the Land Rover – and that was *your* fault,' she added reproach-fully, 'because you said I looked the same shape as a dumpling in that or my warm down gilet.'

'You do and I didn't think you'd need them because I hardly expected you to be eating outside at this time of year! But *that* can't be what made you leave so quickly, so come clean, Poppy – what else did he suggest you do in the garden?'

Poppy's naturally rosy face turned to a shade of dark car-nation. 'Not in the garden, but in the summerhouse, actually. There was one of those wide, wooden-framed loungers at the back, practically like a bed, and that should have given me a clue because you can't leave cotton-covered cushions out in all weathers, can you? If I wasn't so stupid, I'd have realised they must have been there for a *purpose*.'

'That *was* a bit of a giveaway,' I agreed, keeping my face straight with an effort.

'But it didn't occur to me straight away and everything was fine at first: we started lunch and were getting on really well, just like we did in the pub. Then suddenly he said that there was a good reason why our first real date was taking place in the garden: it was because his wife was always there and he wanted her to meet me and continue to feel part of his life.'

While she was talking I had been stacking the parcels of Wishes into the huge and entirely unstylish shopping trolley I used to transport them to the post office, but I looked up at this and said incredulously: 'His wife's the *gardener*? I thought you said he was a widower?'

'Yes, that's what I said to him. So then he said, yes, he *was* a widower, but he felt his wife's presence everywhere in the garden because she loved it so much. And what's more, Chloe, he said her ashes were sprinkled all around the roses next to the summerhouse where we were sitting!'

'That's pretty bizarre, to say the least, Pops. I bet the roses are healthy, though?'

'It's a bit hard to tell at this time of year,' Poppy said, starting to get her sense of humour back. 'I was gobsmacked; but then I said, if he felt that his wife was sort of hanging about watching, didn't he find it off-putting bringing new girlfriends back, and he said no, he was sure she approved.'

'I'm not surprised you made an excuse and left!'

'Oh, but there's more! He said the reason he's sure she approves is because they had an open marriage – and open in more ways than one, because they both liked having sex in the open air, even if not always with each other.'

'He *didn't*!'

'He certainly did – he came right out with it, as if it was really everyday. That's why they had the summerhouse built:

to screen their activities. The back of it is towards the road. And then, Chloe, I was so startled I blurted out that I remembered his lonely hearts advert saying he liked outdoor pursuits and now I could see exactly where he was coming from! And unfortunately that seemed to encourage him, because he pulled his chair round to my side of the table and said he thought a riding mistress sounded fun and he was always open to new ideas. Then luckily Felix rang, and that's when I said I had to go. I'm sure I left with more speed than manners.'

'Serves him right – and he looked so nice too,' I commiserated.

Having got it all off her chest, Poppy was beginning to find it funny. 'It's a pity he didn't have a date with Mum instead of me. She'd have given him a run for his money,' she said, with one of her sudden giggles.

'You never know with Janey,' I agreed. 'He could have been thrown, hogtied and branded before he knew where he was.'

'Still, it's taught me a lesson. I'm starting to think you and Felix are right, and I'll never find a man this way. They'll *all* be weird.'

'Maybe that's because *all* men are weird and most women simply settle for the least weird one they can find,' I suggested cynically.

'No, they're not. Felix isn't weird, for a start,' she protested.

'Any man who is so engrossed in books that half the time he doesn't notice that he's buttoned his jacket up wrongly, or is wearing odd shoes, is just a little on the weird side, even if he's nice, don't you think?'

'Lovable eccentricities are different,' she said firmly, then hesitated and added, 'Chloe, have you thought lately that Felix seems to be . . . sort of looking at you in a different way? I thought I was imagining it, but then the other night . . .'

I sighed. 'Oh, you've noticed? I thought *I* was imagining it, too – I hoped I was. Now he's suddenly decided he wants to settle down, he seems to have fixed on me, for some mad reason. I think it dates back to last year when he bought those old Kate Bush albums at auction in a mixed box with some books, and decided I looked like her picture on the cover. It made him see me in a different light.'

'Yes, I think you might be right,' Poppy said thought-fully. 'It was about then I began to notice it. I expect it made him suddenly realise how pretty you are too – and you *do* get on well together.'

I ignored the pretty bit, which is just Poppy being loyal, and said, 'Of course we do, all three of us get on well, we always have – so it would be just as logical to have a *ménage à trois*, wouldn't it?'

She grinned. 'When you put it like that, I can see how ridiculous it is. He's been a big-brother figure all our lives, it would take quite a bit of doing to make *us* see *him* in a new light.'

'Yes, some very strong magic!'

Poppy giggled again: 'Actually, I've twice found Felix watching an old clip of Kate Bush on YouTube, when she's singing that "Wuthering Heights" song, so she's magic as far as he's concerned.'

'I absolutely do *not* look like Kate Bush!'

'Most people wouldn't mind if they did. I certainly wouldn't!'

'I think I just have an inbuilt aversion to having a *doppel-gänger*. Come on, let's go through into the cottage and have coffee. I'll post these later – there aren't any urgent ones.'

I got out some truffles that I'd been experimenting with. Though I only sell hollow chocolate shapes, I still like to make (and eat) the filled sort – one shelf of my fridge is usually full of them. And there's nothing quite like chocolate for cheering the troubled mind. Poppy went off back to Stirrups with most of her bounce restored.

I trundled my trolley off to the post office with my parcels, trying to think of a way of transferring Felix's interest to Poppy and of making her see him in the light of a lover, not a brother.

But since there was absolutely no chance of making her look remotely like Kate Bush, or him like George Clooney, I was on a bit of a sticky wicket.

Chapter Fourteen

Fairy Dust

Poppy told me that Hebe Winter had received a brief note from the bishop's secretary giving her the date when the new vicar was to take up his duties, which was much sooner than everyone had expected.

So when two huge removal vans rumbled by on the Friday afternoon of that week, heading in the direction of the old vicarage, sheer naked curiosity drove me to walk up there on the pretext of buying a loaf from the Spar on the Green, even though I realised it was probably only the new incumbent's possessions arriving, rather than the man himself.

The drive of the vicarage is quite short, most of the large grounds, which back onto Angel Lane, being behind the house. From the open front gates I could see the vans parked in front of the open porch and men carrying things in through the big central door, though mostly just quite ordinary-looking furniture, apart from a huge, dark, carved wooden headboard that looked very old. But it was hard to tell from that distance and anyway, I saw only that much because the wind lifted the blanket that was draped over it for protection.

There were what might have been large statues too, but they were also enveloped in so much packaging that it was hard to make out what form they took. Still, there's something fascinating about other people's belongings, like a TV game where things slide past you on a conveyor belt and you don't know what's coming next.

But I couldn't stand there for ever, so in the end I had to carry on walking. Perhaps I should get a dog? They are such a good excuse for nosy-parkering! Only then I don't suppose Tabitha would ever speak to me again.

When I got back I knew Jake was home from college and had brought Kat with him, because his long black coat and her half-unravelled-looking woolly wrap thing had been tossed over the back of a chair and then I fell over their bags. There was no sign of them in the cottage, but I could hear Grumps' voice in the museum, so thought they were probably with him.

I had a quiet sit-down with a mug of hot chocolate and then poured out three more, added hot milk, and took them next door to see what they were up to.

Jake was at the top of a stepladder, hanging masks high up on the wall, with Kat steadying it. As usual she was dressed in a frothy, short black frock, black tights and big boots, like a rare species of pretty Goth fairy. So far, Grumps did not so much tolerate her presence about the place as seem entirely unaware of it, but I expect she would impinge on his consciousness eventually.

Grumps was up at the other end of the room, where workmen were finally installing the tracking for the heavy velvet curtains that would divide off the pentagram area, and had pulled up his Gothic-backed wooden chair to the centre of the floor so he could watch them. This they seemed to find unnerving, but I expect that was because he'd already expressed his displeasure in no uncertain terms about all the delays and broken promises.

Fortunately, the rest of the curtains *had* been hung in time for the first magical rite of the season, as it were, so it had gone ahead. (Jake and I had taken care not to venture into the museum while the faint sound of chanting could be heard.)

Tabitha was sitting bolt upright on Grumps' knee, her yellow eyes fixed unblinkingly in the same direction as his. I handed out the hot chocolate and then asked the two workmen if they would like some too, or a cup of tea.

They declined, saying they just wanted to finish the job and get off, which in my experience is almost unheard of. I'd automatically expected a response along the lines of, 'Tea – milk and three sugars, love.' I could entirely see where they were coming from, though – and also that their stay would be indefinitely prolonged if they kept nervously dropping things the way they were doing – so I stayed chatting to Grumps to distract his attention. Not that Grumps really *chats*; he just makes pronouncements, but if you can get him started on a series of those he can keep going for ages.

The museum was really beginning to take shape and most of the glass cabinets were crammed with all kinds of peculiar things, labelled in Grumps' almost unreadable handwriting. (*I* can read it, but that's from long practice, transcribing his letters and chapters.) His collection was already catalogued, so he was now compiling a glossy brochure and several pamphlets from it to sell to the visitors. I anticipated having to type those up before they went to the printers too.

I had to leave eventually in order to have time to eat something before getting ready to meet David, though both Jake and Grumps' unexpressed disapproval made me feel like that song where a husband is begging his wife not to take her love to town. Jake even declined my offer of cooking him and Kat a pizza first.

Their attitude may have coloured my choice of clothes, for while I didn't want to look as if I had pulled out all the stops, I did feel it would be very satisfying if I could instil a tinge of regret in David that he'd let so much gorgeousness slip through his fingers.

Pretty impossible really. In the end, I just chose my newest jeans and a very pretty top sprinkled with sequins in pink and turquoise, and paid a bit more attention to my face than my usual five-minute makeover.

A pair of turquoise earrings that Mags brought me back from Goa last time she was there completed the ensemble. I suspected a guilty conscience, since her presents to me are always nicer than she gives Poppy – or even Felix, who is her own son. But I suppose it was kind of her to bring me back a gift at all, because my own mother never did . . . and I wondered if Mum really was in Goa, as I suspected, and that was the reason Mags kept jetting off there for solitary holidays, just like she used to do to Jamaica right after Mum vanished.

That started me thinking about Mum's blackmailing activities and wishing I hadn't seen the letters and still thought Chas was my father, instead of all this uncertainty. I *wanted* it to be him, but I couldn't just sweep under the mat the possibility that it might not be.

By the time I put on my jacket and went across to the Falling Star, David's red sports car was already parked outside. This was a wiser move than parking in the courtyard, because it doesn't have a lot of manoeuvring room, due to the small meteorite, after which the pub is named, sitting right in the middle of it.

There was no sign of Mrs Snowball behind the little desk that evening but her son, Clive, lifted the flap and came through from the busy public bar just as I entered the snug. David was the only person in the room and had been sitting in the window, but got up when I came in and kissed my cheek.

'Hi, David. I hope you haven't been here long?'

'No, I've only just arrived. What would you like to drink? I thought I'd wait until you got here.'

Behind Clive, who is a small, portly, middle-aged man with hair like grey wire wool, something hissed fiercely. He shifted to one side, proudly revealing a gleaming monster of a coffee machine.

'You might like a coffee, Chloe?' he suggested. 'We've got one of these now. The tourists all seem to want coffee these days, don't they? And I thought there'd be a lot more of them once your grandfather's museum opens. It'll be right good for business at the Star.'

'Yes, I suppose it will, I hadn't thought of that. And I'd love a coffee!'

'Wouldn't you prefer a glass of wine?' suggested David.

'No, I'm not much of a wine drinker and it's too early in the day for me anyway. Coffee's fine.'

'Right you are,' said Clive, then bellowed at the top of his lungs, 'Mother!'

We must have looked startled, because he explained that

141

Mrs Snowball was the only one who could understand the instructions for the coffee machine as yet. 'I haven't had time and Molly doesn't come in today.'

Mrs Snowball shuffled in, wearing her tartan slippers with the pompoms on the front.

'Customers for coffee, Mother.'

'I wouldn't have disturbed you, if I'd known,' I apologised.

She gave me a gappy smile and subjected David to a more prolonged inspection, before saying amiably, 'That's all right. What'll it be then, my loves? Capuchin? Express? Frappy-latty-thingummy?'

'I think we'll have two monkeys,' David said facetiously, and she looked blankly at him.

'Two cappuccinos please, Mrs Snowball,' I said.

'And a brandy, if you've got a decent one,' David added.

'I don't have no complaints about the brandy from my regular customers,' Clive said. 'You sit down, I'll bring the drinks over.'

'One-horse sort of place,' David said, 'and they'll never get the tourists in if they don't smarten up. I can't imagine why you prefer it here to the Green Man.'

'We like it just the way it is,' I said defensively, 'and we often have the snug to ourselves even in summer, while by mid-evening the Green Man is full of Hooray Henry types and tourists.'

'I often meet my friends there,' he said slightly stiffly and I remembered that in the past he'd introduced some of them to me, and they *were* loud Hooray Henry types.

'I've heard quite a lot of local people from that end of the village go there too,' I said quickly. 'Poppy says you can find half the gardeners from Winter's End playing darts in the back bar most nights.'

142

'Well, *any* bar that has you in it is better than one that hasn't,' he said with a smile. 'You look lovely, Chloe – and not a day older than when I last saw you.'

'You don't look much older either, David,' I said, feeling flattered, though my attention was slightly distracted just then by catching sight of Mrs Snowball's reflection in the mirror behind the bar. She had presumably completed her magic trick with the machine and now removed something from her pinny pocket and sprinkled it over the top of one of the cups. It seemed an odd place to keep the chocolate, or cinnamon, or whatever it was . . .

'I *feel* older, though,' David was saying ruefully. 'Lately I've realised that the time has come to settle down – and finally move out of the city too. It's better for bringing up children, for a start.'

'I – I didn't think – I mean, you didn't say you'd got married, David!' I said, startled, though I don't know why I was so surprised.

'I haven't. There hasn't been anyone serious since we broke up, Chloe, though it took me quite a while to accept what a big mistake I'd made in letting you go.'

'Oh, no, I think in retrospect it was a *good* thing,' I assured him cheerfully. 'We just weren't right for each other and it wouldn't have worked out.'

I wonder if all single men, when they get to a certain age, start to think of settling down? If so, maybe it's more a practical impulse than a romantic one and what they really want is someone on tap to look after them as they get older. I certainly didn't believe he had been living a bachelor existence for the last six years!

He gave me another warm smile, his teeth so un-naturally white they probably glowed in the dark and saved

143

him a fortune in light bulbs. 'Somehow, I seem to have been thinking about you a lot lately, Chloe, so it was a wonderful surprise to run into you again.'

'Yes, it's lovely to see you again, too,' I replied, though actually from Zillah's readings I should have guessed it might happen.

Clive brought the coffee and David's brandy just then, on an old battered tin tray painted with the Guinness toucan. His mother hovered anxiously at his elbow.

'This looks lovely!' I said, though I could see mine had missed the sprinkle treatment entirely, while David's seemed to have got a double dose.

'Enjoy! That's what they say on American telly, isn't it?' she cackled, then shuffled off back to whatever she'd been doing before Clive summoned her, and he went back through into the public lounge.

'Strange people,' David commented, one eyebrow raised quizzically, then took a sip of his coffee and pulled a face. 'Strange cappuccino, too!'

'Mine is fine, so I expect she just overdid the sprinkle on yours,' I suggested, though now I came to look at his coffee, it was speckled with greenish stuff that looked more like powdered herbs than anything. 'You'll hurt her feelings if you don't drink it. Here, let me scrape some of it off with my spoon.'

'You're too soft-hearted, Chloe,' he said, but even after I'd skimmed the top off it he still emptied the cup into a jaded aspidistra behind him after a couple of sips. It would probably perk it up no end.

David removed the aftertaste with a good gulp of brandy. 'I wonder if I could ask you a favour, Chloe.'

'A favour?'

144

'Yes, I'm looking for a house around here and I thought you might come and see some of the possible ones with me. I'd appreciate another viewpoint.'

'Poppy's the one who could be really helpful, because her cousin Conrad works in an estate agents and so she—'

He leaned forward and laid his warm hand over mine. 'No, it's *your* opinion I value.'

'You could have both,' I said as the door to the snug opened. 'And here are Felix and Poppy now!'

'So what, exactly, made you two decide to meet up here more than an hour earlier than our usual time?' I demanded when David had gone. He'd seemed disgruntled, as though I had arranged for my friends to arrive, even though it must have been plain that I was as surprised as he was.

'Felix phoned me up and suggested it: we were a bit worried you might fall for him all over again,' Poppy confessed, 'so we thought we would come and see.'

'Yes, and it looks as though we were right. He was holding your hand when we came in,' Felix said pointedly.

'He wasn't, it was only a casual gesture. He'd just asked me to help him look for a country house, because he wants a woman's viewpoint.'

'You're not really going to take up with him again, are you?' Poppy asked anxiously. 'Only we never thought he was right for you the first time round.'

'No, and actually I was quite glad when you came in, because although it was lovely to see him again, we seemed to have even less in common than we had before, and I was getting bored. I expect he has some other candidate in mind for the country house and really does just want a bit of feminine viewpoint when he's looking round them.'

'I think you're naïve, and it's a ploy to get back together with you again,' Felix insisted.

'You're daft. I'm sure neither of us is interested in starting the romance up again.'

'Is that a coffee cup?' asked Poppy, tactfully changing the subject. 'Since when did the Star start serving hot drinks?'

'Just today. They've got a machine behind the counter, but Mrs Snowball is the only one who knows how to use it so far. I'm not sure she's entirely got the hang of it, though, because although mine was fine, David said his was horrible.'

When I got back home, Jake was in the garden practising with the firesticks that Grumps had paid for. The effect in the darkness was very pretty and he seemed quite expert, so I hoped he wouldn't set himself, or anything else, alight.

David rang me while I was watching (we had exchanged mobile numbers) to say that he was sorry he'd had to rush off earlier, but he was feeling quite peculiar, and was positive it was the coffee he'd had at the pub.

'I'm sure it can't have been because I feel fine, and Poppy and Felix had some later too. What *sort* of peculiar?' I asked curiously, but he wouldn't say.

I'd noticed that Mrs Snowball didn't sprinkle anything onto *our* coffees, so I suspected that whatever ingredient she'd added to David's had been at Grumps' instigation. But I'm sure it can't have been harmful, just something *discouraging*.

Chapter Fifteen

Welcome Gifts

Poppy turned up the following Thursday just as I was pouring hot cream onto grated chocolate to make truffles – one part cream to two parts grated chocolate.

She was still wearing jodhpurs and a quilted gilet, but must have been to a Parish Council meeting, since she had changed her usual T-shirt for a fairly disastrous spotted blouse in mustard with a bow at the neck.

'Oh good,' I said, 'I need an extra pair of hands. I'm dividing this mixture in half and I need you to keep stirring the other bowl until I tell you to stop.'

She took the spoon and obediently started to stir. 'This smells lovely! What are you making?'

'Truffles. I thought I might try combining two of my favourite flavours, vanilla and cinnamon, and see what happened. Yours will just have natural vanilla flavouring and I'll roll them in powdered cinnamon, but I'll add both ingredients to my batch and dust with powdered chocolate.'

When they were blended I transferred them to two

labelled plastic boxes ready to be put in the fridge to firm up. 'There we are, I can finish those off later. Now come on, we'll have a cup of coffee and you can tell me all the latest Parish Council gossip. I can see you're dying to!'

She followed me into the kitchen and said, 'Well, it was Mr Merryman's last meeting, because he hands over to the new vicar officially on Monday morning. Miss Winter thanked him and we gave him a present – a loving cup in that blue pottery they sell to the tourists up at Winter's End. But we still don't know who the new vicar is!'

'What, *still*?' I handed her a mug and we went into the sitting room.

'No, apparently he's been in America on business and he's only flying back on Sunday and then coming straight down to Sticklepond. But the exciting thing is that he's invited the whole Parish Council round for drinks that evening! Salford Minchin delivered the invitation to Miss Winter, but the signature was as unreadable as the bishop's, and he just shoved it through the letterbox and cycled off before she could question him.'

'Didn't you tell me he communicated in grunts anyway?'

'He does seem pretty monosyllabic, especially with women,' she agreed. 'Given his history, I suppose that isn't surprising. Miss Winter has been calling up the bishop, trying to find out who the vicar is, but his secretary keeps telling her he is unavailable, so now she suspects that he's appointed someone so disreputable he daren't tell her the name!'

'He can't be that bad, or they wouldn't have ordained him in the first place. And any vicar is better than none, surely?'

'Yes, that's what I said to the others. Anyway, we've decided to take buffet food to the vicarage on Sunday and make it a bit of a welcoming party. Effie Yatton said Maria

Minchin's idea of a canapé was cold cheese on toast cut into triangles, and since the new vicar is a bachelor, he probably wouldn't have thought of food.'

'Is he? At least you know that much about him.'

'That's about all we *do* know – except that he must be well off, of course, to afford all the renovations going on up at the vicarage. *Filthy* rich.'

Her denim-blue eyes were bright and her cheeks flushed. She seemed amazingly excited just because the Parish Council were going to throw a welcoming party for a jaded, ageing, ex-pop star and still-nameless vicar . . . though actually, I was starting to feel a bit left out of things and would have liked to have gone too!

'What are you taking as your contribution?'

'A cake – and I can't imagine why on earth I offered to make one, when it's the thing I'm truly hopeless at!'

'You could hardly turn up at a party with a Yorkshire pudding,' I pointed out, since those are her speciality.

'No, that's true, though there's going to be a pretty weird mix of food anyway. Hebe Winter said she was going to get her cook to make a tray of sushi, because she thought that was the sort of thing the vicar would be used to eating. Her great-niece, Sophy Winter's daughter, spent several months in Japan and she's shown her how to make them. Otherwise it will be sausage rolls, crisps, nuts and olives – and my disastrous cake.'

'It's not going to be a disaster. I have a whole, fresh, uncut fruitcake in the tin right at this moment that you can take. You know Jake loves them, so I'm forever baking them, two at a time.'

'Oh, thank you, Chloe!' she said, her face lighting up. 'Though isn't it a bit like cheating?'

'Not any more than Miss Winter telling her cook to make sushi! But if we ice it now, you will have had a hand in it, won't you?'

'I suppose I will,' she agreed, brightening.

So we covered it with marzipan and roll-out fondant, then added a snow-covered church from my biscuit tin of cake-decorating odds and ends. Poppy was all for adding the stagecoach and horses that originally made up the rest of the Victorian Christmas scene, but I thought that would be over-egging the pudding. Instead she used my set of small metal letter cutters to write 'Welcome Vicar' around the edge in left-over icing, tinted a froggy green, which was the only shade of natural food colour I had in the cupboard.

When we'd finished she helped me to clean up the kitchen, over which icing sugar had drifted like snow, then said, 'I'd like to buy some Chocolate Wishes to take too. Twelve should do it, even including the Minchins.'

'Is that a good idea? Hebe Winter might not be pleased if she finds out where they came from.'

'I don't see why not. She said she didn't mind a chocolate shop, it was only the museum she objected to. Besides, I wanted the angel-shaped Wishes and I can't see why she should object to those. I mean, angels are *good* things, right? That one we saw looked quite stern, but I wasn't frightened of her.'

Poppy used to say that about the maths teacher at school, who *petrified* her. But I hadn't thought our angel was scary, she just looked as if her mind was on other, deeper, things.

'The Lucifer-type fallen angel element aren't so good, Poppy. Don't you remember when we did *Paradise Lost*?'

'Oh, I always rather liked Lucifer. He was just a bit too ambitious.'

I gazed at her, speechless. After a lifetime of being friends, she can sometimes still surprise me.

'But yours are all good angels and the messages inside say only helpful or comforting things, Chloe. So I thought they would be appropriate and *different*. Fun. I bet the new vicar won't have seen anything like them before.'

'No, probably not,' I agreed, and would have given them to her except she insisted on paying. They were a new batch, one I had said the latest version of the chocolate charm over – Mayan specials. I can't really see where the Mayans and guardian angels meet, but I expect they had something similar, even if they did seem to be a violent lot (the Mayans, not the angels).

'Hebe Winter is hoping the new vicar is a much stronger character than poor Mr Merryman, because Laurence Yatton has been surfing the internet and found out all kinds of unsavoury things about the Mr Mann-Drake who is buying Badger's Bolt!'

'Well, we already knew that from the stuff Jake printed out for Grumps, didn't we?' I pointed out. 'Did you see the photograph of him wearing a sort of druid robe, all hollow-cheeked and cadaverous? But perhaps he's just a very peculiar old man with more money than sense, who likes dressing up and holding rather *off* parties.'

'Perhaps,' she agreed doubtfully, then looked at the cuckoo clock and got up. 'Look at the time! I must go – and thanks for the cake, Chloe!'

'I'll save you a couple of the new truffles to try too,' I promised.

When she'd gone, clutching a cake tin, I removed the chilled truffle mixtures from the fridge and rolled teaspoonfuls into little balls between my palms, coating one batch in cocoa powder and the other in the cinnamon. I tasted one of each before putting them back in the fridge and they were equally delicious!

Unfortunately, Jake thought so too, and I had to forcibly remove the last couple from him later so I could save them for Poppy – though, of course, I could always make some more . . .

As a thank you for helping with the cake, Poppy rang early next day and invited me out for a hack, which she does sometimes anyway, when not fully booked up. I originally learned to ride on Poppy's first pony and I enjoyed it, even if I never got bitten by pony-mania as badly as she did.

This time it was just the two of us, with Poppy riding her beloved Honeybun and me on an elderly grey called Frosty. It was a brisk, cold, sunny March day, so it certainly blew the cobwebs away, and we were just coming back along the bridle path through part of the Winter's End estate when we came across Hebe Winter, standing in silent contemplation among a patch of wild garlic.

She looked as if she'd been there for some time – perhaps a decade or two. And I'm not saying she was having an out-of-body experience, but there were no lights on and nobody was home for several long minutes when Poppy stopped to introduce me. Then life slid into her wide, blank eyes as though someone had pushed a slide into a projector: spooky.

'Miss Winter, this is my best friend, Chloe Lyon. You remember I told you about her? She makes chocolates.'

Restored to herself, Miss Winter's searchlight-bright blue gaze rested on me in a way that would probably have totally disconcerted me, had I not had a grandfather like Grumps.

'Gregory Lyon's granddaughter? We have already met, I think – briefly.'

'Hello, Miss Winter,' I said cheerfully. 'Isn't it a lovely day for March?'

'I expected nothing less,' she stated, then turned on her heel and strode off, the greenish tweed of her cape blending with the shrubbery. I'd have liked to have known what she had in the cloth-covered basket over her arm, because it was moving.

Back at the stables, while Poppy was still fussing over Honeybun, her mum, Janey, cornered me in the tack-room.

Though you wouldn't think it, she was a lot closer to sixty than fifty, like Mags and my missing mother, Lou, and slim and attractive in a haggard sort of way. She was wearing buff-coloured, skin-tight breeches and a checked shirt unbuttoned to just south of decent. Her hair is golden, rather than sandy like Poppy's, and although her eyebrows and lashes might once have been pale, she kept them tinted dark brown. I wished Poppy would, because it would take away that permanently startled look.

And it was Poppy she wanted to talk about, which made me feel a bit uncomfortable because since she's my best friend I felt I couldn't really discuss her, even with her mother. So mostly I just listened while Janey chain-smoked in an edgy sort of way, and told me how she wished Poppy could find a decent man.

'She's the marrying-and-settling-down-with-a-family kind, but she's never going to find someone if she doesn't bother more about clothes and makeup, or listen to any of my advice, is she?'

'She's been going on quite a few dates lately, through the dating column in *The Times*,' I said defensively, though two hardly counts as a lot.

Janey shrugged. 'If she has, I bet she's never been out twice with the same man. They don't ask her again, do they?'

'One of them did, but it turned out he was interested in the wrong sort of outdoor pursuits. Still, you have to get out there and look, if you want a partner, don't you?'

'I'm not convinced that the sort of man she needs puts adverts in newspapers,' Janey said, flicking ash about in a way you really shouldn't do in riding stables. I only hoped their insurance was fully up to date and entirely comprehensive.

'Perhaps not, but it's going to work out OK: I've read the Angel cards and Zillah read both the Tarot *and* the leaves for her the other day, and they all say that she'll find love closer, and sooner, than she thinks.'

Janey looked at me through a haze of smoke. 'Then I only hope it isn't one of *my* ex-boyfriends, because I don't think any of them are her type.'

'I'm sure it won't be. Poppy couldn't possibly go out with a man that you had gone out with. She would find it really weird.' And since most of the eligible men in the neighbourhood were Janey's cast-offs, it materially had to lessen her chances of ever finding someone.

'Would she?' She gazed at me rather blankly. 'I don't know why it is, Chloe, but I feel sort of guilty that she hasn't found anyone. I mean, I've always been nice when she's brought a boyfriend home in the past, haven't I?'

Too nice, that had been the problem! Twice when she was

younger Poppy had found some pleasant and innocuous boy who seemed to be on the same wavelength, but they always completely lost interest once they came within Janey's orbit.

'I don't think I've been a terribly good mother, on the whole,' Janey confessed, viciously grinding the cigarette stub out under one booted heel.

I was surprised by this rare moment of introspection. None of the former Wilde's Women were prone to look at their innermost deep feelings, even supposing they had any. I'm pretty sure *my* mother didn't.

'Oh, I don't know, Janey – at least you were always around when Poppy needed you, which was more than Mags or Lou managed. And she had ponies and birthday parties, and you let us camp in the paddock and have midnight feasts and things like that, a bit like the children in an Enid Blyton novel.'

She smiled. 'Thanks, Chloe, I hadn't thought of it like that.'

'I suppose you don't want to tell me where Mum has got to, do you?' I asked hopefully, thinking I would try my luck while she seemed to be in an unusually forthcoming mood.

But a shutter seemed to come down. '*Me?* Why should you think I would know?'

'Because I'm sure Mags does and when one of you knows something, you all know it. Only *she* won't say either, although I suspect it's Goa.'

She neither confirmed nor denied this, simply changed the subject back. 'Do you know what the cards meant about Poppy?'

'I'm starting to have an inkling, but we'll have to wait and see if I'm right.'

Now I could see that Poppy and Felix were made for each other, I only wondered why I hadn't spotted it before.

The only problem was making the two of them look at each other with fresh eyes . . .

I'd have to work on it.

That evening Chas Wilde phoned up again, this time to say he would be in the north soon and would like to pop in for a quick visit.

'It's ages since I've seen you, isn't it?' he said. 'How are you settling into your new home?'

'Oh, I love it,' I said abstractedly, then on a sudden impulse took the plunge and added, 'and I'm glad you rang, because there's something I want to talk to you about.'

'That sounds ominous!' he replied cautiously.

'No, not really, though it is difficult. You see, when I was packing up to move, I found some of Mum's old letters.'

He sighed. 'I think I can guess what you want to talk about, then, and it's long overdue, after all. You want to know how your mother and I . . . came together?'

'Not exactly. Knowing Mum, I can imagine. I also know she got pregnant with me on purpose, as a sort of insurance policy after Wilde's Women disbanded, because she told me so.'

'She would. But I did a wrong thing in a weak moment and I had to pay for it, though I never grudged one penny I gave her to support you, Chloe,' he said sincerely.

'I know that,' I answered, because Chas is a kind, decent man, weak moment or not. 'But the thing is, I've discovered that she also told *another* man that he was my father too, so you might have spent eighteen years paying out for a child that wasn't your own!'

In the long silence that followed I could hear my heart thumping. 'Chas? Are you still there?'

'Yes, I'm here. Look, Chloe, the thought that you might not be mine *had* crossed my mind from time to time – you look nothing like me, for a start. But as I said, I made a mistake and so it was right that I should pay for it. Anyway, I've grown fond of you – you *feel* like my daughter.'

'And I'm fond of you too – which makes it all the harder not knowing for sure what the truth is!'

'Well, we *could* find out with a DNA test, if it matters to you?' he suggested. 'I could organise that.'

'Would you? It would be something to know one way or another. And if you aren't, then I'll have to assume it's this other man, though I suppose she could have been lying to him too!'

'Let's cross that bridge when we come to it, shall we? And we'll hope the test is positive. I'll see about it and I expect you'll have to send a swab or a hair sample or something off to a lab in the post. I'll let you know.'

'Thank you, Chas, *and* for being so understanding too. I thought you might be really angry.'

'With Lou, perhaps, but never with you, Chloe,' he said kindly.

I *so* hoped he was my father!

I was feeling a bit edgy after that, so later, when Jake's phone suddenly played a snatch of Mortal Ruin's 'Darker Past Midnight' I immediately insisted he change the ringtone to something else. I wasn't terribly tactful about it either, so he was miffed and we had a bit of an argument. Then he slammed off up to bed in a sulk.

I suppose it did seem totally unreasonable. It would have been so much easier if I could have told him *why*.

Chapter Sixteen

Dead as My Love

In the morning I apologised to Jake.

'That's OK. I suppose because you hear it everywhere, it just got on your nerves,' he said handsomely. 'I've changed it to something else now.'

'Thanks, Jake. That song just seems to be haunting me. It was even playing on the phone when I was put on hold the other day,' I explained. 'By the way, Chas is calling in sometime before too long – he rang last night.'

Jake knew the situation (or what we thought was the situation!) so he evinced no surprise at this, and went off in Grumps' car to collect Kat. They planned to spend the morning listening to some friends rehearsing their band. If the DNA test proved Chas wasn't my father, it would be time enough to tell him then . . .

When I went to Grumps' study to collect the latest chapter or two of *Satan's Child*, which had recently galloped off in an unexpected direction just when I had thought it was about to come to an end, he was removing the wrapping from a rectangular cardboard box.

'Morning, Grumps,' I said, putting down his cup of tea with the two biscuits balanced on the saucer – after a brief flirtation with Garibaldis we were back to the Jammie Dodgers again, I saw. 'Have you been buying things at auction, or has someone sent you a present?'

'Neither. Nor do I get the feeling that this contains anything good.' He lifted the lid, took a brief look inside, and then slammed it down again as though something evil might escape.

He looked rather pale. 'As I thought!'

'What's the matter, Grumps? Is it nasty?'

'A warning – unwelcome, if not entirely unexpected. Mann-Drake has evidently arrived in the village, for Zillah found this on the doorstep addressed to me early this morning.' He looked up at me seriously. 'Until I have taken steps to protect us all, should he contrive to introduce himself to you, have nothing to do with him. Certainly do not invite him across your threshold – and warn Jake. I will speak to Zillah myself.'

'He might not tell me his name,' I pointed out, starting to feel as if I had suddenly stepped straight into the world of one of Grumps' novels and wondering if he himself could tell the difference between reality and imagination. 'What does he look like?'

'Perfectly ordinary and harmless, though he has a voice that could charm the birds off the trees. In recent pictures from the internet he looks not much different from the last time I saw him, though he was dressed up in some ridiculous outfit, like a conjuror.'

'Yes, Jake showed me those – eerily lit from below, and with a sort of cowl shadowing his face!' I agreed, thinking that Grumps himself always seemed entirely unaware of his own eccentricities of dress, though of course *he* never looked ridiculous, just odd.

He gestured to the box. 'He would have used the powerful conjunction of the ley lines at the Old Smithy for dark purposes, and this shows me the depth of enmity he feels towards me, because I managed to purchase the Old Smithy while he was incapacitated with severe appendicitis. I found it disappointing that it was *not* fatal . . .'

'Grumps!' I exclaimed, staring at him. 'You didn't have anything to do with his illness, did you?' Then I realised what I had just said and added, 'No, of course you didn't! What *am* I thinking of?'

'Ill-wishing can lead to the opposite outcome to that desired, or rebound upon one's head; though it seems to me that to wish something bad upon another person, when your heart is pure and unselfish in its intentions, should not cause such an unfortunate result,' he said ambiguously. 'It is a very grey area.'

'Right . . .' I said. Not that I agreed, it was just that I knew how pointless it would be to get into an argument with him on the subject.

'We must protect ourselves while I consider my strategy, my dear Chloe. Florrie Snowball can help me there, for luckily her one great skill is the very thing we need now.'

'You mean Mrs Snowball from the Falling Star?'

He nodded, so it looks as though I was right in suspecting her of being another of his coven, along with the Frinton sisters. I wondered if there were any more in Sticklepond, whom I didn't yet know about.

'Do you know how the Falling Star got its name, Chloe?'

'Yes, of course. The rock in the middle of the courtyard is supposed to be a meteorite. It's got a brass plaque on it that says so, and that it mustn't be moved because that would be unlucky. But it can't have actually *fallen* there, because then the pub would be sitting in a huge crater, wouldn't it?'

'The sign means that it must never be moved from where it came to *rest*,' he said, which was another of the kind of statements he was prone to make that could be interpreted in more ways than one. Really, sometimes his conversation was enough to make you feel dizzy.

'It's really inconvenient where it is now, because it's right in the middle of the courtyard and cars are always getting scraped against it. I expect stagecoaches did too.'

'It's on one of the ley lines, the last landmark of significance before the conjunction here at the Smithy – and there may be three, for I am currently researching the possibility of an even more ancient one.'

'Oh, right. How exciting for you, Grumps!' I said, though I was still puzzling over where Mrs Snowball's speciality came in. Unless he'd heard about the coffee machine, of course, and thought large amounts of caffeine might sharpen our wits?

'If you could leave me now, Chloe – I must burn this,' he indicated the box, 'and then perform one or two rites to negate its power. You might put some more wood on the fire before you go.'

'OK,' I agreed, because although I was naturally curious about what was in the box, I wasn't curious enough to actually want to *see* it.

Anyway, this whole enmity thing between Grumps and Mr Mann-Drake was really just two old men playing an advanced real-life game of Dungeons and Dragons, wasn't it? Or that's what the logical part of my mind said, anyway!

* * *

On the night of the new vicar's welcome party I was at home in the sitting room, cutting the thin, almost transparent printed sheets of Wishes into small strips and feeling like Billy No-mates, even though it didn't sound like the most exciting event ever. Jake was at Kat's place (doing college work, allegedly) and the telly was absolute rubbish.

In the end, I put the *Bride and Prejudice* DVD on for the hundredth time just for the bright colours, cheery music and Bollywood dancing. I know all the words to the songs, so I could sing along while I was working.

I'd expected Poppy to ring me by mid-evening, but when she didn't I assumed either the party was going on much later than she'd expected, or the new vicar had been a bit of a damp squib in the ex-pop star department.

I suspected the latter. But since we were meeting up at the Falling Star after dinner on Monday night anyway, I supposed she and Felix would regale me with all the details then.

Next morning I woke even earlier than usual and decided to walk up to the Spar to get a newspaper and stretch my legs, before attempting to prise Jake out of bed in time for college, though actually he wasn't quite so bad now he picked Kat up on the way.

It was unlikely that there would be many people around at that hour, so I didn't bother with makeup and just put a jacket on over my working outfit of jeans and a T-shirt, with a blue and white spotty cardigan for warmth, all lightly smeared and fragranced with chocolate – glamour personified. I was closing the door before I remembered I hadn't even brushed my hair, but I didn't bother going back.

The air was cold and damp and the sky was paling into

a reluctant and jaundiced dawn. There was no one about in Angel Lane, though I could hear the steady pestle-and-mortar sound of Mrs Snowball donkey-stoning the flags in front of the Falling Star.

I looked back at her over my shoulder as I turned the corner into the High Street and she grinned and waved a pink, rubber-gloved hand at me. I returned the wave while walking backwards, thinking that it would be a miracle if *I* had that much energy when I was the wrong side of ninety, not to mention the flexibility to be able to get down onto a kneeling mat *and* back up again. She must be one of the livelier members of Grumps' coven . . .

Mrs Snowball's smile suddenly vanished and she pointed behind me, gesticulating wildly. I whipped round, afraid I was about to collide with a lamp-post, but I wasn't – the threat was much, much worse. For there, almost upon me, was a tall, dark figure from my past, the open wings of his long black leather coat flying back with each stride, so that he seemed to swoop down on me like a huge bird of prey.

By his side trotted a small, jaunty white dog, so incongruous that it made me desperately hope that this was all just a really bad dream – until I realised that if it was, then the frantic thumping of my heart would have woken me up by now. There was a loud rushing noise in my ears that sounded like my guardian angel, either arriving or departing – and I sincerely hoped it was the former, because I needed her.

He came to a jarring halt way too close for comfort and stared incredulously down at me as though I were the ghost of some half-remembered and not entirely delightful past.

'Chloe?'

For a second or two I was caught and drowning in those

startled, turquoise eyes, in which swirled a hard-to-decipher mixture of emotions among which, bewilderingly, anger seemed to dominate. Then the light in them died and he took a step backwards, breaking the spell.

'It *is* you,' he said coolly. 'I thought I'd conjured you up from thin air.'

Released, both my wits and the power of speech returned to me with a rush and I didn't need the white clerical collar around his throat, or even the silver crosses that dangled from the rings in his ears, glinting among the long, black curls, to tell me what he was doing here, however unlikely it seemed.

'Yes, it's me – but I'm not the Chloe Lyon *you* once knew, Raffy Sinclair!' I said and then added, with a powerful uprush of bitterness and loathing, 'And of all the parishes in all the country, why did you have to pick *this* one?'

'I didn't – it was chosen for me,' he said, and those oh-so-familiar winged black eyebrows twitched together in a puzzled frown. By now he was probably wondering why I hadn't thrown myself at him with cries of joy, as I'm sure any of his other ex-girlfriends would have done. 'I had no idea you would be here, but I can't see why *you* are upset about it when I—'

But I didn't even wait for him to finish his sentence, instead turning to flee back round the corner into the chocolate-scented sanctuary of my cottage, where I leaned against the door, panting, as though he might attempt to burst in at any moment.

Jake, looking mildly surprised, was standing in the doorway between the sitting room and my workshop, a half-eaten piece of toast in one hand. 'What's up?'

'Nothing – I just ran into the new vicar, that's all!' I said slightly hysterically, my voice wobbling. 'It was a bit of a surprise.' And *that* was the understatement of the year.

'Why, is it someone famous after all?' He went to peer out of the shop window. 'I wouldn't have thought you'd have gone all weak-kneed and groupie over—' He abruptly broke off, then exclaimed, like an awed twelve-year old, 'Oh, *wow*, is that him in the long black coat?'

'He's still there?'

'Well, he was standing looking at the house, but now he's walking past. He looks familiar.'

'It's Raffy Sinclair from Mortal Ruin – the band that did the "Darker Past Midnight" song you had on your phone.'

'Raffy Sinclair? *He's* the new vicar? Cool!'

'No, it *isn't* cool and he's the last man in the world I would have expected to get ordained, let alone turn up here,' I snapped, and he gave me a puzzled look.

'I suppose it *is* weird. I mean, he and his band were pretty wild, in their time, weren't they? But I don't suppose it's going to affect us in any way, so what are you getting your knickers in a twist about?'

'I am *not* getting my knickers in a twist!' I yelled, then managing with a huge effort to pull myself together, added more calmly, 'But of course, you're right, it won't affect us.'

'I'd like to know where he got that coat from,' Jake said enviously, then inelegantly stuffed the rest of the slice of toast into his mouth at once. He looked like a Goth hamster.

Now I was starting to recover my equilibrium and return to surrogate-mother mode, I was amazed that he'd got up without being told a second time and also made himself something other than his usual breakfast. But then, I suppose a constant diet of Pop-Tarts palls after a while, as even Raffy Sinclair seemed to have found out.

'I've got to go. Kat wants to be in college early this morning,' Jake said, picking up his bag and coat. That explained everything.

'Drive carefully, won't you?' I said, fussing as usual as I stood on the doorstep watching him open the Saab door, which he'd left parked by the kerb the previous night.

'Get a life, Mum!' he called out in his usual cheeky way and then roared off as though he'd made a pit stop in a Ferrari.

I was just thinking that fussing over Jake was stupid, since it had completely the opposite effect to the one intended, when a movement in the shadows of the gateway almost opposite caught my eye: Raffy was standing there, the little dog wrapped inside his coat, but now he turned and walked off without a backward glance.

If he'd been waiting to see if I would come out again, so he could speak to me, then he'd thought better of it.

Just as well: we might have had a lot to say to each other once upon a time, but now it was all *way* too late.

Chapter Seventeen

Written on the Cards

'Why on earth didn't you call me last night and warn me who the new vicar was, Poppy?' I demanded, when I finally got someone to answer the telephone up at Stirrups. As usual, her mobile had either gone flat, been trodden on by a horse, or not been switched on at all.

'Sorry, Chloe. I was going to, as soon as I had a minute, only I've been up half the night.' I could hear her stifling a yawn. 'When I got home after the party I could hear one of the ponies banging about in his stall with colic, so I had to get the vet out. Mum wanted me to lie in this morning, but I couldn't leave her to do all the work alone.'

'But, Poppy, the new vicar is *Raffy Sinclair*.'

'Yes, isn't it exciting?' she agreed enthusiastically. 'Though actually, I didn't think you were a huge fan of his, because you've never mentioned him and—'

'Poppy,' I interrupted, 'I came face to face with him in the High Street less than an hour ago and it was such a huge shock that my heart is still racing.'

'Oh, I *know* and I don't blame you, because he's *terribly* handsome, isn't he? His eyes are almost turquoise, like the sea in that Jamaican holiday brochure you got when your mum went missing – quite stunning! And he's really, really nice when you talk to him too, so even if all those stories about him and the rest of his band are true, I'm sure he's put all that behind him now that he's found God.'

'Poppy, it wasn't just a shock, it was a nightmare! Raffy Sinclair—' I began, but she had the bit between her teeth now and was galloping off.

'I expect you felt as stunned as we all did when he walked into the room last night. But I'm sure we'll all soon get used to seeing him around the parish. We'll have to, won't we, since he's the vicar?' She giggled. 'It's going to be such fun!'

'Poppy, stop gabbling for a minute and *listen*! Raffy Sinclair is the man I met at university – you remember, the boyfriend who went off and left me when his band was offered a recording contract, and didn't come back? The one I never, ever, heard from again – unless you count reading about his debauched exploits in the newspapers.'

There was a gasp. '*That* was Raffy Sinclair? I had no idea! If only you'd told me his name instead of clamming up about it, I would have warned you and – oh, Chloe, he seemed so nice too!' she exclaimed, distressed.

But of course Poppy had been away at the crucial time and when she eventually returned I'd lost any desire to share more than the barest details, even with my oldest friend. Only Zillah knew the full extent of what I went through then and I hadn't told even her the name of the man who'd broken my heart.

'I never wanted to see him again!'

'No, and I suppose I can understand that, because *I* still feel a bit sick when I think of the silly way I behaved over that instructor when I was doing my course and I'm sure I'd *die* if I had to see him again,' she agreed.

'That was a bit different, Poppy – I thought Raffy *loved* me. He told me so!'

'I know, and it's terribly sad and romantic, just like a film,' she sighed.

'Yes, one with an unhappy ending!'

'But it *was* an awfully long time ago. I expect you've hardly thought about him for years, it was just the shock of suddenly seeing him that's upset you.'

'Poppy, Mortal Ruin's music is inescapable, so I've never had the chance to forget him!'

In fact, 'Darker Past Midnight' still makes me want to cry, because I'm not the girl in the song he's longing to see again . . . but I didn't tell Poppy that.

'Oh, yes, I suppose that would keep stirring it up,' she agreed. 'But at least you got over him long ago, even if you couldn't forget all about him, and you'll probably soon get used to seeing him about. And after all, now he's been ordained, he must be a totally changed man from the one you knew.'

'I don't care if he's on the fast-track shortlist for saint-hood,' I snapped and slammed the phone down, though I was sorry almost immediately. It wasn't poor Poppy's fault that I was so upset.

Then some slight movement out of the corner of my eye warned me that I was not alone and I saw that Zillah was sitting quietly on a kitchen chair as if she had materialised there, with a large pot pie in a ceramic dish, the ostensible reason for her visit, on the table in front of her.

'Oh, Zillah!' I gasped, wondering just how many shocks a heart could take in one day. 'How much of that did you hear?'

'Enough,' she said, while the roll-up fag dangling from one corner of her mouth shed a long trail of ash that narrowly missed the pot pie. 'Finally I know the name of the man who made you so unhappy. Who deserted you in your hour of need. Who—'

'Let's not go there,' I said wearily, dropping onto the chair opposite. I was starting to feel quite wrung out and the day had barely got going yet.

'And now here he is, masquerading as a man of God,' she said, ignoring me. 'The warning was on the cards!'

'It's a pity they didn't spell it out a bit more clearly, then, because I thought they just meant David. And Poppy doesn't understand why I'm so upset that Raffy's come here, since it was all such a long time ago. She says that since he's become a vicar he *must* have changed a lot since I knew him, but it's hard to believe.'

'Whatever he's become now doesn't excuse what he did in the past. And anyway, Chloe, the past tends to come around and bite you on the bum when you're not looking.'

'Yes, it certainly just bit mine.'

'And it will bite his, in time – his punishment will find him out.'

I looked up quickly at that. 'You're not going to tell Grumps, are you?'

She didn't reply, just grinned at me, golden teeth glinting, and then hoisted herself up leaving a final discarded snake-skin of ash on the table. 'There's a nice pie for your dinner. I'm off out later, so I thought I'd cook early – I've joined the local tea dance club.'

She held out one small foot in a jewelled high-heeled silver sandal for me to admire. 'New, breaking them in.'

'Lovely,' I said, my mind still focused on other things.

'Zillah, you really *won't* tell Grumps anything about what happened between me and Raffy Sinclair, will you? I mean, he doesn't know we ever went out with each other, let alone—'

'You can't hope to keep secrets from your grandfather,' she said ambiguously, which either meant that she thought he was so all-seeing that he would automatically pick up information from the airwaves, or that she told him everything.

I hoped my little Sticklepond Sibyl was wrong.

'So now I don't know if she'll tell Grumps that Raffy's the man who treated me so badly, and if so, whether he'll feel the need to try and take some kind of revenge. Though if he did, Raffy would *totally* deserve it,' I said to Poppy and Felix later in the snug at the Falling Star.

Felix had entirely forgotten that I'd been out with anyone while at university (he too had had other things on his mind at the time, being in the throes of his divorce just then), and was unflatteringly astounded to discover that Raffy and I had been an item.

'But it's all so long ago and anyway, you couldn't really blame the man for going off when Mortal Ruin got its big opportunity, could you?' he said, even more inclined than Poppy to think I should have got over it by now. 'Be reasonable, Chloe!'

'Perhaps not, but I *could* blame him for dumping me without a second thought!'

'But you spent only one term at university, so it was hardly a long relationship, was it?'

'And you were both terribly young, so it probably wouldn't have lasted anyway,' Poppy suggested gently.

'I wouldn't worry about your grandfather doing anything to him, either,' Felix said with his sudden attractively lopsided grin, 'because if he tried to put some kind of curse on all your old suitors, he'd have no time to do anything else.'

Poppy giggled. 'That's an exaggeration, Felix! Chloe's only been out with a handful of men and no one at all for ages and ages.'

'I wouldn't mind if he put a curse on David Billinge,' Felix said. 'I'm sure he's trying to get back with you, Chloe. And you seem to have managed to forgive *him*, even though he jilted you on the eve of your wedding, haven't you?'

'That was because he did me a favour. I realised almost immediately that marrying him would have been a big mistake. Now he just wants to be friends, which is fine by me. He's picking me up on Wednesday afternoon and we're going to look around a few country cottages. It'll be fun – I love looking at other people's homes.'

Felix looked unconvinced, and I'm pretty sure Poppy wasn't listening at all, because she suddenly said, 'You needn't see much of the vicar, Chloe, so it may not be such a problem as you think. I mean, it's not like you go to church, is it? Your paths will hardly cross.'

'They crossed this morning, practically on my doorstep.'

'I expect he was taking his dog for a walk round the block, because the rear drive to the vicarage is just up Angel Lane, isn't it?'

'Yes, so it is. Well, I'll just have to try and keep out of his way. And I expect that even if Grumps does find out and tries to do something horrible to Raffy, it won't work. Besides, he has other things to worry about at the moment.' I told them about the parcel Grumps had received from

172

Digby Mann-Drake. 'He said it was a warning and it must have been something really nasty, because he burned it.'

'Actually, I forgot to tell you that Mr Mann-Drake came into my shop the other day and he seemed very inoffensive and pleasant,' Felix said. 'I didn't even realise who he was until we were chatting and he said he'd bought Badger's Bolt as a weekend cottage, but found the ambience so restful that he intended spending a lot of time there. That doesn't sound very dangerous, does it?'

'But Jake looked him up on the internet and he's really not a very nice person – and Grumps said he could easily deceive people,' I warned him.

'Yes, I think he sounds horrid and Miss Winter should be glad that your grandfather bought the Old Smithy and not him, or we would have him right in the middle of the village,' Poppy agreed. 'But I've just had a thought: Miss Winter is bound to make the new vicar go and visit your grandfather, isn't she?'

'Serves him right,' I said callously, then changed the subject and told them about my conversation with Chas.

'He took it a lot better than I expected. He's such a nice man that I really want him to be my father!'

'There's still a good chance he is,' Poppy said optimistically. 'And at least you'll soon know one way or the other, won't you?'

'If it's not him, what will you do then?' Felix asked. 'Go after that actor, whatever he was called?'

'Carr Blackstock – and he didn't sound particularly friendly. I'll think about that, if it comes to it. One step at a time.'

'Gosh, everything seems to be happening to you at once,' Poppy said.

'Yes, it needs only Mum to turn up on the doorstep to make my happiness complete,' I replied slightly sourly, because it was starting to feel as if my six-year sea of relative tranquillity had been maliciously stirred with a big stick and a whole lot of murky stuff was rising from the bottom.

Chapter Eighteen

Charm

I saw the notorious Mr Mann-Drake for myself the very
next day and, like Felix, I found it hard to square his
appearance with his reputation . . . though, admittedly,
his appearance *was* very odd.

He was going into Marked Pages as I was coming out, after
my usual cup of coffee on the way back from the post office
with the Chocolate Wishes orders. When he made a strange
sort of half-bow and doffed his wide-brimmed felt hat, wishing
me good morning, I guessed who he was even though he
looked nothing like the photograph of him I'd seen.

It must have been taken while he was standing on a box,
for instead of being tall and cadaverous, he was more like
a skull on a short stick, wrapped in a Victorian-style evening
cloak. His hair was dyed even blacker than Jake's and plastered flatly to his head and though his skin appeared slightly
mummified, his eyes were as dark, bright and alert as a
lizard's.

In fact, he looked like an old-fashioned music-hall magi-
cian, except that there was something slightly reptilian about

175

him that gave me the creeps, even though his voice fell like drops of liquid honey into the air. Grumps was right about that.

Poppy rang later that day from her mobile and she must have been up in one of the paddocks, out of earshot of her mother, because I could hear sheep bleating in the background and a blowing noise, which she said was Honeybun being friendly and wanting to say hello. I was only surprised that for once her phone was in working order.

'Did you call so Honeybun could communicate with me?' I asked. 'Only I'm melting couverture and I'll have to turn the temperature down and tip a bit more in, shortly.'

The chocolate spends over an hour being heated and stirred before the next stage, when you put more of the couverture chocolate drops into the Bath to cool it down, and once started on the process I don't stop, short of a power cut.

'No, of course not, it was because Raffy Sinclair's just been here and I thought you'd like to know.'

'What, he's been to Stirrups?'

'Yes, he caught us just as we were having our elevenses. He said he intended visiting every house in the parish over the next few weeks to introduce himself, starting with Mr Lees and the members of the Parish Council. He'd seen Effie Yatton already and after us it would be Felix.'

'That seems pretty keen – he's only just arrived.'

'He certainly is keen. He's already had a meeting with the Parochial Church Council and he's started saying morning and evening prayers in the church every day too, which is more than poor old Mr Harris managed. He said anyone who wanted to join him would be welcome.'

'But doesn't Mr Lees practise the organ in the afternoons?'

'Yes, but he's usually finished and gone for his tea by then, though he sometimes plays it late at night when he calls in to lock up the church on his way home from the pub. People complain about it, but being blind he says day and night are all one to him, and takes no notice.'

'Yes, I've heard him playing once or twice faintly, when the wind has been in the right direction and my bedroom window open. But I thought he was deaf and dumb as well as blind, the Pinball Wizard of the mighty Wurlitzer?'

'Oh, no, he can hear perfectly well, and talk if he wants to – he just doesn't usually want to. He must have talked to Raffy, though, because they're going to the Falling Star for a drink together tonight.'

'What? Raffy can't invade *our* pub!' I protested indignantly.

'They'll go in the back bar and I don't suppose he'll make a habit of it, he's just being friendly.' She paused, then added, apologetically, 'He *is* warm and friendly, you know, Chloe, though I found it a bit hard talking to him, knowing he treated you so badly. I think he noticed there was something wrong.'

I could imagine: Poppy's thoughts and feelings scud across her expressive face like clouds across the sky.

'As soon as Mum went to make him some fresh tea, he told me he'd bumped into someone he knew at university the previous day, Chloe Lyon, and Mr Merryman had told him you were a friend of mine! He said it had been quite a surprise to find you were living in Sticklepond.'

'I bet it was!'

'That's what I said, and then I think he realised you'd told me all about him, because he said it seemed to have given you a bit of a shock when you ran into him in the High Street, but he assumed that you'd long ago forgiven and forgotten and moved on with your life, just as he had.'

'What does he mean, just as *he* had?' I demanded indignantly. '*I* was the wronged one – and I was doing just fine with the moving-on bit until he chose to turn up on my doorstep.'

'Yes, but of course at that point he was assuming you were married, because he'd seen you that morning with Jake and thought he was your son.'

'But why on earth should he—' I began, then remembered. 'Oh, yes, I think Jake *did* call me Mum when he was leaving, the way he does when he's trying to wind me up.'

'I told him you weren't married and that Jake was your half-brother, and you'd practically brought him up single-handed. He looked really surprised.'

'There, that just goes to prove he never even *looked* at the letter I sent him after I got back from university, or he would have known all about Jake! And now I suppose he thinks I've been pining for him all this time and that's why I've never married.'

'Oh, no, I'm sure he doesn't, Chloe! I explained that you'd spent the last few years building up a really successful chocolate business and he'd actually eaten one of your Wishes at his welcome party.'

'I wish it had choked him!'

'You don't really think that, it's just his arrival's temporarily stirred up all the hurt feelings again, that's all. But I'm positive he's an entirely different man from the one who let you down, a *nice* man.'

'Can leopards really change their spots?'

'Yes,' Poppy said simply. 'Even the blackest sinner can repent. And he must have done, or they wouldn't have let him enter the Church, would they?'

'I suppose not,' I agreed reluctantly, only half believing in this metamorphosis from rock god to man of God. 'Did he say anything else interesting?'

'No, there wasn't time, because Mum came back with the fresh tea and a plate of Bourbon biscuits and started flirting with him, which was hideously embarrassing. *And* she told him she was going to start attending church services, though I shouldn't think she ever has, apart from the occasional wedding.'

'She won't be the first. He'll have every woman in the parish drooling over him, just wait and see.'

She giggled. 'Except Hebe Winter! He's going out to Winter's End in the morning and then he said he thought he might visit your grandfather in the afternoon, since she'd made such a big thing of it and he was quite interested in the concept of the museum, anyway.'

'Visiting Grumps might not be the wisest move he's ever made,' I said. 'I have a feeling Zillah has told Grumps everything she knows about Raffy Sinclair. Look, I'll have to go and see to the chocolate now – I'll talk to you later.'

It was late afternoon by the time I'd finished making Wishes and cleaned the workshop up again.

I felt tired and drained, but I went through into the museum because I'd promised to help Grumps check the proofs for the guidebook. It was just a short brochure, but he was now thinking of using the same firm in Merchester to privately print his definitive guide to the history of magic, an old project he was suddenly keen to resurrect, and which had so far been rejected by every publisher he'd sent it to, even the one who published his book on ley lines.

He had the proofs spread out on the desk and they didn't take long to go through. Then, just as we finished, Zillah appeared with Clive Snowball, who was carrying an old cardboard wine box.

'Clive's got something for you,' she said, with one of her gold-glinting smiles. She seemed to be on surprisingly friendly terms with the publican.

'Mother sent these,' he said, dumping the box onto the desk in front of us, then added, without showing any sign of curiosity about the strange objects that surrounded him, 'I'll be off then. There's a delivery due at the Star.'

'I'll see you later at the tea dance club then, will I?' asked Zillah.

'No, I'll pick you up and drive you, love: you don't want to be walking the length of the village in those pretty silver sandals of yours, not in winter.'

I won't say that Zillah simpered, precisely, but there was more than a hint of sashay in her walk as she went off to let Clive out again.

Grumps didn't seem to have taken in any of this exchange but had folded back the lid of the box and was engaged in unpacking thick, greenish, old bottles, the sort that have a glass marble stopper hinged to the neck on a strong wire.

They each seemed to have several objects inside them, but when I held one up to the light I could only make out a slip of paper and what might have been twigs tied together. 'Witch bottles? Is that Mrs Snowball's mysterious magical speciality?'

'Of course. Florrie Snowball makes the best and she's

built up a large stock over the years, because we all felt they would be needed, sooner or later.'

'Oh,' I said thoughtfully, because the purpose of the bottles is to ward off ill-wishing, and they've been found hidden in many old houses. 'Are these supposed to guard us against Mr Mann-Drake?'

'The first line of defence,' he agreed, 'for as boy scouts say: be prepared!'

I couldn't imagine Grumps had ever been a boy scout, but something was puzzling me. 'Grumps, I thought the bottles contained magic to keep witches out. So how come a *witch* is making witch bottles? And if she had boxes full of them in the pub cellar, then they can't be working, can they?'

'They work very well.' He held one up and shook it gently and for a moment I thought I saw a glittering spark of light like a shooting star in the murky depths, but it must have been a reflection.

'But if the charm works, then why isn't it affecting *you* either, Grumps?'

He looked at me in a surprised sort of way. 'Because my heart is pure and my intentions good, though I confess to feeling the odd twinge, should I . . . er . . . *inadvertently* stray over the borders of white magic, even with the best of motives. A little revenge, for instance . . .' He winced slightly. 'It is like a sort of spiritual lumbago. Practitioners of the Old Religion can take two paths and this charm works against those who have taken the wrong one, and protects those of us who have not.'

'Right,' I said, thinking that at least if his coven believed that, then the witch bottles should keep them all on the straight and narrow – or, as straight and narrow as magic usually is: it seems a twisty sort of thing.

Grumps handed me the bottle. 'You'll find a small ledge for that above the museum door, Chloe. In fact, you will find a place for them over every exterior door to the Old Smithy.'

He was quite right, too – there was. I carried the box and he placed the bottles onto ledges above the lintels. 'Made for the purpose, you see, Chloe. Very cautious women, the Frinton sisters. They will have taken their own bottles with them to set up at their new address.'

In my cottage there was a tiny niche carved into the stonework over both my front and back doors, just big enough to hold a bottle. I'd already noticed them and put one of my ornamental angel figures in each. They seemed protection enough to me, but since Grumps showed signs of extreme annoyance when I said so, I placated him by relegating them to the windowsills among the scented geraniums, and replacing them with the witch charms.

'Poppy tells me the new vicar intends coming to see you tomorrow afternoon, Grumps,' I said casually, when that was done, but obviously not casually enough because he gave me one of his sharp looks.

'If he is obeying Hebe Winter's orders, then he is a fool. If he knows of our relationship, then he is a double fool.'

'What has our relationship got to do with it?' I demanded, but he didn't deign to reply to that one. I can't really believe in his omniscience, so it does look as if Zillah has told him something about my past relationship with Raffy, though I sincerely hope not *all*.

'I'm not sure Mr Merryman ever recovered from his visit with you, Grumps. What on earth did you say to the poor man?'

He looked faintly surprised. 'Nothing that anyone could

take objection to, I am quite sure! I was busy when he arrived, so perhaps it was what I was *doing*, rather than anything I *said*. Are you asking me to be kind to the new dolt when he comes to disturb my peace?'

'No: you throw the bell, book *and* candle right back at him, if you want to,' I told him callously.

Chapter Nineteen

In the Mix

My Angel card reading the following morning suggested that I should resolve issues with another and let the balm of forgiveness heal my heart, but if it was referring to Raffy then it had gone beyond the bounds of optimism and into la-la land.

But I supposed it could have meant forgiving Mum instead (though the outcome was equally unlikely), since the postman brought me a small DNA sampling package, organised by Chas. He was quick off the mark!

If Chas *wasn't* my father it would throw the game right open, because if Mum lied to him, she might also have lied to the other man and it would be awful if I never found out who my biological father was. I didn't really know why it felt so important, though, since I never intended having children so I wouldn't be worrying about what genes went into the mix.

Anyway, there was no turning back now, so I followed the instructions and did the swab thing straight away, then sealed it all up again to send off later when I went to the post office with my Wishes.

And at least I wouldn't have to keep a lookout for Raffy that morning when I was out, because I knew he would be at Winter's End. I'd seen him pass the window very early with his dog the previous day and again that day (surreptitiously, from behind the curtain, though he never even glanced at Angel Cottage), so it seemed set to become a regular habit.

That afternoon David was picking me up to go to look at a selection of country cottages, so with a bit of luck I wouldn't even be in the same building when Raffy came to see Grumps, either.

On the way back from the post office I called in to see Felix, as usual, but then almost immediately wished I hadn't, since all he could do was sing Raffy's praises.

They were such opposites that it hadn't occurred to me until then that they would get on so well, but by the time I'd listened to him waffling on about how you wouldn't think Raffy had ever been famous because he was so ordinary (is he *blind*?) and how he felt he'd known him for ever, and how *friendly* he was, it was enough to make my coffee curdle.

Even more than Poppy, he thought I should have long recovered from my bit of history with Raffy and moved on, especially since he must have changed radically before being ordained.

If anyone else mentioned the words 'forgive and forget' to me after that, I swore I'd deck them. Reason and common sense be damned: I just couldn't snap my fingers and say, 'OK, let's forget it!' when even the very mention of his name made me go all bitter and twisted inside. And yes, I did know that was negative and damaging and I'd feel *so* much better if I let it go, but I just couldn't do it.

I was also starting to feel very aggrieved about Poppy and Felix's lack of empathy. These were *my* friends, and whether I was in the wrong or the right, they should be on *my* side and not be the devil's advocate, even if he is cunningly disguised in a surplice. And I was still not convinced there wasn't a Lucifer lurking inside there!

So I said one or two sharp things to Felix, who commented as I left that he'd never seen me quite like this, though he didn't qualify exactly what he meant by 'this'. But whatever it was, perhaps it would have started to make him think twice about my suitability as the right person to sink into middle age with, which would be a damn good thing.

Now I just needed to get him to switch his focus to Poppy instead, and vice versa. I wondered what she'd done with that love potion she got from Hebe Winter. Not that I believed in them, of course, any more than the power of Grumps' magic; but still, if I could manage to get hold of it, there would be no harm in giving it a try, would there?

Raffy must have gone to see Grumps immediately after lunch, much earlier than I'd expected, because there was a knock on my door ages before David was due to pick me up and there he was, standing two steps down on the pavement and disconcertingly eye to eye.

The expression on his pale, chiselled features was guarded, though I noted that he seemed remarkably undisturbed considering where he'd just come from: but then, I already knew he was made of much less yielding stuff than Mr Merryman.

My automatic reaction was to slam the door in his face, except that he foiled that by leaning on it.

'Chloe, can I come in? I think we need to talk.'

'I don't need a visit, thanks. I'm not one of your parishioners!'

'No, I think I've already grasped the message that the
Lyons aren't churchgoers from your grandfather. But I
would like to talk to you – please?'

If I hadn't just at that point inconveniently remembered
what the Angel cards said that morning and hesitated, then
I'm sure he wouldn't have managed to insinuate himself
over the threshold. But somehow there he was, standing in
the middle of the workshop and looking around him in an
interested sort of way.

'It smells delicious in here,' he said appreciatively, 'but I
hope I'm not disturbing your work?'

'No, I don't make chocolate every day, and actually, I'm
going out shortly.'

'Oh? Then I won't keep you long,' he said, but he still
didn't seem in a hurry to come to the point of the visit. I
had plenty of time to notice the changes in him: the fine
lines on his pale, translucent skin, the resolute set of his
mouth and square chin. Boy to man: the past and present
Raffys seemed to coalesce into one before my eyes.

'I'm told this used to be a doll's hospital.'

'It was, but now it makes a perfect chocolate workshop.'

'Yes, your friend Poppy told me all about the chocolates,
and then, of course, I'd already eaten one at the welcome
party. Putting messages inside them is a brilliant idea. I'm
not surprised business is booming.'

'What did your Wish say?' I hadn't meant to ask that, it
just sort of sneakily slipped out.

'That I was never alone,' he said simply.

'No, you wouldn't be: your conscience must talk to you all

187

the time, for a start,' I snapped, and he gave me an unfathomable look.

'It does, but it also tells me that I can't undo what I've done in the past, I can only change my future actions.'

'Comforting,' I said drily, but seeing he wasn't about to leave any time soon I took him through into the sitting room and made hot chocolate, for my own comfort rather than his. I didn't even ask him if he liked it, just made it the way I take it, dark and strong and full of flavour – no milk or honey to sweeten the brew.

He was standing at the window when I went back in. As I handed him the mug he said, 'It's lovely out there, like a secret garden. I can see you're keen on geraniums, too.'

Since they lined the windowsill three pots deep, that didn't take the deductive powers of a Sherlock Holmes. 'Scented pelargoniums,' I said, giving them their proper name. 'I've got apple and mint and attar of roses, but I'm looking forward to getting a lot more when I have a bigger greenhouse to over-winter them in and—' I stopped abruptly, on the brink of forgetting who I was talking to in my enthusiasm. 'But you haven't come to talk about gardening, have you? What *do* you want? And sit down, for goodness' sake – you're giving me a crick in the neck!'

He obeyed, perching on the edge of the window seat and taking a cautious sip from his mug. He'd haunted me for so long that it was hard to take in that he was actually there, big and solid, in my sitting room. I could see now that he was wearing a black T-shirt printed with a white dog collar, which gave the effect of the traditional garb, rather than the actual thing, which was a particularly Raffy touch, even though it still looked incongruous to me.

I felt like throwing something at him, possibly the hot

chocolate, but instead I sat on the small sofa with my feet tucked under me and both hands wrapped around my mug for warmth, though I hadn't felt chilly until just then.

'We need to clear the air, since it's going to be impossible to avoid each other in a small village like this,' he said.

'Especially since you've already managed to ingratiate yourself with my best friends, you mean?'

He grinned unexpectedly, if wryly. 'Same acerbic Chloe, I see!'

'Not quite the same,' I said evenly, because I wasn't a fool for love any more, that was for sure.

'No, I suppose we've both changed in many ways.' He looked at me levelly under those black, winged brows and said, 'I had no idea you lived in Sticklepond when I agreed to come here, though strangely enough I thought of you the day I came to look at the vicarage. I suppose it was because you once told me you lived in Merchester, which isn't far away. And then, when I was in the church trying to make my mind up whether to come here or not, I remembered the way you always read the Tarot cards before doing anything important.'

'I don't read the Tarot any more, they never came right for me. Zillah does, though – she's a relative who lives with us.'

'I've met her. She let me in when I went to see your grandfather and then made me a cup of tea. Everywhere I go, they make me pots and pots of tea,' he added, slightly despairingly.

'Not like Zillah's. Did you drink it?'

'Yes, because she stood over me until I did, and then snatched it back as though she thought I was going to steal the china. Then your grandfather offered me a glass of some special herbal liqueur after that.'

Like a lamb to the slaughter, I thought. 'You drank that too?'

'Not after the tea, and anyway, I don't actually drink much alcohol any more, apart from the odd pint of beer. But I think I could get addicted to *this* stuff,' he said, taking another thoughtful sip of chocolate.

'Do you feel all right?' I demanded, and he looked up, surprised.

'Fine. Why not?'

'Oh, I just wondered . . . Grumps managed to upset Mr Merryman quite a bit.'

'Grumps? Is that what you call him? No, we had a really interesting chat. He's a very original and surprising man.'

'He's all of that,' I agreed.

'I'm fascinated by the way the early Christian Church in Britain absorbed the pagan rituals and festivals into their calendar and Mr Lyon told me that there will be quite a lot of information about that on display in the museum and in the guidebook.'

'Yes, there is – I've proof-read it. One of the separate pamphlets he's writing to sell in the museum deals with it too.'

'Since he's basically just exhibiting the history of witchcraft, rather than actively preaching paganism and the joys of Wicca, I can't really see any problem in having the museum at all. I'll have to try and persuade Miss Winter to see it that way too, though when I visited her this morning she seemed to be coming round to the idea herself anyway.'

'Was she?' I said, surprised. 'Perhaps she's now just more worried about the man who has moved into Badger's Bolt, Digby Mann-Drake.'

'Yes, she told me all about him, and so did your grandfather. I'd already heard of him in London and known one or two people who've fallen for all that black magic posturing and the secret rites stuff at his place in Devon – though actually, it's just burned down.'

'Burned down?'

'That's what your grandfather told me. According to him, the villagers burned it to the ground because he was corrupting the local youth, but I expect it was really only an electrical fault or something like that.'

'Oh, so that's why Mann-Drake told Felix he would be spending a lot more time here than he'd first expected . . .' I mused. 'Badger's Bolt was supposed to be just a weekend cottage.'

'He's still got his house in London, so far as I know,' Raffy said. 'But I agree with Miss Winter and your grandfather that his influence is not one that we want in Sticklepond, even if we discount his alleged occult powers.'

He raised an eyebrow quizzically at me, presumably wondering on which side of the magical fence I fell these days, but I wasn't about to try to explain my ambivalent feelings on the subject.

'Clearly we will *all* have to join forces to combat him, not fight among ourselves, Chloe.'

'I can't see that happening any time soon,' I said shortly, 'and we seem to have strayed an awful long way from the subject of why you wanted to talk to me.'

'That's easy enough to answer: I was puzzled by why you seemed so angry and bitter at seeing me again,' he said, to my complete astonishment.

'You were *puzzled* by it?'

'Of course!' He opened his blue-green eyes wide. 'Because if anything, it should have been the other way round! *You* were the one who broke things off and moved back here to live with an old boyfriend, after all.'

'I did *what*?' I gasped.

'Come on, Chloe!' His eyes took on a sudden stormier hue. 'When I hotfooted it back to the university to find you at the start of the new term, your ex-roommate told me all about it.'

'*Rachel* told you that I'd gone back to an old boyfriend?' I repeated incredulously.

'Yes.' He got up and walked over to the fire, where he stood gazing down into the flames, his back to me. 'It's strange, but even then I couldn't believe you'd do that to me, until she showed me part of a letter you'd sent her and there it was in your own handwriting.'

'Saw what?' I asked numbly. 'What did it say?'

'Oh, I remember every word! You said you weren't coming back, because once you'd met up again with your old boyfriend, you realised you loved him and couldn't bear to leave him again. His name was—'

He broke off and turned suddenly to look at me, his eyes widening.

'Jake,' I finished quietly. 'My baby half-brother – *that's* who I couldn't bear to leave.'

I felt tears welling up in my eyes and slowly spilling, but I didn't brush them away, just sat and looked at him.

'Oh God,' he said quietly, 'Poppy told me you'd brought him up and I never made the connection. So, you mean there *was* no other man?'

'No, there was just Jake. I realised as soon as I got home how much he'd missed me and that I couldn't bear to leave him again.' I looked at Raffy, trying to find a way of explaining the situation so he would understand.

'My mother neglected him – she was forever off with a new lover – but I had the mad idea that perhaps if I wasn't around to take over whenever she wanted me to, if I went away to university, she'd be forced into being a proper mother. But it didn't work out like that, because the second I set out for home at the end of that first term, she dumped Jake with Zillah and took off.'

'But couldn't Zillah look after him?'

'No, Zillah loved him but she isn't good with babies – she'd forget him for hours and then when she remembered, feed him all the wrong things and drop fag ash over him. Besides, I felt really guilty that I'd hardly given Jake a thought once I'd met you, and he'd needed me. I explained everything in the letter I sent you, but you obviously didn't read it.'

His head had been bent over his clasped hands, his long black hair hiding his face, but now he looked up quickly. 'I didn't get any letter!'

'It was enclosed with the one to Rachel. She was supposed to give it to you when you turned up . . . And I was quite sure you would turn up,' I added painfully.

'I did, the very first chance I got. But Rachel never gave me the letter and she only showed me that bit of the one you sent her, to go with her story.'

'So you just believed all her lies?'

'I – well, it *was* in your writing,' he said defensively, 'and she was very convincing.'

'So convincing that you never stopped to think if that was the sort of cruel thing I would do? Or tried to find out if it was the truth?'

My tears had dried and for a moment I felt filled with white-hot rage: for Raffy's credulity and stupidity, for Rachel's duplicity and callousness, and for all the lost years of my teens and twenties, which I'd devoted to Jake.

But I quickly caught myself up on that last thought: I might sometimes have resented Jake's claims on me, but it didn't mean I didn't love him. I'd do it again if I had to.

Raffy sighed. 'No, I suppose I was so mad I wasn't thinking straight and anyway, I didn't see why she would tell me lies.'

'Because she always fancied you,' I said. 'She saw her chance and took it.'

'But what about you?' he asked, suddenly rallying. 'Didn't you wonder why I never wrote or turned up?'

'Not after she told me she'd given you my letter and you hadn't even bothered to read it. And by the way, she said you jumped straight into bed with her, and I don't expect that bit was a lie?'

He looked shamefaced. 'No, I got blind drunk in the students' union bar and then she . . . consoled me. I regretted it next day. Never went back. Went to hell in a handbasket, in fact,' he said soberly. 'What a fool I was!'

'I still can't *believe* you thought I would ask another person to tell you something like that – you must have known I loved you! And for weeks I kept expecting you to turn up, until I got Rachel's letter. And after that the papers were full of all the things you and the rest of Mortal Ruin were up to, so I knew you'd completely forgotten about me.'

'But I hadn't! Lord knows, I *tried*, but you were forever coming back to haunt me.' He sat down again and, leaning forward, took my hands in a warm, firm grasp. 'It took God to make me see just what effects my actions had on other people, and turn me outwards, instead of in. I found it a hard struggle to truly forgive you in my heart for what I thought you'd done to me, but I always hoped you were happy and it had turned out well for you.'

'That's more than I managed for you, because I never forgave you at all! Whenever one of your damned songs reminded me of you, my thoughts were about ninety per cent cocoa solids.'

'I'm guessing they were pretty bitter, then?'

'I think you could say that, with a dash of hot chilli on the side. My opinion of you was that you were a cheap forastero blend and I was probably right!'

'Thanks,' he said drily. 'But I'm truly sorry if things haven't worked out for you. I always pictured you married and with children when I thought of you and—'

He broke off: perhaps something in my expression warned him not to go there.

'I nearly got married, but it didn't work out, and then I had Jake to bring up. I feel I've done my bit in the motherhood and relationship stakes, so now I'm concentrating on my business.'

I suddenly realised that he was still holding my hands between his and it felt as if some powerful current was passing between us . . . until I snatched them away.

'But Felix mentioned that your ex-fiancé has turned up again, so maybe you won't always feel that way?' he suggested.

'David's just a friend these days, that's all,' I said shortly. 'Felix gets the daftest ideas.'

'Right,' Raffy said, and got up. 'Look, Chloe, what's happened, happened, and I can't change that. But I'm so

195

very sorry and I hope eventually that you'll find it in your heart to forgive me for unintentionally hurting you so much, just as I forgive you.'

'*You* forgive *me*?' I stared at him.

'Yes – don't we both share the blame for not trusting in each other's love enough to question what Rachel told us?'

'Some of us are guiltier than others, and I *don't* forgive you, Raffy Sinclair!'

For a moment his eyes flashed and I thought he was about to lose his temper, just as the long-vanished Raffy that I once loved would have done. It might even have cleared the air a bit. But then he gave a long sigh. 'I'm sorry you feel like that, but I'll leave you in peace now and go to the church. I feel a need to pray for both of us – but even more for Rachel.'

I felt more inclined to damn Rachel to the fiery pits of hell for what she'd done to me – to *us*. But then, I wasn't the one with a freshly minted conscience and a matching set of ethics.

'I'd concentrate on praying for yourself after visiting my grandfather,' I advised him. 'You know what they say: if you sup with the devil, you need a long spoon.'

Outside, David tooted his car horn and I got to my feet, feeling about ninety years old. 'I've got to go; I'm going house-hunting with a friend.'

'Of course.'

I put a brass screen in front of the fire and unhooked my coat from behind the door, then he followed me out through the workshop and into the lane. There he paused, looking down sombrely at me, and I stared inimically right back up at him.

'God bless you, Chloe!' he said, then strode off towards

the High Street, past David's red sports car, without even seeming to notice, his dark head bent and his hands in his pockets.

I got into David's car feeling as if I'd gone several rounds in the boxing ring, and his peppering me with questions didn't help, either.

'Wasn't that Raffy Sinclair? Mel Christopher told me he was the new vicar and I thought she was joking! You wouldn't think someone with that kind of lifestyle would suddenly get God, would you?'

'I know, I was surprised too,' I said, the understatement of the century. 'Of course, the band split up years ago, so I expect they've all moved on and done something else. He's been ordained for quite a long time, I think.'

'But why was he visiting you? You don't go to church now, do you?'

'He came to see Grumps, really, and then I expect he thought he might as well call on me. He intends visiting every house in the parish eventually, so at least he can tick me off the list now.'

'I suppose he'll be a seven-day wonder and all the women will go gooey over him.'

'Not me,' I said flatly and he gave me a sideways smile as we drove out along the Neatslake road, passing the sign to Stirrups.

'No, I'm sure he isn't *your* type in the least.'

'So, which house are we going to see first?' I asked, firmly changing the subject. I longed to be on my own, to go over every single nuance of what Raffy had said to me, but until I was, I'd have to try to put a brave face on it.

Chapter Twenty

Fallen Angels

I must have succeeded, even running on automatic response, because David didn't notice anything wrong. In fact, he said the afternoon had been fun – which I expect it would have been, in other circumstances.

It was only later, while we were having tea at a canal marina café, and debating the merits of the two properties we'd seen that day, that it occurred to me that Grumps might have already ill-wished Raffy for a wrong that had turned out to be due to nothing more than credulity and stupidity. Perhaps, if it wasn't too late, I should tell Grumps so? But then, he couldn't *really* do Raffy any harm, could he . . . ?

I returned to the present to find David holding forth on the subject of guest bedrooms and en-suites, neither of which seemed very important to me at the best of times, and not at all at that moment, so I said it was time I was getting back home.

He dropped me off at the door, but even then I hadn't got a minute to myself, because of course Jake came back soon after I did. I'd promised to cook him his favourite dinner – sausage and mash with mustard sauce, followed by a fresh cream éclair I'd bought him from the Spar that morning, which seemed at least a century ago.

But this was probably a good thing, because by the time we were finishing dinner, the urge to weep uncontrollably was all safely dammed up behind a lot of concrete resolve and I'd made my mind up to tell Jake at least some of the truth. Better he heard it from me than as a stray rumour.

'The new vicar visited Grumps today,' I said, scraping plates and then dumping them into the washing-up bowl. 'Then afterwards he called to see me, too.'

'What for?' he asked, looking up from my newest copy of *Skint Old Northern Woman* magazine, which seemed a strange choice of reading matter for a teenage boy – except, of course, that he *is* a fairly strange teenage boy.

'To catch up on old times.' I took a deep breath and confessed, 'You see, we went out with each other years ago. You were only a baby at the time, so you won't remember, but I went away to university and that's where I met him. But then he went off with Mortal Ruin and became a rock god and I . . . came home.'

'*You* went out with *Raffy Sinclair*?' he exclaimed, with the same unflattering amazement that Felix had shown at the news.

'Only for a few weeks, and I haven't seen him since.'

'Oh my God – you mean I might have had Raffy Sinclair for my brother-in-law if you hadn't messed up?' he demanded aggrievedly.

'I didn't mess up, we just . . . drifted apart,' I lied. I certainly wasn't going to tell him all the truth, especially that *he* was the reason I hadn't gone back to university and been there when Raffy returned to look for me. 'And you never wanted a brother-in-law anyway – look how horrible you were to poor David!'

'I wouldn't have wanted one like *him*. He hated me.'

'No, he didn't, he just got tired of all the awful tricks you played on him, and no wonder! He was asking about you today – which university you hoped to go to, and that kind of thing.'

'He was probably hoping it wasn't one near home,' he said acutely. 'Then he wouldn't have to have me around much if you got back together.'

'We're not getting back together,' I said firmly, though strangely enough I was starting to think I might have been reinstated on David's current list of suitable brides, despite not meeting any of the criteria: I preferred living alone, I'd lost any desire for motherhood after bringing up Jake, and my idea of a good time was curling up on the sofa at home with a box of truffles, wine, and my favourite Georgette Heyer novel. Sophisticated I was not. That Mel he kept mentioning sounded a much more suitable candidate.

'I'm not what he's looking for. In fact, I'm not what *anyone* is looking for,' I assured Jake.

But he was now staring at me critically, as though he'd never seen me before in his life, even ignoring the cheese board and the bowl of grapes I'd put in front of him to fill up any empty crevices. 'I suppose you were quite pretty when you were young.'

'I'm way too old to remember,' I snapped, and he grinned and started on the crumbly Lancashire. He had an amazing capacity for putting away food; he'd already eaten most of my dinner since, unsurprisingly, I wasn't that hungry.

Kat was coming round to watch him practise in the

garden with his firesticks while I was out at the Falling Star, so before I left I warned him not to set anything alight, including himself.

I'd been tempted to ring Poppy and say I had a sudden rush of Wishes orders and couldn't go out tonight, but I knew if I did she and Felix would only come to the cottage instead.

Unfortunately, I'm not terribly good at fibbing. And anyway, by now I'd gone through the angry, tearful and distraught stages and was feeling fairly numb, with just a piquant hint of bitterness.

Maybe I could invent a new chocolate line: BitterSweets for dumped lovers?

Poppy and Felix were just turning into the entrance to the Falling Star together as I came into the High Street, so I ran across to join them. Mrs Snowball switched the coffee machine on and started bustling about with the cups and saucers the second we opened the snug door so I, for one, hadn't the heart to tell her that after the day I'd had I really felt more in need of a double brandy than a cappuccino.

'I saw that young man you brought in here, dropping you off earlier in his posh little sports car,' she said to me conversationally. 'He hasn't been back since. Didn't he like my coffee?'

I suppose a man in his early forties *did* seem young to Mrs Snowball. Oddly enough, although I hadn't really noticed the age difference between David and me six years ago, I was now much more conscious of it. All David's tastes, ideas and attitudes seemed to be terribly stuffy and set in stone, and he just assumed I would automatically agree with them as if there weren't other, and usually *better*, options.

'David loved your coffee and I'm sure he'll want to come again. But we'd been house-hunting and he had to get back home.'

'Oh yes, I'd forgotten you were doing that today,' Poppy said.

'*I* hadn't.' Felix gave me a pained look, as if I'd done something not quite nice.

Florrie Snowball turned from fiddling with the steaming, hissing chrome monster and looked at me. 'So, you're moving in together already? I know you used to be engaged, because that Zillah told me. And who can blame you if you've taken up with him again – a handsome feller like that?'

'No, it's nothing like that. It's just that he wants to move into the country and I enjoy looking at other people's houses, that's all.'

'Well, who knows, his heart might soften towards you again,' she said, so clearly she had a romantic heart concealed behind her Maidenform corset. 'You bring him back in soon and I'll make him some extra special coffee,' she promised, with a gappy grin.

'It looks like David has made a conquest,' Poppy said when we were sitting out of earshot in the window. Felix was paying for this first round, which involved a lot of checking of various pockets and counting out of coins.

'Funny, I didn't get the feeling at the time that she liked him that much.'

'She certainly likes Felix – look at her going all flirty at him again,' Poppy said.

'But even he doesn't get extra sprinkle on his cappuccino,' I observed as Felix sat down with his cup. 'David did, though actually you're not missing anything, Felix, because it was funny, speckled greenish stuff, not grated chocolate or cinnamon.'

'I wonder what it was, then?' Poppy said. 'What would have green speckles in it?'

'Perhaps she mistakenly used rancid powdered milk substitute, or something like that?' I suggested. 'It didn't look very nice and he poured most of it into that plant behind you. He dashed off home, too, and rang me later to say he didn't feel well.' And now I came to look at it, the aspidistra was looking pretty ropey.

'I wanted a pint of best bitter, not a coffee,' Felix complained, 'only I couldn't hurt her feelings. I mean, I've got my own coffee maker in the shop now – I can drink it all day if I want to, for free. She seems to be in love with that machine.'

'The novelty will probably wear off soon, now that Molly and Clive can both work it,' Poppy said. 'Look, she's going, so we can have something else in a minute.'

But Mrs Snowball paused in the doorway to deliver a parting shot. 'I hear the new vicar nearly bought it this afternoon: squashed flat by an angel!'

She could be heard cackling like the wicked witch in a pantomime even after the door had shut behind her.

I turned to the other two and demanded, 'What on earth does she mean? Has Raffy had an accident?'

'It's OK, he's fine. It missed him by a mile,' Felix said. 'Effie Yatton came into the shop later and told me about it.'

'Yes, and she rang me at home, too. She always knows everything first – she's the village voice!'

'But *I* don't know *anything*,' I said impatiently. 'What angel? When?'

'It was one of the marble monuments in the graveyard

and it fell across Raffy's path on his way to the church this afternoon,' Poppy explained. 'It blocked the left-hand path, where it divides. Effie thinks it was a sign.'

'Yes, a sign of mole activity,' Felix put in, grinning.

'Raffy saw Grumps this afternoon,' I said thoughtfully. 'I don't suppose that had anything to do with it.'

'I know your grandfather is a gentleman in a velvet jacket, just like the old Jacobite toast, but he's no mole,' Felix said. 'Didn't he and Raffy get on well?'

'I don't know, but that's not what's bothering me. If Zillah told Grumps about Raffy and me, he might be impelled to try and take a bit of revenge on my behalf.'

'But there isn't anything he *can* do really, is there?' Poppy said. 'Magic doesn't really work, we know that.' But she didn't sound entirely convinced.

'Of course it doesn't,' agreed Felix uneasily. 'It's a load of mumbo jumbo.'

'It would be pointless anyway now, because Raffy came to see me after he'd been next door and we – well, we've cleared the air,' I confessed, though I didn't mention that there was still a sulphurous haze hanging about.

'Oh, I'm *so* glad,' Poppy said. 'Are you friends again?'

'No, I think it would be going quite a bit too far to say that, but I understand now that he didn't behave as badly towards me as I thought he did.'

Then I explained about Rachel's lies, and Poppy, her soft heart stirred, said, 'So it wasn't really his fault, then? Oh, but it's all so terribly sad!'

'Yes, that's what Jake thinks now I've told him about it, but only because he's devastated to think he missed out on having Raffy for a brother-in-law! But I don't suppose our relationship would have lasted anyway, he wasn't the constant type. I mean, look at the way he took everything Rachel told him at face value and then slept with her.'

'That *was* pretty bad,' Poppy allowed, 'but he told you he was drunk and angry at the time.'

'Maybe, but even when he was sober it never seemed to have occurred to him to come to Merchester and look for me – and, since there was only one family of Lyons in the place, wouldn't have been hard to find.'

'But you didn't go and look for him, either, did you?' Felix said.

'I couldn't. He was brought up by an aunt and I had no idea where she lived. What was I supposed to do, follow the band around the country like a groupie, hanging out at stage doors in the hope of a word of explanation?'

'No, I see what you mean,' Poppy said, 'and by then, of course, you'd accepted Rachel's version of what happened – and what a truly horrible person she must be!' She sighed. 'Oh, well, it's all past now, isn't it?'

'Yes, all passion spent, and the rest of it,' I said wearily. 'Raffy said he was going to the church to pray after we'd had our talk and I expect that's when the angel nearly fell on him. I only hope, wherever Rachel is, one fell right on top of her.'

'And *I* hope that now you and Raffy have talked things over, you can both draw a line under it,' Felix suggested optimistically.

'You keep saying that, but it's easier said than done. How would you both feel if your past turned up on the doorstep? I mean, you've never told us any details about your divorce, Felix, except that your wife was unfaithful, but what if she suddenly moved to Sticklepond with the man she left you for?'

'Actually, it was a woman,' Felix confessed. 'That seemed to make it even worse.'

'Oh, *poor* Felix,' Poppy said sympathetically. 'My horrible experience in Warwickshire wasn't half so bad, even if it was hideously embarrassing. I didn't think anyone had noticed I had an almighty crush on that riding instructor until I overheard him laughing about it with his friends – *and* his wife! He used to flirt with me too, and try to kiss me, but he didn't tell them that. And yes, I would *loathe* ever having to see him again.'

'It's funny how we all went through a different sort of hell, more or less at the same time, isn't it?' I said.

Poppy nodded. 'And even stranger how we've all ended up living so near together.'

'There does seem to be a congruous pattern to our lives,' agreed Felix.

'I don't know about you two, but I could do with a stiff drink,' I said, with a sigh. 'Perhaps a double whisky will magically fill me with magnanimity?'

'Or make you maudlin,' Felix suggested. 'But I'll join you anyway and we'll risk it.'

'I'd better not, I'm driving,' Poppy said. 'By the way, it's the first Parish Council meeting with Raffy as vicar tomorrow. I'll pop in afterwards and tell you what happens, Chloe.'

'Always supposing another angel doesn't get him first, fair and square,' I said.

I didn't so much fall asleep that night as plummet into a dreamless stupor, waking up with eyelids ruched like Viennese blinds and a headache so powerful I felt as if my head was nailed to the pillow.

I staggered to my vantage point behind the workshop

curtains just in time to watch Raffy walk past with his dog, and thought resentfully that he didn't look like someone nearly felled by an angel, though the marks of a sleepless night showed where the blue shadows lay like bruises under his eyes.

Good.

Once Jake had gone off to college I went to collect the latest chapter from Grumps. I hoped this book was nearly finished, because it seemed to me to be much longer than usual. But every time it appeared to be winding up to a conclusion, it galloped off again at a tangent.

'What did you think of the new vicar?' I asked him, gathering scattered pages.

'Oh, surprisingly intelligent. Can keep his end up in a conversation. I don't mind if he visits again . . . if he is able to.' And then he shifted a little in his chair and winced.

'What's the matter?' I asked suspiciously.

'Just a touch of sciatica. What are these?' he added, prodding the biscuits in his saucer.

'Lemon cream puffs.'

'I can't dip a lemon cream puff into my tea,' he objected.

'Yes you can, but it will taste pretty weird,' I said, and left him to it.

'Zillah,' I said on the way back through the kitchen, 'a marble angel nearly fell on the new vicar yesterday in the churchyard, soon after he left here: was that Grumps' doing?'

Zillah was sitting in the old armchair by the hearth, in front of the flat-screen TV, with Tabitha limply draped across her lap like a small, moth-eaten fur rug.

'How would he be able to cause that, in a churchyard, on hallowed ground?' she asked, the inevitable fag hanging out of the corner of her mouth barely moving as she spoke.

'I suppose it is silly, when you think about it,' I conceded.

'I read the vicar's leaves and the Tarot – did he say I gave the cards to him to hold?'

I shook my head. 'How did you know I'd seen him?'

'I know everything,' she said complacently. 'The cards showed me clearly that he has a heart washed clean of sin and a vital part to play in the events that will unfold.'

'His heart must have been through a carwash on Extra Long, then,' I said sourly, then told her what had happened between us the previous afternoon. 'So I'm still furious with him,' I concluded, 'because he was so credulous and never gave a thought about me afterwards. He even slept with Rachel! And I certainly haven't entirely forgiven him, either, though maybe I'll be able to get my head around it eventually . . . in a decade or so.'

I remembered something she'd said. 'And what did you mean, he has a vital part to play?'

Zillah shrugged, and the lime-green shawl she was wearing slid off one shoulder. It would have looked quite racy, except for the double layer of pink and magenta cardigans beneath.

'As vicar, I presume. Gregory says we must all join ranks together against Digby Mann-Drake, and Raffy can't do that if he's been flattened by an angel, can he?'

'It would certainly make it difficult,' I agreed.

Chapter Twenty-one

Garnish

While I was in the post office sending off the latest batch of Chocolate Wishes I heard that notices had been posted on the gates of both the lido field and the tennis courts overnight, saying that when the leases expired in April the current owner, Mr Mann-Drake, intended closing them to the public.

Everyone was up in arms about this and I detoured on my way home to read the notice on the tennis court gate. It was on laminated fluorescent orange card so it would have been a bit hard to miss, but I was only just in time, since Effie Yatton drove up in her old green Morris and removed it just as I'd finished.

An energetic, grey-haired woman with a thin, eager face like a whippet, she nodded to me and said concisely, 'Disgraceful! I'm taking the notices to the Parish Council meeting later, to see what can be done!'

Then she tossed the notice onto the passenger seat on top of another one, presumably from the lido field, and drove off. I have a feeling taking them down was illegal, but when I told Felix about it while scrounging a free cup of coffee, as usual, he said he expected she would return them later and it looked like being an interesting Parish Council meeting, for once.

I had to wait much longer than usual to find out whether it was or not. In fact, it was getting so late by the time Poppy arrived that I'd just about given her up, but she explained that she'd gone to church afterwards.

'Raffy says evening prayers at five thirty every day except Sunday, so he was going straight there, and Felix and I thought we would go too.'

'*Felix* went?'

'Yes, he likes Raffy; they seem to get on really well. There were one or two other people there and it was a short service: he read out a daily office, a bit like an extended "Thought for the Day". He has a lovely speaking voice, hasn't he? Sort of deep and mellow and warm . . . It was lovely and peaceful and I felt *so* much better afterwards. You should try it, Chloe.'

'I don't think so!'

'Perhaps not,' she conceded contritely. 'Sorry, I wasn't thinking!'

'That's OK.'

'Things are obviously going to be different at the Parish Council meetings with Raffy there, Chloe. He didn't exactly take charge, but somehow the power shifted over from Miss Winter to him . . . or maybe it will be a power-share?' she said doubtfully. 'Raffy is quite quiet, but you certainly know he's there.'

'Bit hard to miss him, seeing he's six foot four.'

'You know what I mean!' she said, then gave me a

rundown of what had happened. 'Felix said you already know about the notices that were put up by Mann-Drake?'

'The whole village knows about them now. They're almost as much a talking point as Raffy being the new vicar.'

'It's a pity Mr Grace died before we could raise enough money to buy the tennis courts and lido for the village. Now we don't know if the notices are meant as a threat to try and get a much higher lease next time, or because Mann-Drake intends trying to sell the two sites for housing development.'

'Could he do that? The Parish Council are hardly likely to approve, are they?'

'No, but he could appeal over our heads, because they're within the village boundaries.'

'What, even the lido? I would have thought that was *right* outside it.'

'Before the Black Death the village was much bigger, though a lot of the houses have vanished since and now they're just bumps in the fields.'

'So the ones dotted around the edge are just those left?' I said.

'Yes. Anyway, Miss Winter is going to write to Mann-Drake expressing how the council and the whole village feel about it, and Raffy says he will go and talk to him as soon as he can too. But meanwhile, he's very generously offered the tennis club the use of the vicarage court.'

'I didn't know there was one.' Mind you, the vicarage gardens are such a jungle there could be a lost civilisation in there, complete with a stepped pyramid, and no one would know.

'It's at the back, near the rear gate. He's going to get the men who are cutting back the trees and bushes to clear it as a priority and have the little pavilion renovated. Effie

Yatton runs the tennis club and she was really grateful – so grateful that she confessed that she's been using the vicarage drawing room to hold her Brownie pack meetings in when the village hall was otherwise engaged!'

'But isn't there an annexe to the village hall she could have used?'

'Yes, but the roof is leaking and it needs rewiring. Raffy was really funny about the Brownie meetings. He said he'd wondered why there were giant papier-mâché mushrooms in one corner of his drawing room and a pile of hula hoops. And then he said he would have the annexe repaired – he is being really kind and generous about everything!'

'I expect he can afford to be,' I said acidly.

'I don't know. I wouldn't have thought he was *mega* wealthy,' Poppy said thoughtfully. 'I mean, he has just bought the vicarage, and the renovation bills for a crumbling Victorian wreck must be huge, mustn't they?'

'I expect he's still raking in royalties, because he wrote all of Mortal Ruin's songs, and you hear them everywhere, especially that one from the car advert. It's never off.'

'It's still generous,' she insisted. 'He was pretty laid-back about your grandfather and the museum too. He said Mr Lyon had no intention of trying to impose his own beliefs on anyone else, and the museum and guidebook would include a lot of interesting material about the overlap between paganism, witchcraft and early Christianity.'

'Well, that's true, it does.'

'Then he said he thought your whole family, especially your grandfather, should be encouraged to become part of the community. I said *you* already were, since you were a regular at the Falling Star.'

'That's probably not quite what he meant, Poppy! But I

do think his suggestion about involving Grumps in village affairs was a good one,' I allowed. 'It's better to have him on your side than against you, though since he's not terribly gregarious, I'm not quite sure how it's going to happen.'

'Zillah seems to be joining things already, doesn't she?'

'Yes, Clive Snowball took her to the tea dance club, but I can't see Grumps following her there any time soon.'

She giggled. 'No, nor I, though he would instantly be besieged by partners if he did, because apparently there's always a shortage of men.'

'*And* he's tall and still very handsome.'

'So is Laurence Yatton, the Winter's End steward – *and* he's single. Pity he's more than forty years older than me! But speaking of tall and handsome, Effie has fallen for Raffy and brought him some of her home-made vegetarian sausage rolls to the meeting today, because she said she knew Maria Minchin couldn't cook.'

'I shouldn't think she's alone in that.'

'She certainly isn't, because Raffy told me and Felix later that he kept finding food offerings on the doorstep – jam and cakes and all kinds of things. He gets stuffed full of cake and biscuits when he visits people, too, so I said he'd soon be able to get into *The Guinness Book of Records* as the fattest vicar!'

I couldn't imagine a fat Raffy, even though he's not one of those tall, skinny men who look like a taper – he does have broad shoulders. 'Maybe he could have an imaginary doctor prescribe a gluten-free diet for him?' I suggested. 'And at least I won't be leaving a cake on his doorstep any time soon. He's safe from me.'

'But I thought you'd made your peace, even if it is difficult having him about?'

'I wouldn't put it quite like that, though I suppose I'll get used to it eventually. I just need more time.'

'Zillah must like him,' she said with another giggle. 'She left a parcel of bouquets garnis on the doorstep with handwritten instructions to Maria to put them into every stew and casserole she made, and Maria was so mad I think she tossed them straight into the rubbish bin, though don't tell Zillah that.'

'It was actually probably a wise move . . .' I said thoughtfully. 'I don't suppose there were any more falling angels?'

'No, but strangely enough Raffy himself fell into a trench on the way back from church later that same day. He said he stayed on for a while after evening prayers, so it was quite dark by then. You know where the workmen have dug a hole right outside the gate and put a metal plank across?'

'Yes, I think there's a leaking water pipe. And Raffy fell into it?'

'The *plank* fell into it and he went with it, then when he tried to pull himself out, the side of the hole caved in on top of him and practically buried him in earth and pebbles! He said if anyone was watching, it must have looked like a slapstick film.'

'But it could have been dangerous!'

'He was all right, and he rang Mike up from the vicarage as soon as he got home, so a barrier and lights could be put up around it until the workmen came back. He said he wasn't usually accident prone, so perhaps he deserved it and it was some kind of punishment,' she added, 'though it was quite mild as far as fiery pits of hell were concerned.'

'*Punishment?*'

'For hurting you so much in the past and then putting the blame on you all these years, when it was his own selfish action in going away with the band that started the whole

214

thing unravelling, whatever came afterwards. I thought that was a very generous admission, but Felix doesn't seem to see things quite the same way and he said Raffy shouldn't talk nonsense.'

But I'd stopped listening and instead was busily counting up incidents. 'I suppose that was three things – the angel, the plank and then the cave-in? And bad things usually come in threes . . .'

Or fours? For a mad moment I wondered again about Zillah's bouquets garnis, but Lucretia Borgia she was not, so they were probably just some weird but entirely harmless invention of her own.

'He only told us two about the trench thing, because he didn't want to get the workmen into trouble, and luckily all the bruises were where you couldn't see them. He is so brave and kind!'

She sounded so admiring that I asked with sudden suspicion, 'Poppy, *you* aren't falling for Raffy, are you?'

'Of course not! Whatever gave you that idea?' she said, opening her blue eyes wide with amazement. 'I like him, but he's not a very *comfortable* person, somehow, is he? You feel he's a bit world-weary and . . . well, I don't know how to describe it, but you feel that he's been everywhere and done everything.'

'Yes, I know what you mean, and he probably has.'

'But now he's a reformed character, I expect his past experiences make him able to deal with all kinds of things. He seems to have resolved the situation with Miss Winter and your grandfather already, doesn't he? She even said she thought she might have been a bit hasty in condemning Mr Lyon, when clearly Mann-Drake is a much greater threat to the happiness of the village.'

'That was pretty magnanimous.'

'She's found out a bit more about Mann-Drake and those rumours of some kind of not-so-secret society at his Devon house – the one that's just burned down – did I say? Probably divine retribution!'

'Maybe it was, in which case, Mann-Drake is clearly on the wrong side!'

'She's afraid he will try and start his goings-on here in Sticklepond. Raffy says he is going to go and talk to him when he comes back from London, though none of us is convinced that's really a good idea, or that it will have any effect.'

'No, if Mr Mann-Drake is styling himself somewhere between Aleister Crowley and Sir Francis Dashwood, I don't think he'll be swayed by a bit of a chat with the vicar, even if he *is* Raffy Sinclair.'

'I hope Mann-Drake isn't going to hold orgies at Badger's Bolt,' she said earnestly. 'Apparently he's converting the cowshed into some kind of big room, very oddly decorated.'

We couldn't say any more then, because Jake and Kat came in and, since it was dark enough, Jake offered to demonstrate his firestick technique to Poppy before she left.

'Stay for dinner?' I offered. 'Kat is, and we're having pizza and ice cream in front of the TV tonight.'

'I suppose I could. Mum was going out later and the work experience girl is there to help her at the moment, so I don't suppose she'll mind – if she notices at all.'

She went into the garden with Jake and Kat while I lingered behind and rifled the battered leather rucksack that does duty as Poppy's handbag, removing a tiny bottle of viscous fluid from the junk at the bottom. 'To induce love in the eyes of another' it said, in a small spiky hand on the label: 'Two drops to happiness.'

She'd seemed sincere about not falling for Raffy, but he didn't appear to have lost much, if any, of his considerable charisma, so if there was even the slightest risk of her succumbing to it, then I needed to divert her attentions elsewhere.

Of course, this stuff probably wouldn't work, any more than Grumps' magical efforts ever did, but I would lose nothing by giving it a go as soon as I got her and Felix together and had the opportunity . . .

The revelation that Raphael Sinclair was the new vicar of Sticklepond appeared in the local paper and spread like wildfire around the further reaches of the district, relegating the news about the lido and tennis courts to second place, though in the village people were still seething about that, of course.

It didn't seem that I could go anywhere without hearing Raffy's name, and even dropping in for coffee with Felix meant I had to listen to a lecture on being grown-up and moving on, and how great it was that someone like Raffy should deign to come and lord it over our lowly little village!

'Though the whole thing will probably be a seven-day wonder, because of course he's been out of the public eye for years now, even if his music hasn't,' he said. 'I don't suppose any of the younger people will be very excited, it will be just us oldies.'

'Jake is,' I said, wondering gloomily if I now ranked with the oldies.

'Jake's different. And I've told Raffy that if he wants to join us at the Falling Star tonight – or any other night – he's welcome,' he said, slightly defiantly.

I stared at him. '*I* certainly won't be going if he does!

What were you thinking of? It's always been just the three of us!'

'There's no reason why it can't sometimes now be four, is there? I didn't think you'd mind. You said you would have to get used to seeing him about.'

'Yes, but seeing him walking about in the village is one thing,' I said (I turned tail and fled whenever I glimpsed him in the distance), 'but having him sitting opposite me in the snug at the Star is another!'

Felix was looking at me with unwonted criticism. 'Raffy said you might still feel like that, and he wouldn't come unless you said you didn't mind.'

'Well, I do mind having my personal space and my social life – what there is of it – invaded! My forgiveness doesn't stretch that far yet.'

'Aren't you being a bit petty?'

'I don't think so – and I thought you understood how I felt,' I said, and after that we came as close to an argument as we'd ever got in our whole lives.

That was all Raffy's fault, too.

Chapter Twenty-two

Darker Past Midnight

When I went to collect Grumps' chapter on Saturday morning (all days of the week being equal, as far as Grumps and I were concerned) Zillah, who was sitting at the kitchen table shuffling the Tarot with practised skill, told me he had gone out.

'*Out?* But he hardly ever goes out in the mornings!'

'Another change. That Hebe Winter came to see him yesterday – you could have knocked me down with a feather when I found her on the doorstep, looking down her long nose at me. And then there's a phone call and off he goes up to Winter's End right after breakfast. Drove himself too, and he doesn't often do that, either.'

'His sciatica wasn't bothering him any more, then?'

'Cleared up completely.'

Grumps' visiting seemed very odd, but I supposed they were discussing ways of defeating the encroachments of Digby Mann-Drake, for which an alliance of sorts evidently needed to be forged. He hadn't looked as if he could do anything more exciting than pull a rabbit out of a hat, but appearances can be deceptive.

Zillah, pushing aside the remains of her breakfast, had begun to lay out the cards into a familiar pattern, but she looked up and added, 'He said the latest chapter was on his desk.'

I was sure this book was twice as long as any of his others. And was it my imagination, or had his writing taken a darker turn? I only hoped his hero was up to the challenge!

Grumps returned in an expansive mood and when I took his printed chapter back he informed me that Hebe Winter had invited him to attend an emergency meeting of the Parish Council on Tuesday, in an advisory capacity.

'But they had a meeting only on Thursday!'

'Events regarding Mann-Drake have taken yet another turn since then, and there is no time to be lost, Chloe. I knew of his plan to close down the tennis club and some picnic field or other, but now he is trying to levy a charge on the householders living along the edge of the Green, simply for driving across a strip of grass to their property.'

'How on earth can he do that?'

'He is trying to resurrect some obsolete ancient right conferred with the Lord of the Manor title. Six houses are affected, and each has received solicitor's letters demanding either a one-off payment of fifteen per cent of the house's value, or a very steep annual rental fee. It is, as they say, money for old rope.'

'I've never heard of such a thing, but I would have thought they needed a good lawyer, rather than a warlock,' I suggested, and he gave me a stern look.

'Fortunately, the vicar is more far-sighted than you, for it was he who suggested consulting me about Mann-Drake. I find myself quite liking him.'

'*I* wouldn't go that far, but I absolve him from everything in the past except stupidity and self-centredness. I hear your sciatica has magically disappeared, by the way, Grumps?'

'Quite vanished,' he agreed. 'A momentary twinge . . . or three.'

Felix said he couldn't meet us in the Falling Star that evening, because he was going to play darts with Raffy and the gardeners from Winter's End in the Green Man instead. He did do this sometimes, only not on a night when he usually met us, so I supposed he was still sulking over our spat.

But at least it meant that Poppy and I could have a good girls-together session, when she told me all over again about the things she was looking for in a man. It was a fairly modest list really, and all the qualities and assets were possessed by Felix, such as not living with his mother (he rarely even *sees* Mags and has never lived with her) and having his own hair and teeth.

'I'm even starting to feel desperate enough to try the lonely hearts columns one more time,' she confessed, so it was a pity Felix wasn't there, so I could have tipped the love potion straight into his drink – and probably hers too, for good measure – then maybe banged their heads together. It was so blindingly obvious to me now that they were made for each other, that I didn't see why *they* hadn't realised it.

'Don't do anything hasty,' I counselled.

'But the time is slipping by faster and faster and I would really love to have children,' she said sadly. 'I can't leave it too late and right now I'm starting to think I'd settle for a Mr OK, never mind Mr Right!'

'Give it just a little more time,' I suggested. 'Remember what the cards said about patience paying off in the long run?'

'Yes, only I'm running out of patience. But what about you?' she asked, then said Jake had confided in her the other night that he was afraid I was falling for David all over again.

'I suppose he could be *your* Mr OK, if you wanted to settle down,' she said doubtfully. 'But you keep saying you don't want to get married or have children.'

'No, I don't. David may have some thought of us getting back together – I'm not sure – but he's forever talking about a woman called Mel Christopher, so on the whole, I think not. Do you know her?'

'Yes, she rides a grey horse and she has the worst seat in the county. She was widowed a couple of years ago and then married Hebe Winter's great-nephew, Jack Lewis, but it was a brief mistake and they're getting divorced. Or perhaps they are divorced by now? I don't know. She's beautiful, though, with blonde hair and brown eyes.'

'That rings a bell. I think I may have seen her about.'

'I wouldn't have thought she'd want to marry again so quickly, so perhaps it *is* you that David's interested in. Aren't you seeing him again tomorrow?'

I nodded. 'We're going to look at a couple of properties a bit further towards Appleby Bridge. But it isn't like a date or anything. I've made it plain I'm happy on my own, I only want friendship.'

'Well, you know how stupid men are at picking up signals, Chloe. You practically have to hammer bulletins into their heads to get the message through.'

Raffy must have managed to pick some of my messages

up, though, because now he seemed to be doing his best to stay out of my way.

Whenever I caught sight of him in the distance, I only had to blink and he'd vanished again: now you see him, now you don't.

On Raffy's first Sunday the church was packed to the rafters at both services. Most of the villagers turned out, right down to the Catholics and Methodists, while the curious from further afield crowded into the aisles, so that according to Poppy they were packed in like sardines and if anyone had fainted from the massed body heat they would still have stayed upright.

Felix was there, Janey went with Mags, and had my own mother been around, I expect she would have gone too, brazen sinner or not. Even Jake went, with Kat – he'd flirted with the Church briefly at junior school and got himself baptised, so he didn't see why he shouldn't.

Mr Lees played them all in with a favourite fugue, though to everyone's astonishment at the end he broke into a lively rendition of 'I Do Like to Be Beside the Seaside'. Something must have come over him, probably Raffy.

After the Sunday morning service Jake and Kat lingered behind to look round the church, which may have seemed odd of them, but they *are* both keen on history and it *is* very old. Apparently there's an almost unique very early sixteenth-century Heaven and Hell window and lots of interesting monuments.

Raffy came back in and chatted to them, then invited them over to the vicarage for coffee while he waited for Maria Minchin to finish burning his lunch. He showed them round the house too, and I'm ashamed to say that I pumped Jake for all the details he could remember.

'Well, it's not as huge as I thought it would be from the front, because it's long rather than deep,' he said. 'There's an enormous drawing room and a dining room at the back with a door onto the terrace, which he's going to make into a sort of den, I think. He's turned part of the cloakroom into a mini-kitchen, so he can make a drink or snack without disturbing the Minchins.'

'That might be vital, if Maria Minchin's cooking is as bad as they say. Go on, what else is there?'

'Only a library in that turrety thing at the end, plus four or five bedrooms upstairs. The workmen have just about finished and the decorators moved in, so his furniture is all piled in the middle of the floors, covered in dustsheets, but he says he hasn't got enough yet, most of the stuff from his flat in Notting Hill wouldn't have looked right.'

'So he's still living in what was the servants' hall?'

'Yes, but he'll be able to move into part of the main house by next week and then the Minchins can spread themselves out a bit more. He says their flat is quite cramped. That's about it, he hadn't got time to show us the garden, though he talked about it quite a bit.'

He evidently intended doing most of the gardening himself once the jungle had been tamed, even growing his own fruit and vegetables, which wasn't quite the rock-and-roll lifestyle Jake had envisaged, though he was still enthusiastic about Raffy Sinclair.

Everyone was, except me.

'I told him I knew he'd been out with you when you were young,' Jake confessed. 'But of course, since it was forever ago, I knew you must have practically forgotten about each other until you met again.'

'Yes, our romance had completely faded into the realms of ancient history,' I agreed.

'That's pretty much what Raffy said. Me and Kat are joining the tennis club when it starts up in spring, by the way. The vicarage court should be ready by then.'

'You don't play tennis!'

'I play squash and there's no reason why I can't play tennis too, is there? Kat plays tennis.'

I supposed there were a lot worse things he could be doing.

By this time we were late for Sunday lunch, which we have with Grumps and Zillah, but luckily she was running late with the roast duck, *petits pois* and crunchy roast potatoes.

There was lemon syllabub afterwards, possibly my most favourite pudding, so I was so stuffed that I could barely drag myself out of the house and into David's car to go house-hunting afterwards, and certainly couldn't eat a thing when we stopped for tea.

It was odd how I never used to notice how much he talked about himself, but now I could see that we didn't have conversations, it was all monologues! And I didn't know if he was sizing me up for a possible resumption of our engagement or not, but I took Poppy's advice when the current monologue veered round to which houses were suitable for raising families in, and reminded him that *I* had decided never to marry or have children, because I was perfectly happy with my lifestyle.

He laughed at that as though I'd made a joke, and for one moment I thought he was going to pat me on the head and tell me *he* knew what I needed better than *I* did, in which case I would probably have bitten his hand.

I was starting to realise what a very narrow escape I had

had six years ago – what *had* I been thinking? I would probably have been arrested for murder by now, had the marriage gone ahead.

Apart from the night following my revelatory conversation with Raffy, when sheer emotional exhaustion overcame me, I had not been sleeping well. Whenever I closed my eyes the past came back to haunt me in inglorious Technicolor. The only good parts were when I imagined what I would do to Rachel if I could lay my hands on her, scenarios generally involving boiling oil and thumbscrews.

Instead of sleeping I'd spent large portions of the night hours making Chocolate Wishes in the workshop, with the radio on for company. The quiet sound of the melted chocolate being churned about in the Bath was quite soothing, as was the rich scent that filled the air. I'd been making and eating an awful lot of truffles too – my bill for cream was *astronomical*.

I'd printed out the updated version of the chocolate charm that Grumps gave me, and could now say the whole of it over the chocolate while I was tempering it. Not that I thought it would have any effect, but I invoked it more from gratitude for the kind thought and sheer force of habit, than anything.

Jake kept wandering downstairs in the middle of the night to check on me: I was sure he was worried, but he didn't say anything.

Meanwhile, I was stockpiling an awful lot of Wishes!

I hadn't called at Felix's shop on my way back from the post office since our little spat, but then on Monday he came to the cottage to see me and tendered a very handsome apology for his lack of understanding, which I accepted, though it was subsequently slightly soured by discovering that I owed it to Raffy. He'd told Felix that he quite understood if I couldn't yet bear to see him among my friends, but hoped that one day I would change my mind.

Magnanimous of him. And it had the effect of making *me* look like the petulant child and *him* the grown-up!

Chapter Twenty-three

Pax

Hebe Winter collected Grumps in her white Mini car and took him to the emergency Parish Council meeting. Afterwards Poppy brought him back and dropped him off at the house, before coming through the museum to the cottage. I was just clearing up after a chocolate-making session and had to stop her absently eating the couverture chocolate drops from the open sack, like sweets.

'How did it go?' I asked, firmly closing the sack up again and putting it away.

'Oh, fine, though Miss Winter, Effie and Laurence were in Elizabethan dress ready for the Re-enactment Society later, and what with that and your grandfather's strange outfit, it all seemed a bit surreal somehow.'

'You should try living with him and Zillah: my whole life seems surreal. Was the emergency about this right-of-way thing?'

'Yes, though I can't see why it couldn't wait until the ordinary meeting on Thursday, because there isn't a lot we can do about it yet. Miss Winter seems to be calling extra meetings whenever she wants to get something off her chest, lately! But Laurence has found some similar cases on the internet and Miss Winter's solicitor is going to look into it and report back. And we are awaiting a reply to the letter she sent to Mann-Drake about the lido and tennis courts, but he's still in London.'

'Mann-Drake has really stirred up a wasps' nest in Sticklepond with all his money-making plans,' I said. 'The latest move may only affect half a dozen houses, but everyone is wondering what he will do next, and there's a lot of anger.'

'Yes, Hebe Winter not only looked like Elizabeth the First today, but I thought she was also going to launch into the "I know I have the body of a weak and feeble woman, but I have the heart and stomach of a king" speech and then lead us out to battle! She asked your grandfather to give us his opinion of Mann-Drake and it was pretty much the same as Raffy's, apart from more of an emphasis on his magic powers and how Mann-Drake only wanted to buy a house in the village because of its powerful position on the ley lines.'

'Well, that's probably true – combined with the chance to make a quick buck or two.'

'Raffy said there were always people attracted to the occult, though magic's only real power lay in suggestion and superstition,' Poppy said, 'and Mann-Drake's "supernatural powers" were nothing more than a mixture of personal magnetism, drugs, alcohol and fear.'

'That probably went down well with Grumps and Hebe Winter!'

'Miss Winter always *says* she's a herbalist,' Poppy said doubtfully. 'Mr Lyon said that at least we could all now see that *he* was no threat to the community in comparison to Mann-Drake.'

'No, I'm sure he's not.'

She frowned in an effort of recollection. 'He said something else, about how later religious practices were like lichen growing on an old tree, feeding off the vital sap and obscuring the essential truth, though not completely hiding its shape . . . or something.'

'That sounds like Grumps,' I agreed. 'I think it's just his twisty way of saying live and let live.'

'Yes, he did say that in some cases the two could become interdependent, so he meant well. Raffy told him he couldn't agree with that viewpoint, but he looked forward to discussing it at more length some time.'

'What did Grumps say to that?'

'Only that he looked forward to that too.'

'Oh? He must have been in a surprisingly mellow and amenable frame of mind!'

'He advised us all to buy witch charms from Mrs Snowball and put them over our doors, just like yours,' she told me. 'Do you think that's a good idea?'

'It certainly can't hurt. Was that the end of the meeting?'

Poppy gave one of her infectious giggles. 'Yes, except that Mr Lyon suddenly said that he had been considering something the vicar had said to him about joining in with village life and had decided to join the Elizabethan Re-enactment Society! He's going to become John Dee to Miss Winter's Virgin Queen.'

'Good heavens – did he? How did they take that?'

'They were initially stunned.'

'So am I!'

'Yes, but once that wore off, I think Miss Winter was quite pleased, really.'

* * *

230

Our usual threesome met at the Falling Star a couple of days later, all sulks forgotten, and Mrs Snowball, who was minding the bar in the snug until Molly arrived, told us that she'd done such a roaring trade in her witch bottles since the last Parish Council meeting, that she'd had to order a fresh consignment of empty ones.

'Though they're not the same as the old. It takes some of the mystery out of it when the glass is thin enough to guess what's in there, though they'll work just as well. But the old Bellarmine pottery ones were the best.'

'Yes, Grumps has got one of those in the museum. I remember it in the catalogue.'

We'd tried to get in our drinks order quickly, before she had a chance to switch the coffee machine on, but she insisted on giving us cappuccinos on the house, 'seeing as I'm raking in the money for me charms!' And she cackled like an old hen.

'You can rake in some more, because I need two extra bottles,' Poppy told her.

'Ah, but I've put me prices up!' she said cunningly.

'Couldn't I have a discount for bulk?' wheedled Poppy. 'These will make five I've had.'

'I suppose I *could* let you have them at the old price, seeing as you're a good customer at the Star.'

'Thanks, Mrs S! I need to protect the stable yard next, you see: I can't have the horses exposed to anything nasty going around, can I?'

'You make Mann-Drake sound like a contagion,' Felix said.

When Molly came in Mrs Snowball disappeared, only to return a little while later bearing two of the original thick, greenish bottles, which she handed to Poppy after wiping the dust off with a corner of her flowered pinny.

'Here you are, from the last of the old stock I laid in years ago. I found a box right at the back of the cellar that got overlooked behind a pile of broken crates.'

Poppy paid for them, then immediately gave one of the bottles to Felix. 'This is a gift, but you have to promise me to put it over your shop door. In fact, I'll come back with you and make sure you do!'

'Poppy, you shouldn't waste your money like that,' he protested. 'Mann-Drake's already been in my shop and of course nothing dire happened, so I really think it's—'

'Oh, stop being so macho,' she said. 'Better to be safe than sorry, don't you think, Chloe?'

'If Grumps says it's a good idea, then it probably is,' I agreed. 'You don't lose anything by having one, do you, Felix?'

'Except for a possible new customer,' he grumbled. 'But, OK, since you both seem determined on it, I'll move some of the books from the shelf over the door and put it there.'

'You'd better attach the bottle to the shelf too,' I suggested, 'or some over-curious customer might try and lift it down, or knock it off.'

'Good idea,' Poppy agreed.

In Mrs Snowball's absence Molly had let us have beer and then later, when Felix went back to the bar to fetch crisps and Poppy was in the loo, I seized the moment and quickly whipped out the little bottle of love potion. I managed to get a drop or two in each glass before they came back, though the creamy tops acquired a faintly oily iridescence. It seemed a harsh way to treat best bitter, but it must have tasted all right because they drank it down without a murmur (or any noticeable effects whatsoever).

Then we all went back to Marked Pages and Felix cleared

a space on the shelf over the door. Despite his protests, I firmly removed the toolbox from his grip and, standing on a chair, screwed an eyelet into the back of the shelf, wired round the bottle and attached it.

'There! It won't fall down, no one can pick it up, and the light-fingered will need a screwdriver or wire cutters if they want to nick it.'

'They'd probably be cursed if they did,' Poppy said with a giggle. 'Well, I'd better get off home now, because Mum's gone to Hot Rocks on the pull with Mags, and I don't like leaving the horses unchecked for too long.'

'Yes, I'd better go too, though Jake doesn't exactly need my company these days, now he's got Kat!'

'They *are* sweet together,' Poppy said soppily.

'You incurable romantic!' Felix smiled at her and their gazes seemed to meet and lock for a long moment . . . But then they both blinked dazedly and looked away and the moment – if there was one – was broken.

Maybe I imagined it?

The following Tuesday Grumps went to his first Re-enactment Society meeting and Jake and Kat offered to drop him at the village hall on their way to have dinner with her parents. Having initially been alarmed by the first sight of Jake (not to mention his relationship to Grumps, when they got to know about it) they had now done a complete about-face and seemed to be trying to adopt him. Any mother of a teenage son would understand exactly how I felt about having someone else shoulder part of my food bills – *deeply* grateful.

'OK, and I'll come and fetch you later, Grumps, if you ring me,' I told him.

Luckily his eccentric taste in clothes meant he hadn't had

233

far to look among his collection of garments to find something suitable for the role of John Dee – an embroidered,
tasselled cap and a long, velvet robe fitted the bill quite
nicely. He was a natural for the role.

Before they left I checked him over, a bit like an anxious
parent whose child is off on a first date, making sure he
had my phone number and a little money. 'You may have
to use the public phone at the back of the village hall and
also there's probably a kitty for refreshments,' I explained.

'Dear me, yes,' he said, 'I seem to have got out of the
habit of social engagements, but I am sure it will do me
good to get out into the world occasionally.'

I'm not sure the Sticklepond Re-enactment Society
counts as the world, but it's a start.

It was Laurence Yatton who called me later to tell me
Grumps was ready to be picked up and, when I collected
him, he seemed to have had a good time.

'There were six kinds of biscuits, two of them home-
made,' he said approvingly, the cookie connoisseur. 'Hebe
Winter said that when she told her niece, Sophy, that I was
to assume the role of John Dee, she suggested that I might
occasionally go to Winter's End dressed in character, when
it is open to the public. They would rope off a special area
where I could work and everyone would think I was drawing
up a birth chart for the Queen, or some such thing. Just
for an hour or two, as a special treat for visitors. They
already have a Shakespeare, who makes an occasional
appearance, as does Hebe in her role as Elizabeth the First.'

'Would you do that?' My reclusive old Grumps was
constantly surprising me lately!

'I don't see why not. Many of the society are also Friends

of Winter's End and work there in full costume as volunteers throughout the open season, but I would not, of course, have time for that, for I will be fully occupied with my own work and with the museum.'

I could tell he was now quite fancying himself in the role!

I still felt furious that Raffy should have burst back into my life just as it had begun to settle down into a pleasant pattern, and that feeling didn't seem to be wearing off at all. In fact, every time I caught sight of him my heart gave a sudden jolt and then started thumping away at twice its normal rate, which couldn't be good for me.

It must have puzzled Poppy and Felix (and presumably Raffy too), that a boy-and-girl affair that ended so long ago should still make me act this way, but I couldn't explain it to them. And while I could force myself to *say* I forgave Raffy, that wasn't going to extinguish the bitter, lonely flame that was burning in my heart for what was lost, was it?

I was sure Raffy was trying to keep out of my way, just as I was trying to keep out of his, but of course that was impossible in a small place like Sticklepond. He buzzed around in his little un-rock-god Mercedes hatchback, presumably going to church-related meetings and making calls. He buried, christened and said prayers but so far, hadn't married (no takers till spring had sprung), and he walked his little dog past my cottage very early every morning, without fail. I knew this, because I watched him from behind the shop window curtain. It still seemed strange to me to see the white gleam of the clerical collar at his throat, even if it was just printed onto a black T-shirt: it was a symbol of what he had now become, however improbable . . .

According to Poppy, Raffy was still determinedly carrying on with his scheme of visiting all the houses in the parish, which could prove to be his life's work once he reached the scattered outskirts and set out into the countryside.

He and Felix really had struck up an unlikely friendship, too. I'd found Raffy in Marked Pages more than once myself, although he'd always hurried out as I went in.

He was paying contractors to clear the worst jungly bits of the vicarage gardens, I'd also seen him out there, hacking down overgrown shrubs side by side with them.

Anyway, he was suddenly ubiquitous . . . or do I mean omnipresent? No, I suppose that's God. Anyway, Raffy was *everywhere* and a huge, huge success – with the female parishioners in particular. They may have been dubious initially, but they couldn't resist that smile, it had been the downfall of many and *I* should know.

And evidently it was a well-known fact that a single vicar, in possession of a modest fortune, must be in need of a wife.

'Raffy visited Grumps again the other day,' I told Poppy, though I didn't mention that he'd looked my way as he passed the shop window while I was working, and this time given me a tentative wave. 'They seem to enjoy the verbal sparring, and even Zillah's warmed to him, since the cards told her he's got a vital role to play in what is to come.'

'He's bound to play a part in everything, now he's the vicar, isn't he?' she pointed out.

'She just meant the Mann-Drake situation, I think, though she might have interpreted the meaning wrongly.'

I heaved a sigh. 'Even simply knowing Raffy was in the area would have been difficult enough, without *seeing* him all over the place. I suppose I ought to have started to get used to it by now, but I haven't.'

'Oh, I don't know, I've been thinking it over and I'm sure the way you feel now isn't just to do with *him*, it's about lots of unresolved issues,' she said, suddenly surprising me with an insightful comment, as she sometimes does.

'What do you mean?'

'Well, you lost your first love, you were jilted by your second and your mother abandoned you, to all intents and purposes.'

'Yes, but she wasn't much of a mother to start off with.'

'Maybe not, but you're bound to have resented the fact, because it meant you had to stay home and look after Jake – so then you weren't there when Raffy went back to find you.'

'Actually, I expect Jake would have survived with Zillah and Grumps if I *had* gone back to university.'

'Survived, but not turned out so well, even if you could have brought yourself to leave him. And I'm sure he'd have gone off the rails at some point if you'd abandoned him like his mother did.'

'Perhaps,' I admitted. 'He's turned out quite well, hasn't he?'

'He's a lovely boy,' she said warmly. 'By the way, have you heard anything from Chas about that DNA test?'

'Only an email saying he'll be calling in soon when he's up in the north on business, so he can't have got the result yet. It'll be odd seeing him and not knowing . . .' I sighed. 'It's just another damn issue to resolve, isn't it? But I really *do* hope Chas is my father, because at least he cares a little for me and I'm fond of him.'

'I think if you could find out the truth about who your father was and come to terms with that, manage to forgive your mother for being so useless and then, finally, forgive Raffy for letting you down all those years ago, then you'd probably feel like a whole, fresh new person!'

'That's a bit of a tall order! I think I'd have to *be* a different person,' I said with a wry smile, not mentioning that the Angel cards were in at least partial agreement with her, since they kept coming up with the unambiguous message that I should forgive Raffy. I couldn't read it any other way.

'You could do it,' she said encouragingly, 'and then perhaps we could *both* look for nice men, before they're all gone. There *must* be two left on the shelf still, don't you think?'

'Of course there are – like Felix,' I suggested sneakily.

'Well . . . yes, I suppose so, because he's single and there's nothing *wrong* with him, is there?'

'Absolutely not. But *I* don't want a man. I've had enough of them. Or children either, because Jake was enough. No, I love my little groove of pub, chocolate, friends and a lovely garden to play with.'

Seeing her face fall I added quickly, 'But we could go further afield occasionally, or even join something, so we would meet new people?'

'They do have afternoon and evening classes at the village hall,' she suggested doubtfully, 'but they seem to be things like napkin folding and paper flower making.'

'I don't think either of us has quite reached those levels of desperation yet, have we?' I asked.

Zillah, having decided that we needed Raffy, took the matter of reconciliation into her own hands.

The following day she knocked on the inner door that led to the museum, stuck her head in and announced loudly, 'Gentleman caller!'

Then she pushed Raffy into the room and shut the door firmly behind him.

'Sorry to disturb you,' he said, looking at once startled and entirely unsure of his welcome, as well he might. 'I can see you're busy and I didn't *mean* to come in. I called in to leave something for you with Zillah, but she insisted—'

I'd got over the first heart-jarring shock of his unexpected appearance by now, so I said evenly, 'It's all right, there's no point in resisting Zillah if she decides you should do something. I don't make chocolate every day and at the moment I'm only cutting out the Wishes to go inside.'

Seeing he wasn't about to be immediately ejected, he came over to look.

'I get them printed on sheets of this thin, shiny paper and cut them out myself,' I explained. 'There are lots of different ones, so no two boxes of Chocolate Wishes are identical. I make a random selection.'

'So, how do you get them inside the chocolate shell?'

'I mould the shapes in two halves, then I put the Wish in one and stick on the top with a little melted chocolate.'

'Easy when you know how.'

'Yes, though you have to use tempered chocolate, or a white line could develop around the join and spoil the look of it.' I was talking slightly too fast, unnerved by his nearness. I'd forgotten quite how tall he was too, until he was inches away, looking down at me . . . 'I sell them in boxes of six or twelve.'

'Felix says you shift them by the bushel-load so you have to go to the post office with parcels every day.'

'Yes, the number of orders snowballed after my Chocolate Wishes got a mention in an article in *Country at Heart* magazine and I've been advertising in it ever since. You have to keep on top of them, even when they're not urgent, and I usually call on Felix on the way back – it's the lure of his new coffee machine.'

'I know, I'm getting into the habit of doing the same, only earlier, after I've said morning prayers in the church.'

'Do you have to say prayers every day, morning and evening?'

'I don't *have* to, I *want* to; it's different,' he said with a smile. 'By the way, did Jake tell you he'd been round to the vicarage with that nice girlfriend of his?'

'Yes, and he said you were about to move back into the main house.'

'I already have, into one bedroom and a small downstairs room at the back, while the decorators finish the rest. Jake's an interesting young man – lively, intelligent and outgoing. You've done a good job with him, because he can't have been easy.'

'No, he certainly wasn't that,' I agreed.

'Felix told me some of the tricks he used to play – very inventive!'

I reflected that Felix seemed to have been telling him *way* too much! 'He's grown out of them now and he'll be going to university in the autumn, assuming he ever puts any revision in for his exams and gets the grades. But luckily his girlfriend's keen on studying. They're applying to the same universities, but I don't know how that will work out.'

Raffy had now caught sight of the chocolate spell stuck to the cupboard door next to him and was reading it. 'Interesting!'

'According to Grumps, that's some sort of magical incantation that the Mayans used when they were making their chocolate, and it was brought back by the *conquistadores*. He has a Spanish archivist chum who's cataloguing the books and papers of an ancient, titled family and he found the manuscript among them. He and Grumps have deciphered most of it between them and now he insists I say it over every batch of chocolate I make, to improve it.'

'And do you?'

'Yes, though I don't see how it could have any effect. They're working on the last part now, though that may be a later addition. I only hope they don't find any more after that, or I'll be muttering like a witch over the cauldron for hours every time I make a new batch.'

Raffy laughed deep in his throat. I'd forgotten the way he did that but it made my heart do the flippy thing again. I realised I'd slowly relaxed while we were talking, and there was a pile of snipped, shiny Wishes in front of me that I didn't remember cutting.

Raffy dug a hand into the pocket of his black greatcoat and handed me a small, tissue-wrapped package.

'This is what I wanted Zillah to give you. I've been searching the packing cases for it, I knew it was in there somewhere. Jake told me you loved angels when we were in the church looking at the stained-glass window, and when I was here I noticed there are an awful lot of them in the cottage, so . . . well, I thought you might like one more for your collection. I picked it up abroad.'

I unwrapped it, disclosing an exquisitely carved dark wooden angel, perhaps three inches high, her beautiful face calm amid a swirl of delicately carved draperies.

'But it must be terribly old and probably valuable,' I

protested, though I immediately coveted it. I expect that's a sin: all the best things are.

'The ribbon the angel's holding says "*Pax*",' he pointed out, with a hint of the old glinting, Raffy smile. 'So it's a peace offering and entirely appropriate that you have it. An offer you can't refuse.'

And he was right because somehow, although I wanted to, I couldn't.

Chapter Twenty-four

Gift Bag

I kept going to look at the angel. Her serene expression amid the whirlwind of draperies, like the perfect stillness at the heart of a storm, seemed to epitomise how I would like to feel, however unattainable that now seemed. I had thought I'd won through to a quiet, happy, contented phase in my life after we moved here, until Raffy came along and tossed me back into the maelstrom.

But eventually I came to the conclusion that, by accepting the angel from him, I'd taken at least one faltering step in the direction of total forgiveness, and even finally acknowledged that what happened between us in the past wasn't entirely his fault.

When I said as much to Zillah, she replied, 'Then you can take another giant step tomorrow, if you like, love, because I told Raffy me and your grandfather are making something special for him and he's to call for it in the morning.'

'One step will do for me at the moment, thanks! And what sort of something special are you and Grumps cooking up? It's not nasty, is it?'

'No, the opposite,' she assured me mysteriously. 'I told him I'd leave it with you, because I'm going out in the morning and Gregory won't answer the door.'

'*Out?* Out where?'

'I'm going to the cash-and-carry with Clive Snowball, just for the ride . . . and maybe a catering-sized jar of piccalilli and some biscuits.'

'Then Raffy can collect it when you're back.'

'No, he might need it earlier,' she said mysteriously, then added, 'It's your birthday soon.'

I stared at her. 'Has that got anything to do with it?'

'Nothing at all, our Chloe, I was just making conversation,' she said, and since she was evidently in one of her more obtuse moods, I went to see if I could get any sense out of Grumps, though let's face it, that was a forlorn hope.

I was still packing the day's Wishes orders in the morning when Raffy tapped quietly at the door to Angel Cottage. I'd intended to hand him the small padded envelope Zillah'd given me without inviting him in, but there was a bitterly cold early March wind and the little white dog at his feet was shivering.

'Come in,' I said, opening the door wider.

Raffy hesitated. 'No, that's OK, thanks. I didn't mean to disturb you, and anyway, I've got Arlo with me.'

'Look, just come in out of the cold, will you?' I snapped. 'Grumps said I was to make sure you read the note with the package anyway and *I'm* not freezing on the doorstep while you do it. And why don't you get your dog a coat? He looks chilled to the bone!'

In fact, he was now shivering pathetically all over my

feet and, when I bent to pat him, licked my hand and gave me a piteous look.

'Arlo won't wear a coat, he rips them off and eats them. He's putting all this on for your benefit. Look at him – he's so greedy he's got a layer of blubber two inches thick to keep him warm.'

Indeed, he was as fat and glossy as a seal, and once the door was shut he stopped shivering and looked perfectly happy to the point of smugness: I'd been had. Story of my life, really.

'You'd better come through into the sitting room, because I shouldn't really have animals around the chocolate workshop.'

'But I've obviously interrupted you when you're busy and that's the last thing I wanted to do,' Raffy protested.

'I'm packing orders, but I've almost finished and I'll be off to the post office with them shortly.' In fact, another ten minutes, and I would have been on my way when he knocked at the door, so he'd have had to come back later, when Zillah had returned.

He followed me through and Arlo immediately curled up in front of the fire as if he belonged there, though his ears twitched when he heard the crackle of the envelope I handed to Raffy. He probably hoped it was biscuits.

I sat down and watched him open it. I had, of course, prodded and fingered the package and so had a reasonable idea of what it was.

He took out a small, square sachet, looked blankly at it, then passed it to me.

'A herbal teabag?'

'I don't think so. Better read the note,' I suggested, but from the look of it, it was just as I thought: several

245

ingredients – probably herbs, but possibly something more revolting – had been pulverised and then enfolded in a small square paper packet on which Grumps would have written a spell. Zillah had then sewn it into a covering of white cotton.

'Your grandfather writes, "I must insist that you carry the enclosed in the pen pocket of your shirt at all times, but especially when you visit Mr Mann-Drake later today."' Raffy looked up. 'He doesn't say why, and unfortunately, there's a slight problem.'

'I know – you don't wear shirts, with or without pockets, do you?' I said. He was wearing the black T-shirt with its printed dog collar, black jeans and trainers, and the long leather coat that Jake had so admired when he first saw him. He could have done with another, warmer layer on top of the T-shirt on a day like this.

'I only wear a real shirt for official occasions, when I have to. The other snag with your grandfather's gift is that it's presumably some kind of protection charm, which as a vicar I probably shouldn't have anything to do with, though it's a kind thought.'

I went into the kitchen to brew hot chocolate, but it was only two steps away, so I could carry on with the conversation while I made it. 'Yes, and at least it means he's got ill-wishing you out of his system, thank goodness, before you got more than a few bruises. I *told* him not to do it, and it didn't do his sciatica any good, either.'

'Ill-wishing me?' he said, his voice sounding amused. 'Can you possibly mean . . . when the angel fell on me?'

'And when you fell in the trench. Poppy and Felix told me about that. I expect Grumps thinks it was his doing, but it was probably just coincidence.'

'A series of unfortunate events? But thank you for calling him off, anyway.'

Arlo had heaved himself up and followed me into the kitchen, presumably in the hope of food, but he was so fat he rippled under his velvet coat so I hardened my heart . . . to the point where I only gave him *half* a biscuit.

I took the cups of chocolate through and put them down on the brass tray table.

'I don't see why you can't carry the charm, since it's a goodwill thing, Raffy. It can't do any harm, can it?'

'I suppose not. I could pin it inside my coat.'

'That would be fine, except that you don't wear it all the time and if you don't take it off when you visit Mann-Drake he'll think it odd. I know – you can pin it inside your jeans pocket, only you'll have to remember to switch it over when you change clothes.'

'Yes, and try not to blow my nose on it,' he agreed gravely, though his turquoise eyes gleamed mischievously. 'And, Chloe, it's nice to hear you say my name again!'

My newborn state of forgiveness was still such a precarious thing that I wasn't quite at the stage of replying to that yet, nor did I offer to help him attach the charm, in case I was tempted to ram the pin into a delicate area. I just handed it to him, silently. It would have been a lot easier if he'd taken his jeans off, but I certainly wasn't going to suggest *that*, either.

I looked down at his bent head, where the long, black curls had swung forward exposing the strong, pale nape of his neck. His shoulders seemed broader and his back under the T-shirt more muscled than I remembered . . .

'I wish you wouldn't go to see Mann-Drake,' I said involuntarily.

He straightened and pushed the hair back from his face with both hands in a familiar gesture. 'Why, you don't *really* think he has any magical powers, do you?'

'No, but I do think he sounds a really horrible man and also terribly persuasive.'

'I think that probably sums up how I used to be, doesn't it? So I should be largely impervious,' he said drily.

'You were never horrible or evil, just young, hedonistic and totally self-obsessed.'

'Thank you for that tribute: I feel so much better now,' he said with un-Christian sarcasm, draining his chocolate and getting up. 'I'll be off on my dragon-slaying right away.'

Arlo seemed to want to stay put, which rather spoiled Raffy's grand exit. In the end, he had to carry him out.

Unsurprisingly, I felt very unsettled after he'd gone, as if all my emotions and ideas were shifting about into new patterns, all on their own. And I was really on edge . . .

Felix was talking to customers when I passed his shop on the way back from the post office, so I didn't stop, just went home and typed up Grumps' latest chapter instead.

After a bit I wandered in to see Zillah, who was back and sitting at the kitchen table riffling the Tarot pack. Cartons of biscuits, catering-sized tins of fruit salad and giant jars of pickles surrounded the urban consumer squirrel. I only hoped I wasn't getting any of that lot, gift-wrapped, for my birthday – especially the pickled eggs.

'So, did you give Raffy the charm?' she asked, looking up.

'Yes, but wouldn't he need more than that to protect him when he visited Mann-Drake?'

'Stop fussing. The cards said he came to no harm, so it worked. Your grandfather, Hebe Winter and Florrie

Snowball dreamed that one up between them. It was powerful.'

I felt the tension I'd carried round with me all day evaporate a bit. 'Maybe *God* made him invincible and it was nothing to do with the charm?' I suggested, and she gave me one of her looks.

'You can ask him tomorrow,' she said, for there was to be a general meeting of the villagers to discuss the future closure of the tennis court and lido field, and everyone would be there. Sticklepond has never needed much encouragement to party, so following the meeting there would be tea, coffee and a buffet, when everyone could chat.

Zillah's reassurance still didn't stop me walking back up the High Street later, on the pretext of giving Felix a jar of my chocolate and ginger spread, pausing at the vicarage gates for long enough to see that Raffy's small silver car was parked before the door.

Physically, at least, he must still be in one piece, and I hoped for his sake that his immortal soul was still hanging on in there too.

And with a bit of luck, even if Mr Mann-Drake had taken exception to what Raffy had been saying to him, he would be too much occupied in the near future with all his money-making schemes to do anything about it.

Chapter Twenty-five

Mixed Bag

Apart from Zillah's reassurance (for what it was worth) I knew Raffy really was OK because Poppy popped in after the latest Parish Council meeting and said his visit to Mann-Drake seemed to have been a bit of a damp squib.

'I mean, I don't know what Miss Winter and your grandfather were imagining would happen to Raffy, but he just said that Mann-Drake had been polite, but unforthcoming about both his personal beliefs and his business plans.'

'I knew Mann-Drake hadn't turned him into a frog, because he couldn't have driven back if he had little stumpy legs and webbed feet,' I said, and she giggled.

'I can't see Raffy as a frog, can you? Anyway, a queue of women a mile long would instantly form, ready to kiss him back into a prince. Effie Yatton would be one of them. She called him "dear boy" twice at the meeting and she keeps bringing him food.'

I pushed the box of truffles we were sharing back in her direction and she selected one covered in chopped nuts, then said, 'We had some really good news for the householders on the Green that Mann-Drake is trying to extort money from. Miss Winter's solicitor found a similar case that had been recently successfully contested.'

'That *is* good news,' I agreed.

'Yes, and the Rights of Way Act was changed after it, so that if you've had at least twenty years' right of access across common land, no one can impose a charge – and that's all of the houses along there.'

I'd picked up another truffle, a rum one but, feeling slightly sick, put it back again: you can have too much, even of good chocolate. Poppy's complexion, however, remained a healthy pink although she had eaten twice as many as I had. 'So Mann-Drake hasn't got a leg to stand on?'

'Not even a little, green, stumpy webbed one,' she agreed happily. 'The solicitor is going to send a letter to him pointing this out, though he thinks he probably already knows about it and just hoped to panic everyone into paying the charge before they discovered it.'

'So that's one problem solved, at least,' I said.

'We're going to announce it at the meeting tomorrow night in the village hall – you are going, aren't you?'

'Yes, it looks like we're all going and I'm taking a big chocolate cake as our contribution to the buffet.'

'Oh, good! I love your chocolate cake,' she said, taking a last truffle and tucking it into her cheek like a hamster. Then she got up, dusting cocoa powder off her hands. 'Better go,' she said indistinctly. 'See you tomorrow!'

I didn't see Raffy again until the meeting, unless you counted brief, early morning glimpses when he walked Arlo past my window – or rather, dragged him past, since Arlo always seemed determined to come in.

I think I may have become what they call a curtain-twitcher.

We Lyons were out in force at the meeting: Grumps, Zillah and Jake had decided to go, and Kat was there with her parents, so we would all get to meet them at last – and vice versa. Janey arrived under her own steam and even Clive Snowball was there; he must have left his mother and Molly in charge of the pub.

Raffy chaired the meeting, with the whole Parish Council, including Felix and a very self-conscious Poppy, sitting on the stage and taking questions. As usual, Miss Winter answered most of them, though she did graciously defer to the vicar from time to time.

There was lots of indignation about this stranger daring to come into their midst and trying to change things, though one or two of the local businesses that he patronised were slightly more forgiving.

'I spoke to Mr Mann-Drake myself,' Raffy said, 'and he was adamant that he intended selling the tennis court and the lido land for housing development. He seemed confident that he'd be able to obtain planning permission on appeal, because the areas are within the village boundary.'

'The junior tennis club gives the kids something to do in summer,' a man's voice called from the back of the hall and someone else said, 'That's right, and most of us have learned to swim up at the lido, and the Guides and Scouts have their annual camp there.'

'The tennis club problem is easily solved,' Miss Winter announced. 'The vicar is renovating the court at the rear of the vicarage, which he has generously offered to let us use instead.'

'The court and pavilion should be ready by the end of

next month, when the lease on the other site runs out,' Raffy agreed. 'I'm making access to it by the side gate onto Church Way, and Miss Yatton will have the keys and run it as before.'

'In fact, I think it will be a distinct improvement,' Effie said. 'The current one floods most of the winter, so there's always a lot of clearing up to do in the spring.'

'But of course!' Laurence Yatton exclaimed. '*That's* why the tennis court land was never built on – seasonal floods! They affect the edge of the lido field too. I'd quite forgotten, and I don't suppose Mann-Drake would know that at all, not being from the area.'

'We will have to make sure any potential property developers *are* fully aware of it,' Hebe Winter said thoughtfully.

'Hear! Hear!' someone called, and there were echoes around the room.

'I can speak to my cousin Conrad,' suggested Poppy. 'He'll probably learn about any interest in the site first, being the main local estate agent – or he can find out.'

'That would be really useful, thank you, Poppy,' Raffy said, and she went quite pink with pleasure.

'Isn't there a line on the side of the tennis pavilion, marking the highest floodwater levels?' asked Mike, the village policeman.

'I think it just shows how high the great flood of '36 got,' Effie said. 'There's a plaque too, but its paint has peeled off.'

'It should be repainted so it's nice and clear,' suggested Felix, and someone in the hall volunteered to do that.

Then Laurence Yatton proposed that a group could be organised to go and picket the Town Hall in Merchester and protest about the lido field, and by the end of the meeting there was a general air of having declared battle and of everyone being ready for action, once they knew exactly in what direction to proceed.

The main business of the meeting wound up with Hebe Winter graciously thanking the vicar for coming to the rescue with the tennis courts and also for taking on the repairs to the village hall annexe.

Everyone enthusiastically gave three loud cheers and then made a dive for the refreshments while Mr Lees, who had been sitting at the piano next to the stage with his black Labrador sprawled across his feet, now lifted the lid and played a Beatles medley, to everyone's amazement.

Kat introduced her parents to Grumps, who was gracious, Zillah, who grinned glintingly from ear to ear, and then to me, by which time they looked slightly stunned, though they told me what a nice boy Jake was. Then they left, taking him with them, which was probably easier than trying to disentangle him from Kat.

'That went really well,' I said to Felix and Poppy when I caught up with them by the buffet table. Felix had piled his plate up so high that it looked like one of those Continental choux pastry wedding confections. 'It doesn't sound like the tennis courts are going to be quite the valuable asset Mr Mann-Drake thought they would be, does it?'

'No, and I'm sure we can get lots of protesters out with placards, and coverage in the newspapers if any developers show interest in building there, or on the lido field,' Felix agreed.

Poppy said earnestly, 'Yes – I mean, it's not that we're against having *any* new homes in Sticklepond, just that they look so much better slotted in here and there, rather than a whole estate of little boxes dropped down in one place.

I'll see if I can get Conrad to be my mole about what's happening.'

'I wonder if there were houses on the lido field before the Plague?' I mused. 'I could ask Grumps to look on one of his old maps.'

I noticed that Felix and Poppy seemed to be sticking together much more than usual, though there was no sign of any special awareness between them, so either the love potion didn't work, which was just as I thought, or I simply hadn't put enough in. But there was still a little left and I had it with me . . .

'I'll get you both some more coffee, before it runs out,' I suggested. 'Back in a mo.'

The crowd had thinned out over by the urns and, by keeping my back to the room, I managed to pour the last drops of the potion into two cups . . . only to find Zillah at my elbow, watching me with interest. I started guiltily.

'What are you doing?'

'Poppy got one of Hebe Winter's love potions and I stole it, because I think she and Felix would be perfect together!' I hissed. 'I put some in their drinks the other night, only it doesn't seem to have worked, so I'm doing it again.'

'We all hoped you and Felix would get together, because he's a nice man and better than that David. But I see things working out differently in the cards now.'

'I don't want either of them,' I told her, then noticed that Poppy and Felix were coming over. 'Sssh!'

'Here you are,' I said, handing over the coffee. 'Sorry I was ages. I got talking to Zillah.'

'But I'm off now,' said Zillah. 'I only came over to tell you Clive's giving your granddad and me a lift back, so you don't have to bother.'

'Grumps has been the sensation of the evening, hasn't he?'

'Yes, I heard several children ask their parents if he was Gandalf or, even better, Dumbledore,' Poppy said.

'I got you the last sausage roll.' Felix handed it to me wrapped in a greasy paper napkin. He had three on his own plate, but you have to love a man who thinks of snaffling you the last savoury from under the nose of the hungry masses.

Mind you, most of the female half of those masses were currently clustered ten deep round Raffy, with Janey practically plastered up his side like a poultice.

As if he felt my gaze, he suddenly turned his head and gave me a half-despairing and somehow strangely intimate smile . . .

I turned away abruptly and said brightly to the others, 'It's early yet. Shall we go to the Falling Star for a while?'

As soon as Chas arrived next day I knew that he'd found out the results of the DNA test and it *wasn't* good news, because it was written all over his naturally lugubrious face so that all his features seemed to be sliding sadly downwards, like tears.

However, I kissed his cheek as usual, made him the strong Indian tea he likes and cut him a slice of fruitcake.

'This is really nice,' he said, looking round the little sitting room. 'And is the Chocolate Wishes business booming?'

'Yes, I'm making very good money and for something I love doing, so it couldn't be better. I still do a bit of secretarial work for Grumps too, which I can fit in easily enough. He's been so kind and he's even giving me this cottage.'

'That's great – a home of your own! And Jake is well?'

'Yes, he's actually working quite hard, which is the

influence of his new girlfriend,' I said. I never asked about Chas's wife, or his children, who were all grown up and off into the world, and he never volunteered the information.

'Good, good . . . I'm glad everything is going so well,' he said abstractedly and sipped his tea, looking utterly miserable.

'You've had the DNA results, haven't you?' I asked, and he nodded.

'And you're *not* my biological father?'

'No,' he admitted. 'And I can't say it was a complete shock, because I've often wondered about it over the years, especially since you've never looked like me in the least.'

'But you still came to see me and brought me presents anyway?'

'Well yes, but I *could* have been, and anyway, I grew fond of you. And now I *feel* like your father, even if I'm not.'

'You're the nearest thing to one I ever had and I wanted it to be you, Chas. You've always been kind, though it can't have been easy, especially when your wife found out about me.'

'It was a difficult time, but she forgave me,' he said and smiled reassuringly.

He is such a nice man, despite his weak moment with Mum!

'But now that we know it isn't you, and Mum lied about that, I'm wondering if she also lied about this other man she was blackmailing. My biological father could be someone else entirely!'

He looked up from his tea. 'Who is the other man – would I know him?'

I hesitated. 'He's still married too, with four children.'

'I have complete fellow feeling with him – I wouldn't tell anyone else.'

'No, of course not. His name's Carr Blackstock and he's a Shakespearian actor, but he's done a bit of TV work, too.'

Chas frowned. 'Yes, I think I know who you mean, though I haven't met him. I expect I know friends of friends of his, it's a small world. I could get an introduction and try and talk to him for you, if you like?'

'Oh, *would* you? I don't know how to go about it without sounding as if I'm after something, or about to make a big scandal. I don't want to meet him, or hear from him, or *anything*, only to find out the truth, one way or another.'

'I'll do my best and let you know.'

Zillah, who likes Chas, had seen his car outside and came in to say hello. I asked her once why Grumps hadn't tried to ill-wish Chas for getting his only daughter pregnant. She replied that the words 'fly' and 'spider' came to mind where Chas and Lou were concerned and it was hardly worth bothering with the fly once it hit the web, because it was a doomed victim.

After she'd gone, Chas pulled out a little gift-wrapped parcel and a card and gave them to me before he left. 'Happy birthday in advance,' he said, kissing my cheek and, oddly enough, at that moment he felt more like my real father than ever before.

We agreed that we were not going to let this discovery change things between us, so if this Carr Blackstock did turn out to be my real father it would suit me very well, since evidently he wanted nothing to do with me.

Chas was father enough.

My life has been a really mixed bag lately, just like my mother.

Later I went up to Stirrups in search of Poppy and a shoulder to cry on, and luckily found her alone. Janey could be distantly seen in one of the paddocks, putting her bay horse through an odd dressage manoeuvre that made it look as if it was trotting on the spot.

Poppy was very sympathetic when I told her about the DNA results and understood exactly how I felt. 'I hoped it was still Chas too, but it's lovely that he feels the same way even though he isn't – that you *both* feel the same way.'

'But now – assuming he agrees – I've got to go through the same process with this other man and it might not even be him!'

'If you remember, Felix and I did think we saw a resemblance between you and Carr Blackstock in those pictures you showed us. And actually, Felix looked him up on the internet too, and found photographs of him with his family, and you look very like his daughters.'

'How strange that feels!' I shivered. 'But at least if it *is* him, then once I know I can simply forget all about it.'

'Yes, let's hope Chas manages to persuade him to co-operate.'

'I gave Chas a letter assuring him I only wanted to know the truth and would keep it a secret.'

'Apart from me and Felix.'

'Of course.'

'It's odd,' Poppy said pensively, 'but I keep having this urge to go and see Felix, though I can't imagine why. He's not worrying about anything, is he? He came up here earlier, for no particular reason, so perhaps he wanted to tell me something.'

'And he didn't?'

'No, but I think I'm going to teach him to ride.'

'What, *Felix*?'

'Yes, he said he had a sudden impulse to try something

new. It'll have to be Atlas, though; he's the only horse we've got big enough to carry him.'

'That's a turn-up for the books, isn't it? He's not usually a sudden impulse sort of man.'

Or he hadn't been until lately. But now he and Poppy seemed to be acting strangely, as if compelled to spend more time in each other's company, though not exactly in the way I was hoping for. But I supposed that as long as Felix didn't break his neck falling off the enormous Atlas, who had feet the size of dinner plates, then perhaps romance might follow.

'Have you asked Janey if she can manage without you on my birthday?' I asked.

'Yes, it's fine. But what are we going to do?'

'I've decided it's time we got out of our rut, and I've got it all planned. We're going to have a day of hair and face makeovers and shopping in Southport.'

'But—' she began to protest.

'It's all booked,' I said firmly.

'But, Chloe, I can't afford—'

'Janey's paying for yours. I asked her and she thought it was a *great* idea.'

Or she had once I'd tweaked what passed for her maternal instincts and appealed to her guilty conscience, by suggesting it was something positive she could do to help Poppy find the right man.

Poppy was in a panic and really didn't want to come, but she couldn't refuse me when I said if she didn't it would spoil my birthday, because I couldn't go alone.

'I need a new look, or at least freshening up a bit,' I insisted and, goodness knows, it was time Poppy lavished a fraction of the care and attention she gave to Honeybun on herself.

'Then we're going to hit the shops of Lord Street and find something new to wear.'

'Do you need something new?'

'We *both* need something new, so that when we meet Felix at the Falling Star afterwards, we'll knock him dead!'

She giggled, warming to the idea. 'If he even recognises us.'

Chapter Twenty-six

High Maintenance

Grumps was all excited about his post, because his Spanish chum had managed to translate the last bit of the manuscript.

'It's quite clear now that the part we have is the original Mayan invocation, as translated and brought back by the *conquistadores*. The rest of it, which is in a different hand, is an embellishment from perhaps a century or two later.'

'I suppose the original charm, invocation, or whatever it is, wouldn't have meant much when it was first brought back, because chocolate didn't take off until much later, did it?'

'No, the document would just have been put away as a curiosity, until this man found it, and appended a few lines of his own. As to whether they add anything to the *power* of the original, I do not know, but I would try it with caution, my dear Chloe. You are quite safe with the original Mayan invocation to the gods to give the chocolate special powers. The rest . . . well, it reads more like a blessing. The author may well have been a priest, as well as secretly a practitioner in the Old Religion.'

'OK,' I agreed. I don't suppose the extra bit will make any difference, but it's odd to think of some old coot, the Spanish version of Grumps, necromancing away so many centuries ago. If he *was* a priest too, then he was playing a very dangerous game.

I decided to try that blind-tasting experiment on Felix and Poppy: I'd make three identical batches of chocolate: one with nothing said over it at all; one with the Mayan incantation and one with the whole thing, including the later addition. I didn't suppose there would be any difference.

Meanwhile, I'd just keep on using the original charm for every day, which can do no harm at all.

The chocolate tasting can be my birthday evening's entertainment!

Digby Mann-Drake had somehow managed to insinuate himself into David's group of local friends that he met at the Green Man, and he had invited David to dinner at Badger's Bolt, together with one or two other of his chums.

He rang to ask me if I would like to go with him and got quite huffy when I turned him down, even when I pointed out it was my birthday and I had the whole day planned out already. Then I warned him about Mann-Drake, but he just laughed in a condescending sort of way and said, 'You really shouldn't listen to rumours! And you're so terribly unsophisticated, aren't you, darling?'

I expect I am, if the idea of dinner with someone who gets his kicks from holding pseudo-black magic rites spiced with sex, drugs and, for all I know, rock'n'roll, does not strike me as a pleasurable outing.

'Apart from the unsavoury rumours, he's also a money-grubbing little weasel, haven't you heard?'

'Oh, that's just business, and you can't blame him for trying to make an honest buck! And if you were only planning on meeting your friends in the pub later on your birthday, then you could cancel that and come to the dinner with me instead, couldn't you?'

'Absolutely not. I'm having dinner with my family before I go out, I always do,' I said. 'Birthday cake and everything. And if you've any sense, *you* won't go anywhere near Mann-Drake either.'

He finally got a bit miffed at that and said he would take someone else.

'That's an excellent idea, David,' I said emphatically, which didn't exactly pour oil onto troubled waters.

I made the chocolates for the tasting experiment: solid hearts, which I put in plastic boxes, marked A, B and C.

Strangely, there was just enough chocolate left from the whole incantation batch to mould the two halves of a large hollow angel, though I'm positive I used equal amounts of ingredients for all three!

Isn't that weird?

I put it away, unfinished, until I wanted to do an Angel reading for someone *really* special.

My birthday morning started out really well. Jake managed to haul himself out of bed without being called, then gave me a lovely little white velvet teddy bear with angel wings and a lopsided silver halo.

'I bought it before Christmas, and I think it's supposed to hang on a Christmas tree, because there's a loop on the back between the wings,' he explained.

'It's perfect!' I said, and reached up on tiptoe to kiss his cheek, which he suffered stoically while wolfing down a chocolate spread toastie, washed down with half a gallon of orange juice. Then he remembered that Kat had sent me a gift too, a 'Who needs men when you've got chocolate?' fridge magnet. I thought I must use that phrase way too much . . .

I opened my other presents while he finished eating breakfast. Chas's was a little book of gardening tips with funny cartoon illustrations, and Zillah's a porcelain bell shaped like an angel. It seemed a bit irreverent, having a clapper up your skirts, but it was a pretty thing. There is generally a bit of an angel theme going with my presents, and at this rate I would soon run out of room to display them all.

Grumps' gift was different – a gold charm shaped like a cocoa bean sliced in half, on a chain. I'd never seen anything like it, so I'm sure he must have commissioned it, especially since it seemed to be hollow and rattled slightly when shaken . . . I put it on straight away, though I'd have to wait to thank him and Zillah later, at the birthday dinner.

I'd already packed up the urgent Chocolate Wishes orders at the crack of dawn, so I could dash to the post office with them before driving out to Stirrups and picking Poppy up for our Day of Beauty.

When I arrived, she looked terribly nervous. You'd think we were going to spend the day having major dental work done, rather than being glammed up!

She needn't have worried because when we came back several hours later, exhausted but happy, we'd had a *wonderful* time.

It wasn't something either of us could do on a regular

basis – high maintenance we were not – but it would be fun as an occasional treat and we decided we'd repeat it every six months or so.

I'd acquired a subtle new makeup and had my hair cut in a shorter, more feathery style, which suited me, though it was the same very dark brown as before, just shinier. And my eyebrows were reshaped, which made an amazing difference. I mean, I like them natural, but they had started to look *too* natural, like escaping hairy caterpillars.

Poppy was the real revelation, though: her hair had been given golden highlights and now fell into long, natural curls rather than the damp-sand-coloured frizz. She had lots of new makeup too, though in different shades from mine, being so fair. But the most stunning difference was that her eyelashes and brows had been dyed brown, which made her eyes seem brighter and the blue much deeper.

She has a good figure, even if it is a bit sturdier than the current fashion for lollipop-shaped women dictated, but her everyday garb of quilted jackets and gilets made her look top heavy and thick-waisted, which she really wasn't. Her attempts to look smart usually involve bunchy skirts and pussycat bows but now, in slim dark jeans and a pretty jersey top, she looked lovely.

It had taken us ages to find dresses we actually looked good in, the current fashion being all ruched and smocky, like baby clothes. What had happened to fashion for adults since I'd last looked? Did designers not think women over thirty bought clothes? This is why I subscribe to *Skint Old Northern Woman* magazine – it's for real women who aren't necessarily thin, teenage, rich, London-based or almost entirely self-absorbed. I now advertise my Chocolate Wishes in it too, since they're the thinking woman's after-dinner mint.

Eventually we went to a shop known for having very individual stuff, and spent more than the rest of the day had cost us put together, on an outfit each. I only hoped Janey's cash flow was up to it. I wasn't sure about mine, unless the bank had inserted some elastic since I'd last checked.

'I'll see you in the Falling Star at eight,' I said, dropping her off at Stirrups in the late afternoon, laden with shopping bags. 'Don't wash the makeup off, or brush the curl out of your hair, or do *anything* to your face before you come. And wear the dark jeans with the white and blue floaty top and the chunky necklace. We'll save our dresses for something really special.'

'Yes, boss,' she agreed, 'but my hair feels funny.'

'It doesn't look funny, it looks great. You'll have to keep using the conditioner and serum, because you can't possibly go back to frizz, now.'

'I do like the way it looks,' she admitted.

'OK, I'd better get off so I'm not late for the birthday dinner with the family, so I'll see you and Felix later   and don't forget, tonight is the blind chocolate tasting.'

'Should be fun!'

Janey, who had just come out of a loose box with a bucket, and the usual fag hanging out of the corner of her mouth, gave a scream at the sight of her daughter. As I drove away, I tried to decide whether it was from delight, or dismay that suddenly Poppy had turned into a younger, fresher version of herself. Or maybe it was a combination of the two?

Back at the cottage, Zillah had taken in a flower delivery for me from David, one of those tortured arrangements featuring a couple of dark and diseased-looking orchids and a twisted sprig of bamboo. I don't think he has *any* taste at all.

Even when we were house-hunting, his ideal of a lovely home looked more like a factory unit than a cottage. If he bought something with original features it would be gutted like a fish in no time, so he might as well stay in his minimalist flat in the first place.

He was clearly not a wellies-and-chicken-run sort of man.

Chapter Twenty-seven

Pure Criollo

Zillah had stuck my birthday candles (way too many) into the top of a lemon cheese Pavlova, a recipe culled from one of her favourite magazines. It was . . . interesting, shall we say, but I appreciated the effort and thanked both her and Grumps for their presents too. I was wearing the little gold cocoa bean at the neck of my new black pleated chiffon tunic top and it went nicely with the low-slung chain belt around my hips. My new, big leather bag was gold too – maybe I should have married a man with the Midas touch?

Poppy was feeling really self-conscious about her new image and so she called for me after dinner so we could go to the Falling Star together. Jake, who was just about to go up to Kat's house, where he was staying the night, looked gobsmacked when he saw her. Mine can't have been such an amazing transformation, since none of the family had commented on my changed appearance, except to hope I had enjoyed my day.

When Poppy and I walked into the snug, Felix was standing at the bar. He looked up with his usual welcoming smile, then his jaw dropped and his eyes practically came out on stalks – and it wasn't me he was looking at but Poppy, all pink, blonde and delectably feminine.

'*Poppy?*' he gasped.

She blushed. 'Hello, Felix. I've had a makeover – we both have.'

'I can see that,' he said slowly, still gazing at her. I don't think he'd looked properly at me once and I was so amused by this, that at first I didn't even notice that Raffy was sitting in our usual window seat.

Then Felix, recovering his wits with an obvious effort, asked him what he wanted to drink, then said to me slightly challengingly, 'I invited Raffy. That's OK now, isn't it?'

Before I could answer, Raffy was on his feet. 'Actually, no, I'm not stopping, thanks. I didn't want to butt in on your celebration, Chloe, only Felix mentioned that it was your birthday and I wanted to wish you many happy returns and give you this.'

'This' was a small, rectangular parcel and it's hard to tell someone to go away when they've just handed you a present . . . especially when they're standing looking down at you with grave, hopeful eyes, a bit like a large dog who knows he's done something wrong, is not entirely sure what, but hopes to be forgiven anyway.

'No, do stay,' I said resignedly. 'We're going to have a blind chocolate tasting session in a bit. You can be an extra guinea pig. But you shouldn't have bought me a present – you've already given me that lovely angel.'

'*Which* lovely angel?' Poppy asked, as we sat down around the table.

I coloured slightly. 'I forgot to tell you: Raffy gave me a carved wooden angel the other day, for my collection.'

'Yes, you *did* forget to tell me that – how lovely,' she agreed, looking at me strangely. 'You should have seen the disgusting flowers *David* sent her, Raffy!'

'They weren't disgusting, just weird,' I said. 'I'd rather have had a pot of geraniums. Oh, and David has gone to have dinner at Badger's Bolt tonight with some of his friends, and he invited *me* to go too! I told him what Mann-Drake was like, but he didn't believe me. He's met him at the Green Man a few times, I think.'

'I wouldn't have thought he was the type for that sort of stuff,' Poppy said, but she was clearly distracted by the way Felix kept turning round from the bar to stare at her.

She giggled: 'Did you see Felix's face when we came in? I thought he was going to have a seizure.'

'When *you* came in, you mean. He barely spared *me* a glance.'

'You both look extra lovely tonight,' Raffy said, amused.

'We should do, we've spent practically the whole day having our hair done, and our faces retreaded, and bought new clothes,' Poppy explained. 'I didn't think I'd enjoy it, but actually, it was great fun.'

Felix came back from the bar and distributed drinks.

'Orange juice?' I said to Raffy.

'It's not that I'm a recovered alcoholic or anything, just, I think I mentioned, that I suddenly decided I didn't much like alcohol, except beer. It only took me half a lifetime to realise – and now I've even given up beer, for Lent.'

Then I saw what Felix had got for me and Poppy. 'Why on earth Babycham?'

'Closest thing to champagne they'd got,' he explained.

'I *like* Babycham,' Poppy said, and smiled at him.

He blinked, still staring at her in a puzzled sort of way.

'I just can't get over how different you look. It's as though I've never really seen you before!'

She went pink and I said, 'You're embarrassing her. Give over.'

'You're both even more dazzlingly beautiful than before,' Raffy said gravely. 'I wish I'd worn my sunglasses.'

Poppy laughed and said, 'I don't think *I* was ever beautiful, but Chloe always looks pretty, even when she's not trying.'

'So she does,' he agreed.

'Now you're embarrassing *me*,' I protested.

Felix gave me his birthday gift – a Georgette Heyer novel in the original dust cover – and, since Poppy had given me hers earlier (a bamboo wind chime for my garden that made a lovely soft, musical clunking sound), that just left Raffy's: a small, framed reproduction of one of those mysterious and magical Dadd paintings.

'It's Oberon and Titania, and I don't know why, but I just thought you'd like it,' he explained.

'I do, very much – thank you.' It was odd that Raffy, who I'd known briefly (if intensely) so many years ago, should instinctively choose something I would love, while David hadn't had the foggiest idea and had probably phoned a florist and left it to them to choose.

He drained his glass. 'Good, but as I said before, I didn't intend stopping, so I'll leave you to it now and I hope you enjoy the rest of your evening.'

'No, don't go – have a chocolate,' I said, rattling one of the small plastic boxes I'd put on the table, a bit like Poppy does with oats in a bucket when she's trying to catch Honeybun.

'Really?' He paused uncertainly, raising one dark eyebrow.

'Yes, really. I need another guinea pig for an experiment.'

So he went and bought another round of drinks, ducking his head to avoid the low beams and looking a bit like Gulliver in Lilliput. Through the hatch I caught sight of Zillah in the public bar, and she flapped her hand at me. If she was playing cribbage again, they had better watch out.

When he returned, we got down to the chocolate tasting. 'Right, I want to know which one of these three kinds of chocolate you like best. I've marked A, B, or C on little stickers on the foil, so you can put the wrappers in the preferred order. Right, off you go.'

They started off fairly soberly, but pretty soon Felix and Poppy were feeding each other bits of chocolate and getting distinctly silly, in a way even two Babychams and a couple of pints of best bitter couldn't account for.

Raffy was taking it seriously, though.

'You're not eating any,' he pointed out.

'That's because *I* know which is which.'

'But you can't have made up your mind which you like best, or you wouldn't be having this test, would you?'

When I opened my mouth to reply he snapped the heart he was holding in two and popped one half into my mouth. I couldn't very well spit it out, even if I could hear Janis Joplin in my head helpfully belting out 'Take Another Little Piece of My Heart', so I chewed and swallowed. It was, if I say it myself, chocolate perfection. 'Which one was that?'

'B,' he said softly, his eyes holding mine. 'My favourite – dark, lovely, fragrant, delicious . . .'

'It's ours too,' Poppy broke in brightly and, when I checked, all three of them had put their wrappers in the same order.

'So it's B, A and then C?'

'Looks like it,' said Raffy. 'Are you going to tell us what the different types of chocolate are now?'

'Oh, they're all exactly the same, aren't they, Chloe?' Poppy said. 'The only difference is that she's said different versions of a Mayan chocolate spell over each pot.'

'Yes, though I didn't say anything over one batch – C. I said the whole of it over A, and then added an extra blessing for the last lot, the B batch, which Grumps and his Spanish friend have just finished translating.'

'Is that *really* all the difference?' Raffy asked. 'That's . . . surprising.'

'To say the least,' agreed Felix. 'You must have done something different, or added a little extra ingredient?'

'I didn't, I used the same blend and amount of couverture chocolate drops, heated and tempered it at the identical temperatures and for the same length of time. *I* can't understand it either.'

I nibbled a bit more from the A and C boxes, absent-mindedly passing the remainder on to Raffy, and agreed that not only was B outstanding in flavour, it also looked glossier than the others and had a crisper snap when I broke it.

'I find it impossible to believe that an ancient charm could change the taste of your chocolate,' Raffy said.

'Oh, but the Chocolate Wishes business only really took off when Chloe started saying it over the melting pot,' Poppy said, 'and that was just the *first* part of it! So obviously the complete thing must make a difference.'

'I think the Chocolate Wishes taking off was due more to the internet and getting a mention in *Country at Heart* magazine,' Felix suggested.

'Yes, and now I advertise regularly in *Country at Heart* and *Skint Old Northern Woman*, I get even more orders.'

'But they do all taste completely different,' Raffy said slowly.

'Yes, and it can't *all* be in the mind if you and I didn't know they were the same chocolate,' Felix said.

'That's right. So we've proved magic really works!' Poppy announced. Her eyes were sparkling and her cheeks now so flushed that I wasn't sure she should be driving home afterwards.

Felix, I noticed, had his arm resting along the back of her chair . . . while Raffy was still looking at me with a hint of that dog-waiting-to-be-forgiven expression in his eyes, sort of puzzled and hopeful together.

We didn't stay late, and when we came out into the cool night air it was a magical sort of evening: there were a lot of stars in the velvety sky and everything smelled crisp and clean and hopeful.

'Anyone want to come back to Marked Pages for a cup of coffee, or something stronger?' Felix offered hospitably.

'I'd love to,' Poppy said. 'I haven't had a whole day off for yonks.'

'Actually, I think I'll call it a night. I seem to have packed a lot into today,' I said.

'Me too, and I'll walk you to your door, seeing I'm going that way,' Raffy said.

It was hardly likely that I would get mugged in the few paces between the corner where the other two left us and my cottage door, but it only took me half that distance to make my mind up that there was something I needed to do – and do *tonight*.

'Come in,' I said, cutting Raffy off in mid-farewell and unlocking the door. 'That is, if it's OK for vicars to be seen vanishing into single women's houses straight from the pub at night?'

'I got ordained, not elevated to sainthood, and I don't think they excommunicate as long as the vicar is single too.' He looked down at me in a puzzled sort of way. 'But Jake will be there to chaperone us anyway, won't he?'

'No, he's staying up at his girlfriend's house tonight. I think her parents now want to adopt him.'

I led him through the workshop to the sitting room, flicking on lights as I went and dropping my coat and birthday presents on the nearest chair. Then I turned to face him.

'What is it, Chloe? Do you want me to try and get your boyfriend out of Mann-Drake's clutches?' he asked, puzzled.

'What? Oh, you mean David? No, it's nothing to do with him. It's just . . . well, there's something I haven't told you – something about *us*.'

His eyes on my face, he said slowly, 'You know, I had an idea there might be something more, but I couldn't imagine what.'

By now I was feeling my resolution starting to drain slowly away, but having started, I was determined to finish. 'Poppy said recently that I was putting the blame for every-thing that had gone wrong in my life onto you, and she was right.'

'Well, some of it probably was my fault and, if it's any consolation, I don't think there have been many weeks that have gone by since we parted when I haven't regretted losing you, Chloe.'

'It didn't make you live like a monk, though, did it?' I snapped, forgetting the whole forgiveness bit for a minute.

'No,' he said evenly, 'it didn't do that.'

I turned away and paced up and down, then swung round and faced him. 'Look, Poppy thinks I'll only be happy if I come to terms with everything, so here goes: as I told you, I realised as soon as I got back from university that I couldn't leave Jake again. But I also discovered something else – that I was having your baby.'

He looked stricken and his already pale complexion completely blanched. 'That explains a lot . . . it explains *everything*. Oh, Chloe!'

'We were a bit careless that last week, weren't we? All that arguing and making up,' I said ruefully, though the tears were pricking painfully at the back of my eyes. 'It wasn't something I could put in a letter, but I thought when you came to find me I could tell you about the baby and somehow we could work it all out. I can't imagine how – I couldn't have left Jake behind, and you wouldn't have wanted to be saddled with two children when you were just starting off on your career!'

Raffy had sunk down into a chair, his head between his hands, but at this he looked up. 'But I never came back and you got Rachel's lying letter instead . . . But the baby,' he asked suddenly 'You didn't . . . ?'

'I didn't abort it. I hadn't even got as far as wondering whether I wanted it or not, before I miscarried, right after I got Rachel's letter.'

'I wouldn't have blamed you, whatever you chose to do,' he said gently.

'Only Zillah knew about it, because she helped me, though it was so early that it was quickly over . . . And I did want it – only I didn't understand that until I'd lost it!'

My voice broke and the welling tears spilled over to run slowly down my face. Raffy sprang up, took one hasty stride and pulled me into his arms. 'Oh, darling, I'm *so* sorry! So very, very sorry! I should have thought of that!'

I gave a sigh and rested my head against his broad shoulder, feeling quite drained and empty.

'I don't know how to make it up to you,' he said helplessly.

'You can't, it's past.'

'But how can you ever fully forgive me? And can I forgive *myself*?'

I felt his lips brush my hair and without conscious thought turned mine up to meet them in a long, slow kiss. His arms tightened around me and time stood still, with the past, however temporarily, forgotten . . .

Then suddenly he wrenched away. 'Oh God, I don't know what I'm doing! I didn't mean to— Oh *hell*, I seem to do nothing but say I'm sorry!' He pushed his hair back from his pale face with both hands in that achingly familiar way.

'I – it's all right,' I said, slightly dazedly.

'No, *nothing's* right. To think *I* felt angry with *you* all these years, and yet—' He broke off again. 'I'd better go. But at least now I understand and I promise not to bother you any more and keep out of your way as much as I can.'

'No, really – I feel much better now everything's open between us,' I protested, which suddenly I did. It was like seeing a dark cloud lift, revealing an edge of light.

'You're very brave and forgiving, but *I* feel damnable – or damned – and I need to go and pray.'

I thought he might also have a few blasphemy issues to address too, but I didn't say so, since he seemed distraught enough as it was.

He kissed me again, but this time very chastely on the forehead, while cupping my face in his hands, then out he went like a troubled spirit into the night.

The breeze brought the faint sound of a Bach fugue from

the direction of the church where he was headed: I thought it would suit his mood wonderfully.

And it's just possible that he's not a cheap blended forastero chocolate after all, but a criollo.

Chapter Twenty-eight

Home Alone

I woke up after a deep and dreamless sleep to an empty house, Jake being still at Kat's. I felt . . . I didn't quite know . . . empty, perhaps, and as if I'd undergone some great catharsis, which I suppose I had.

But I also felt anticipatory and about to embark on a new phase of my life. Last night I'd managed to crawl out of my shabby chrysalis of bitterness, anger and blame to emerge, if not as a carefree butterfly, then at least as a halfway decent moth. Poppy had been right: I could now move on.

Unfortunately, though, the previous night had also revealed to me just how easy it would be to fall in love with Raffy all over again, going by the traitorous way my body had responded to his. *He* had broken that kiss, not me. In fact, *I'd* probably kissed *him* and not the other way round.

But now I'd recognised the danger existed, I could guard against it, because there was no way I was making the same mistakes all over again. I would have to make it clear that a casual friendship was all I wanted and then the kiss could be forgotten.

Raffy took his early morning walk with Arlo as usual, but didn't so much as glance sideways at Angel Cottage. The pale, translucent skin of his face was again shadowed and bruised under his eyes as if he hadn't slept much, though this time I was sorry to see it.

Arlo was feeling friendlier, because he obviously wanted to cross over and call in. I suspect he had every house tagged where he'd been offered food.

Poppy rang me later, and I deduced that she was giving the first of her Saturday morning lessons in the indoor riding school, since there was the muffled thump of hoofs on sawdust in the background and every so often she removed her mouth from the phone and bellowed things like: 'Change legs!' 'Trot on, George!' and 'Kimberly, sit up *straight!*'

'So, did you enjoy your birthday?' she asked, between commands.

'Yes, it was all lovely – and wasn't Felix stunned when he set eyes on you!'

She gave her infectious giggle. 'I don't think he'd ever actually seen me as a *woman* before.'

'No, but he has now, and if you carry on looking so pretty, he won't be the only one, either. Honestly, if a bit of slap and a new hairstyle is all it takes, it just goes to show how shallow men are.'

'To be fair, I hadn't really seen Felix in any other light except brotherly before, but he's quite handsome when you look at him objectively, isn't he?'

'Very,' I said encouragingly, though actually 'attractively homely' would sum him up better. 'Funnily enough, when you were telling me about the qualities you'd like your Mr Right to have, I suddenly realised that Felix had them all – isn't that strange?'

'Mmm . . .' she said thoughtfully. 'But I thought he had his eye on you, at one time?'

'If he did, he doesn't any more.'

'I slept there last night, at Marked Pages,' she said pensively.

'What, with Felix?'

'Not *with* Felix, I just fell asleep on the sofa, and he must have covered me up and left me to it. I let myself out really early this morning before he was awake and came home, and Mum hadn't even noticed I was missing. I hadn't had that much to drink, so I'm sure your chocolate had the weirdest effect on me!'

'I think it might have had an odd effect on me too,' I admitted.

'It made me feel as though I'd drunk lots of champagne and everything was sparkling and magical – and I still do, a bit, this morning. Do you feel like that?'

'No, it just made me understand everything clearly for the first time, probably a bit like when Raffy suddenly got God.'

'Perhaps it has a different effect on different people?' She broke off to yell, 'Kimberly, get up and get right back on! No, you're not in shock. Butterfly's legs are only a foot long, you didn't have that far to fall.'

'Has she fallen off?' I asked.

'She slides off over his shoulder every time he stops, that's why I put her on a Shetland. What were we saying?'

'That you thought my chocolate gave you a champagne buzz.'

'It was that Box B. You'd better be careful who you sell it to!'

'*I* didn't get all giggly and flirty.'

'No, but you suddenly seemed to be getting on better with Raffy – I saw you feeding each other chocolate hearts! And you let him walk you home.'

'A few yards across the road? Though actually, I invited him into the cottage because I needed to tell him something,' I said and then I told *her* about the lost baby too, and her commands to her pupils to change legs or trot on became inextricably mixed with soft cries of: 'Oh my goodness!' and 'Poor Chloe, but why on earth didn't you tell me?'

'You weren't there, and by the time you got back I didn't want to talk about it any more. But now the air's well and truly cleared I feel better, though unfortunately I think Raffy's gone the opposite way. He looked absolutely stricken and rushed off to the church to pray.'

'Well, he's a vicar, that's how they deal with things.'

'I suppose it is. And now we both know everything, I've forgiven him and can let the past go, just like you and Felix kept telling me to. But Raffy didn't seem to understand that, because he said he would do his best to avoid me. And by the way, don't tell Felix about the baby, will you? Zillah is the only other person who knows . . . I *think*. She *might* have told Grumps.'

'I won't tell him unless you say I can, though it would help him to understand, because we've both been puzzled about why you hadn't got over it, when it was clearly more that Rachel's fault than anyone else's.'

'Yes, my forgiveness doesn't so far extend to her. I'm not sure it ever will.'

There was an anguished howl. 'I'd better go,' Poppy said resignedly. 'Butterfly has got fed up and is standing on Kimberly's foot, looking stubborn as a rock, and I don't blame him.'

I told Grumps about the blind chocolate tasting trial and that Poppy was convinced the full spell gave the chocolate extra magical powers, and he said approvingly, 'That girl's not as stupid as I thought she was.'

'She isn't stupid at all,' I replied indignantly. 'She simply has an innocent, trusting nature, even though that's pretty astonishing, considering Janey brought her up.'

'Mmm. And you say the vicar was there last night, too?'

'Yes, and I invited him back to the cottage afterwards. We've cleared the air between us, Grumps – there are no more secrets. I've put the past behind me.'

'You have, have you?' he said, with one of his sharper looks, confirming me in my belief that Zillah had long ago told him everything. Then to my surprise he added, 'Good, good . . . I believe his punishment has already found him out, so now we can all concentrate on removing that carbuncle Mann-Drake from our midst.'

'Zillah said we needed Raffy for that. He would be vital.'

'He certainly has a part to play. As to the chocolate, perhaps you had better be careful when using the additional blessing,' Grumps said thoughtfully. 'Keep it for special recipients.'

'Yes, I'd already decided to use only the Mayan bit for the Chocolate Wishes.'

Not, of course, that I thought my chocolate really did have magical properties, but it was better to be safe than sorry.

* * *

When I went into Marked Pages after posting my parcels, Felix asked me, slightly indignantly, what I had said to upset Raffy, because when he had seen him after morning prayers he'd been really down and almost morose.

'Nothing! As far as I'm concerned, the past is now the past, the slate's clean and he's just the new vicar and nothing more. That's what you wanted, wasn't it? I'm ready to start again and be friends.'

'Is that what you told him? So how come he seems to have gone into a tailspin?'

'I can't imagine,' I said untruthfully.

'Oh, no?' he said sarcastically. 'He said he now under stood why you didn't want to see him and he was going to keep out of your way as much as possible. And then he said he wished you all the happiness in the world with David. What did he mean by that? You haven't got engaged again, have you?'

'I keep telling everyone that I'm just friends with David, nothing more. Honestly, I don't think you listen at all! In fact, although I love looking at houses, I think I've had enough of that now too and I haven't really got the time anyway, because I get more and more chocolate orders every day.'

'But David—'

'Look, can we forget about him?' I said wearily. 'Let's talk about *you*. Poppy says she spent the night here.'

He went pink. 'She fell asleep on the sofa and it seemed a shame to wake her. But she left so early, I didn't see her go. She got back all right?'

'Yes, fine – I spoke to her this morning when she was giving a lesson.'

'*I* have my first one this afternoon. I'm shutting up shop specially.'

'Be prepared to eat your meals off the mantelpiece for the next few weeks,' I advised him.

'It's not that bad, is it?'

'Believe me, you'll use muscles you never even knew you had. But it'll give you a peachy bum.'

'I already have one of those,' he said with dignity.

David called at the cottage unannounced especially to apologise for being a bit short with me when I refused to go to Mann-Drake's dinner party with him.

'No really, I didn't mind at all,' I assured him truthfully, 'and thank you for the lovely flowers.'

Actually, that wasn't a total lie because I quite liked the bamboo. I'd put it in a tall, thin glass vase on its own and it seemed to be sending out roots.

He still lingered in a hopeful sort of way so I felt I had to invite him in, even though I was working. I sat him down and then carried on brushing chocolate into winged heart moulds.

'The party was quite fun, actually,' he said. 'Digby – he asked us all to call him that – is such an interesting man, and some of the things he told us about over dinner were quite fascinating.'

'Like what?' I asked, but he didn't seem to be able to remember specifics. I suspect he and the rest of them were hypnotised by that golden voice. I didn't ask him who he took as his dinner partner either, because if it wasn't Mel Christopher, I'll eat all my scented geraniums.

'To show you forgive me, I thought you might come with me for a second look at that cottage near Rainford, and the converted barn near Scarisbrick,' he suggested. 'Those were your favourites, weren't they?'

'Yes, but that isn't important, is it, because *I* won't be living there. It's which one *you* preferred.'

'I think you have a better eye for these things,' he insisted. 'Do come with me. I'll arrange later viewings on Wednesday afternoon and then we can go and have a drink in the Green Man afterwards – even dinner?'

I tried to get out of it, because I was now not only entirely sated with house-hunting but had started to find poor David terminally boring. However, he made it impossible to get out of, though I did insist that I had to get back home after a quick drink at the pub. 'I can't leave poor Jake on his own all the time!'

'He's an adult now, certainly old enough to take care of himself,' he pointed out.

This was true and I had started to feel a pang or two at the thought of him grown up and off, just like any empty-nester. I didn't mention that 'poor Jake' was usually either up at Kat's house, like a Goth version of the Fresh Prince of Bel-Air, in the Old Smithy kitchen being stuffed like a Strasbourg goose by Zillah, or foraging perfectly successfully for himself at home.

Instead I tried to make it plain to David that this would be my last house-hunting expedition with him, because my business was now so busy that I simply didn't have time any more. We must have seen everything for sale in his price bracket in the entire county by now anyway.

He didn't seem to take in what I was saying and I was just psyching myself up to be much more blunt when Zillah waltzed in, beaming away like a lighthouse.

'Ah, David – how lovely! Are you well . . . just at present? I remember when you used to come out in the most 'alarming rash every time you came to see us,' she said, then settled down as if she had all day to chat.

Only five minutes later he was roaring off in his noisy sports car as if the devil himself was after him.

'He didn't have to leave,' Zillah said, looking vaguely surprised. 'I only came to see if you and Jake fancied coming over for beef and carrots later, followed by fruit salad with marshmallows.'

'*Marshmallows?*'

'Those tiny ones that you see sprinkled on hot chocolate in cafés,' she explained – or rather, didn't explain. Some magazines have a lot to answer for.

'I think you might have to have Kat too, because she and Jake offered to help Grumps unpack and display all that stuff he bought from an auction this afternoon, and it's bound to take ages.'

'That's all right, there's plenty. Gregory seems to have quite taken to Kat since she started redoing all the museum notices with her calligraphy pen and volunteering to help run it when it opens at Easter.'

'It's getting really close, but it's almost ready to open, isn't it? We just need some more stands for books and gifts behind the desk, and a postcard rack.'

They were to stock my Chocolate Wishes, though I would also throw open my workshop doors to the public on the afternoons when the museum was open and sell the chocolates direct. I intended to make a stock of treacle toffee cat lollies, too, which Zillah thought would be bestsellers even though young children were to be excluded from the museum.

Raffy was now not so much avoiding me as turning tail and fleeing whenever he glimpsed me, so I had no way of letting him know that I really had forgiven him. I didn't know if I was making him feel so guilty he couldn't stand the sight of me, or if he thought my kissing him was a sign that I expected him to take up where we left off . . . or maybe both?

But no, on reflection, I thought he was just indulging in a major guilt trip. And I was . . . sort of missing him, which was odd, since I hadn't seen much of him to miss since he moved here. I even told Felix that he could invite him to go to the Falling Star with us any time he wanted, and he did, but Raffy said I didn't really mean it!

But actually, I did, because something strange was happening between Poppy and Felix and I was starting to feel such a gooseberry that a fourth person would have been very welcome – even Raffy!

Poppy had stuck to the moisturising and minimal makeup routine she'd learned on my birthday and said she was never going back to frizzy hair again, now that she'd realised that conditioner and serum would instantly make her look more Pre-Raphaelite than unshorn sheep.

Chas emailed me to say that he'd pulled some strings and finally managed a quiet chat with Carr Blackstock, but it had been a really tricky meeting. For a start, he'd been angry that Chas knew anything about him and Mum, until he learned that Chas had been in the same boat. He was also very suspicious of *my* motives, though Chas reassured him that I only wanted to know whether he was or was not my biological father, but had no interest in him other than that. And, of course, I'd sent a letter for him via Chas that said the same thing.

Chas said it was clear he firmly believed he wasn't my

father and in the end agreed to provide a DNA sample to prove it once and for all. But actually, I hoped it was him, even if he was horrible, because then I'd be able just to draw a line under it and forget all about him!

Chapter Twenty-nine

Rites

When I went to collect Grumps' chapter on Wednesday morning he was highly pleased with himself and insisted on showing me an old map of Sticklepond that he had acquired from Felix the previous day.

'Have you found a new marker for your ley line?' I asked, helping to hold down one curling end.

'No, no – something quite different. A piece of extremely useful information about the lido field that I have passed on to Felix, so he may tell the rest of the Parish Council.'

'Right,' I said, putting his tea down on a corner of the map.

'See here?' He pointed, the large red stone in the silver ring he wore on his index finger glinting dully. 'The so-called lido field has never been built on for it once formed the gardens of a long-gone small monastic house. But *this* map was drawn up later, after the first wave of the Black Death had swept the land, and you can see here that the area is now clearly marked as "Plague Pit Field".'

'Plague Pit Field? You mean there was a mass grave there

for plague victims?' I asked, startled. 'I suppose they did have to bury them quickly.'

'Precisely. And then over the years the name has been forgotten, until eventually the area became a popular local picnic spot, leased from the owner of Badger's Bolt, by the council, as a public amenity.'

'But how odd, to think what is there, forgotten.'

'And it may well save the field from development – siting houses on top of a mass grave, however ancient, would hardly be popular with either the local people or potential purchasers.'

'It certainly wouldn't!' I agreed.

Halfway through viewing the first property, while David was waffling on about knocking down walls and installing en-suite bathrooms, I told him I wouldn't have time to come out house-hunting with him again. But unfortunately he took that as a sign that I was still piqued because he'd taken someone else to the Mann-Drake dinner party.

The song 'You're So Vain' could have been written for him and he seems to have the hide of a rhinoceros.

'No, I really *meant* it when I said I didn't mind about that, David. Why on earth should I, since we're only friends? It's just that Chocolate Wishes is so busy now that I won't be able to take so much time off in future, and once the museum opens I will be even busier.'

He gave the indulgent laugh that made me want to hit him and said he'd already realised we would have to wait until Jake goes to university before we could move our relationship onwards.

Honestly, I can't imagine why I once found him pleasant, easy company! But things really came to a head in Rose

Barn, the second property, because he tried to kiss me while the estate agent was tactfully waiting downstairs.

I fended him off with more vigour than tact, and he got a bit huffy . . . once he'd got his wind back.

'What on earth did you do that for?' he demanded, his eyes watering. 'It was only a little kiss!'

'A kiss too far and it was you who told me I wasn't sophisticated, if you remember,' I pointed out. 'Put it down to that. But never mind, I expect several of your posh friends don't object to a bit of random dalliance.'

'You're jealous!' he said, enlightenment dawning all over his handsome face, and this mistaken belief seemed to cheer him up no end. I tried to disillusion him, but since I stopped short of saying outright that he was now boring me practically into rigor mortis, which would have been a bit brutal, it had no effect at all.

He turned into the Green Man car park afterwards as if everything was fine between us which, as far as he was concerned, it was. *I* was resolved that this was going to be the fastest drink ever, especially when he said as we were going in that some of his friends were down for the weekend and might already be there. They were, too – I could hear loud confident voices and braying laughter as soon as I opened the door.

I vaguely recognised one or two of them from six years ago, but I'd forgotten quite how awful they were – and *they* had clearly forgotten *me* entirely.

Mel Christopher – she of the grey horse, blonde hair, brown eyes and amazing figure – was one of them, and it became obvious in about three seconds flat that I was right about David taking her to Badger's Bolt instead of me.

She was sending me clear signals that she could take

David away from me any time she wanted to and I tried to signal back that she could go right ahead, with my blessing, but I think she could only transmit, not receive.

She also gave me the impression that I had a shiny nose and bird's-nest hair, so after a bit I went to the ladies to check, which meant going through the foot part of the L-shaped room, where most of the locals gather.

There I discovered Raffy playing darts with the Winter's End gardeners, as well as Hebe Winter's great-niece, Sophy, and her husband, Seth Greenwood. I'd seen him at the village hall meeting and he's tall and a bit scary-looking until he smiles: then he's gorgeous and you know *exactly* why she fell in love with him. Sophy, who I've met occasionally in Marked Pages, waved at me, but Raffy just gave me a sombre look before turning and flinging his darts randomly at the board. One fell out and everyone jeered, but in a friendly way.

I'd rather have joined them than go back to David's friends, because they seemed to be having much more fun. When I returned, Mel was telling the rest of them what they'd missed at Mann-Drake's dinner party, though most of them had evidently met him at one time or another anyway, either here or in London.

'He's one of the Devon Drakes, darling!' as Mel put it. So obviously it was a case of 'never mind if he's utterly perverted, so long as he's in Debrett's'.

They all thought him 'great fun'. He was to hold a house-warming party at his cottage at the end of next week, to coincide with some magical ceremony or other – possibly *very* other – which they were remarkably eager to be invited to.

'He's had the stone outbuilding behind his cottage

converted – he showed us after dinner,' Mel said. 'The décor is modelled on a Mithraic temple, though the frescos are copied from that Indian temple – you know the one!'

I thought I could have a good guess.

'He said we could bring one or two friends, so if any of you wanted to come . . . ?' she invited. 'It'll be fun, won't it David?' She gave him a warm, intimate smile that was meant to exclude me.

'I expect the ceremony will be a lot of nonsense, but Mann-Drake's very entertaining and hospitable,' he agreed, then said to me, 'You could come with me this time, Chloe.'

'Oh, no, thank you,' I said hastily. 'I'm not much of a party animal.'

'I'd have thought it would be right up your street – isn't your grandfather Gregory Warlock, who writes all those lurid novels?' asked Mel, and they all laughed rather offensively. 'But never mind, if you can't make it, then David can be my dinner partner again, can't you, darling?' She flashed him a Helen of Troy look that would have instantly scuttled my boat, had I been trying to float one.

'Lovely, I hope you have a great time,' I said. 'Now, if you'll excuse me, I'd better get on my broomstick and fly off, because I've got an early start tomorrow morning.' This was only partly an excuse, because I was going with Zillah to a psychic fair in Southport next day.

It took very little effort to persuade David to stay, since not only was it still so early that there was no need for him to see me home, but Mel was now making an outright play for him and he was finding it hard to keep his concentration on me.

In fact, I was so keen to get out that I didn't even notice

that Raffy was leaving too, until I collided with him just outside.

We disentangled ourselves and he said quickly, 'Sorry, I'll – go the other way.'

'But I might get mugged on the way home on my own,' I said plaintively. 'Could you reconcile that with your conscience?'

He looked down at me uncertainly. 'You're not serious? Nothing's likely to happen to you on the streets of Stickle-pond, is it?'

'Who knows?' I said, though it was profoundly unlikely and anyway, according to Grumps, nothing at all could harm me while I was wearing the peculiar little gold cocoa bean he gave me on my birthday. I could only think he had something put inside it, though what, how, or when, was anyone's guess. A bit like me and my messages in the Wishes, it was easy when you knew how.

'You're leaving early,' he said, though he did fall in beside me, his hands driven deep into the pockets of his long, black coat and his expression rather sombre. 'I suppose you're meeting your friends at the rival hostelry?'

'No, they've gone to see a film. I would have done too, except I'd already agreed to go house-hunting with David one last time.'

'You mean – you've found the right house?' He gave me an unfathomable sideways glance.

'No, and I'm not sure any more how serious he is about finding a country place – but if he is, he'll have to do it without me from now on. But I'm glad I ran into you, because there's something you need to know.'

'Something *else*?' he said slightly despairingly.

'About Mann-Drake, not us.'

I told him what I'd learned about the proposed party.

'So, you're worried about your friend being drawn in, is that it?' he asked when I'd finished.

'No, though I would have thought he was the last man to get involved in anything like that. But Mel Christopher seems to be able to twist him round her little finger, so I expect he'll end up staying on afterwards, when apparently there's to be some kind of pseudo-magical initiation rite. I just thought I'd tell you because, as vicar, you ought to know what's happening in your parish, that's all.'

We had reached my door by then. 'Thanks,' he said. 'I'll have to think about it . . . And I *could* talk to your boyfriend, if you wanted me to?'

I'd been toying with the idea of asking him in to supper, which was an extendable curry I'd made earlier (assuming Jake hadn't decided to wolf most of it down in my absence) but instead I now snapped through gritted teeth, 'He is *not* my boyfriend!' and went in, slamming the door.

'Was that Raffy you were yelling at?' asked Jake, caught frozen in the act of removing a treacle toffee cat lolly from one of the big sweet jars on the worktop.

'Yes, but I wasn't yelling – and don't eat the stock.'

'*Who* is not your boyfriend? I hope you mean Deadly David!'

'Yes, of course I do. I keep telling everyone until I'm blue in the face that I'm *not* going out with him, *not* going to get engaged to him again, *not* doing anything with him, even seeing him again as a friend! In fact, I think he's about to be snaffled up by the village siren.'

And I told him about the Green Man and Mel Christopher while I heated the curry and cooked rice and he laid out plates and cutlery, though when I got to the bit about Mann-Drake's house-warming party and the ceremony for special guests afterwards, his face darkened.

'We met him when we were out walking Kat's dog earlier and he invited *us* too! It turns out she's chatted to him a few times when she's been on her own, but she hadn't told me.'

'You haven't argued, have you?' I asked, concerned.

'Yes, but we've made it up again. I can see he comes across as totally harmless and she was just being polite, because he's so old. But I hear he's also invited one of the girls from Dolly Mops to his party, so he seems to be spreading his nets pretty wide.'

'I only hope someone has warned her about him.'

'Oh, most people my age wouldn't be interested – it's hardly going to be a rave if there's a geriatric in charge, is it?'

'Perhaps I should speak to Kat tomorrow too,' I said worriedly.

'There's no need. I've told her not to even say hello to him in future, just turn round and walk away if she sees him coming,' he said firmly. For a moment, with his flashing brown eyes and black hair, he looked like a Mafia version of Grumps.

Chapter Thirty

Grave Concerns

'And my blood is still boiling at the sheer cheek of the man – first of all ingratiating himself with Kat and then daring to try and draw my Jake in too!' I said to Poppy while we waited in the snug of the Falling Star for Felix to arrive. He'd had to go off somewhere after the latest Parish Council meeting.

'Oh, Jake is much too sensible to be drawn in by someone like that, especially since he knows all about Mann-Drake,' she assured me, 'and I expect Kat was just being polite to someone so much older than herself. I hope the Dolly Mops girl is too – I'd already heard about that invitation from Effie Yatton, and that the old cowshed has been turned into a kind of pagan temple.'

'Effie Yatton seems to know an awful lot!'

'It's because she runs the Brownies – it means she has moles everywhere! She says it's clear that Mann-Drake is trying to corrupt our youth. He's even invited the son of the farmer next to Badger's Bolt too, so he's casting his nets wide, isn't he?'

'He's already drawn in David and some of his friends, but I'm not worried about them because they're old enough to know what they're doing.'

'I wouldn't have thought it was David's kind of thing?'

'It isn't really. I think it's Mel Christopher's influence.'

'Hebe Winter wanted Mike to stop the party, but of course he can't unless they break the law in some way. Raffy said some of the rumours he'd heard about the meetings Mann-Drake used to hold at his Devon house weren't very savoury and I thought he meant orgies, though I shouldn't think the cowshed is big enough for that.'

'I wouldn't know, I've never been to an orgy.'

'That's what Raffy said when I asked him,' she said innocently. 'Then Felix said Mann-Drake ought to be careful about inviting young people to his parties, because there have been cases where teenagers have posted the details on internet sites and hundreds of uninvited guests have turned up.'

'Yes, I've read about that – parents coming back and finding their homes trashed.'

'We all agreed it would be *terrible* if that happened to Mann-Drake's party,' she said meaningfully.

'Right . . .' I said. 'Did Felix tell the Parish Council about Grumps' big discovery? He's highly pleased with himself!'

'Oh, yes – it was amazing about the plague pit. Fancy it being forgotten! Though the Palm Sunday procession has always stopped there for special prayers, so that's probably a throw-back to that time. Raffy's going to see if there's anything about it in the church records. But it is quite nice in a way that generations of families have played and picnicked there, where their ancestors are buried, isn't it?'

'I suppose it is. And it will certainly put a crimp in the plans to build homes there, I would have thought.'

'Yes, Conrad told me that the developers, Mango Homes, are coming to look at the lido field on Tuesday morning at ten and Mann-Drake is meeting them there. Hebe is organising a protest and newspaper coverage, and then they are going on to picket the Town Hall in Merchester afterwards. We'll have to make banners and go.'

'Are Mango Homes the ones who call the roads on their estates after fruit?' I asked. 'Like Raspberry Road and Galia Gardens?'

'And Plum Place for the posh end?' Poppy giggled. 'Yes, those are the ones and they usually stucco their houses and paint them in ice-cream colours, so it would look like a chunk of the Cornish Riviera had been transplanted to Sticklepond.'

'That wouldn't fit in with the local houses at all.'

'No, that's what we all said. That was about the end of the meeting then, and I came out with Felix and Raffy. But Felix said he had to go and see a customer and dashed off, and although I asked Raffy to join us here later, he said he was very busy at the moment. Easter does seem to be, for vicars,' she added. 'But before he went, he said he was a donkey – that was a bit odd.'

'A *donkey*?'

She nodded, her curls, which had now permanently replaced the frizz, bobbing. 'I'm not sure why, unless I misheard, though I *had* told him about the Palm Sunday walk earlier and he asked me then if the donkey was compulsory.'

'He *is* a donkey if he's avoiding me, because I keep telling him I forgive him.'

'Perhaps he needs time to forgive himself, now he knows the whole truth?'

'Maybe, but I think he's wallowing in it a bit too much. And he still seems to think that David and I are an item, no matter what I say.'

'I think even Felix has now grasped that you aren't!'

'No, I'm not remotely attracted to him now – and thank God I never married him!'

'So your mum actually did you a good turn, there,' she pointed out with a grin.

'Yes, unintentionally, I suppose she did.'

Poppy looked restively at the door for about the twentieth time. 'Felix is *ages*, isn't he?'

'You're getting just like Siamese twins, joined at the hip! How did the riding lesson go?'

'I don't think he's a natural, but he didn't fall off and he quite liked it, really,' she said, giggling, then her eyes went back to the door and glazed over.

'Felix!'

'*Poppy!*' he replied, in a soppy voice.

They gazed meltingly at each other for a few moments (which is clearly as far as things have progressed), until he came to his senses and kissed us both in a brotherly way on the cheek and said how nice we were looking – which we were, because ever since Southport we've made a bit more of an effort when going out in the evenings.

'I just called in to see Jake,' he said, slightly self-consciously, since this wasn't something he made a habit of. 'That's why I'm late.'

'Ah . . .' I said, 'and I suppose you suggested that he spreads the word about Mann-Drake's party?'

'Well . . . sort of,' he admitted.

'Poppy's just been telling me all about the meeting – that's how I guessed – but I don't want Jake to get into trouble.'

'He won't – I didn't *ask* him to do anything,' Felix said. 'In fact, he said he knew someone at college with millions of Facebook friends, who couldn't keep a secret, and he would have to be careful not to accidentally tell him anything about it.'

'Right,' I said, and though I was still angry over Mann-Drake's attempt to draw my little brother into his orbit (he would have regretted it if he had), I said no more about it.

'Great news about the plague pit, isn't it?' Felix said brightly.

'Yes, wonderful. Grumps told me about it this morning and I don't see how they could build there now, because the whole village would be up in arms.'

'And what with that and the river being prone to flooding in winter at the tennis courts and one edge of the lido field, there's not really a lot you could do with either of them, is there?' he said.

'Perhaps in the end the village will get them back again, one way or another,' Poppy suggested optimistically.

There was no sign of Mrs Snowball tonight, so Molly allowed us to have drinks other than coffee, and it was just another nice evening like we've so often had before ... except that somehow the dynamics of our little trio was subtly changing, so that I was starting to feel sort of ... lonely.

I asked Jake when I got back what he intended to do about Felix's suggestion and he smiled in a really mysterious and annoying way and said I should keep out of it, but that he'd just accidentally pressed 'reply all' when he emailed Kat about the party, so the news had gone to his entire contact list.

Then he warned me that he'd heard weird chanting from the museum and a strange smell of incense was seeping under the adjoining door, so if I'd thought of popping in to see Zillah, right then probably wouldn't be a good moment unless I went all the way round the front of the museum.

However, Grumps' coven had been meeting frequently to counter Mann-Drake's threat, so I was quite used to it by now, even if the idea of a lot of old wrinklies standing hand in hand in a circle next door, starkers and chanting, did gross Jake out.

By the time the Mango Homes people and Mann-Drake arrived at the lido field on Tuesday morning, Hebe had organised a reception committee of placard-wielding villagers, with Felix, Poppy and me among them. She and Raffy awaited them, flanked by a reporter and photographer from the local paper, ready primed.

The placards said things like 'Honour Our Dead!', 'Leave Our Ancestors in Peace!' and 'Sacrilege!'

Mine read 'Grave Concerns!' I was quite pleased with that.

Hebe buttonholed the property developers the moment they got out of their car and, in her terribly clear and carrying voice, told them all about the plague pit and the winter flooding, talking right over the top of all Mann-Drake's attempts to interrupt.

Then Raffy put his oar in and said that the whole village would like the lido field and the bodies of their ancestors left in peace and we all cheered.

After that, it wasn't surprising that the Mango Homes people didn't stay long, because a new estate built on a plague pit was never going to be easy to market, Pustule Place and Bubo Bank not having quite the right ring, especially since the river edge of it would have to be mounted on stilts.

Mann-Drake, however, switched tack and tried sweet-talking his way around everyone but, finding it wasn't working, was eventually driven away too, by a languid and leached young man who was either his PA or acolyte, or possibly a strange hybrid of the two.

Hebe and some of the villagers went on to Merchester to picket the Town Hall, with the reporters in close attendance, but Felix, Poppy and I had to get back to do some work, and Raffy apparently had a big annual church council meeting to go to, because *he* dashed off as well.

The coverage in the local papers on Thursday was wonderful ('A plague on you – Sticklepond wants its dead kept buried!') and was syndicated to a national daily.

There were lots of great photos, including one of Hebe Winter and Raffy ('Sticklepond's ex-pop star vicar!'), and a long shot of the protesters including me and my placard, with all the feathery fronds of my hair blown upright into a Mohican.

The papers had also dug a few stories out about Mann-Drake, hinting at dark deeds and secret societies, and somehow managing to suggest that his house in Devon was burned down by a firebrand-waving mob of locals, but without actually coming out and directly saying so.

There was an interview with local bookseller and anti-quarian Felix Hemmings on the historical importance of the Plague Pit Field, which I knew about, but also, to my surprise, one with novelist Gregory Warlock.

He gave his books and the museum's imminent opening a good plug, and then pointed out the harmless – and frequently benign – effects of magic down the centuries, as opposed to the pernicious nonsense of pseudo-magical mountebanks like Crowley and Mann-Drake. He was also quoted as saying that magic, when properly practised, could happily marry with a Christian way of life, which I can only put down to Raffy's influence. All those visits must be paying off!

Grumps has an amazingly good eye for publicity, though according to Zillah he might have got a trifle carried away by his enthusiasm, and led the reporters to believe that some kind of semi-satanic orgy was to take place at Badger's Bolt on Saturday night . . .

In a moment of compunction I phoned David up early on the Saturday morning to suggest that he cry off Mann-Drake's party, though since I couldn't *really* say why, he just thought I was jealous again. I might as well have saved myself the trouble.

Jake went to Kat's house early in the evening, where they would have a ringside seat, since the side gate faced onto the lane that led to Badger's Bolt.

He phoned when the dinner guests arrived, including David with Mel Christopher, and said several very strange people were already staying at the cottage.

'I'll tell you what happens in the morning,' he said, then rang off, before I could tell him not to leave Kat's parents' house that evening, though they seemed very sensible people.

The village was really quiet for ages after that, until suddenly there seemed to be a huge number of vehicles making their way through the narrow streets. Then later, just as I was falling sleep, I could hear sirens in the distance . . .

Chapter Thirty-one

Party Animals

'When loads of people started to turn up, me and Kat went out for a look,' Jake said when he returned next morning. 'There were cars right up the lane and parked along the road for miles.'

I was glad I hadn't known that the night before, because I would have been worried about him! 'You didn't get too close, did you?'

'No, we just stood back and watched as people burst into the cottage and started partying. Mann-Drake and his guests were in the barn by then, but he must have heard the noise because he came out, saw what was happening, then ran back inside. Then some of the revellers got into the barn the back way and suddenly he and his guests all came running out of the front, half naked. It was the funniest thing! There were reporters and a local TV crew there by then, and they got the full-frontal effect.'

'They were *half naked*?' I repeated.

'Well, they all had thin, wrap-around silk robes on, but it was clear there was nothing underneath, because it was a pretty breezy evening,' he said, with a reminiscent grin.

'Didn't the police try and stop it? I heard sirens.'

'A load of police cars arrived, but that was latish, after we'd gone back to Kat's house. Your friend David and some of his mates rang the doorbell and wanted to come in, but Kat's mum wouldn't let them any further than the driveway, because they were barefoot and in robes and looked as if they were out of their heads on something.'

'How awful! But you can't blame her, can you? What did they do?'

He shrugged. 'There was nothing they could do, except hang about until the police got rid of the gatecrashers, which took quite a while, and then they all went back to the cottage. Most of the cars had gone from the lane this morning, so I presume they got home in the end.'

'So it's all quiet again now?'

'Yes, though the cottage has been well and truly trashed. I saw that policeman, Mike Berry, on my way back this morning and he told me. Mann Drake had to spend the night in a hotel, so let's hope he found some clothes, first.'

The whole village was abuzz with the news and Mann-Drake's party not only made the newspapers, but also got onto local TV – a brief shot of the guests running from the barn, including Mel and David, their thin silk robes clutched about them, eyes wide. The cameraman had rather focused on Mel . . .

Apparently the damage to the interior of the cottage was so bad that the renovations were all to do again. It was to be hoped that Mann-Drake's house and contents insurance covered damage by uninvited and mainly off-their-heads visitors, though it didn't sound as if his guests were in a much better state.

Oh, David, I thought, what *have* you been up to?

I met Felix and Poppy in the pub right after the Parish Council met to discuss it.

'I feel a bit deafened,' Poppy said, sinking into her seat with a sigh of relief. 'The meeting was in the vestry because the drain problems were being fixed at the village hall, and Mr Lees played fugues on the organ really loudly all the way through!'

'That up-tempo version of "The Girl from Ipanema" as we were leaving was a bit of a turn-up for the books, though,' Felix said.

'He does seem to be lightening up sometimes,' Poppy agreed. 'Look at the Beatles medley he played after the protest meeting in the village hall! It must be Raffy's influence.'

'Did you see the TV coverage of Mann-Drake's party?' I asked.

'Or *un*-coverage, in Mel Christopher's case,' Felix said with an unbecoming smirk, and I gave him a look.

'Mike said he had to wait for reinforcements before trying to get rid of the gatecrashers and it was only much later, when the guests could get back into the house, that they found several items including their wallets, were missing.'

'Yes, I heard a bit through Jake. He and Kat watched most of it happening and David and Mel tried to take refuge at Kat's parents' house, only her mother didn't like the look of them and wouldn't let them in.'

'I'm not surprised,' said Poppy. 'I heard the cottage was such a mess that Mr Mann-Drake and his chums had to spend the night in a hotel, and they left for London this morning.'

'Let's hope he doesn't come back,' I said.

'That's what Hebe Winter said. She hoped his failure to extort money from the householders on the Green or make a killing from property developers, combined with having his home wrecked, would give him a distaste for Sticklepond.'

'I should think it might well!'

'She's got one or two more tricks up her sleeve if he comes back,' Felix said. 'The water supply to Badger's Bolt is from a spring and the pressure isn't good, but it used to be even worse until the last owner illegally diverted a stream into it. Now the Winters have discovered the original plans for a Victorian water garden on the estate just where the spring that feeds that stream surfaces and have decided to restore it, so I'm afraid the supply at Badger's Bolt will soon be a trickle again.'

'When Mann-Drake called in at the cottage to look at the damage in daylight before he went back to London, Mr Ormerod – the farmer next door, whose son was invited to the party – had a slight accident with his slurry spreader and the whole front of the cottage was sprayed with it,' Poppy said.

'You can't blame him for being mad,' Felix said, grinning. 'Several fences were broken down last night too, and some cattle got out onto the road.'

'What happened about the slurry?' I asked.

'Sluiced off with a water tanker later,' he said. 'But the smell lingers: muck sticks!'

Grumps was collected for the next Re-enactment Society meeting by Laurence Yatton and his sister, Effie, and brought back by Hebe Winter herself, in her white Mini.

I can't imagine how she can get behind the steering wheel in a farthingale, unless perhaps she has a hooped petticoat that she slips on once she arrives. But it would be *lèse-majesté* to enquire.

Grumps was in very good humour and seemed quite convinced that Mann-Drake was well on the way to being repelled, though he put that down almost entirely to the efforts of himself and his coven.

When you live with someone with a sense of humour like Jake's, you wake up on April Fool's day with the certain knowledge that at some point he will fool, surprise or amaze you – or even frighten you half to death.

This year he'd outdone himself, because when I opened my eyes there was the most enormous spider sitting on the pillow by my cheek. Being still half awake, I gave a blood-curdling yell and leaped out of bed.

The scream didn't wake Jake up but *I* did, by shaking him ruthlessly. 'How could you do that? I nearly died when I saw that huge spider!'

'Realistic, isn't it?' he said, with a sleepy grin.

'Very – but did you have to put it on my *pillow*? I could have had a heart attack.'

'I didn't put it on your pillow,' he said, looking at me as if I was mad.

'Yes you did!'

'You've been having a nightmare – mine's in the bath.'

I wasn't sure I believed him, but when I checked there *was* a huge rubber spider sitting in the bath, so I made him get up and look in my bedroom, but of course by then there was no sign of the first one.

He was just saying, 'There you are, I told you you imagined it,' when out it sidled from a fold of duvet. It was big enough to saddle.

Of course I screamed again and ran out, but when Jake asked me a minute later to open the bathroom window I did, then watched from a safe distance as he tossed the invader out.

'I don't know how you can touch them with your bare hands,' I said with a shudder. 'Now, remove the one from the bath, too!'

He was hoping to catch Kat out with it later, and I only hoped she gave him hell when he did.

Easter was rushing towards us – and so was the opening day of the museum. The Easter period is generally a time of big celebrations with Grumps anyway, because he says it's really all about the Saxon fertility goddess, Eostre, and that's where the rabbits and eggs come in, too. One of the pamphlets he'd written for the museum dealt with the subject and of course it formed part of the display showing the overlap of Christian and pagan festivals.

That afternoon, just as I was about to go through into the museum to help Grumps, David knocked at the cottage door, all repentant and shame-faced.

'Hello, Chloe. Can I come in?' he asked humbly. 'I've come to say I'm sorry I didn't listen to your advice about the party, and made such a fool of myself.'

He looked so miserable that I had to let him in, though I was finding it hard to keep my face straight, after all that media coverage.

'That picture of you running out of the barn with Mel made most of the dailies as well as the local paper and TV. It must have been a quiet night for other stories,' I commiserated.

'You can't imagine how hideously embarrassing it's been – and still is, Chloe! I don't know how . . . I mean, I'm not *excusing* anything, but I'm *positive* there was something in the drink we had after dinner, before we went to the barn for the ceremony. Then Mann-Drake passed another large cup of something round and we were all supposed to drink from it in turn. We shared one of those Far Eastern pipe things, too.'

'Like a hubble-bubble?' I said helpfully.

'My memories of what happened immediately after that are a bit hazy, but by the time the gatecrashers arrived, things were getting a bit . . .' He petered out, flushing.

'Uninhibited?' I suggested.

'Well, yes, I suppose so,' he admitted. 'But as soon as I got out in the cold air, my head cleared and I felt stupid without my clothes. *Mel* persuaded me to put the robe on,' he added resentfully, 'and then when we could finally get back in the cottage, my wallet had vanished and all our clothes had been piled up in the middle of one room and . . . rendered unwearable.'

'You mean they *peed* on them?' I asked incredulously, not having heard about that.

'We needn't go into it,' he said hastily. 'My car keys were still there, fortunately, so we could get home. It's lucky for me that Mel came out much clearer in the pictures than I did. They seemed to focus on her.'

'Didn't they just!'

'Only a handful of people have recognised me – but that's enough! Rumours have got about and people are talking.'

'It'll all die down soon,' I said soothingly. 'If anyone mentions it, deny it's you.'

'I already have. But I just wanted to ask you to forgive me for being so stupid and to tell you that I've learned my lesson. I'm obviously running with the wrong crowd these days and if I'd listened to you, none of this would have happened.'

'But of course I forgive you – there's nothing to forgive,' I said lightly. 'And I'm sure you'll make it up with Mel too.'

'I don't think so,' he said shortly, so clearly she had spectacularly fallen out of favour, though I wouldn't bet on her not being able to win him back round, if she wanted to.

Then he smiled at me, kissed my cheek and said, 'You're kinder and more generous than I deserve – and I know you didn't really mean it about us seeing less of each other, it was just because I was being stupid with Mel. But now—'

I heard the door to the museum open behind me and then Raffy called tentatively, 'Chloe, are you there? Your grandfather wants to know—'

He broke off on seeing David, and the two men eyed each other. Feeling glad of the interruption, I said, 'Have you met? David Billinge, Raffy Sinclair, our new vicar. Now, if you'll excuse me, David, I promised to help Grumps in the museum this afternoon.'

'Yes, of course, and – we're friends again, aren't we?' he asked.

'Of course,' I said, ushering him out and closing the door with a sigh of relief.

'Sorry to interrupt,' Raffy apologised, then added darkly, 'and I wish it was as easy for you to forgive *me*.'

'I *have* forgiven you – I *told* you so,' I insisted, but he was so deep in his guilt trip that I could see he still didn't believe me and thought I was just being kind. 'Did Grumps send you to fetch me? And what are you doing here? Poppy said vicars are run off their feet at this time of year!'

'We are, but your grandfather felt a sudden urgent need to discuss an aspect of the pagan/Christian significance of Easter, though I can't stay much longer.'

'Had any luck with the donkey for the Palm Sunday

procession?' I asked as we joined Grumps in the museum, and Raffy grinned suddenly, more like his old self.

'Apparently the donkey isn't compulsory. I hope you'll all come and join in the procession. I'm going to say special prayers over the plague pit.'

'Sounds like fun,' Grumps said, and I wasn't sure if he was serious or not. I never am.

Raffy didn't stay much longer but it was clear that I was going to have to take some positive action to show him that I really do forgive him, I'm not just saying it, or he's going to be wallowing in guilt for ever.

So after dinner, while Jake was upstairs in his room playing music too loud and allegedly doing coursework with Kat, I got out the two halves of the large angel I'd made with the leftover chocolate from the taste test, the one with the added va-va-voom.

I wrote a message on a slip of paper, put it inside and stuck the angel together with a little melted chocolate. It wasn't tempered, but then, I didn't expect the angel to stay in one piece long enough to start showing a white line round the join.

Then I called up the stairs to Jake and Kat that I was going out and not to do anything they shouldn't. (Why *did* I keep saying these pointless things?) I wasn't sure that they heard over the music, but they were unlikely to miss me anyway. I put on my coat and set off for the vicarage.

I intended leaving my angel of peace, in its special gold box, on Raffy's doorstep. Ringing the front doorbell and running away seemed like the best plan, then he could digest both the chocolate and the message on his own.

Chapter Thirty-two

Delivering Angels

I went the front way to the vicarage, so I could check that there was no sign of Raffy before I nipped up the drive and left the angel in the porch.

Unfortunately Maria Minchin must have spotted me, because she bounced out of the front door just as I'd put down the box and rung the bell, ready to dash away. She's a big woman and it didn't reassure me that she was brandishing a rolling pin. I had to remind myself that it was her brother who had murdered someone, not her.

'Just as I thought!' she declared. 'What is it *this* time? A cake? Goulash? Sausage rolls? Anyone would think I'd starved the last vicar, but let me tell you, he died of old age and not my cooking!'

'No, it's not . . . I haven't . . .' I stammered, taken aback by this onslaught.

And then Raffy's deep voice, behind her, said, 'What is it, Maria?'

'Another damned fast-food delivery and I'll not have it

in *my* kitchen!' She pushed past him and then the door to the kitchen wing closed with a reverberating slam.

'Chloe?' Raffy said, surprised to find me on his doorstep. Then his eyes dropped to the gold box at his feet.

'It's something for you, and I was just going to leave it when Maria got the wrong idea.'

'So I heard.' He picked up the box. 'Is it chocolate?'

'Yes. You gave me an angel, so I thought I'd return the compliment and I happened to have a large one already moulded, so . . .' I shrugged, and would have turned away except he reached out a long arm and more or less dragged me in, shutting the door behind us.

'No, you don't,' he said, examining me curiously in the hall light. He was not looking particularly vicarish tonight, since he was wearing jeans and a plain sweatshirt . . . In fact, he looked much more like the old, once-familiar Raffy, from dishevelled dark curls to bare feet in heelless Moroccan leather slippers, which was quite disconcerting.

He drew me through another door into a small, warm room at the back of the house, which seemed to be a combination of den, library and music room. A guitar leaned against a bookshelf and there was a piano in one alcove with a heap of handwritten music cast down on top of it.

'Take your coat off,' he said absently, opening the gold box and looking down at the dark chocolate angel inside.

'It's a peace offering,' I said, but I didn't take my coat off since I wasn't stopping.

'But why? *I'm* the one who needs to make peace, not you.'

'Yes, well, when you've quite finished enjoying the little self-flagellation trip you're on, you might like to read the message inside,' I suggested. 'I'll leave you to it.'

'No, wait!' he said as I turned to go. 'Look, I'm sorry—'

'So you keep saying!'

He ran both hands through his hair distractedly, pushing it back off his face.

'Look, *please*, Chloe, sit down while I read my message: all right?'

'I suppose so.' I took my coat off and sat reluctantly right on the edge of the sofa, which was low and squishy, with a kelim cover.

'It seems a pity to break this lovely angel,' Raffy said, but he did, then read the message inside aloud, his face inscrutable.

'"Get over yourself, you prat! We were both young and stupid and it didn't help that Rachel was a lying cow. We're two entirely different people now, so let's see if we can manage to be friends – OK?"'

He looked up and his long, mobile mouth twitched at the corners. 'That's not exactly poetic, but I think I've got the message,' he said and then came to sit down next to me.

'Before we bury the subject for ever, can I just say that I always meant to go back for you? I truly loved you,' he said. 'I should have believed in you, whatever Rachel said.'

'And I should have believed in you too. But I did want the baby, despite everything.'

'Oh, darling!' he said softly, pulling me into a warm, wordless hug, and I cried into his shoulder for ages, while he held me. I suppose I'd bottled that particular grief up for so many years, it was bound to come out sooner or later.

After a bit, feeling better, I sat up and mopped my face. 'I think we need to eat the angel, now,' I said, reaching for the box. 'It will make us both feel *much* better.'

I have a strong belief in the therapeutic power of good chocolate.

'Will it?' he said doubtfully, but he still ate the piece I passed to him and then another. We munched in a cathartic and companionable silence.

'You make *great* chocolate,' he said after a while. 'I've been trying to get up the nerve to ask you to make some for me, for ages.'

'You want some Chocolate Wishes?'

'Not exactly Wishes. Poppy told me you made Easter eggs for Jake when he was little, with messages inside.'

'Yes, it gave me the idea for the Chocolate Wishes in the first place.'

'Wasn't celebrating Easter a bit anti-pagan?'

'I never said *I* was a pagan – I'm nothing at all, though having never been christened and Grumps being a warlock, I'm probably barred from the Church for ever.'

'Oh, I don't think so.'

'Anyway, there's nothing much Christian about choc-olate eggs, is there? Especially if you listen to Grumps!'

'Yes, he did rather rub my nose in the whole Saxon goddess of fertility stuff this afternoon, though it was just a coincidence that the Christian Easter fell at the same time of year as the Eostre festival. But about Easter eggs . . .'

'Oh, I don't make them now Jake's grown up, or only a few big ones filled with truffles for my nearest and dearest. It makes a change from hearts and angels.'

'Yes, this angel obsession of yours seems a bit out of keeping with your upbringing, somehow, Chloe.'

'Actually, if you read Grumps' history of paganism, they do sort of tie in together. Anyway, I've got a guardian angel, so I know they exist.'

That confession sort of slipped out and surprised me: it wasn't the sort of thing I usually talked about, because people would think I was as mad as a box of frogs.

'Have you?' Raffy said, looking interested rather than amazed. 'So have I! Mine first appeared to me one night when I was on tour with the band and at a low ebb. He scared the shit out of me.'

'*He* did?'

'Yes, he seems to be male.'

'Mine's sort of female . . . but not scary.'

'I don't suppose you'd done anything to be scared about, like I had. His message was to clean my act up, or else. I'd grown out of the rock-and-roll lifestyle bit by then anyway, so I did, but life seemed hollow, somehow – a bit like your Chocolate Wishes, only with no message inside.'

'You said that was the *first* time you saw him?' I asked curiously.

'Yes, he came back, much later. I'd seen sense and done what he'd told me by then . . . but the other three band members didn't. You remember Nick?'

'The tall, fair one, played the bass guitar?'

'Yes. He died of a drugs overdose, leaving a young family. And then, the night after his funeral, the angel turned up again and . . . well, this time it was my Road to Damascus moment. I saw what I needed to do, what I had to give – and then the right path just opened out in front of me: the one leading to ordination.'

'I bet that was a popular decision with the rest of the band!'

'You'd be surprised,' he said soberly. 'Nick's death was a real wake-up call, and by then they were all marrying, settling down and having families. Life on the road is disruptive.'

He looked at me, eyes serious. 'But we've gone a long way from what I meant to ask you, which was if you would make me some chocolate eggs with special messages inside them, so I can have an Easter egg hunt in the churchyard early on Easter Sunday morning?'

'It isn't long until Easter,' I objected.

'I'll even pay for extra moulds, if you need them.'

'I've got moulds . . . though I'd need more if you wanted a lot of eggs.'

His turquoise eyes locked with mine. 'Please, to show you've really forgiven me in your heart, will you do this for me?'

'I suppose I *could*,' I conceded. 'And they had better be milk chocolate because most of the children won't be used to the dark stuff.'

'Whatever you think,' he said, smiling warmly at me.

'I'll wrap them in coloured foil, but if it rains they'll have to go into little cellophane bags and I'd have to charge you extra for those.'

'Fine. I'll print out the messages to go inside and bring them over at some point. I'm going to make some Easter rabbit footprints here and there on the flowerbeds that morning too, for the children to find.'

'Won't you need a rabbit for that?'

'Only a rabbit's foot, and Effie Yatton says I can borrow her lucky kilt pin if I get desperate.'

'But you might get it dirty!'

'Yes, I'm hoping to find an alternative. And, Chloe, since you are making the eggs for the hunt, I would love it if you also helped me to hide them too, early on Easter Day.'

'What, *me*? I've never even been in the churchyard!'

'Haven't you? Even just from a historical perspective the church is well worth visiting and the churchyard is like a potted history of the local families, with some very interesting inscriptions.'

'Yes,' Jake said.'

'There are several lovely angel monuments – you really should see them. And you said yourself that you're not a believer in anything in particular, so there's no reason why you shouldn't go into the church, is there?'

'Granny used to go to services occasionally, but I always felt there was too much of Grumps' influence in me, and if I even went in, then the tower would crumble, or the windows implode, or something.'

He laughed. 'I don't think much of your grandfather's influence *has* rubbed off on you – and *I'm* the one things fell on, angels and all.'

I flushed guiltily, even though I didn't see how Grumps could have pulled any of those incidents off. 'Zillah went to your first church service, didn't she? She isn't in Grumps' coven, though she used to take flasks of hot tea when they met in the open air, just like Granny did, to thaw them all out afterwards.'

'Really?' Raffy looked fascinated.

'Grumps is a naturist, not up to anything kinky – he just thinks you can get closer to the essential powers skyclad. Granny never minded, though she put her foot down when he wanted to initiate Mum, and later me, into the coven, and I did the same for Jake. Luckily he's just fascinated and interested in magic from a scholarly viewpoint – he wants to do a history degree.'

'So am I, and in the way religions sort of weave together – or the good elements do. It's only man who reinterprets any of the religious teachings to cause harm or misery to others.'

'Aren't we suddenly swimming in deep waters?' I asked.

'Not really, I'm just trying to prove that there's no reason why you shouldn't help me with the Easter egg hunt.' He gave me a serious look. 'Unless, of course, you really hate the idea and if so, I'll stop badgering you.'

'You aren't badgering me, but I'm sure some of your myriad new fans among the parishioners would fall over themselves to help.'

'I think my novelty's wearing off, though they have all been very kind – *too* kind, some of them. You saw how Maria feels about all the food people keep giving me. She thinks it's a reflection on her cooking skills.'

'How *is* her cooking?'

'Fairly dreadful, but it usually falls just this side of edible. I'm wondering if there's a tactful way of sending her on a cookery course.'

'Poppy said the congregation is still a lot larger than it used to be with Mr Harris, though nowhere near the crowds you first pulled.'

'It'll be down even more when they realise how boring I really am, but not as far as it was before, I hope.'

'*You'd* stop attending if every service opened and closed with an organ fugue,' I said. 'Poppy told me all about Mr Lee, and sometimes even I can hear him, if the wind is in the right direction.'

He laughed. 'Oh, he's great! I told him I thought fugues were fine for when everyone is arriving – providing it isn't a wedding – but I thought we needed to lighten up when they were on the way out again, and he took it on board. It helped that he used to play the organ at Blackpool Tower ballroom at one time.'

'I didn't know that! But Miss Winter will probably go

with that, so long as you don't play the guitar and get people to clap. She nearly had Mr Merryman run out of the village on a hurdle for doing that.'

'I don't play the guitar in public, only here, when I'm writing music – I still write songs for other people.'

For I moment I thought bitterly that that had been the story of my life since we parted, listening to songs he'd written for other people. Then I caught myself up: no more looking back.

'If I do the Easter eggs, you have to do something for me,' I said, picking out the last shards of chocolate from the box and handing him the angel's feet, while popping a wing tip in my own mouth.

'What's that?'

'Come to the Falling Star with me and Poppy and Felix tomorrow,' I said.

'What time do you call this?' Jake demanded when I went home, striking a pose like an irate Victorian papa and curling an imaginary moustache. 'I took Kat home ages ago. We ate all the cheese, is that OK?'

'Yes, I'll get some more tomorrow. And I was just delivering an angel. To the vicar.'

'I would have thought he'd already have a monopoly on those,' he said, but he looked strangely thoughtful.

Chapter Thirty-three

Candy-Coated

That night I lay awake for ages turning over what had happened in my mind, but when I finally fell asleep it was to dream, comfortingly, of angels. I woke up with a strong yearning to see the ones in the churchyard and the stained-glass window – and really, I didn't see why I shouldn't. Raffy was quite right!

I mean, just because Grumps had damned himself to the fiery pits of hell, assuming the God crowd *had* got it right, it didn't necessarily follow that his entire family was doomed to follow him there, did it?

The cottage was quiet, since Jake had left that morning for the Lake District with Kat's family, who were keen walkers. I couldn't exactly imagine Kat and Jake stomping around the lakes in their big boots, but I'd packed him off with lots of unwanted advice and loads of pocket money. Grumps probably had the same idea, but the advice would be different. Jake would be back in time for the museum's opening.

By mid-afternoon I'd finished making the first batch of

chocolate eggs (I'd already ordered extra moulds to be express delivered tomorrow) and both kinds of Wishes.

I was still candy-coated when I pulled on a warm jacket over my work clothes and walked up the High Street to the churchyard, which has a soft buff sandstone wall with flowering plants growing out of the crevices, and a weathered lich-gate.

Inside, it looked all neat and mown, with ancient graves mingling with more recent ones, and I saw what Raffy had meant about angels: even from the gate I could see the one that had almost fallen on him, a severe, asexual creature with firmly folded wings, holding a book. Its nose was freshly chipped but it had been fixed to its pedestal again.

When I got further in I found one or two smaller angels and I particularly liked a white marble one that seemed to be either taking off or landing in a positive whirlwind of draperies, a bit like the carving Raffy had given me. That was a Winter grave. There were, unsurprisingly, a lot of those.

It was very peaceful, with no one else around at all, so I thought I would just pop my head in the church to see if I could spot the famous Heaven and Hell window that Jake had said was over the altar.

The old door was enormous, with a heavy iron latch, and inside the smell was curiously but pleasantly compounded of flowers, lavender polish and old books, the latter explained by the wooden shelves of prayer books next to me.

It had been quiet outside, but it was totally silent in there, though no drastic events happened at the intrusion of an infidel – no bolts of lightning struck me, nothing crumbled. Instead, it was somehow warm and safe, and I suddenly had that rare but uplifting feeling of being folded in downy wings . . .

327

I drew closer to the window over the altar and became lost in the bright, fragmented, primary colours. There was so much going on – wistful angels at the top and merry little devils below, who were feeding people to monsters, flames or other damnations, a bit like a backlit Bosch painting.

I thought of Raffy, praying in here after I'd told him about the lost baby, and wondered whether he had found comfort . . .

When I finally emerged, the light outside felt very bright and harsh. Raffy was sitting waiting for me on a table tomb, which seemed a little irreverent.

'Hello, Chloe. I saw you go in, but I didn't want to disturb you. I'm so glad you came!'

'I wanted to see the angels and the window. You piqued my curiosity.'

'For whatever reason, you're always welcome here – and now you can see that there're lots of good places to hide the Easter eggs too! You *are* going to come and help me, aren't you?'

'Yes, all right,' I agreed. 'I've started making them already.'

'Good. Well, time to go and say evening prayers,' he said, getting up, then paused and added questioningly, 'You could come in, if you wanted to?'

I backed away slightly. 'No, thanks.'

'OK, let's not rush things,' he said with a smile. 'You just go in whenever you want a quiet minute. All Angels welcomes everyone, for whatever reason.'

'Yes, that's what I felt,' I agreed, then added lightly, 'But then, so does the Falling Star! See you there later.'

On the way home I popped in to tell Felix that I'd persuaded Raffy to join us at the pub, and found Mags, his mother, reclining on the leather settee in the front room of the shop like an abandoned mannequin, all angular limbs.

'Sweetie!' she said, in her usual casually friendly way. 'I haven't seen you for ages. Great hairstyle! I saw Poppy too the other day and barely recognised her.'

'We had makeovers,' I explained.

'It was worth every penny,' she said earnestly, then hoisted herself back onto her four-inch stilettos. 'I'm afraid I'll have to go. Thanks for the coffee, Felix darling.'

She looked pretty good, considering she was a lot nearer sixty than fifty, just like Janey and my mother. Goodness knew what Lou looked like by then: probably much the same – well preserved, if not pickled.

On impulse I said casually, 'Give my regards to Lou when you next ring her.'

'OK, I—' She stopped abruptly and stared at me aghast through blue-fringed eyes.

'Just as I thought! She's in Goa, isn't she?' I demanded.

Mags looked suddenly a little frightened. 'I can't say – you'd need to ask your grandfather about that.'

Then she picked up her huge woven leather bag and shot out into the street.

'Grumps *knows*?' I said slowly, staring at Felix.

'Sounds like it,' he agreed. 'Mags has always been nervous of him.'

'Well *I'm* not, and I'm going back to ask him where Lou is, right now!'

'And when I did, he admitted he'd known where she was for the last two years!' I told the others, including Raffy, at the pub that evening.

'She left Jamaica after a few months, on someone's yacht,

and eventually washed up in Goa, where she's running a bar with another man she's picked up. She contacted Grumps a couple of years ago, and he's paying her an allowance on the understanding she doesn't come back or contact me. He said he thought we were all much happier without her.'

We were all sitting round our usual small table in the window, sipping coffee. Mrs Snowball was in charge and had insisted: the machine's novelty was proving surprisingly long lasting.

She seemed to have taken one of her fancies to Raffy, even though he was, spiritually speaking, playing for the other team.

'That's true, but even so, he might have told you,' Poppy said sympathetically. 'He shouldn't just have let you carry on wondering.'

'The worst thing is, he *did* tell Jake, when he turned eighteen, because he was a man! How chauvinistic is that? But he swore him to silence first, so he couldn't pass the news on to me.'

'But look on the bright side,' said Felix. 'The mystery is cleared up, but she can't come back and mess up your life again, even if she wants to, because your grandfather holds the purse strings.'

'I don't think she wants to, and if she did she'd have to be repatriated, I think, because she hasn't got a passport any more. She left hers on the cruise ship with Mags, and it's expired.'

'At least you know now that *she* hasn't expired,' pointed out Felix, who was clearly in male Pollyanna mode.

'Perhaps, when you've got used to the idea, you could go out there and see her?' suggested Raffy.

'I don't *want* to see her, specially since I've had *another* bombshell tonight: Chas had the second DNA test back, and Carr Blackstock *is* my biological father.'

I'd quite forgotten that Raffy knew nothing about all that, but Poppy, seeing his blank expression, quickly explained the situation to him.

'And Felix and I thought we could see a likeness to photographs of this actor. We just didn't really want to say so when Chloe hoped so much it would be Chas.'

'Your mother did that?' Raffy asked, staring at me. 'Blackmailed two men into paying maintenance?'

'Yes, and in a way it's a relief to know it *is* actually one of those two, because she might have been lying about that as well, which would have thrown the field *wide* open, and I might never have found out.'

'I know one of Carr Blackstock's daughters,' Raffy said. 'Her husband's in the music business.' He looked at me consideringly. 'Come to think of it, your eyes are the same colour as hers and there is a slight resemblance, though the Blackstock girls are all tall – comes from their mother's side of the family.'

'She's from a famous acting dynasty, isn't she?' I said. 'I looked them up. But I'm not about to try and claim him as my father or anything, I just needed to know who he was.'

'Of course,' Raffy agreed. 'That's perfectly natural.'

'Chas – this is Chas Wilde, the man I thought was my father – says Carr Blackstock has agreed to meet me, only I'm not sure if I want to, because apparently he still half suspects I'm going to be wearing a secret microphone and sell the details to a newspaper, or something!'

'He's not that famous, is he?' said Felix. 'I'd barely heard of him before all this.'

331

'I think you should meet him, just the once,' Poppy said.

'Poppy's probably right and – well, would you like *me* to arrange it?' Raffy suggested. 'I could be the intermediary and even stay with you during the meeting, if you wanted me to. I just thought he might find the presence of a vicar reassuring.'

'That seems like a good idea,' Felix said.

'Oh, would you?' I said gratefully. 'He gave Chas his email address. That's the only contact I have for him.'

'If you let me have it, I'll approach him tactfully. I still haven't sold my flat in Notting Hill, so we could use that as neutral territory for the meeting. It's partly furnished with the stuff that I didn't think would fit in the vicarage and I can drive you down there. In fact, you could stay there overnight and we'll come back next morning. I'll go and stay with a friend nearby.'

'But I know you're so busy at the moment,' I protested, remembering what Poppy had said.

'If I can set it up for early next week, I'll be able to do it. We can leave right after morning prayers and then perhaps Mike will say the evening ones, if he's free, or people can just have private prayer if not. We'll be back next day. But if it's not early next week, then it will have to be after Easter, I'm afraid.'

'Thank you, that would make everything very much easier,' I said, because I found I *did* want to see the man who had so carelessly fathered me, from sheer curiosity if for no other reason, even if I was also very nervous about it.

Raffy walked me back home and came in for long enough to get Carr Blackstock's email address. I gave him a jar of my chocolate and ginger spread too, since I'd made enough for Jake as well as Zillah, forgetting he was going to be away. It doesn't keep that long.

I only hope Maria Minchin doesn't come after me with a steak tenderiser, but I don't really think murder runs in families, and anyway, Salford's was a *crime passionnel*, not a spat over a jar of ganache.

Raffy came back again next day – or rather, he visited Grumps and then Zillah let him through the museum door into the cottage.

'Gentleman caller!' she announced, just like last time.

'Hi,' I said from the desk, where I was just finishing typing up Grumps' latest chapter of *Satan's Child*. Unless he suddenly went off at a tangent again, tomorrow's chapter should be the last.

I rattled off the final sentence and pressed save, then swivelled round. 'Finished! Come through to the sitting room. Tea? Coffee? Hot chocolate?'

'I didn't want to disturb you, if you're busy.'

'I'll have to start packing chocolate orders in a minute, but I would have had a drink and ten minutes first, anyway. So, what's it to be?'

'Not tea – I've had enough of that doing my visits. It's usually either that or very weak instant coffee.'

'It was pretty keen of you to decide to visit everyone in the parish. I mean, most of them don't go to church at all, and those who do probably go to a different one.'

'You'd be surprised how welcoming most of them are, though. I just want to meet them all and say I'm there for them, no matter what denomination they are, and also that they are welcome to join me at evening prayers, if they want to.'

'And do they?'

'Quite a few drift in and sit for a while. Perhaps they find a moment's peace after a busy day.'

'Mmm . . .' I was brewing up hot chocolate, while thinking that I still found it hard to replace the old Raffy with the new one. He may have had a Damascene conversion, but I hadn't. Sometimes I managed to get one transparency on top of the other, but then they would suddenly slide apart again.

'You know, for years I thought you were a cheap blended forastero chocolate, but then I started to think maybe you were a reasonable criollo, after all.'

'I'll take that as a compliment,' he said with a grin. That smile and the sparkling eyes must have been laying waste to the hearts of his female parishioners.

He'd come to tell me that he'd emailed Carr Blackstock on my behalf and already had a reply. We were to have our meeting at Raffy's Notting Hill flat after lunch on Tuesday!

'My name obviously didn't mean anything to him, but he seemed reassured that your vicar would vouch for you having no intention of trying to profit from the relationship.'

'Thank you for organising that,' I said gratefully.

'We'll set out early in the morning, right after prayers, if that's OK? I've already spoken to Mike and he's free to go in that evening, and Mr Lees will make sure the church is unlocked in the morning and locked at night, as usual. I'll leave Arlo with the Minchins, because he's really taken to Salford. He's taken to you too – he tries to drag me in here every time we pass.'

'I expect it's the smell of the chocolate, though it isn't good for dogs.' I paused. 'It really *is* kind of you to set all

334

this up and go with me to London. I feel much braver knowing you'll be there, because Carr Blackstock doesn't sound terribly friendly.'

'It's the least I can do – and don't worry,' he said reassuringly, 'I'll look after you.'

I finally told Zillah about the letters I'd found, and my father turning out to be someone other than Chas, and she was not in the least surprised. I expect she'll tell all to Grumps too, which will save me having to do it.

'I always knew it wasn't Chas Wilde,' she said.

'I only wish it was,' I replied, and then when I explained about Raffy arranging the meeting and mediating, she insisted on reading my cards again. They looked complicated, but she read them quickly, while I was still trying to figure the meaning out upside down, then whipped the pack back together.

'Just as I thought,' she said darkly, but then infuriatingly refused to explain.

Felix and Poppy would probably barely register my absence. They kept drifting together like two magnetic ladybirds, but without seeming to get any further. What kind of push would it take actually to propel them into each other's arms?

Perhaps, I thought I should get Raffy, in his capacity as vicar, to ask Felix if his intentions towards Poppy are honourable.

Practically the whole village turned out for the Palm Sunday walk around the boundaries, brought together by a spirit of solidarity and, in my case, gratitude to Raffy and a desire to distract myself from worrying about Tuesday's meeting.

The local press and TV station were out in force to cover the blessing of the Plague Pit Field, which Raffy performed very movingly, speaking with a sincerity you couldn't mistake, while also looking ravishingly handsome with the wind catching his black hair and flipping his white surplice about.

I reckoned I was slowly getting used to this new, improved Raffy . . .

Chapter Thirty-four

Melting Moments

What do you wear for travelling down to London with your ordained ex-rock star former lover, in order to meet a father you only just found out about?

A minor point, perhaps, but I wasted a lot of time on it, and then decided it didn't matter after all. Jeans would do, and a favourite, flattering top for confidence, worn with heeled boots so I didn't look quite so insignificant.

Raffy, as befitting his role, wore one of his vicar T-shirts with black jeans. His long, black coat was slung in the back with the overnight bags and a small carton of milk, coffee, tea and biscuits, which *he* had thought of, not me.

'Supplies,' he explained, as we headed down the motorway. 'Someone goes in to clean the flat and I told them to switch the fridge on. We'll stop for sandwiches or something on the way down, then we could have dinner out this evening before I go off to my friend's place.'

But I was so nervous I hadn't eaten any breakfast and my throat closed up when I tried to eat lunch, though I did drink several cups of tea. My hands felt cold and clammy and my heart kept racing. I really hadn't expected to feel like this!

Raffy's flat was nice, on the first floor and very light, with funny little wrought-iron balconies outside the long windows. He said he remained undecided whether to sell it or let it out.

The sitting room was still furnished, and the spare room where I dumped my bag. I smartened myself up a bit while Raffy made tea and opened a packet of biscuits, and I managed to eat one or two of those, though they tasted like sawdust in my dry mouth.

The clock was ticking towards the hour . . . and then the bell rang.

'This is it,' Raffy said. 'You stay here and I'll go and let him in. Remember, if you want me to leave you both alone at any point, just say, OK?'

'OK,' I echoed hollowly.

I expect Raffy's appearance surprised Carr Blackstock, even if he didn't recognise who he was, but his manner and the dog collar must have reassured him because I could hear the low sound of their voices, then the unfamiliar light tenor one said impatiently, 'Very well!' and in they came.

Carr Blackstock was a lot smaller in real life than I had thought, but conversely had a lot more presence, even if he was currently wearing the defensive air of the found-out villain of the piece.

For a long moment we just stood and took stock of each other. He was a well-preserved man of about sixty, at a guess, with handsomely greying locks, the same unusually light grey eyes as mine and, it has to be admitted, the same pointed, elfin ears.

'Would you like me to leave you alone?' offered Raffy tactfully. 'I could make some tea, perhaps?'

'No, don't – I'd much rather you stayed,' I said, quickly linking my arm in his to physically keep him there at my side.

'I, too, would prefer it if you stayed,' my newly discovered and evidently extremely reluctant father said, looking at me with a kind of chilly distaste. 'I'm not sure quite what etiquette demands we say on these occasions . . . er, Chloe, since I suspected I was being bled dry all these years for a child that wasn't mine, only to find that I was wrong, after all. It has all been quite a shock.'

'It was an even greater shock to me when I found out that Chas Wilde wasn't my father,' I told him, 'because I'm fond of him. In fact, when I discovered it was you instead, it wasn't just a shock, it was a *huge* disappointment!'

He didn't seem interested in how I was feeling. 'My chief concern, as it has always been, is that my wife and daughters don't hear about this.' He began to pace up and down, as if he was about to give birth to a Shakespearian monologue. 'But Chas Wilde and your vicar here both assure me that you don't want anything from me, either money or recognition?'

Raffy put his hand over mine, where it lay on his arm, and squeezed it reassuringly.

'No,' I said steadily, 'I have a very good business of my own and a loving family. I certainly don't want to upset your apple cart, just because my mother caught you in a weak moment and I was the result.'

'We were staying in the same hotel one night,' he explained abruptly. 'We met in the bar and I'd had a drink or two – it was just one of those things.'

'That's pretty much how I thought it must have been.'

'So, what *do* you want?' he demanded testily.

'Nothing!' I replied, surprised. 'Chas said *you* wanted this meeting!'

'He told me that *you* wanted to see *me*!'

'Chas has clearly engineered this meeting with the best of intentions, trying to bring you two together,' Raffy said.

'Well, if you don't want anything except to satisfy your curiosity, then the whole thing seems pointless,' Carr Blackstock said coldly. 'You didn't expect me to have any fatherly feelings for you, at this late stage, I suppose?'

'No, certainly not. In fact, I wish I could pay back the money you gave my mother!'

'Since you turned out to be my mistake, I suppose it was right that I should pay for it, after all,' he said with a shrug.

'Then look on the bright side: at least you'll never have to see your mistake again,' I said tartly, and he looked a bit shame-faced.

'Before you go,' Raffy said, 'perhaps Chloe would like to hear if there are any hereditary health problems she should know about?'

Carr Blackstock looked insulted. 'Absolutely none! Healthy stock on both sides.'

'Then I think that's all we need to say to each other,' I said. 'You're nothing to me, or me to you, except for an accident of conception, so there's no reason why our paths should ever cross again.'

'That suits me very well!' he said. He seemed furious, but I suppose guilt takes some men that way.

I was certainly glad to see the back of him and I could hear Raffy talking as he showed him out, though I couldn't imagine what he was saying.

By the time he returned, I'd found a bottle of Armagnac in his drinks cabinet and swiftly sunk the very large snifter that was burning its way right down into my empty stomach and doing something to dispel the cold shakiness that must have been a delayed reaction to the tension.

'For someone who doesn't drink, you keep a pretty good stock of booze,' I said, trying to sound normal, but he wasn't fooled.

'Chloe, I'm so sorry it turned out like that!' he said, giving me a comforting hug and it was only then that I realised that there were tears running down my face.

'I can't imagine why I'm crying, because I'm angry more than anything else! I know finding out I really was his daughter wasn't a welcome surprise, but it wasn't *my* fault.'

'I know,' he said softly, his arms encircling me as I leaned against him. 'I'd hoped he would be nicer about it all, but unfortunately he seems a very self-centred and mean-spirited sort of man. He doesn't deserve a daughter like you, and I told him so.'

'I bet that went down well,' I said, 'but I think I'm starting to get over it. Could I have another brandy? It seems to be helping.'

He held me away slightly and looked down at me with some concern. 'Do you think you should? It might be better if we went out and had something to eat first, before you start on the spirits.'

'I'm still not hungry, but maybe we could have some-thing sent in later?' I suggested and, my legs going a bit wobbly, sank down onto the sofa while he fetched me a more modest slug of brandy – in fact, it was more of a damp glass. He sat down with one arm around me, in a brotherly sort of way, and I put my head on his shoulder and sighed. 'I'm *so* glad you were there, Raffy!'

'And I'm glad I was there for you, too. I'll *always* be there for you, now that I've found you again – even if you marry that stupid David Billinge!'

I turned my head and stared at him a little fuzzily, since the second glass of brandy had gone to my head, rather than my stomach. Alcohol can be *so* perverse. 'You're quite mad! I'm not even going out with him – he was just a mistake from the past.'

'Like me?'

'You're not so much a mistake, more like unfinished business,' I said, and then, I'm not quite sure how, suddenly we were in each other's arms and locked in a long, long kiss.

Finally he drew back and started to say, 'Chloe, this is *really* not a good idea—'

But I didn't even let him finish the sentence, just wrapped myself more firmly around him, running my hands up his back under his black T-shirt, and kissed him again . . .

After a while we transferred our activities to the spare room, though I'm sure at that stage he intended doing the honourable thing and leaving me there alone, while he found some food to soak up the brandy.

But since I had an unbreakable grip on him and most of his reservations seemed to have been discarded along with his clerical T-shirt, he came down onto the bed with me where, in some respects, he proved to be very much the old Raffy . . .

I slept right through to early next morning and woke feeling truly awful: my head ached and my stomach howled like a banshee. Then memories of the previous day all rushed in at once, like a very mixed bag of unwelcome visitors.

There was no sign of Raffy, but someone was clashing things about in the kitchen and a few minutes later he appeared with a tray of coffee, toast and orange juice. *And* aspirin, I was happy to see. His eyes were anxious and he was frowning, but he set the tray across my knees carefully, when I dragged myself up a bit, then stepped back.

I wasn't wearing anything, so I tucked the edge of the duvet around myself to preserve any modesty that might have escaped last night's conflagration.

'I feel like grim death,' I groaned.

'Yes, I know, but I thought you'd feel better if you ate something, so I went out to the local shop. Don't take the aspirin until you've at least had some toast.'

Someone – most definitely not me – had picked up yesterday's clothes and folded them carefully over a chair, and I wondered just how long Raffy had been awake. Going by his expression, long enough to get himself back into his vicar T-shirt and his coat of many scruples, at least.

Sipping strong coffee between the hammer blows of my headache, I realised that the pain I was feeling wasn't entirely physical. Last night had shown me that I still loved him – I suppose I always had, and always would. But even if he felt the same way about me, which I was pretty sure he didn't, it was never going to work out.

'Last night . . .' he began, while I winced at the sound the toast made when I crunched it, like a whole platoon of soldiers marching over gravel.

'I know – you were just comforting me. It's all right. I was too full of brandy to think straight.'

'But I feel I took advantage of you when you were upset,' he said guiltily.

'No,' I said, feeling a rosy blush spreading upwards from the duvet, 'I think actually it was the other way round. Don't give it another thought. We'll pretend it never happened.'

'But, Chloe—'

I managed a smile, probably not a terribly convincing one, but a smile. 'No, really, I'm fine. I just grabbed at you for comfort . . . though maybe I should take one of those morning-after pills?' I added, suddenly remembering that unscheduled actions can sometimes have unexpected outcomes. You'd think I would have learned that lesson the hard way.

Raffy went white, which was interesting, since he's naturally pale anyway. 'Oh my God!'

'Tut, tut, aren't you taking the name of the Lord in vain?' I said, dipping my toast into the coffee to see if it was quieter to eat that way.

He ran both hands through his hair distractedly. 'Yes, but . . . I never even gave it a thought, Chloe – and *I* was the sober and presumably sensible one!'

'Don't worry,' I said, giving up on the rest of my breakfast and lying back with my eyes closed. 'I don't take after my mother.'

'You wouldn't have to blackmail *me* into anything. I'd marry you tomorrow!'

'That's kind of you, but I couldn't even if I wanted to,' I said firmly, still feeling like grim death and in no mood to deal tactfully with fits of gallantry and guilty conscience. I pushed the tray away and leaned back, closing my eyes again. 'Have you forgotten? You're a vicar and I'm the daughter of Gregory Warlock, author of sensational occult fiction and the proprietor of a museum dedicated to paganism and witchcraft: does jumping the broomstick with me *really* sound like something your bishop would favour?'

That was a pretty unanswerable question, because even if he had loved me back, it was clearly impossible: it would be a marriage if not made in hell, still destined to descend there pretty quickly – so I wasn't surprised when he didn't reply.

When I opened my eyes, he had quietly vanished with the tray, presumably back to the kitchen and his own breakfast.

We had a fairly silent journey back. Raffy was remote and tight-lipped at the wheel whereas I was just tight, the effects of the brandy not having quite worn off. My headache had now reached aspirin-defying proportions.

He dropped me off at home at about midday and I crawled straight into bed, instead of checking for urgent Chocolate Wishes orders among the avalanche that awaited me on the computer: poor business technique. Poor *anything* technique.

Zillah must have come in at some point while I slept, because when I woke up a couple of hours later, there was a note on the kitchen table and a hotpot with a pastry crust sitting in the fridge.

By then, I was suddenly ravenous, and by the time I'd eaten that and a good wedge of crumbly Lancashire cheese, I felt like a new woman. Not a particularly *good* one, but definitely new.

This was just as well, because Poppy called in.

'I can't stay long – we switched the Parish Council meeting to today, because of Maundy Thursday being busy for Raffy,' she said. 'I only hope he's remembered

345

it! I'll have to go straight home afterwards – the vet's coming out – so I thought I'd look in on you now to see how things went in London . . . and actually,' she added, taking stock of the way I looked, which was probably worse than I felt now I was on the mend, 'clearly it didn't go well!'

'*Parts* of it went with a bang,' I said wryly, and told her all about the meeting with Carr Blackstock.

'So that's that: I didn't feel a thing for him or he for me. All he could think about was himself, and how it would affect him if the news got out. But his coldness did upset me quite a bit . . . In fact, so much that afterwards I took advantage of Raffy.'

Her blue eyes went round. 'You *what*?'

'Oh, *he* thinks he took advantage of *me*, so he's all full of honour and scruples now and even offered to marry me! But he hadn't thought it through: I mean, he's a man of God and I'm Gregory Warlock's daughter – I ask you!'

'Perhaps he loves you, that's why he asked you?' she suggested, the incurable romantic.

'No, he was just comforting me and it got a bit out of hand. *I* got a bit out of hand, to be truthful. The marriage bit was just an impulse when I said I ought to take a morning-after pill.'

'Oh gosh, so you should!'

'I was going to, but I'm well past the age where you get pregnant at the drop of a condom,' I said, trying to be flippant, 'so I'll spare my body the chemicals – I've already nearly poisoned it with brandy.'

'But it is still a risk, and you keep saying you don't want children. What if you *are* pregnant?'

'I don't know . . . I was sure up to this morning that I

346

didn't want a baby, but now . . . I find I *do* want Raffy's, just like I did the first time. So I'd keep it, but I think I'd have to move somewhere else, for his sake.'

Poppy was looking at me with dawning realisation. 'You still love him, don't you? Despite everything?'

I sighed. 'Yes, but even if he loved me back it wouldn't work out, so I'll just have to try and put last night's mistake out of my head and settle for friendship: Onward Christian Bloody Soldiers.'

'I suppose you aren't exactly ideal vicar's wife material,' she admitted. 'Gosh, I won't know how to look him in the face, now I know what you've been up to! You don't think of your vicar as a *man*, somehow.'

'I think you'll find that most of the other women around here don't have a problem with that,' I told her drily. 'And what about you and Felix?'

She went scarlet. 'What about me and Felix?'

'Ever since my birthday you seem to be constantly together, and I suspect your feelings towards him have changed.'

'Yes, I suppose they have: I suddenly seemed to see him entirely differently – not like a brother at all. It was really odd.'

'But he obviously feels the same way about you too, Poppy – it's love, love, love! Why aren't either of you doing anything about it?'

'Because you're wrong and I'm sure he doesn't love me *that* way, we've just become even better friends than before.'

Actually, that sounded like a description of the *best* kind of love to me, but who am I to judge? And maybe pushing them together was now best left to the gods, or the magical Mayan chocolate, or Hebe Winter's love potion, or whichever was in charge of that department.

Chapter Thirty-five

Proposals

Being incurably kind-hearted, Poppy phoned me to see how I was as soon as she got home, while waiting for the vet.

'Raffy did remember we'd changed the Parish Council meeting to today, but he looked a bit pale and distracted . . . but then, he is naturally pale, isn't he?' she said. 'And Holy Week is bound to be busy. But I was terrified he would catch my eye and then he would know that *I* knew what you two got up to in London!'

'But you didn't?'

'No, thank goodness. And funnily enough, no one else mentioned about you two going off together overnight like that at all – isn't that strange?'

'Perhaps because they're all gossiping like mad behind our backs instead?' I suggested.

'Well, perhaps,' she agreed. 'Anyway, the good news is that Mann-Drake has put Badger's Bolt up for sale again – Conrad told me. Only now the sluice gates up at the Winter's End water gardens have been repaired, the water supply is dodgy, to say the least. Plus Mr Ormerod, the farmer next door, has put a gate across the lane at the road end. He says it belongs to him and he can do what he likes with it.'

'That's going to make the property really hard to sell, isn't it?'

'Very, and the lido field and tennis courts are now pretty worthless, so the money Effie Yatton had collected to buy them might be enough. Miss Winter is going to get her nephew, who is some kind of property developer, to put in an offer for them, because she says he's good at getting bargain property. In fact, I seem to remember there was a bit of a scandal a year or two ago, because one of those rogue dealer programmes caught him out on camera buying properties from elderly people at knockdown prices and then developing them at a huge profit.'

'Oh? Well, *he* should be able to get them for a song, then!'

'Yes, everything is turning out really well, isn't it and—' she broke off. 'Sorry, Chloe,' she said contritely. 'I forgot that things aren't going too well for you.'

'I'm all right,' I said, more stoically than I felt.

I was now suddenly finding I could no more keep away from Raffy than Poppy could bear to be parted long from Felix. We were obviously both in a bad way, though at least there was hope for Poppy, because *I* could tell that Felix reciprocated the feeling, even if she couldn't.

So, despite it being only a matter of hours since Raffy dropped me off at the cottage, I found myself slipping into the back of the church when he was saying evening prayers. Luckily the door was left ajar so people could come and go silently, and I was sure he didn't see me, because I hid behind the carved screen at the back. It had a handy eye-level hole in the pattern, like a leper's squint, which seemed appropriate: I think I might be a moral leper after sleeping with the vicar.

I sneaked out later when his back was turned, picking up a list of the Easter services on my way. He was certainly going to be busy, starting with Holy Communion on Maundy Thursday evening. On Good Friday there was an early family service, then a long mid-afternoon service – after which I expected he would go and say evening prayers as usual! It all kept going pretty well non-stop until Sunday evening. I hadn't realised quite how energetic the clergy were, it was a real eye-opener.

I didn't see where he would fit collecting the Easter eggs for the hunt into that schedule, so when it was starting to get dark, I put them in a big wicker basket and set out to deliver them . . . And, OK, I admit that it was an excuse because I really just wanted to talk to him again, so there was clearly no hope for me.

Off I went along Angel Lane with my basket of goodies like Little Red Riding Hood, and up the back drive to the vicarage, past the newly revamped tennis courts. I didn't want to risk another run-in with Maria Minchin, if I could help it.

You have to go up steps to the terrace at the back of the house and there was a light in the room that Raffy had taken me to when I delivered the chocolate angel.

Through the glass door I could see him, his head bent over a guitar, and hear him singing softly, but I'd actually lifted my hand to tap on the french door before I realised what the song was – 'Darker Past Midnight'!

Tears suddenly welled and I was filled with an overwhelming sense of desolation at the futility of my rekindled love. My hand fell back down to my side and I took a quick step back into the darkness.

Then Arlo barked sharply, once, and the music stopped mid-chord. Raffy flung open the door.

'Chloe, wait!' he said urgently, and caught me in two long strides, drawing me back into the light and warmth of the room.

'I . . . just brought you the Easter eggs,' I said weakly, keeping my head bent. 'I thought you might not have time to collect them.'

He took the basket and put it down on the nearest chair without letting go of my arm, as if afraid I might run out again into the night. Then he gently turned my face up to his and said softly, 'What's the matter?'

'N-nothing, it's just that song you were singing always made me cry, because the girl in it wasn't me.' I tried to smile. 'Stupid, I know . . . and I haven't done it for ages.'

'But – it *is* about you,' he said, looking astonished. 'Of *course* it is! I wrote it when I thought I would never see you again. That whole *Dead as My Love* album is about you!'

'Me?' I laughed uncertainly. 'No, I don't think so!'

'I can prove it. Look – sit there.' He pushed me down onto the sofa and I watched as he went to a bookshelf that held a whole row of familiar, black-bound Moleskine notebooks, the sort he'd always used to jot his musical ideas down. He pulled one out and flicked through the pages. 'Here we are,' he said, coming back over and sitting next to me. 'Read that!'

It was the rough outline of 'Darker Past Midnight', with its haunting words of loss and regret – only here, in this early draft, it was called 'Song for Chloe' and dated soon after we'd parted, just as he'd said.

'I called it "Song for Chloe" first, but since the pain of missing you always seemed worse after midnight, I changed it . . . and why are you crying again?'

'Because it *was* me, after all!' I choked.

And then we were in each other's arms and he was saying, between long, slow, lingering kisses, 'I love you now even more than I did then, if that's possible!'

'You do?'

'Yes, of course. Wasn't it obvious that I couldn't resist you in London, despite my best intentions?'

'No, I thought you just felt guilty about it. And *I* seduced *you*, if I remember rightly . . . though I hadn't let myself admit I still loved you until then.'

He smiled down at me wickedly. 'I was more than ready to be seduced!' he said, then kissed me again, and we had a blissful cuddle on the sofa until he suddenly remembered that he hadn't drawn the curtain over the French door.

'It's still early and occasionally Effie or someone else will walk up that way to see me.'

When he came back he put his arms around me again but said, 'Just as well we cool off a bit anyway, since this is as far as we go until you marry me – and I think that had better be *really* soon!'

'Isn't that a bit old-fashioned, not to mention an extreme case of shutting the stable door after the horse has bolted?' I asked, snuggling back up to him again.

'Maybe, but it feels right. I want the whole, traditional church wedding, with you walking up the aisle and Poppy as bridesmaid, though I can't somehow see your grandfather giving you away. Perhaps Jake will do it?'

'But Raffy,' I said, dismayed, 'I told you that was impossible in London, given our situation! Can't we just make the most of what we've got?'

'Things have changed quite a bit, but it would still upset some of my parishioners if I lived in sin with you,' he pointed out. 'And anyway,' his square jaw hardened stubbornly, 'I *want* to marry you – and in church. We're not going to have a hole-and-corner affair.'

As evidence of this, he firmly removed my hands, which I had slipped under his soft chambray shirt, but he kissed them before he let them go.

'Your bishop really wouldn't like me,' I said with a sigh.

'*I* like you, that's the main thing – and there's the parable about the one lost sheep that was found,' he reminded me. 'Things have changed and I'm unlikely to be excommunicated for marrying the granddaughter of Gregory Warlock, though your grandfather might disown you.'

'He might, though I'm never sure quite how Grumps will see things. He seems to quite like you.'

'So long as he doesn't try and insist on some kind of second pagan ceremony. That really might upset the bishop.'

'There isn't even going to be a *first* ceremony,' I insisted. 'It's all impossible.'

'I don't feel anything is impossible any more. We'll find a way around it. Come on, I'll walk you back home.' He got up and pulled me to my feet.

'Are you sure? The village is probably buzzing with gossip about us going to London together already!'

'Then a bit more won't hurt, will it?'

Arlo, who had given up hope of the biscuits that often accompanied a visitor, was curled up asleep in the corner, but he woke when we got up and followed us out into the night, vaguely pleased at the idea of an extra walk.

'I'll come and help you with the Easter egg hunt on Sunday,' I said as we crunched down the gravel, hand in hand.

'And you could even come to one of the services?' he suggested, adding with a smile, 'I saw you at evening prayers.'

'But I was behind the screen! How on earth did you know I was there?'

'I always know when you're around,' he said simply. 'Will you come?'

'I'll think about it,' I promised.

As we turned into Angel Lane, he said, 'By the way, Felix told me today that he was in love with Poppy, but he didn't think she felt the same way about him and only saw him as a brother!'

'She said much the same thing to me earlier, about Felix!' I said, laughing. 'Honestly, it must be obvious to everyone else that they've fallen in love! What did you say to him?'

'That I could see that Poppy was in love with him, of course,' he said. 'I thought that at least he and Poppy would have a happy ending, even if I didn't. But now I know that you love me too, I'm sure it'll work out for all of us.'

And, despite being in full view of anyone who happened to be looking, he gave me a kiss and another rib-cracking hug.

'But, Raffy . . . !' I protested helplessly.

He grinned. 'Love *will* find a way,' he said, and strode off, Arlo at his heels.

Next morning, when I drifted into Grumps' study on a cloud of pink, fluffy unfounded optimism, he handed me the final chapter of *Satan's Child*, accompanied by a searching look. In return, I gave him his tea and two Oreo cookies.

'You look *glowing*,' he said. 'That is surprising, considering what reception your father gave you in London. Zillah
has told me about it . . . *and* about some other things
she has read in the cards, though I find them hard to
believe.'

'Like what?' I asked suspiciously.

'An outcome that is unexpected, though perhaps, remembering that the festival of Eostre is upon us and the goddess
might well take a hand in proceedings – maybe even already
has – I should not have been so surprised.'

'I can't imagine what you're talking about, Grumps!'

'What are these?' he demanded, looking at his saucer.

'Oreo cookies.'

'A strange combination of colours, and the outside looks
like a dog biscuit,' he said disapprovingly.

'They don't taste remotely like them, though,' I assured
him, and left him tentatively dipping one into his tea.

Zillah was disinclined to enlighten me about what she'd
seen in the cards too. Although I'd told her about the
meeting with my father yesterday I hadn't, of course, shared
what I'd got up to with Raffy while in London.

And now I said nothing about last night, partly because
I wanted to hug our love to myself for a while longer, and
partly because I still couldn't see any way we were ever
going to have a traditional, happy-ever-after resolution.

At least there were to be wedding bells for Poppy and Felix.
Spurred on by Raffy's advice, Felix had driven out to Stirrups
that very morning and, finding Poppy in the yard cleaning
out Honeybun's hoofs, had gone down on one knee and
proposed.

'Janey was so stunned she dropped her fag into the bale

355

she was hefting and it caught fire,' Felix said when they came to tell me about it.

'Yes, we had to put it out with buckets, but after that she found a bottle of bubbly and we celebrated, though she drank most of it herself,' Poppy said, then showed me her magnificent diamond solitaire ring.

'I had some money put by from the sale of a first edition,' Felix explained.

'I'd better not wear it when I'm working!'

'I think diamonds are pretty indestructible,' I said. 'Oh, I'm so pleased for you both!'

Felix had to tear himself away and go back to open the shop, but Poppy lingered long enough to wish I could be as happy as they were. So then I confessed that Raffy and I had discovered we *did* love each other, though for reasons that must be obvious it was a love that not only dared not speak its name, but couldn't even have a secret affair.

'I'm sure you'll find a way round the difficulties, Chloe, and I don't think there *are* any traditional vicar's wives any more.'

'That's what Raffy says.'

'There you are then,' she said, beaming. 'He's a very alternative kind of vicar, and you would be an extremely alternative vicar's wife!'

I no longer hid behind the curtains to watch Raffy and Arlo go by in the early morning, but instead brazenly smiled and waved at him. I didn't expect him to stop, not with his current workload, but instead we texted each other all the time.

Poppy and Felix were going to the afternoon service on Good Friday, along with about half the parish from the sound of it, but I spent the day making Wishes and catching up with orders.

Just after lunch Kat's parents dropped Jake off on their way back from the Lake District, together with about a ton of dirty washing and a backpack full of Kendal Mint Cake. It was lovely to have him back again, even if the cottage would smell like a laundry for the next two days.

He went to see Grumps and Zillah after lunch, then later we both helped them to put the final touches to the museum, ready for tomorrow morning's grand opening ceremony, when Hebe Winter would cut the ribbon and the local press would capture the moment for posterity. Then, it being also the first day of the season for Winter's End, she would have to dash back for that.

I would be opening Chocolate Wishes to the public in the afternoon for the first time too, so I was a bit nervous about that, though the shelves were stocked ready.

The museum looked wonderful – the glass-fronted cabinets were stuffed full of enticing treasures, masks grinned down from every wall, the desk gleamed, the display of Grumps' novels added a bright note and his other books, pamphlets and postcards, together with a stack of my Chocolate Wishes and jars of treacle toffee cats, were invitingly arranged. The roll of tickets lay ready to hand and a float of small change was in the cash drawer.

We were ready.

When Jake and I went back to the cottage after a family dinner, I told him about Carr Blackstock turning out to be my very reluctant father, and that Raffy had taken me to London to see him – only to find that Zillah had got in with the information first.

'I know all about it,' he said, buttering a toasted hot cross bun to fill in the gaps that Zillah's substantial, but slightly odd chicken Caesar salad and zabaglione hadn't reached. 'He sounded a total waste of space. I think I'm better off with my unknown Italian waiter for a father, because at least he looks cheerful and friendly in those holiday snaps Mum gave me.'

'Yes, she did say he was a lot of fun,' I agreed, though of course her definition of the word 'fun' was probably not the same as ours.

Then Jake said it had been kind of Raffy to drive me there and let me stay in his flat, and he hoped we'd managed to have a good time despite the dodgy session with Carr Blackstock.

'Yes, we're . . . friends again now,' I said, blushing faintly.

'So I've heard.' He gave me a grin and popped yet another hot cross bun in the toaster, and I wondered exactly *what* Zillah had been telling him . . . ?

We settled in with a DVD, while next door Grumps and his girls were celebrating the festival of Eostre with a crescendo of chanting and a pervasive, but not unpleasant, reek of incense.

My mind wasn't on the film at all, because I was feeling as if I was sitting in the middle of a tug-of-war between two opposing religions, with my guardian angel as referee. While I'm sure Raffy is perfectly capable of accepting Grumps as a member of his family, and Grumps could probably reconcile himself to my marrying Raffy, how the Church would view it was another matter entirely.

The phone rang when I was in the kitchen making a drink and Jake picked it up. I thought it was Kat, because I could hear him talking away, but then he stuck his head through the kitchen door and said, 'It's Raffy – don't make me a drink, I'm going round to talk to him. By the way,' he added, grinning wickedly, 'he asked me if he could marry you, and I told him that was fine by me, so long as he paid the bride price first.'

I threw an orange at him, which was the nearest object to hand, and he ducked and laughed annoyingly. 'See you later!'

'Jake Lyon, come back here!' I yelled, but he was gone.

'Raffy, are you still there?' I asked, picking up the phone.

'Yes, and I could hear what Jake was saying,' he said, laughter in his voice. 'I take it he's on his way here now? He took the news pretty well, though he seems to have the dowry idea the wrong way round.'

'There isn't any news,' I said weakly, 'and I didn't think Jake could surprise me any more after all these years, but evidently I was wrong. What on earth does he want?'

'Nothing I can't afford to give,' he said mysteriously and refused to say more.

When Jake came back a short time later, he was wearing Raffy's long leather coat, and looking very pleased with himself: I am clearly worth my weight in cowhide. He took it up to bed with him, but not before suddenly remembering that Raffy had sent something for me and fishing a small box out of his pocket.

Inside was a small and very plain gold cross. I stared at it for a moment, then reached for the phone.

'Raffy? You hadn't gone to bed, had you?'

'No, I thought you might ring me.'

'You shouldn't have given Jake your lovely coat!'

'I think it looks a lot better on him than it did on me,

and it's probably more than time I stopped looking as though I'd just escaped from *The Matrix*. After Jake, I'm now wondering what your grandfather might demand from me, apart from my immortal soul?'

'Don't be silly, he's not a satanist,' I said with dignity.

'I know, I'm just joking.'

'Are vicars allowed to joke about that kind of thing?'

'You should hear the bishop,' he said. 'We're allowed a bit of levity these days. Did you like your cross? I thought you could hang it on the chain with the little gold cocoa bean.'

'The bean's hollow and I'm pretty sure Grumps has put some kind of charm in it.'

'That's OK: my gift is to reflect the other side of you, the spiritual one that believes in angels. Hebe Winter always wears a pentacle and a cross, haven't you noticed? They seem able to balance witchcraft and Christianity quite easily in Sticklepond. I expect you get used to it.'

'Maybe, but I think Hebe Winter is a law unto herself,' I said doubtfully.

It was getting very late and it would be a big day tomorrow, but I still consulted the angel cards before I went to bed. They told me it was safe to love and be loved, but they didn't mention how to reconcile pagan grandfathers and irate bishops, and I couldn't help being afraid that Raffy was being too sanguine about how either of them would take the news.

Chapter Thirty-six

Behind the Scenes at the Museum

Saturday dawned with the promise of a bright, sunny, perfect April day. Just as well, because Poppy and I had decided to wear the dresses we had bought on my birthday for the occasion. They might be a little over the top for a Saturday morning in Sticklepond, but in comparison with Grumps I was sure we would fade into sartorial insignificance.

I'd hung the little cross on the chain with my cocoa bean and tucked them into the neckline of my dress, not feeling quite ready for a showdown with Grumps yet, but sometimes they made a faint, melodious chiming as I moved, to remind me they were there.

By ten, quite a little crowd had gathered outside the museum to watch Hebe Winter, in full Elizabethan regalia, declare Sticklepond's newest tourist attraction open.

She said a few gracious words (and since she was as astute as Grumps, several of them advertised the opening of Winter's End to the public that afternoon) and then cut the ribbon across the entrance door with a pair of silver scissors shaped like a stork, to the accompaniment of clicking camera shutters and much applause.

Then we all went indoors, where there were bowls of punch of Zillah's devising and slices of fruitcake of mine, and a party atmosphere began to develop. The guest list had been wide, and ranged from Kat's parents, wearing what seemed to be a perpetual air of bewilderment, to the entire Sticklepond Re-enactment Society, who were instantly recognisable since, like Miss Winter, they were already in Elizabethan dress ready for the opening of Winter's End, where they would act as volunteer staff.

Mrs Snowball and Clive, having supplied the alcoholic element of the punch, now assisted in drinking it, along with several elderly women I didn't recognise, but strongly suspected were from Grumps' coven.

Felix and Poppy might have been anywhere, since they were moving about in a little cloud of bliss and congratulations, while Janey was moving about in an overpowering cloud of Yves Saint Laurent's Opium. I've seen horses sneeze when she walks by.

Jake and Kat took charge of the desk and the rest of us stood around listening as Grumps was interviewed. As usual he managed to get in a good plug about the re-issue of his backlisted novels, as well as mentioning his most recent one, *The Desirous Devil*. And yes, I know it sounds like a Mills and Boon, but apparently it's sold better than all his previous books put together. The lurid, fifties-style cover may have had something to do with it and goodness knows what they will put on the front of *Satan's Child*. The mind boggles.

Raffy arrived just as they had finished and the reporter immediately asked him about his reaction, as vicar, to a museum dedicated to the history of paganism.

His eyes passed over the crowded room until they found me and he smiled. My knees jellified and I had to take a quick gulp of punch to steady myself, nearly choking on a bit of orange-scented geranium leaf – I'd wondered what Zillah had wanted with those this morning.

'Actually, I think that a museum exploring the way in which people, throughout the ages and across diverse cultures, have reached out to God, can be no bad thing, don't you?' he said. 'And probably most so-called witchcraft in the past was just the application of herbalist knowledge, passed down orally.'

Hebe Winter and Grumps fixed their eyes on him, a little like lazy lions wondering whether to chase a gazelle or not, but said nothing.

The reporter left immediately after the interview and Raffy came straight over to where I was standing.

Impulsively, I pulled the chain out of my neckline, displaying the gold cross and the cocoa bean nestling together on the end of it. 'There you are, Raffy – an unholy alliance. Just as well the reporter's gone.'

'What's that?' said Grumps, who had ears like a bat, despite his age. Then his gaze sharpened. 'And where did you get that cross from?'

'It was a gift from Raffy, Grumps.'

'Was it, indeed?' he said, turning that inquisitorial stare on Raffy.

'And why shouldn't she wear one, Gregory?' Hebe Winter looked at me approvingly and I would have bet even money that her own pentacle and cross were reposing on her narrow bosom, under the finely goffered ruff.

'Why are you giving my granddaughter unsuitable gifts, young man?' Grumps asked, unappeased, and Raffy put his

arm around me and announced, brazenly, 'It's *very* suitable, in the circumstances, because I want to marry her.'

'You're engaged?' exclaimed Poppy, clapping her hands
and beaming. 'Oh, that's lovely! Congratulations.'

'No! I *can't* . . . I mean, the bishop would never approve
of me . . .' I stammered, flustered at this sudden public
announcement.

'*I'll* speak to the bishop,' Hebe Winter stated.

'That's very kind of you, Miss Winter,' Raffy said. 'I rang
him yesterday, so it won't come as a total surprise, but if
you could put in a word for us too, that would be great.'

'I notice that no one has asked *my* opinion – or my
permission,' Grumps remarked with deceptive calmness,
because I could see he was ruffled, though that might simply
have been at the prospect of having his comfortable life
disrupted.

'Raffy asked mine and I gave it,' Jake told him. 'I think
it's a really good idea.'

'You do, do you?'

'I warned you this was coming, Gregory,' Zillah pointed
out. 'But did you believe me?'

'And I intended coming to speak to you about it before
this,' Raffy told Grumps, 'only Easter's been a bit hectic. But
I hope you don't have any real objections?'

'It doesn't matter whether he has or not, Raffy, does it?'
I said. 'Since *you* will only marry in a church and *I* can't
very well do that!'

'Why not?' asked Zillah, to my surprise. 'You were christened in All Angels, so there's no reason why you shouldn't
marry there.'

'What?' I exclaimed.

'Your granny and the last vicar, old Mr Harris, arranged

it between them, just like they had when your mother was a baby.'

'And I was told *nothing* of this?' demanded Grumps, outraged.

'She knew you'd only kick up a fuss, and what you didn't know couldn't harm you.'

Raffy gave me a squeeze and smiled down at me. 'There, you see? I knew you were always on the side of the angels, and now there's nothing to stop us getting married.'

'I . . . suppose there isn't,' I agreed slowly. 'Please say you don't mind, Grumps?' I begged. 'It needn't change anything: I'd only be living a few yards away and I'll still be coming over every day to type up your chapters and make Chocolate Wishes.'

'I perceive that this is yet another example of Christianity absorbing paganism,' Grumps said darkly, 'but I suppose if you must, you must.'

'Oh, thank you, Grumps!' I said, and gave him a kiss on the cheek, which he suffered, rather in Jake's manner.

'And you will come to the wedding?' Raffy asked.

'No, but I will be at the reception. You can hold it here in the museum.'

'That seems a reasonable compromise,' Raffy agreed.

'We could even have a double wedding,' suggested Poppy. 'But you can't marry yourself, can you, Raffy?'

'Not really,' he said with a grin. 'But I have a friend who would love to come and perform the ceremony.'

'It had better be *soon*,' Zillah put in.

'Why?' I asked, looking at her suspiciously.

'Never you mind!' she said. 'But the sooner the better, you mark my words.'

'That's fine by me,' Raffy said, and then everyone drank

a toast to our engagement, and Poppy and Felix's engagement, followed by one to the museum's opening . . . and by that time, only the people who were driving were entirely sober, and the Winter's End contingent had to leave.

Raffy had to go soon after, too, kissing me before he did, which felt very odd in public.

I was still in a bit of a trance while the room slowly emptied and we closed the doors for lunch, but when finally recalled to the land of the living, it appeared that we had made an inordinate amount of money already, despite no one having paid an entrance charge.

Grumps' books and pamphlets, which he had been signing with a flourish every time one was shoved under his nose, had sold like hot cakes and so had several boxes of Chocolate Wishes and practically a whole jar of treacle toffee cats, though I couldn't imagine who had bought them out of the morning's assembly. I could see Kat and Jake had had one apiece, because the sticks were in the waste-paper basket under the desk.

'We'll have to put a fresh stock of books out for this afternoon, Grumps,' I said, 'and you could think of expanding the stock of things you sell, with some witch-related souvenirs.'

'Yes, I think you'd really clean up with more gifts for the visitors to buy,' agreed Jake.

'I will give it some thought,' Grumps said. 'And perhaps a greater variety of postcards too. I have been asked if there are ones of myself.' He stroked his beard rather complacently, looked at us and added, 'All that went very well, don't you think? Apart from Chloe's intention to enter into holy matrimony as opposed to anything more logical, and I expect I will grow accustomed even to that, eventually.'

'You'd better – I *told* you it was on the cards,' Zillah said.

'You didn't tell *me*,' I complained, as we followed the others through the door to the house. 'And what did you mean by saying to Raffy that we ought to marry sooner than later?'

She took my arm to hold me back and whispered something in my ear. I felt my eyes widen.

'But – the cards aren't *always* right,' I protested.

'They are, it's only the interpretation that's sometimes wrong,' she said. 'I keep telling you!'

After lunch, which I didn't eat much of, Jake drove Grumps to Winter's End, where he made a guest appearance dressed as John Dee.

Kat and Zillah held the fort at the museum and I opened up Chocolate Wishes to the public for the first time and switched on the Bath, so that soon the rich fragrance of criollo couverture was wafting through the door into the museum, drawing in visitors like a magnet.

We were all pretty exhausted by closing time, so it was just as well we were only opening four afternoons a week after this! I still had to finish cleaning up in the workshop and Kat kindly came and helped me, whispering away in her chatty fashion: I only wished I could hear more than one word in five of what she was saying!

We all had dinner together – a hotpot that Zillah had made the day before – and then Jake, Kat and I retired back to the cottage.

The day had been an emotional roller coaster and it wasn't over yet, because Felix and Poppy had persuaded me to go to the late Saturday night service at All Angels when Raffy would light the Paschal Candle.

*　　*　　*

And I was glad I did go, even if I *was* in a trance of such tiredness that everything seemed to be waving about slightly, a sort of underwater ripple effect.

Whether knowing I had been christened there made a difference, I don't know, but tonight entering the church felt like going home, and there was a moment when I was *sure* I could see the flickering of angel wings in the candlelight . . .

And Raffy looked tired and pale, but also tranquil and happy, as if he'd just received the answer to a really important question.

Chapter Thirty-seven

Gran Couva!

It was only just light on Easter Sunday morning when we met in the churchyard like a pair of conspirators. Raffy was carrying the big basket of chocolate eggs.

'What, no Easter Bunny costume?'

'Couldn't get one big enough,' he said with a grin, kissing me. 'And look!' He held aloft a small wooden object.

'What is it?'

'A wooden rabbit's foot! An elderly parishioner who carves walking stick handles made it for me. It'll save getting Effie's lucky rabbit's foot brooch dirty and be much easier to make paw prints in the flowerbeds with.'

We went around hiding the eggs in crevices, under bushes and in low tree branches.

'Isn't this a bit irreverent?' I asked, as he inserted one between the feet of the marble angel that had almost fallen on him.

'No, because Jesus said, "Suffer little children to come unto me," and since the church is his house, this is his garden.'

'I suppose you're right,' I said, reflecting that I was going to have to get used to this sort of conversational gambit, now it came with the whole new Raffy package. 'What about keeping a few eggs back, in case one or two of the children don't find any?' I suggested.

'Good idea. OK.' He looked at his watch. 'I'll take morning prayers in a minute – it's just a short service today, because the big one is mid-morning and only a couple of regulars will show up. Then the egg hunt will be directly afterwards.'

He gave me a kiss and went off into the church, and a few moments later Effie Yatton arrived to help, with a big roll of Easter Bunny stickers, a picnic table and folding chair, which she erected just inside the gate.

By the time he came out again, there was quite a crowd of excited children and their parents waiting for the off, and Effie had absent-mindedly eaten one of the spare chocolate eggs.

Later that evening an exhausted Raffy and I were sitting on my little sofa, with Arlo curled up and snoring in front of the fire. The lights were off and the curtains open, so we could see Jake and Kat in the garden. He was getting extremely good with the firesticks, weaving intricate patterns in the darkness.

'I don't really want to leave my little cottage and walled garden,' I said drowsily.

'You don't have to. Presumably you will still come over here every day anyway, to make Wishes?'

'Yes, and type up Grumps' books,' I said. 'And Jake can either stay with us, or here in the cottage, in his university holidays, can't he?'

'Whichever he prefers,' Raffy agreed. 'I think he should

have his own room at the vicarage, though, so he knows he's always welcome. And I'm going to get plans drawn up to install a proper kitchen in the main part of the house, so Maria can just do the cleaning and housekeeping and not the cooking, after we're married!'

'You only want me because you think I'm a better cook,' I accused him.

'No, I want you because I can't resist your chocolate,' he said, kissing me.

'And I can't resist you.' I returned the kiss enthusiastically. 'You've gone from being forastero to criollo and now – gran couva!'

'I hope that's a *good* chocolate?'

'The best,' I said simply, then groaned as the phone at my elbow rang. 'Who on earth can that be?'

'Chloe, is that you?' asked a once-familiar, brittle voice.

I sat up straighter. '*Mum?*'

'Yes, it's me. Mags said the gaff was blown, so I thought I might as well ring you.'

'Why? What do you want?' I demanded suspiciously.

'Nothing – only that I hear you haven't got a man yet, so if you want to come out to Goa for a holiday with Mags, I can guarantee to find you one.'

Typical! Six years of silence and then the only thing she's interested in is whether I'm still single or not!

'That's all right,' I said, relaxing back into Raffy's embrace, 'I think I've found one for myself.'

Chloe's chocolate spread

This is a simple ganache of cream and chocolate. Make it in small quantities, since it does not keep for more than a couple of weeks in the fridge.

You will need double cream and chocolate. While Chloe used couverture chocolate, patisserie or any type with a good percentage of cocoa solids will work perfectly well. I prefer very dark, bitter chocolate, but choose the kind *you* like best.

Have a clean jam jar ready.

For a firm but spreadable consistency, you need roughly equal parts of double cream and chocolate. Grate the chocolate into a bowl, or chop it finely.

Heat the double cream until it is hot but not boiling and then pour it over the chocolate. Stir well until the mixture is smooth and glossy.

At this stage you can add powdered ginger to taste, to make Chloe's chocolate and ginger spread, or experiment with flavourings like rum or vanilla.

Spoon into the clean jar and allow it to go completely cold before covering and putting it in the fridge.

Making a chocolate Easter egg

This is great fun to do and very easy, if messy!

You will need an Easter egg mould – I have metal and plastic ones in various sizes and they work equally well. Rub the insides with a piece of kitchen paper.

Couverture or patisserie chocolate are best for making hollow shells, but again, any good chocolate will be fine.

Melt the chocolate in a double pan or in a bowl over a pan of simmering water. Do not let steam or water get into the chocolate!

Coat the inside of the moulds with the chocolate. My moulds have a deep, embossed pattern, so I prefer to coat the insides with a pastry brush, just as Chloe did. The alternative is to spoon melted chocolate into the moulds and swirl it around to cover. Whichever method you use, apply three or four coats, then clean any runs from the edges of the mould.

When it has set slightly, turn the moulds upside down on a wire rack and leave them to harden. They will contract slightly as they do so and a little pressure at one end of the mould should release them.

You can stick the two halves together, either with a little melted chocolate, or by heating a baking tray and briefly touching the edges to it before sealing them together. (I put solid chocolate rabbits inside mine before sealing the two halves.)

You can decorate the outside with a ribbon, piped icing – whatever appeals to you. I have made Fabergé-style jewelled eggs, sticking on cake decorations, like little silver balls and frosted, coloured diamonds, using sugar paste. Or simply put the egg inside a cellophane bag with a ribbon tie.

And the very best thing about working with chocolate is that you can eat your mistakes: have fun!

Ten fascinating facts about chocolate

1. Chocolate can have distinctly different flavours depending on the species of the cocoa bean and the conditions in which the bean was grown.
2. It is scientifically proven that chocolate contains the 'love-chemical' phenylethylamine, and by eating it you receive a similar feeling to when you are in love. Some might even say it is better than a hot date . . .
3. A cocoa pod contains roughly 40 to 45 cocoa beans. It takes up to 270 cocoa beans to make 500g of chocolate.
4. In general, darker chocolate contains a higher percentage of cocoa solids and is more expensive than milk chocolate.
5. 90% of the world's cocoa is produced by just 9 countries, the majority of which are African.
6. Cocoa butter melts just slightly below body temperature at around 33°C, which is why it melts in your mouth.

7. The world's largest Easter egg was created in 2005 by a Belgian chocolate manufacturer and displayed in New Jersey, USA. It weighed in at a colossal 27 feet tall, 21 feet wide and weighed 4,299 pounds. That's a lot of chocolate . . .

8. The first chocolate bar was created in 1847 by the Bristol company Fry & Son.

9. More than twice as many women eat and crave chocolate than men.

10. If stored in warm conditions, chocolate can develop a white film called bloom. This occurs because the cocoa butter separates out and melts sugar onto the chocolate's surface.